Twenty-Nine and a Half Reasons

Twenty-Nine and a Half Reasons

A Rose Gardner Mystery

Denise Grover Swank

CROOKED
LANE

NEW YORK

Published in the United States by Crooked Lane Books, an imprint of The Quick Brown Fox & Company LLC.

Crooked Lane Books and its logo are trademarks of The Quick Brown Fox & Company LLC.

The Library of Congress Cataloging-in-Publication Data is available upon request.

978-1-62953-220-2
978-1-62953-376-6

Cover design by Louis Malcangi
Book design by Jennifer Canzone

Printed in the United States.

www.crookedlanebooks.com

Crooked Lane Books
2 Park Avenue, 10th Floor
New York, NY 10016

First Edition: September 2015

10 9 8 7 6 5 4 3 2 1

Chapter One

Having a boyfriend was supposed to make my life easier.

Instead, I buttoned Joe's white shirt on Monday morning, forlorn. This was the fifth time he'd left for Little Rock after a weekend with me, and each time was even harder than the time before. I rested my cheek against his chest and sighed. "I wish you didn't have to go."

He lifted my chin and leaned down to kiss me, making me want him to stay even more. "You should quit your job at the DMV, which you hate anyway, and come stay with me in Little Rock."

I sighed again. We'd had this conversation before. "Joe . . ."

He kissed me again, knowing full well his lips were my Kryptonite.

Muffy, my eight-pound guard dog, whined at my feet. She always did have good timing. "I'll take you out in a minute, Muff." I pulled away and looked at the clock. "It's seven, and it'll take you two hours to get to Little Rock. You need to get goin'."

"You still didn't answer my question."

I rested my hands on his chest and looked up into his face with a playful grin. "An intelligent police detective such as yourself should know full well that wasn't a question. And besides, you know my answer. We've only been dating a month. It's too soon. And then there's Violet . . ."

"Your sister is a grown woman with a family of her own. You spent twenty-four years living your life to please your mother, Rose. It's time to think about you."

"I can't leave Violet to deal with all the estate stuff from Momma's death. That wouldn't be fair to her."

"You sell the house and divide the assets. It's not that hard, Rose."

I took a step back. I didn't want to sell the house. "That still doesn't address the length of time we've known each other. It's only been—"

"A little over a month." Joe ended with a sigh. "I know. How long do you need? Two months? A year?"

"I don't know, Joe." I said, frustrated I didn't know that answer.

He pulled me against his chest and nuzzled my neck. "I'm sorry. I didn't mean to push you. I just miss you so much durin' the week and the weekends don't last long enough."

"I know." My stomach flip-flopped in my confusion. I missed him, too. Terribly. Why didn't I want to move to Little Rock with him? I settled into his chest, the soft rhythm of his heart filling my ear with comfort and reassurance. I needed to soak it in to last me through the rest of the week. Four nights without him—the thought filled me with loneliness, but the thought of moving to Little Rock filled me with terror.

He kissed me again, reminding me of what I'd be missing for the next five days. I knew full well that was his intent when he pulled back and gave me his ornery grin.

"You play dirty," I said with a grin of my own.

"You better believe it." Joe dropped his arms and turned away. "OK, I need to go before I throw you into the car and take you with me anyway." He rummaged around on the kitchen counter.

"That's called kidnapping, Detective Simmons. You of all people should know that. What are you lookin' for?"

"My keys." He opened the junk drawer and shuffled through the contents. "Here they are." He clutched them in his fist and pulled out an envelope. "Fenton County Courthouse. This looks important."

I grabbed the envelope. "Oh crappy doodles! I completely forgot. I have jury duty on the eleventh. What's today?"

He raised an eyebrow. "The eleventh."

My stomach twisted. "Oh no! I didn't tell Suzanne, and I don't have vacation time left. She'll never let me off."

"Suzanne has to you let you off. It's the law—and it won't be vacation time either, so don't worry about that. She'll understand."

I wasn't sure she would understand at all. Suzanne, my coworker and nemesis, had been promoted after our old boss's extortion arrest. I'd been involved in uncovering the crime, and had suffered some injuries. When I'd returned to work after a week off, sporting a bruised and battered face, Suzanne tried to bond with me, thinking we were sisters in boyfriend abuse. But when she found out I'd gotten beat up in the bust of a sting operation instead, and that Joe was an undercover cop, she hated me again. It didn't matter that I'd been accidentally dragged into it; all that mattered to Suzanne was that I'd become big news in town and had stolen attention from her. Of course, it didn't take much to be big news in Henryetta, Arkansas, population 11,000. Before the Daniel Crocker mess, the biggest news had been Samantha Jo Wheaton lighting her cheating husband's boat on fire in their front yard.

"Just call in and tell her you forgot. Besides, you'll probably only be at the courthouse half a day and be at the DMV in the afternoon. They'll hardly miss you."

"Yeah, you're probably right . . ." Other than the crime ring bust, which involved a couple of deaths—my momma's and a bartender at Jasper's Steakhouse—and a few break-ins at my house, there wasn't much crime in Henryetta or Fenton County. Did they have jury trials for jaywalking?

Muffy whined again, and Joe reached down to rub her head. "I hear you, girl." Joe grabbed my hand and gave it a squeeze. "I gotta go. Walk me out?"

I glanced down at my skimpy pajamas. "And give Mildred, president of the Busybodies Club, something to talk about after she watches you kiss me goodbye? Yeah. I'll walk you out."

We stepped into a July sauna, Muffy bolting through the door in front of us.

"It's gonna be another scorcher," Joe said. "They say it's the hottest, driest July on record."

"Hmm." I was too busy already missing him to care.

We waited for Muffy to do her business, stalling for more time together. Joe pointed to the house next door. He'd lived there while he was undercover, working as a mechanic and building evidence against Daniel Crocker so the state police could bust his statewide car parts ring. "Any news of who's movin' in?"

"Mildred says a family with five boys is moving in this week."

"In that tiny house?"

"If Mildred says it's true, it's gospel."

Joe shrugged. Even in the short time he'd lived there he knew nothing slipped by Mildred.

We finally reached his car, and he pulled me into a hug.

"You're not doing undercover work this week, are you?" I looked up into his face to make sure he told the truth.

He smiled. He knew how much his job scared me. It had almost gotten him killed by the Henryetta crime ring. I had no idea if there had been any other near misses. He refused to tell me. "No, darlin'. Not this week."

"You wouldn't lie to me to make me feel better, would you?"

He kissed me lightly and murmured against my lips. "No, Rose. I swear I'll never lie to you."

"Good." I gave his chest a light push. "Now go on before I drag you back into the house and lock you up."

He lifted an eyebrow with a wicked look. "Are you going to tie me up?"

I titled my head. "Would you stay if I said yes?"

Laughing, Joe opened his car door. "My life was utterly boring before I met you, Rose Gardner."

"You say that like it's a bad thing, Joe McAllister." I shook my head. "I mean Simmons. I don't think I'll ever get used to your real last name. You'll always be Joe McAllister to me."

He sat in his front seat looking up at me, the beautiful brown of his eyes accented by scattered dark flecks. It still stung a little that Joe thought I might have been the extortionist and had kept up his cover for so long.

The sunlight caught his brown hair, enhancing his natural coppery highlights. I asked myself for the thousandth time why I wasn't going with him. He was a good-looking man, all alone in the city. Any woman would kill to be with him. I was crazy. But I was also stubborn.

He grabbed my hand and rubbed the back of it with his thumb. "I don't want to leave you like this with us rememberin' the bad times."

"I'm sorry. I don't want you to go with us like this either."

He scooted his seat back and pulled me in to sit on his lap.

"Joe!" I squealed.

"Let's give Mildred something to talk about that will last all week." He slipped his fingers into my hair and pulled my mouth to his, making me forget we'd been arguing. After a good half a minute he whispered against my lips, "We'd better stop before I take you back inside. I'm gonna be late as it is."

I sucked his lip into my mouth and he groaned. I should have felt bad torturing him; instead, I took delight in the fact I had the power to do so.

"Maybe I'll just rip your clothes off right here in the car."

I grinned. "You wouldn't dare."

"Darlin', you keep kissing me like that and I make no guarantees." His hand slid up under my shirt. I giggled as I tried to jump off his lap, but his arm around my waist kept me in place. He laughed, but the look in his eyes told me he wasn't completely teasing.

I stared into his face, soaking in the memory, wanting it to last through the week. My breath sucked in with a familiar tingle in the back of my head—the warning a vision was coming on. My peripheral vision blacked out and then an image filled my sight. I was seeing through Joe's eyes—my *gift* always showed me possible futures of whoever I was physically close to. This time, I was in an office, sitting at a desk, clenching my fist in anger. An older man stood in front of me. "It's not personal, Joe. If you hadn't broken the rules in Henryetta, the job would be yours."

As the vision faded away, I said, "You're not gonna get the job." My head fully cleared and I groaned. I'd give anything if I could stop from blurting out whatever I saw in a vision. For some reason my second sight was connected directly to my big mouth, and that thoroughly annoying trait was what got me into most of my trouble.

The smile fell from his face.

"I didn't know you were lookin' for a new job, Joe."

"It's a transfer, Rose, and it's not like it matters now."

I wanted to ask where he wanted to be transferred to, but I knew it had to be closer to me. There's no way he'd be looking for a job farther way. "You of all people know what I see doesn't always come true. I saw myself dead. I saw you dead. We both lived. We changed it."

He looked hopeful. "You really think I can change it?"

Why did I tell him that? "No. I'm sorry. The man said it was because you'd broke the rules in Henryetta." Breaking the rules had been my fault. Joe had disobeyed orders and helped me escape from Daniel Crocker. He'd saved my life. "I'm sorry, Joe."

His mouth lifted into a crooked smile. "Hey, don't worry. It'll all work out." He kissed me and looked into my eyes. "I wouldn't have changed a thing, except maybe trust you a little sooner."

I smiled, tears in my eyes. I couldn't imagine not having him in my life. I climbed out of his lap and shut his car door.

"Have a good week, Rose. Call me tonight and tell me all about jury duty."

I put a hand on my hip and teased, "And you can tell me absolutely nothing about your day. All that top secret police work."

Shaking his head, he grinned. "If you only knew. It's mostly boring."

"Nothing about you is boring, Joe Simmons."

He winked, a mischievous glint in his eyes. "Gotta keep the intrigue going." He shut the door and gave me a half-hearted wave as he drove away.

"Your mother'd be rollin' over in 'er grave."

I turned to the voice across the street. Mildred, my eighty-two-year-old neighbor, stood on her front porch wearing a pink, fuzzy bathrobe and curlers, holding a watering tin in her hand. I realized I was wearing pajamas consisting of a spaghetti-strapped tank top and short shorts. "Good morning, Miss Mildred."

"There ain't nothing good about a mornin' when you wake up and find a porno show in front of your house."

I released a heavy sigh. "It wasn't a porno show, Miss Mildred. I was tellin' Joe goodbye."

She shook her head, and even though I was too far away to hear, I knew she was clucking. "Fornicatin' is what you was doin'."

"Times have changed, Miss Mildred."

"Times are always changing, Rose Anne Gardner, but the Good Book don't and it says that what yer doin' is fornicatin'. You was raised better than that."

"I'll keep that in mind. You have a good day now." I gave her a small wave and called Muffy to come inside. As I entered the air-conditioned house, her words hung heavy on my conscious. Mildred was right. I'd been raised to believe lots of things, much of which turned out to be untrue. Still, I couldn't ignore the weight of my guilt pressing on my shoulders.

Why didn't I want to move to Little Rock to live with Joe? What held me back? I didn't know. I only knew I wasn't ready.

My stomach balled in knots as I picked up the phone to call my boss. She answered on the second ring, already knowing it was me from caller ID.

"What is it this time, Rose? A motorcycle gang? Did your Great Aunt Tilly die?"

I swallowed. "Jury duty."

After a second pause, her voice returned, flat. "Jury duty. Today?"

"Suzanne, I'm sorry. I plumb forgot." My grip on the phone was so tight I worried it would snap in two.

"I bet ten dollars and a lemon cream pie you don't have jury duty, Rose Gardner. I suspect you're just wantin' to stay in bed with your highfalutin' boyfriend all day. And when I find out I'm right, I'm firing your ass."

First of all, I knew she couldn't fire me. I worked for the state of Arkansas, and government jobs didn't work that way. I had an exemplary work history, considering they didn't count busting your boss for extortion as a demerit. Although I'm sure my old boss, Betty, might disagree.

"I'll see if the courthouse will give me a note to bring when I come back this afternoon. Okay?"

Suzanne responded by hanging up.

I kind of hoped jury duty lasted long enough that I didn't have to go back in for the rest of the day. I'd rather wrestle a starving razorback in the woods than face Suzanne.

While I showered, I thought more about Joe. He was right. I did hate my job, and Suzanne had always scared the bejiggers out of me, even more so now that she had all the power that went with being the temporary acting supervisor of satellite branch #112 of the Arkansas Department of Finance and Administration.

Why didn't I get a new job? There was nothing keeping me there. After Momma died, I'd found out that I'd inherited over a million dollars from my birth mother, yet I hadn't touched a dime of it. With the few expenses I had, I could afford to quit my job and to stay home for months until I figured out what I wanted to do with my life. But I'd never do it. I was raised to be more practical than that.

Some lessons can't be unlearned.

Chapter Two

Muffy stunk up the house while I got dressed, prompting another trip outside before I left, and stealing the extra ten minutes I had planned to get to the courthouse on time. I drove around the Henryetta town square looking for a parking spot close to the Fenton County Courthouse. It usually only took a few minutes to find an empty space, especially in the morning, but today every spot was filled. The first meter I found was several blocks away. Digging through my purse for change, I only came up with a dime and dollar bills. Of course, the meter took quarters.

The parking spot was situated in front of the floral shop where I'd bought Momma's funeral flowers only a month before. A bell on the door announced my presence when I entered. I basked in the air conditioning, slightly chilled by the beads of sweat on my arms. Joe had been right. It might have been July, but the day was going to be hotter than usual. It already was.

A young woman wearing an apron emerged from the backroom. "May I help you?"

"Hi, I'm parked out front there." I waved to my old Chevy Nova at the curb. "And I don't seem to have any quarters. Would you mind breaking a dollar for me?"

She pursed her mouth in disapproval. "Sorry, we don't give change."

"But I have to be at the courthouse for jury duty and I'm running behind already, if you could just—"

"We only give change to customers."

9

A trail of sweat trickled down my neck, and I lifted my hair to take advantage of the cool air. "But I was a customer a little over a month ago, for my momma's funeral. Agnes Gardner." If she didn't remember me, I knew she'd know about Momma. Her death had been big news. It wasn't every day someone was murdered in Henryetta, let alone with a rolling pin.

The girl shook her head with a disapproving glare. "You're not Mrs. Gardner's daughter. I remember when she came in to order the funeral flowers. She was a dowdy thing."

She was right. When I'd come in to order the flowers, it was before Aunt Bessie had cut my hair. Before I'd bought all new clothes that didn't make me look like an old lady. And before I'd decided I'd wasted my entire life trying to make my momma happy.

That Rose seemed like a totally different girl.

I lowered my hair and self-consciously tugged at the waist of my floral skirt. "It was me, I swear it. I've just changed since then."

"Customers only."

"Fine," I dug into my purse and pulled out my wallet. "What's the cheapest thing you have?"

"You can buy a carnation for a dollar."

After I handed her two dollars, she handed me a white carnation and change.

"Have a nice day," she said as she turned and walked to the backroom, but her tone didn't sound like she meant it.

I opened the door and found a police officer standing by the parking meter, writing out a ticket.

"Wait! I was gettin' change." I waved the coins at him.

He turned around to face me, and my mouth dropped open before I quickly closed it. The policeman writing my ticket was the same one who'd tried to handcuff me after Momma's murder. He would have done it, too, if Joe hadn't stopped him. "You," the officer said, narrowing his eyes and bending over his tablet. "Once a lawbreaker, always a lawbreaker."

His glare caught my breath before I wheezed out, "I didn't have any quarters. I had to get change."

"Then why do you have a flower in your hand? Looks to me like you thought you could park here illegally, pop into the store to make your purchase then leave, stiffing the city of Henryetta."

"No! That's not it at all and even if I did, it's only a quarter."

"Sure, it starts with a quarter today and the next thing you know you're a drug-addict robbing the Dollar General to get your next fix." He lifted his chin, a hard gleam in his eyes. "The law's the law, Ms. Gardner." He ripped the ticket off his tablet in an exaggerated motion and handed the paper to me. "But like I said, once a lawbreaker, always a lawbreaker."

I took the ticket and he walked back to his car, which he'd illegally parked behind mine. "But I wasn't a lawbreaker! I was innocent of my momma's murder and didn't do anything wrong this time."

He stood next to his open car door and pointed at the curb. "The parking meter says different. Have a good day." Then he got in and drove away, watching me in his rearview mirror.

"Why does everyone keep sayin' that when they don't mean it?" I stomped my foot and my ankle collapsed. The heel of my shoe had broken and flopped to the side. "Crappy doodles!"

Three blocks from the courthouse, I hobbled a half block before I finally caved and took off my shoes, carrying them in my hand. I pulled out my cell phone to check the time. 9:05.

Half running and half jogging, by the time I reached the majestic steps to the old stone courthouse, I was a sweaty mess. The reflection in the window told me my hair had fallen from the stifling humid air, and the sweat on my forehead had plastered the strands onto my face.

After passing through the massive wooden front doors, I stopped at security. An elderly security guard lifted a hand in warning. "You can't come in without shoes, ma'am."

I waved my heels. "I have shoes."

"You have to be *wearin'* shoes." He raised his bushy eyebrows.

"Don't I have to send them through an x-ray machine?"

The man leaned forward and narrowed his eyes. "This ain't the *airport*, ma'am."

"But my shoe's broken." I demonstrated the floppiness of the heel.

"No shoes, no entrance."

"But I'm due for jury duty at nine!"

"Then you're in a heap o'trouble. You don't show and they'll issue a warrant for your arrest. As it is, you're already late."

I bet Officer Barney Fife would volunteer to carry that warrant out. *Once a lawbreaker, always a lawbreaker* echoed in my head. "Fine," I muttered, bending down and slipping my feet into my shoes. I limped past the guard.

"Hold up there! You can't just go in. We need to examine your purse."

I handed it over with an exaggerated sigh.

The guard looked me up and down before putting it on the conveyor belt. "Come around this way." He waved to the end of the machine.

I walked over and waited as he ran the belt back and forth, back and forth, until he finally rolled my purse out and examined the contents.

"If you could just hurry a bit." I said. "As you already know, I'm late for jury duty."

His face lifted from studying my purse and he watched me for a second. "Security can't be rushed, ma'am. Are you wanting me to hurry 'cause you're tryin' to hide something?"

"No! *No!* I swear, I'm just so late—"

He closed my purse and pushed a button on his radio strapped to his shoulder. "Ernie, I'm gonna need some assistance. Gotta 10–66. Over."

"Copy that. I'll be there in five. Over." The radio crackled.

"Ma'am, if you could have a seat." He waved to a plastic chair against the wall.

"What? I can't go?"

"No, I need to do a pat-down and I need another officer present to ensure that you're not sexually harassed."

"*What?*"

"Ma'am, take a seat or I'll be forced to inform the judge that you're obstructin' justice."

I flopped in the chair, indignation rising. He was discriminating against me because of my shoes. After sitting for several minutes, I realized I hadn't been to the bathroom since I'd gotten up, and I'd had two cups of coffee. "Do you think I could go to the bathroom really quick?"

He shook his head. "Nope. The restrooms are located in a *secure* area."

The entryway was hot and I waved my hand to try to cool off with little success while I crossed my legs back and forth. Thinking about having to go only made it worse. I watched the minute hand on the industrial wall clock move slowly around the face. Over ten minutes had passed and no Ernie. I stood. "Look, I really need to go report for jury duty. If you could just let me go—"

"Sit."

"You can even pat me down, I swear I won't sue you."

"*Sit.*"

I was about to protest when I heard a familiar voice. "Well, well, well. It didn't take you long to get into more trouble." The police officer who'd given me the ticket hooked his thumbs into his belt and rocked back on his heels with a smug smile. "I can't say I'm surprised."

The security guard pointed toward me. "You know this one, Ernie?" His voice rose.

"Oh yeah, I just gave her a ticket for illegally parking."

"I was gettin' change," I huffed.

"Then last month, there was the whole business with her mother's *murder*." He half-whispered the last word.

The security guard raised his eyebrows and appraised me with the new information. His hand rested on the butt of his gun.

"I was innocent! Daniel Crocker killed Momma."

"Ma'am, I'm gonna need you to stand and spread your feet and hold your arms out, away from your body."

I considered protesting. This was unfair, but I figured if I put up a fuss Officer Ernie would be only too happy to haul me down to the police station, a place I had no intention of going back to. "Hey," I said as the guard started patting my sides. "This is the county courthouse and you're a city police officer. What are you doin' here?"

Ernie shifted his weight. "Robbie is off with gout so I'm dropping in to help Ol' Matt when he needs assistance. Not that it's any of your business."

The guard moved down my legs and finally dropped his hands. "She's clear."

"You sure?" Officer Ernie asked. "She's a sneaky one."

"Yeah, I'm pretty sure."

Ernie stuck out two fingers in the shape of a V and moved them from his eyes to me and back again. "I'm watchin' you."

Rolling my eyes, I picked up my purse off the end of the conveyor belt and hobbled to the elevator. The postcard said to report to room 226.

As luck would have it, the elevator moved slower than Ol' Matt performing his security checks. By the time I reached the second floor and opened the door to the room, it was nine-thirty and I was about to pee my pants. Since I was already late, a couple more minutes wasn't going to hurt anything.

I spotted the women's restroom halfway down the hall but saw the *Closed for cleaning* sign just as I was headed in. "Excuse me!" I called into the restroom.

A Hispanic woman appeared in the doorway and pointed to the sign. "It's closed."

"I *know*, but I really need to go," I pleaded.

Pinching lips in disgust, she shook her head. "No, you go downstairs."

I groaned as she spun around and dismissed me. I didn't have time to hobble downstairs and find another restroom. The men's restroom was next door. I glanced up and down the hallway. No one. Sticking my head in the doorway, I called out in a whisper-shout, "Hello! Is anyone in there?"

Silence.

Should I? *Could* I? Shoot, weren't men's restrooms just like women's except for those little porcelain pots on the wall? Besides, I was sure I'd paid for at least one of them with my tax dollars. Not that I wanted to use a porcelain pot on the wall. The stall would work just fine.

Tiptoeing into the room, I closed my eyes and opened them a crack in case someone was really in there. Empty.

I hurried into the stall to do my business. As I was finishing up, someone shuffled in and stopped at the urinal next to my cubicle. I looked down and saw a pair of men's dress shoes. My eyes widened and I picked up my feet, knowing that if whoever was out there saw my heels, he'd know the restroom had been inhabited by a woman. Unless I was a cross-dresser, which wasn't likely in the Fenton County Courthouse on a Monday morning. But then again, what did I know about cross-dressing? I'd worn my first lacy bra and panties only about a month ago.

A cell phone chirped and I nearly fell off the toilet before I realized it was ringing outside the stall.

He answered the call while I heard a stream of water and grimaced at the thought. A few moments later, it was clear he'd finished his business but continued chatting on the phone. I restrained a groan. Didn't he know I had to report to jury duty?

"No, don't worry," he said. "You're gettin' worked up for nothing."

Being over thirty minutes late to jury duty qualified for something to get worked up about as far as I was concerned.

"This thing will never go to trial."

I pulled out my cell phone and switched it to silent, checking the time. 9:34. Had they already sent the police out to arrest me?

And that's when I felt it coming. A vision. I braced myself against the side of the stall.

I sat at a beat-up table in an old kitchen. Dirty dishes spilled out of the sink and onto the counter. My left hand held a pen, a half-finished crossword puzzle in front of me.

A cat jumped onto the table, nearly bumping over an ashtray with a burning cigarette. I heard a man say, "We have nothing to worry about."

My hand picked up a piece of food and held it toward the cat. "Don't you worry, Felix. They'll never figure out who that lapel pin belonged to. How many pins got dogs on 'em with a bird and a tree?" I took a drag of the cigarette, blew the smoke out the side of my mouth, then put it down and picked up my pen. My left hand, which had a long jagged scar from my wrist to my forearm, filled in the word *buzzard* on the puzzle. I laughed. "We're goin' to get away with murder."

My vision faded and I was back in the stall. "You're gettin' away with murder." I clapped my hand over my mouth in horror. Had he heard me?

I froze, straining for any sound. He was no longer talking on the phone. I placed one foot on the floor without my heel clicking, then the other—not an easy task since my heel was flopping.

15

Lowering my head, I looked for the man's legs and found nothing. He'd left the bathroom.

With a long exhale, I opened the stall door and hurried to wash my hands. What had I just seen?

Had someone really committed murder, and was he going to get away with it?

Then again, *getting away with murder* was an expression everyone used. It probably meant nothing. So why was he talking about a trial?

I pulled my juror letter out of my purse and ran out of the bathroom. I didn't want whomever it was to come back and realize I knew his secret, if he actually had one. Besides, I was already late and hoping to avoid getting arrested. I'm sure Officer Ernie would love to give me a strip search, looking for stray rolling pins.

In my haste, I didn't look before I exited the restroom and ran into something hard. Stumbling backward, I screamed at the top of my lungs, tripping on my broken heel, and fell to the floor as papers floated around like a sudden snowstorm.

The murderer had come back to get me.

Chapter Three

"Watch where you're going!" a voice snarled above me.

The papers settled enough for me to stare into the angry blue eyes of a man wearing a dark suit, a white shirt and a crisp yellow tie. His dark blond hair was short but styled. He leaned down and I couldn't help my involuntary squeak as I scooted back in fear.

"This is a courthouse, not a barroom brawl."

"I . . . I'm sorry . . ." I stammered, caught off guard by his hostility. I reached for the paper closest to me.

"Don't touch those!" He reached for the sheets, his shirtsleeves pulling back to reveal his wrists. No scars. He was scary enough without worrying that he was the man in the restroom.

Jerking my hand back, I got to my knees and grabbed the wall to pull myself up. "I was only tryin' to help. No need to be nasty about it."

His entire face puckered as he squatted. "You've helped quite enough. *Thank you.*" Even with his snotty tone, his cultured Southern accent was evident. He appeared to be in his early thirties, but his attitude and haughtiness reminded me of the women in the Henryetta Garden Club. The ones from old Southern money.

"I'm sorry. It's just that I'm late to jury duty—"

A throaty snort erupted. "Of *course* you are. Why am I not surprised?"

Indignation squared my shoulders. "It's obvious that your mother raised you better than this. What do you think she would say, knowing you were treatin' a lady this way? You should be ashamed of yourself. Mr. . . ." My eyebrows rose as I waited for him to answer.

His jaw dropped halfway through my tirade and his cheeks pinkened, making him look younger and less hardened. "Deveraux."

"Mr. Deveraux." I pursed my lips in disapproval. Any properly raised Southern gentleman was terrified of his mother's wrath. Especially when the combination of poor manners and women were involved. "I suggest you brush up on your manners." I turned left and started down the hall only to realize, to my horror, I had gone the wrong way. I stopped midstep and squeezed my eyes shut. This whole morning had to be a nightmare, just a bad dream. Situations like this didn't happen in real life.

Only, in my life, they did.

Sucking in a deep breath, I spun around and headed the opposite direction, teetering on my broken heel. With my jaw thrust forward, I tried to pass Mr. Deveraux with as much dignity as I could muster.

Mr. Deveraux, to his credit, ignored me as he continued to scoop up the papers and stuff them into manila folders.

Just when I thought I was home free, I heard a smug voice behind me. "Fourth door on the right."

The sound of my *click-thud* steps echoed off the hard surfaces in the hallway, but I continued walking, in spite of my billowing mortification. It's hard to look dignified when you're swaying like a sailor. Finally, I reached the fourth door. I glanced down at my letter to make sure I had the right room, not trusting Mr. Crabbypants, but my hand was empty.

I'd dropped the letter.

Closing my eyes with a sigh, I wondered how this day could get worse.

"Lose something?"

A groan escaped before I could squelch it. I opened my eyes and plastered on a smile.

Mr. Deveraux handed the paper to me with a smirk. "A gentleman always helps those less fortunate, Miss Gardner." He tilted his head toward me before moving briskly down the hall. "You're late. You better get in there," he called out, looking straight ahead.

I closed my gaping mouth and opened the door.

The room was packed and a man in a police uniform stood in front. ". . . it's your civic duty." He watched me enter the room, along with about seventy-five other people.

When would I stop asking if things could get worse? "I'm sorry I'm late."

The man gave me a stern, disapproving look. "Jury duty started at nine o'clock sharp, miss."

"But I—"

"*If* you are chosen for jury duty, you will be expected to show up before the check-in time, which I have already told the other citizens who were considerate enough to show up when they were supposed to. Now if you will please take a seat."

I hung my head in embarrassment. As I made my way to the back, a hand reached out and grabbed my wrist. I almost screamed again, choking to stop the exhale. In a coughing fit, I looked down at a middle-aged woman with short, fluffy red hair, sitting at a desk. "I need your juror letter," she whispered.

I handed her my paper, and she marked my name off a list and handed it back, glancing over the desk and down at my shoe. Opening her desk drawer, she pulled out a small metal tube and handed it to me.

Super glue. At least something was going my way.

The woman leaned forward. "You can find a seat, darlin'. And fix your heel." She winked.

"Do I hear talking?" the man in front asked.

The woman at the desk widened her eyes in mock surprise and grinned. When no one responded, he resumed talking.

I scanned the back of the room, searching for an empty chair. I found one in the second to last row, between an elderly man in overalls and a girl who looked close to my age. She had long blonde hair, with curls all over her head that had probably taken forever to curl, and a little more makeup than she needed. But she smiled at me as I made my way down the aisle toward her.

"He's got a corn cob stuck up his butt today, don't he?" she whispered as I sank into the chair.

"I guess . . ."

"Do I hear talking in the back?" the man called out, scanning the room. His eyes rested on me for half a second. I stared straight ahead, pretending to latch onto his every word.

When he seemed certain he had everyone's attention, he continued lecturing. "Your pay will be eight dollars for the *day*. No, that is not eight dollars an *hour*. There will be no complaints that this is below minimum wage. Not only is this your civic duty, but it is a privilege." He looked at his watch and cleared his throat. "That's it. I'll turn this over to Marjorie Grace."

The woman, who had checked me in, walked to the front of the room. "Thank you, Bailiff Spencer, for fillin' in for Judge McClary at the last minute."

But Bailiff Spencer didn't hear a word. He'd already rushed out the door.

"Judge McClary usually comes in to address the potential jurors. But the judge was detained in chambers so Spencer had to come and brief y'all instead. It's supposed to be like a pep talk, but he seems to have put the fear of God into everyone instead."

I looked around the room. Mostly I saw the backs of people's heads, but the few faces I could see looked shell-shocked.

Marjorie Grace tried to lighten the mood. "Well, now, looks like Bailiff Spencer forgot he was addressin' jurors and not the defendants."

A nervous laughter spread throughout the room.

"I assure you that we in the Fenton County court system welcome you and thank you for volunteering your time to make our system of democracy the best in the world. Now, if I can ask you for your patience as we wait to see if there are any cases to be tried today. You may get up and walk around, but don't wander too far. We'll need to call you back in to let you know what's going on."

Marjorie Grace walked back to her desk, and the buzz of hushed voices filled the room.

The girl next to me held out her hand, her fingernails painted in a bright pink. "Neely Kate Rivers."

"Hi, I'm Rose." I shook her hand, purposely omitting my last name.

She didn't seem to notice. "I live outside of Henryetta, but I work here at the courthouse, which is how I know all about Mr. Corn-Cob-Butt." Neely Kate giggled.

"Can you get picked for jury duty if you work here?"

"Shoot no, but I figured I'd get out of a morning of work so I didn't try to get out of it. My boss Frank has been crabbier than usual lately, so I could use a morning off with pay. It doesn't matter anyways. They aren't goin' to pick anyone for jury duty. The only trial on the docket this week is an armed robbery and murder. The defendant is sure to plea-bargain. I checked."

"Oh. Can you do that? Check on a case?" The phone conversation in the restroom came back to me, reminding me that I'd been fleeing before I ran into Mr. Crabbypants. The mystery man had mentioned a case not going to trial.

With a playful grin, she leaned forward and whispered. "What some people don't know don't hurt 'em." She sat back up. "What do you do?"

My imagination was working overtime. How many murderers were running around Henryetta, scot-free? Hopefully, none since Daniel Crocker was in jail. "What? Oh, I work at the DMV."

Neely Kate's perky nose scrunched up. "Eww." Then her eyes flew wide in horror. "Oh, my stars and garters! I am *so* sorry. My momma says I don't have a lick of sense, just sayin' whatever pops into my head. She says I need an internal censor."

I waved my hand. "That's okay. I don't like my job, and I dislike my new boss even worse. I keep thinking I'll get another one, I just can't figure out what I'd like to do."

She rested her hand on my arm. "Honey, you have no idea how much I understand your situation. I work down in the Property Tax Department, and it ain't no picnic these days, so don't you be worryin' about where you work. Everyone in the courthouse has been a bear to work with since human resources announced last year that the county pension money was lost in bad investments. Some of 'em were like fools hangin' laundry on the line when a storm's coming, pretendin' like nothing happened, but just last week they made the official announcement that it's all gone."

Her frown turned to a big grin. "But I'm getting married next month. See?" She thrust her left hand in front of my face, showing me her diamond engagement ring. "After I get married, I'm hopin' to quit, so I don't need to worry about a pension." Neely Kate patted my hand. "So, what about you? Are you married?"

I shook my head. "Oh, me? No."

"Boyfriend?"

My face heated. I still wasn't used to admitting it.

"You're blushin'. That's so cute!"

While I glued my heel, Neely Kate continued talking about her fiancé, her momma, the house she hoped to buy, her cat, her car, a dead deer she saw on the side of the road, and the donut she'd dropped on her lap on the drive to the courthouse that had left a stain resembling an unfortunate bathroom accident. She leaned forward, raising an eyebrow and whispered, "If you know what I mean."

If she wasn't so cute, I might have found her annoying. Instead, I found her wonderfully distracting. I forgot about my vision and I didn't have time to feel sad about Joe.

"If I could get everyone's attention." Marjorie Grace called from the front of the room. "I've just gotten word that there's a case on the docket and we're going to pick the jurors from the jury pool."

"What?" Neely Kate whispered. "There wasn't supposed to be any trials this week." She turned to me with a mischievous smile. "Maybe I'll get the whole day off now."

Once everyone had returned to their seats, Marjorie Grace stood next to a giant wire sphere filled with numbers, just like the bingo balls at the VFW. Marjorie Grace explained she would call out numbers and if it matched the number on our jury letter, we would be part of the juror panel. But it was only the first step to being on a jury. If our number was called, we were to gather our things and go to the front of the room.

"Fourteen."

A woman stood and walked to the front.

"Thirty-seven. Forty-four. Seventy-two."

One by one, people started lining up at the door.

"Twelve."

"Oh!" Neely Kate shouted in glee, like she'd won a prize. "That's me!" People laughed as she walked past me. "It was nice meetin' ya, Rose."

Person after person filed to the front and I was sure I was going to escape selection, though I was already dreading seeing Suzanne.

"Twenty-nine."

I looked down at my paper to verify I wasn't mistaken. Marjorie Grace had just called my number.

"Number twenty-nine," she repeated.

I picked up my purse and stood.

Marjorie Grace smiled. "And that concludes the jury panel selection. The rest of you are dismissed."

I followed the other panelists into the hall, trying to ignore the dread burrowing in my gut. I had a sneaking suspicion my day was about to get even worse.

The bailiff, Mr. Spencer, led us to an empty courtroom and had us sit in the audience chairs. Once we were seated, he passed out clipboards with attached questionnaires.

"Answer all the questions honestly. If you lie, Judge McClary will find out and throw you in jail for perjury," the bailiff said.

More than a few heads popped up in alarm.

Mr. Spencer continued, "We'll collect your questionnaire when everyone's done."

The questions were simple enough. My age, my occupation. I had to give more time to *Have you ever been a victim of a violent crime? If yes, please describe.*

After the questionnaires were collected, we were escorted back to the original room. Neely Kate sat next to me. "There's no way I'll get picked. I know too much about this case, not to mention I work in the courthouse."

An hour later, Marjorie Grace announced that we needed to go back to the courtroom.

The bailiff had us line up against the wall. "Will the following jurors please sit in the juror box . . ." He paused, scanning the lineup. "This doesn't mean you've been picked for jury duty, it just means that the attorneys wanna ask more questions." He looked down at the clipboard. "Four, twelve, twenty-three, twenty-nine, thirty-three . . ."

The rest of the numbers faded as I walked to the juror box, more than a little frightened. What could they possibly ask?

Once everyone was settled in their seats, men filed through the door and sat at the two tables in front of the judge's bench. One of the men was Mr. Deveraux.

My stomach knotted into a ball. This couldn't go well.

"All rise," the bailiff announced. "The Honorable Benjamin McClary."

A middle-aged man with salt and pepper hair and a stout body that wasn't helped by his black robe entered through a door in the back wall. Once he sat at the judge's bench, the bailiff motioned for everyone to sit down.

The judge looked out into the gallery, folding his hands on the counter in front of him. "I'm Judge McClary. I apologize for not being able to meet with you earlier, but I was told that Bailiff Spencer filled in for me." He nodded to the bailiff, then turned his attention to the jurors. "Thanks to all of you who've taken time out of your busy schedules to fulfill your civic duty. I'm sure it wasn't easy for many of you, but rest assured, your effort hasn't gone unnoticed. Okay then, first I'm going to swear you in."

We raised our right hands and repeated the short oath.

I knew I was just a potential juror, but being sworn in made me nervous.

"I'm going to introduce the attorneys for this case, as well as the defendant. If you know anyone here, I'll need you to raise your hand and tell us how you know him. I hope I don't need to remind you that you're under oath and lyin', either through your words or by omission, is grounds for perjury, which can be punished with time in jail."

A few potential jurors looked anxious.

"First is Mr. Mason Deveraux III, the assistant district attorney of Fenton County, who will be prosecuting this case. Does anyone know Mr. Deveraux, or had any dealin's with him?"

I squirmed in my seat, unsure what to do. I'd never met him before this morning, but I *had* talked to him. Did that count? Judge McClary said I could go to jail for not telling him things and I wasn't so sure Suzanne was required to give me time off to sit in county lockup. Biting my lip, I raised my hand.

Mr. Deveraux's eyes just about bugged out of his head.

"Yes, miss," Judge McClary said. "Which juror number are you?"

"Twenty-nine."

"How do you know Mr. Deveraux?"

"We weren't actually formally introduced."

The judge's eyes darkened. "That's okay, seein' as how you aren't goin' to a cotillion. Just tell us how you know him."

I urged my racing heart to slow down, not that it paid attention. Maybe this wasn't such a good idea after all. "We met this morning. I was late to jury duty because I got a parking ticket, and then my heel broke, and I had to use the restroom . . ." I looked at the judge. "I didn't mean to be late, I swear it, but then Ol' Matt in security held me up until Officer Ernie showed up to watch Matt frisk me so I wouldn't sue for sexual harassment, even though I swore I wouldn't."

The judge's eyebrows rose.

"So I had to wait for Ernie to show up, and the elevator was slow and when it stopped I really had to go to the bathroom and I . . ." I decided to keep the men's bathroom out of it. "I ran right into Mr. Deveraux, causing his papers to fly everywhere. And that's when I had an interaction with him." I glanced over at Mr. Deveraux, whose face had turned a shade of red that resembled the red peppers in Miss Mildred's garden.

"That's it?" the judge asked.

"Yes, Your Honor."

His eyes roamed around the room and he seemed uncertain what to say. He cleared his throat. "While I appreciate your honesty, miss, I was looking for something a little more substantive than that." He looked around the room. "Anyone else?"

A couple of people raised their hands. One man was his neighbor. Another was a woman who regularly served him at a restaurant where she waitressed. When the judge asked if they could be impartial in spite of their association with him, the man said he couldn't and the judge dismissed him.

He next introduced the defendant's attorney, William Yates. When the judge asked if anyone knew him, he looked at me with raised eyebrows. I studied Mr. Yates to be sure. He was a short, older man with thinning grayish-brown hair. His mouth was turned into a frown. Since I'd never seen him before, I gave Judge McClary a tight smile. Several potential jurors raised their hands, saying they knew him, all saying they couldn't be impartial. The judge dismissed them, too.

"The murder victim was Frank Mitchell. He was the evening manager for the hardware store. Did anyone know Mr. Mitchell or have any dealings with him that would affect your impartiality?"

No one raised a hand.

"And now this is the defendant, Bruce Wayne Decker. Mr. Decker has been charged with aggravated robbery and murder in the second degree. He's been accused of killing Frank Mitchell at Archer's Hardware store after the store closed. Take a good look at Mr. Decker. Do you know him or does he look familiar to you?"

He looked like he was in his twenties, and even though he wore a dress shirt with a tie, the way he tugged at his collar suggested he wasn't used to wearing it. Mr. Decker had a wild look in his eye and his hand twitched. When he realized we were all watching him, he stuffed his hand in his lap.

Both the judge and Mr. Deveraux looked at me, but it wasn't me they needed to worry about. Out of the forty jurors in the original panel, about fifteen raised their hands. Quite a few were vague about how they knew Mr. Decker, but when asked if they could be impartial, almost all answered no. The judge told them they could go.

Mr. Deveraux looked miffed. The number of potential jurors was dwindling fast.

Judge McClary said next they would ask questions of some of us based on our responses to the questionnaire. Lucky for me, I was first.

Mr. Yates stood. "Ms. Gardner." He looked over the top of his reading glasses. "You listed that you'd been a victim of a violent crime."

I swallowed. "Yes, sir."

He peered at a paper in his hand. "You were involved in the big bust of the marijuana and stolen car parts ring that occurred about a month ago." He looked up again.

I nodded.

"Miss, you'll need to answer out loud so the court reporter can record your answer." The judge motioned to a woman sitting to the side.

"Yes, Your Honor."

"Was that a 'yes,' you were involved?"

"Yes, sir."

Mr. Yates cleared his throat. "You didn't elaborate much on this. Could you tell us more about your involvement?"

I told him how Daniel Crocker thought I was the anonymous informant he'd paid money to but who was withholding the promised information. And how the undercover policeman living next door to me thought I was involved, too. But I left a lot out, perjury or not. He'd never believe it was my visions that got me in the mess in the first place.

Mr. Yates sat on the corner of his table and crossed his arms, staring straight at me. "Ms. Gardener, since you've been a victim of a violent crime, we're concerned you're incapable of being impartial. This isn't a judgment on you or your character. We think it would be best if you recuse yourself from the case."

My face burned, not believing what I'd heard. "Excuse me?"

Mr. Yates leaned forward and enunciated his words. "Recuse means to excuse yourself."

Resentment at his insult burned deep. "I know what recuse means. What I'm confused about is why you think I can't be impartial."

"I've already explained that to you."

"Then I obviously didn't understand it. Maybe you should explain it to me again."

I caught Mr. Deveraux smirking as he gave the paper on the table in front of him his full attention.

"All right, Ms. Gardner." Mr. Yates stood and walked toward me. "My client has been accused of armed robbery and murder. Since you were the victim of an assault and your mother was a murder victim, I'm having some trouble believing that you can judge him without bias. Wouldn't you say that you'll be more inclined to find him guilty and suggest a stiffer penalty because of the ordeal you yourself have been through?"

The fact I'd had the worst morning in the history of mornings didn't help me hold back all the things I wanted to say to that shortsighted, arrogant man. But every eye in the room was focused on me, waiting to hear how I was go answer. That is, with the exception of Mr. Deveraux, who looked like he was choking on something. I refused to embarrass myself.

I plastered a sugary smile on my face and looked the defense lawyer straight in the eye. "I'm sorry, Mr. Yates, but I was under the assumption that Mr. Decker was innocent until proven guilty. Are you sayin' that he's not?"

Mr. Deveraux broke into a coughing fit as half the courtroom burst into laughter.

Judge McClary banged his gavel. "Order in the courtroom. Settle down, people." He turned to me. "Ms. Gardner," he exhaled my name in a long breath. "You must understand Mr. Yates's concern."

"I do, Your Honor, but he has to understand mine. Although I've never served on jury duty before, I was taught the defendant is innocent until proven guilty beyond a shadow of a doubt. Isn't the juror's duty to listen to the evidence and make a decision based on what's presented?"

"Well, yes . . ."

"How can I be biased against the defendant if I believe he's innocent until it's been proven otherwise?"

"I'm sure you *feel* that way, Ms. Gardner," Mr. Yates drawled. "But once you start hearing evidence about crime scenes and victims' testimonies, memories of your own *unfortunate* experience are bound to resurface, makin' it difficult for you to concentrate on the case at hand. It's nothing to be ashamed of. No one thinks badly about you recusing yourself."

"I'm a lot stronger than I look, Mr. Yates, and I never said I was recusin' myself."

"Ms. Gardner—"

I lifted my chin. "I'm not gonna do it."

Mr. Yates turned to face the judge, clenching his fists at his sides. "Your Honor!"

Judge McClary leaned forward on his elbows and rubbed his forehead with his hand. "Ms. Gardner. No one's doubting how strong you are, but when evidence is presented, you might experience some fear or animosity toward the defendant."

"And I might get struck by lightnin' in the next thunderstorm, but that doesn't mean it's gonna happen."

The judge rubbed his eyes then looked up with a pained expression. "Ms. Gardner, can you see how it would be in everyone's best interest if you'd just recuse yourself?"

"Your Honor, with all due respect, you're askin' me to lie, which you told me only a few moments ago was perjurin' myself."

Raising his eyebrows in frustration, Judge McClary looked at Mr. Yates. "Short of throwing in her in jail for disrupting the court, I can't make her do it. And considering the fact she thinks she has to lie to recuse herself, I'm gonna let this stand. If you don't want her on the jury, Mr. Yates, just put her on your exclusion list."

Mr. Yates looked flustered with the judge's decision. He took his seat and tapped his papers on the table before he asked another juror a different question. Mr. Deveraux tilted his head to look at me, his earlier disdain replaced with something I couldn't decipher.

Their voices faded to a murmur as my hands began to shake in my lap. I couldn't believe I'd stood up to Mr. Yates. What had gotten into me over the last month and a half?

After the attorneys asked their questions, we filed out of the courtroom and back into our original room while we waited to find out who made the final jury cut. Not that I had to worry. There were only sixteen of us left, but there was no way I'd make it into the pool of twelve and one alternate.

Neely Kate had been dismissed during questioning so I didn't have her to distract me. Instead, I thought about Joe. I wondered what job he'd applied for, and guilt crept in. It didn't seem fair that he would change his job to move closer to me and I wouldn't even consider moving for him. But that wasn't true. I had considered it, but every time I did, fear gripped me like a boa constrictor.

Thank goodness I planned to eat dinner at Violet's house. I didn't think I could face a night alone.

After about an hour, the bailiff stood at the entrance to the door. "Will the following jurors please gather your belongings and follow me: Five, Fourteen, twenty-two, twenty-nine, thirty-three . . ."

I stood in a daze. He'd called my number.

"The rest of you are dismissed."

I stopped at Marjorie Grace's desk on the way to the door. "I'm sorry, but I think there's been a mistake. The bailiff called my number."

"Oh no, honey, there was no mistake. If your number was called, then you've been selected for jury duty."

My eyes widened in surprised and I slowly shook my head. "Oh, no. There's no way they would have picked me."

Marjorie Grace cast a glance at the departing group. "You better hurry along now. It wouldn't do for you to be late twice now, would it?" She winked with a grin.

I hurried to catch up to the last of the jurors trailing out of the room. I had no idea how I'd been picked for jury duty, but somehow I knew it had something to do with the smirk Mr. Deveraux wore as he watched me leave the courtroom.

Chapter Four

Sandwiched between a large man on my right who smelled like he hadn't showered since the Clinton administration—the governorship, not the presidency—and a grandmother on my left who reeked of arthritis cream and cat food, I resisted the urge to wave my hand in front of my face. The air conditioner was on the fritz and a stifling heat filled the room.

After the bailiff swore in the jurors, the judge addressed us with a stern look. "While hearing this case, jurors are not allowed to discuss anything about the trial to anyone. You are not to research the case in any way, including internet searches or visiting the crime scene. If you choose to disregard the rules, you can be found in contempt of court and can be subject to time in jail."

More talk of going to jail. I never knew being on a jury could be so dangerous.

Mr. Deveraux paced in front of the juror's box, his hands behind his back as he spoke. Beads of sweat dotted his forehead, his face lightly flushed. He'd shed his jacket, but his tie rested firmly against his throat.

Tired from the heat and another night of little sleep with Joe, my eyelids drooped. I concentrated on the steady tap of Mr. Deveraux's fingers into his open palm.

"We cannot allow such a travesty!" he shouted.

Startled, I jumped in my seat.

He cast an irritated look my direction as he continued with his speech, telling us Mr. Decker was a menace to society. It was our duty to side with reason and keep Mr. Decker from hurting other unsuspecting citizens.

I studied Mr. Decker from the corner of my eye. He was skinny and on the short side. The tan lines on his neck and cheeks suggested that his neatly trimmed dark brown hair wasn't his usual style. He fidgeted in his seat and his attorney scowled. Mr. Decker stopped and glanced up, catching my gaze. Between his pointy nose and tiny eyes, and the way the corner of his mouth twitched, he reminded me of a mouse. It was hard to imagine him murdering anyone.

Mr. Deveraux stopped pacing and he paused to look at each juror one by one. His eyes rested on me and quickly moved to the cat lady on my left.

"Your job is simple. Listen to the evidence and come to the logical conclusion." His gaze stopped on my face.

Why was he staring at me?

"Thank you." He returned to his table and picked up his papers, tapping them on the table as his assistant leaned over and whispered in his ear.

Mr. Yates stood and tugged on the lapels of his grey suit then adjusted his tie. "Ladies and gentlemen of the jury." He paced parallel to Mr. Deveraux's path, as though he might be contaminated walking in the same route. "The state has circumstantial evidence linking my client to the crime. While Mr. Decker does have a criminal record, I will show the jury that nearly all of Mr. Decker's previous arrests and convictions were minor offenses. My client does not have a history of violent crime, and is in fact, incapable of committing such an act."

I knew I had to judge the case on the evidence presented, but I had to admit that I agreed with the defense attorney. Mr. Decker cautiously lifted his hand onto the table and touched the blank legal pad in front of him, as though he was scared of getting a paper cut.

When Mr. Yates sat down, the judge announced a recess, giving us an hour and a half lunch break. "And let's hope they have the confounded air conditioning back on when we come back!" he bellowed.

After Marjorie Grace told us to report back at one-twenty-five, we left the juror room in a slow moving pack. The heat hit me before I stepped through the doors, sticking my breath in my chest. No wonder the courtroom was so miserable.

I was undecided about what to do with my lunch break. I knew I should go home and let Muffy out, given her constitutional issues that morning, but the thought of walking three blocks to my car seemed like trekking across the Sahara Desert. Besides, going home would only make me sadder, facing the unbearable quiet without Joe there. Merilee's Café seemed like my best option—it was just across the street and bound to be cooler than the courthouse. On the way, I called the DMV to tell Suzanne that I didn't know when I'd be back to work. I thanked the stars above when I got her voice mail, but I knew I'd still get an earful later.

When I entered the café, I realized I wasn't the only one with the same reasoning. A crowd of people in business attire stood in the entrance waiting for tables. I turned to leave when someone called my name. I looked over my shoulder and found Neely Kate, sitting alone at a tiny table for two, waving her arm over her head. "Rose! Come sit with me."

Pushing my way through the crowd, I lifted my hair away from my face. There were so many bodies in the restaurant, I wasn't sure it was any cooler than the courthouse. I sat in the chair across from her and released a heavy sigh.

"It's hotter than a flapjack on a griddle." Neely Kate picked up the laminated menu. "Do you need one of these?"

I nodded. Merilee's didn't offer much selection and most people already knew what they wanted before they even sat down. Seeing how I hadn't been there since Daddy died several years ago, I needed to reacquaint myself.

"I heard you got picked for jury duty."

I glanced up from the menu, my mouth dropping open. "How—"

She tilted her head to the side with a playful grin. "I hear things."

"Oh."

"Let's be honest, working in the Property Tax Department is boor-ring and it's not really that hard to know what's going on. I just keep my ears open." She tapped her earlobe to prove her point. "You'd be surprised what people say when they don't think anyone is listening."

"Which is how you knew about the case this morning."

"Exactly."

The waitress took my order and left.

Neely Kate folded her hands on the table. "I heard you had a run in with Mason Deveraux."

I hesitated. I wasn't supposed to discuss the case with anyone, but I guessed talking about Mr. Deveraux wasn't the same thing. "Yeah, I literally ran smack dab into him."

"I heard you gave him a tongue-lashing."

"But how . . . no one else was in the hall . . ."

"I told you. I know things." She waved her hand vaguely. "Don't question my methods."

For twenty-four years I had known things and people questioned every utterance that came out of my mouth, yet Neely Kate, who knew things that no one should know, self-assuredly sat there telling me to accept it.

I loved her already.

"Yeah, he was a bit snippy."

"Rumor has it he's like this all the time. He's the new assistant D.A., but he doesn't want to be here. He had a job up in Little Rock workin' in the state courts. But something happened up there—something so top secret *I* can't even find out. Now he's stuck here in Fenton County and he's takin' it out on everyone. I guess I can't say I blame him. I'd do anything to get out myself."

I shrugged. I used to think that too.

"His name is Mason Van de Camp Deveraux *the Third*. Could you imagine having such an awful name? No wonder he's so crabby. Anyways, he just started a little over a month ago. About the time that big crime ring got busted."

I pinched my mouth shut, but my guilty look alerted Neely Kate. She shrieked, pointing to me. "Rose! Rose *Gardner*! Oh my stars and garters! You're her. How did I not realize it before?" She covered her mouth with her hand with a dramatic swoop then just as quickly dropped it. "Did you really find your mother dead on your sofa?"

I refrained from asking her how she didn't know already, but I suspected she did. She just wanted the firsthand account. Glancing down in embarrassment, I fiddled with a sugar packet. "Well, there's really not much to tell."

Her hand covered mine. "I'm so sorry, Rose. There I go again, buttin' into things that aren't my business."

Her sincerity grabbed my heart and I found myself wondering if we could actually be friends. "No, it's not that. Honest. It's just that I haven't really talked about it with anyone but Joe. Not even my sister."

"*Really?*"

I shrugged.

"You're kind of famous. You were one of the few to beat the Henryetta police."

"What do you mean?"

Her eyes widened and she bobbed her head. I swore she missed her Broadway calling, sticking around Fenton County. "Once they make up their mind someone's guilty, nothing sways their opinion. But you proved them wrong, not to mention you helped bust that crime ring that was going on right under their noses."

No wonder Officer Ernie hated me so much.

"It was nothing. Honest. It was mostly Joe."

Her eyebrows rose in excitement. "*Joe?* I see the way your eyes twinkle when you say his name. He's your boyfriend, isn't he? Spill it."

The rest of our lunch period I told her about Momma's murder, my Wish List, and how Joe helped me with it even though he thought I might be the extortionist. And I told her about Daniel Crocker and the flash drive. I even told her about Hilary, Joe's old girlfriend, and how she worked for the State Police with Joe and how I couldn't help being jealous of her.

"Why would you be jealous?" Neely Kate asked, licking chocolate pudding off her spoon with big sweeps of her tongue. I suspected Neely Kate did everything in an exaggerated manner.

"Well . . ." I hated to admit such ugly feelings. What possessed me to confess it? No wonder Neely Kate knew so much. She had a way of making people forget themselves and say whatever popped into their head. "She's really pretty for one thing. And obviously smart."

"You're pretty. And you must be smart to not only put Mason Deveraux III in his place today but Mr. Yates too." She shook her head in amazement. "You keep it up, Rose Gardner, and you'll be a local legend."

My face heated.

She laughed. "I don't know why you're so worried. If your Joe wanted to be with Hilary, he'd be with her, not you."

"But they have history."

Patting my hand, she laughed again. "So do you! How many couples bust up a crime ring?"

I smiled as my chest burned with gratitude until I felt the first signs of a vision. *Oh no.* I walked into an office and a man shouted, "Where have you been, Neely Kate? You're ten minutes late!"

"You're gonna get in trouble for getting back to work late," I blurted as the vision faded.

Neely Kate giggled. "Everybody knows that! I get in trouble every day." She pulled out a rhinestone-covered wallet and put her money on the table. "Since this case went to trial, it's bound to last all week. You want to have lunch together tomorrow?"

I nodded, grateful she hadn't flipped out over my vision. "Yeah, I'd like that."

"Yay!" she squealed, jumping out of her seat. "I'll see you tomorrow, Rose."

She flew out of the cafe, people parting to let her through like she was a movie star. Neely Kate was a force to be reckoned with.

To be on the safe side, I arrived in the jury room ten minutes early. Marjorie Grace sat at her desk, touching up her lipstick while looking into a compact. She glanced over with a smile.

I handed her the tube of super glue. "Thank you for this. I think I officially had the worst morning ever."

She laughed and tucked her lipstick into her purse. "I heard about your encounter with Mr. Deveraux in the hallway."

The blood rushed to my cheeks. "How does everyone know about that?"

"Maria from janitorial services was in the women's restroom and heard it all."

So much for Neely Kate's superpowers.

"No wonder you were surprised you got picked for jury duty."

"Did you also hear about my encounter with Mr. Yates?"

Her mouth gaped.

I guessed not and filled her in. When I finished, she burst out laughing, tears streaming from her eyes. "What I wouldn't give to have seen that! That man is a pain in the ass." She clapped a hand over her mouth with a laugh and looked around to see who had heard. Only a few other jurors were in the room and they huddled around the oscillating fan in the corner. Marjorie Grace lowered her voice and winked. "But you didn't hear that from me."

I held up my hands in surrender. "I didn't hear anything."

"Good girl." She lowered her head. "He hates his job and was close to retiring until he found out he wasn't going to get his pension."

"Why not?"

"He's a public defender and works for the county. He doesn't get paid much anyway, but when he found out he lost his retirement money . . . Let's just say he's not been very happy."

Fifteen minutes later, we filed into the courtroom, the heat so intense I felt like I was either Shadrach, Meshach, or Abednego headed into the fiery furnace. Only I suspected that an angel of God wasn't going to swoop in and save me. The windows were tilted open, not that it did much good. And while several fans had been set up around the room, the courtroom was too big for them to do anything other than stir up the hot air and make the room more like a convection oven.

Mr. Deveraux and his assistant had removed their jackets and loosened their ties, as had Mr. Decker and his attorney. Judge McClary's face was red, his round body covered in his black robe. I worried he was about to have a heat stroke.

After the judge banged the court back in session, he tossed the gavel across his desk. "As if it were even possible, this room is hotter than before lunch. How hot is it in here, Spencer? What's the temperature?"

The bailiff jumped. "I don't know, Your Honor."

"Well, find out! These conditions are inhumane."

I wasn't about to disagree.

Bailiff Spencer whispered in the ear of a nearby deputy, who hurried from the room.

"We'll do what we can to keep this trial movin'," the judge said. "Call the first witness!"

Mr. Deveraux frowned then stood. "The state calls Detective Kurt Taylor."

The back doors to the courtroom opened and the detective who'd been certain I killed my mother walked down the aisle. A chill traveled down my spine at the sight of him, and I reminded myself that I wasn't on trial and had nothing to worry about. After Detective Taylor was sworn in, he settled in the witness stand. Mr. Deveraux paced in front of the bench as he asked questions. I swear that man didn't know how to stay still.

"What did you find when you arrived at the crime scene on April 19th?"

Detective Taylor cleared his throat. "I arrived at the crime scene at 11:41 p.m. and found the rear emergency exit standing open. Upon entry, I discovered the victim, later identified as Frank Mitchell, near the door to the office, lying on the floor in a pool of blood, a concave wound on his right temple."

"And did you find the murder weapon on the premises?"

"We did not."

Mr. Deveraux turned to the judge. "Your Honor, the state would like to present evidence A-1, a photo of the victim at the crime scene."

Cat lady on my left, also known as Mrs. Baker, stopped fanning herself with her paper accordion, her eyes wide in anticipation.

A picture of the victim appeared on a wall screen. He lay on the concrete floor in a dark puddle, surrounded by pieces of PVC joints and tubes. His eyes were open, staring at nothing, his mouth twisted in an odd shape.

An image of Momma on our old sofa filled my head. She sat in the dark, a goose-egg-sized dent in her head, and blood splattered on the walls and furniture. I wondered how right Mr. Yates had been that I would find the evidence in the trial upsetting. But I caught him watching me, and I stiffened my back even though I felt like I was gonna barf. I was consoled to see that half of the jury looked like they were about to lose their lunches too.

"Did you find anything else?"

"We found an open safe, with a small amount of cash missing."

The deputy walked in with a white box. Within seconds, the box beeped repeatedly.

"What in tarnation is that racket?" the judge growled.

Bailiff Spencer's shoulders hunched. "It's a thermometer, Your Honor."

"Well? How hot is it?"

"Ninety-one degrees."

Judge McClary swore under his breath. "Mr. Deveraux, continue on until you're done with your questioning, and Mr. Yates," he looked across the bench, "you can cross-examine the witness tomorrow morning. It's too damn hot to think in here."

"Yes, Your Honor."

Mr. Deveraux's face had frozen in a scowl. It was a wonder his face wasn't permanently stuck that way, seeing how he wore that scowl ninety percent of the time. "And did you discover anything else, Detective Taylor?"

"Yes, we found a small lapel pin with a dog and a bird in a tree."

The vision I'd had in the restroom came crashing back into my memory.

Don't you worry, Felix. They'll never figure out who that lapel pin belonged to. How many pins got dogs on 'em with a bird and a tree?

We're going to get away with murder.

My eyesight faded to black, but it wasn't because I was having another vision. Mr. Decker was innocent and I'd peed next to a murderer.

Chapter Five

I woke up with Cat Lady waving her paper accordion in my face and a stench that made me gag. Just above her fan were the faces of Mr. Deveraux and Mr. Yates. While Mr. Deveraux looked concerned, Mr. Yates looked angry. I'd done it now.

I realized my head was in the lap of the man on my right, explaining the terrible odor. I jerked upright.

"Careful, now." Mr. Deveraux reached over the wall in front of the juror box, his hand resting on my arm as I swayed.

"I'm okay." I insisted, smoothing back my hair.

"See, Your Honor?" Mr. Yates screeched, pointing at me. "I told you she couldn't handle being on the jury."

"Oh, for God sakes, Yates," Mr. Deveraux boomed. "I was questioning the witness about a pin." He turned to me with a glare, his eyes daring me to contradict him. "Did all that talk about pins frighten you into a faint, Miss Gardner?"

In that moment, I realized a couple of things. One, Mr. Deveraux had put himself on the line by getting me on the jury, although for the life of me, I couldn't figure out why. And two, Mr. Deveraux knew my name. "No, of course not. Don't be silly." I swayed for effect, flapping the front of my blouse. "I got too hot, is all."

"That's it!" Judge McClary shouted, banging his gavel with more force than necessary. "I can't have jurors droppin' like flies. Court is adjourned for the day!"

Voices buzzed throughout the room and Mr. Yates wandered back to his table, but Mr. Deveraux watched me for a moment, his face expressionless, before he turned away.

After we got back to the juror room, Marjorie Grace pounced on me like a cat on a ball of yarn. "Are you all right, Rose?"

I waved my hand, thoroughly embarrassed. "Yeah, I'm fine. It was just so hot in there."

"Thank God you passed out," Cat Lady said, fanning herself, although her paper was now limp and damp. "I was *dyin'*."

"I can't believe they expect us to sit in there," another woman said.

Marjorie Grace pushed me into a chair and placed a wet paper towel on my forehead.

I looked up into her warm eyes. "I'm so sorry. I didn't mean to cause a fuss."

She leaned forward with a smile. "Don't you be worryin' about it."

"But Mr. Yates was so angry and Mr. Deveraux . . ." Mason Van de Camp Deveraux III confused me. One minute he was meaner than a coon dog attacking a copperhead, and the next he actually looked worried about me. I still couldn't get over the fact that he'd wanted me on the jury. He'd probably had to fight to get me since Mr. Yates was so adamant that I recuse myself. Maybe that was the answer right there. Mr. Deveraux could have done it just to tick off Mr. Yates.

"Both of those cranky butts will get over it. Word has it Judge McClary was about to pass out himself."

Marjorie Grace told everyone to report at nine o'clock the next morning but held me behind. "Are you sure you're okay? Was it just the heat?"

I knew what she was asking, and if I hadn't gotten squeamish looking at the photo of the dead man, I might have been insulted. Still, I couldn't tell her I'd seen a vision in the men's restroom, confirming my suspicion Bruce Wayne Decker was an innocent man after all. What would Mr. Yates think of *that*? But more importantly, who was the man outside my bathroom stall and how was it that Mr. Decker had been arrested instead?

I shook my head. "I'm fine, Marjorie Grace. I think it was a combination of the heat and the toxic cat food fumes comin' from Mrs. Baker."

Marjorie Grace laughed. "That'd do it right there."

I grabbed my purse and stood. "I'm gonna go home to my air-conditioned house and take a long cold shower and a nap."

"Take it easy tonight."

I wasn't looking forward to the walk to my car, but it wasn't much hotter outside than in.

When I pulled onto my street, I saw a U-Haul parked in front of Joe's old house. I gasped. No matter how much I'd prepared myself, I still wasn't ready for the final evidence that Joe was really gone.

Don't be silly. He sleeps in your house, which is better than sleeping next door any day.

Yet I couldn't swallow the lump in my throat as I pulled into the driveway. Three little boys played in the front yard, running around two men who were carrying a dresser from the truck.

"Heidi Joy!" one of the men shouted. "Come get these kids!"

A young woman appeared in the doorway with a baby on her hip and a toddler clinging to her leg. "Andy, I'm trying to unpack the house!"

"We're gonna be short a kid or two if we drop this damned dresser on 'em."

"Boys! Go in the backyard. Now!" the woman shouted.

The boys continued to run in circles, ignoring her.

Heidi Joy stepped on the porch. "Don't be makin' me get the wooden spoon!" She turned my direction and her eyes flew open in horror.

I waved, then pointed to my house with my thumb. "Hi, I'm Rose and I live next door."

She hobbled down the steps, the toddler still clinging to her leg. "Benny, you're gonna have to let go." The little boy dropped his grip and wailed.

Heidi Joy sighed in exasperation and grabbed his hand, tugging him to the yard. "Hi," she said when she reached me. "I'm Heidi Joy Blankenship, and that's my husband Andy."

One of men nodded.

"And these are my boys." The kids crowded around her, curious. The baby on her hip grabbed a handful of Heidi Joy's long black hair and stuffed it in his mouth. Heidi Joy didn't seem to notice.

"Hi," I waved again.

A wide-eyed boy who looked like he was four or five peeked between Heidi Joy's legs. "Do you have any kids?"

"What? No. No kids."

The boys groaned in disappointment.

"But I have a dog, Muffy, who desperately needs to come out. Hold on just a second." I unlocked my door and opened the bathroom door. Muffy made a beeline for the ajar kitchen door and squatted next to a bush at the corner of the house.

"Eww!" the boys shrieked. One of them wandered over and peered down at the pile, grinning. He petted the top of Muffy's head. "What's his name?"

"He's a she and her name is Muffy."

"She's ugly," the boy peeking through Heidi Joy's legs said.

His mother reached behind her and swatted the top of his head. "Keith! Don't be sayin' things like that! Tell the nice lady you're sorry."

"Sorry," he mumbled.

Muffy *was* kind of ugly, but that didn't mean other people could say so. "I'll have you know that Muffy is an intelligent dog and understands more than most people give her credit for. You might have hurt her feelings."

The little boy bit his lip, remorse in his eyes.

"I'm so sorry!" Heidi Joy gushed. "They're completely out of control today. Although it doesn't seem like it, they're good boys. They won't be causin' you any trouble."

"That's okay." I smiled. "I have a niece and a nephew so I know all about kids."

"Are you married?"

"Me? No." Why did that question always catch me off guard now? "I have a boyfriend. In fact, he used to live in your house until he moved back to Little Rock."

"If he's your boyfriend, how come he moved away from you?" the oldest boy asked, scrunching up his nose.

"Andy Junior!" Heidi Joy grabbed his arm and jerked him toward her.

"Well, his job here was temporary and when it was done, he had to go back. He comes down on the weekends."

Heidi Joy covered her chest with her hand. "So you met him while he was living here? That's so romantic." The baby stared at me, a handful of hair still in his mouth. Drool dripped off his chin.

"What's his job?" Andy Jr. asked.

"He works for the state police."

"He's a cop?"

"Yeah." The chaos of the little boys was getting to me, not to mention the heat. And talking about Joe reminded me how desperately I needed to get his advice on how to handle the Bruce Wayne Decker situation. I couldn't sit around and let an innocent man go to prison, but I also couldn't see Mr. Deveraux dropping all the charges. Somehow I didn't think he'd appreciate the significance of my vision in the men's restroom. "I should probably take Muffy inside now. It's awfully hot today. I can't even imagine moving in this heat. Can I get you anything? Some tea?"

"Thank you, but we're good. It was nice meeting you and I hope I see you again." Heidi Joy said, her eyes widening in desperation.

"Don't worry. I'll be around."

I cajoled Muffy inside even though she wasn't done sniffing the boys. Once I got her in, I dug my cell phone out of my purse. She looked up at me with a pout.

"I'm sorry! But I *really* need to call Joe."

Muffy laid on the floor and set her chin on her paws with her *you always say that* look. Okay, so maybe I did, but this time was really important.

Joe's phone rang until it went to voice mail. I almost left him a desperate-sounding message, but I worried that he'd drive down to check on me instead of just calling back. He was already in enough trouble with his job. Instead, I tried to make it light. "Hi, Joe. The good news is I got out of work all day at the courthouse." Tears burned my eyes. I really needed to talk to him. "The bad news is I miss you." My voice broke. "Call me."

After I took a shower, I laid on the sofa to watch TV, hoping to take my mind off of Bruce Wayne Decker. I pictured him sitting in his empty concrete cell on a cot, a toilet in the corner. It hit me that it could have been me there if I hadn't proved my own innocence in Momma's murder. I could be sitting in jail right now waiting to go to trial so Mason Deveraux could prosecute me in front of a jury of my peers while William Yates defended me.

Who was going to prove Mr. Decker's innocence?

I checked my phone for the twentieth time, wondering if I'd somehow missed Joe's call. Sitting around my house moping wasn't doing any good, so I decided to go to Violet's house early.

The new neighbors were still moving in furniture when I pulled out of the driveway with Muffy. I had no idea how they planned to get all that furniture and those kids into such a tiny house, not that it was any of my business. I'd let Mildred worry about it.

My niece, Ashley, met me at the door with squeals of delight. "Muffy!"

"Hey," I protested, watching her and Muffy race for the back door. "What happened to the days of you shouting *Aunt Rose?*"

"That was before you agreed to share your dog with her." Violet called from the kitchen. I found her wearing a pink ruffled apron with "Happiness is Homemade" embroidered across the top. She was making a salad while Mikey sat on the floor eating cheese crackers from a small plastic bowl.

I opened the refrigerator and pulled out a pitcher of sweet tea.

Violet focused on chopping carrots. "How was your day?"

It was a trick question. If she'd heard about my courthouse drama, she'd want details. If she hadn't, she'd be angry I hadn't told her. I decided to test the waters. "I got picked for jury duty."

Her head popped up and her eyes focused on me. "I didn't know you had jury duty."

I shrugged and grabbed a tomato. "I plumb forgot about it until Joe found my jury notice this morning." I pulled a knife from her drawer and sliced the tomato in half on a cutting board. "Did you know you can get arrested for not showing up for jury duty?"

A frown puckered Violet's mouth. "Joe was at the house this morning?" Her tone was accusatory.

I sighed. While this particular conversation was new, it was really a rehash of several previous arguments. "Yes, Joe was there, seeing how he spent the weekend with me, which you *knew* since we saw you at the park on Saturday and we were *together.*"

If possible, her lips pinched even tighter.

I stopped cutting and glared. "We're not having this conversation again, Violet."

Violet's husband, Mike, walked in from the garage and ducked his head. "Don't mind me. I'm heading back to change clothes." He shot past us and down the hall.

Violet peered around the corner, her scowl deepening. "For heaven's sakes, don't come out in clean clothes, stinkin' to high heaven. Take a shower, Mike!"

The shower water turned on down the hall.

Violet whacked the poor carrots with her knife as though she was beheading them. "Fine by me, Rose Anne Gardner, *I'll* do all the talkin' because I've already heard everything you've had to say."

"And I could say the same, Vi."

She blew a strand of hair out of her face, rolling her eyes. "Rose, Joe is your first boyfriend."

"Yes, Violet, seeing how I don't suffer from either short-term nor long-term memory loss, I'm very well aware that I never had a boyfriend until I was twenty-four."

"Which means you're inexperienced."

Looking up, I grinned. "Not anymore."

"*Rose Anne Gardner!*"

I crossed my arms. "Well you were the one who suggested a couple of months ago that I sleep with someone."

"And I also said you shouldn't sleep with just anyone. You need to find a boy with a nice solid family."

"You don't know anything about Joe's family."

She pointed her knife at me. "No, and neither do you, or you didn't at least last time I heard. Has that changed?" Tilting her head, she waited with a smirk.

Her question sobered me. "No." Joe refused to say much about his family other than he had a sister in Little Rock and his parents lived in El Dorado. In fact, he hardly said anything about his life before me. "Besides, what does it matter what his family's like? I'm datin' Joe, not his family."

"A man's family becomes important when you get married."

"Nobody said *anything* about getting married." I hadn't let my mind wander that far into the future. I didn't want to jinx us.

Violet's face softened. "Look, Rose. Joe's the first man you've dated. You're young. Have some fun."

"But Mike was the first boy you ever dated and look at you now."

The shower water turned off. Violet stared at me for several moments before she put her knife down and opened the back door. "Ashley, come inside and wash your hands for dinner." She picked Mikey up from the floor and set him in the high chair. Pausing, she looked around the kitchen, then turned to me, a sadness creeping into her eyes. "Give yourself a chance to explore your choices, Rose. Just don't settle, okay?"

The unspoken *like me* hung in the air, even more ominous in its silence. My chest filled with dread. Violet and Mike were one of the happiest couples I knew. I swallowed the lump in my throat. "Okay, Vi. I'll think about what you said."

Mike carried in a giggling Ashley and we sat down to eat. Without mentioning the details of the trial, I told them about my day at the courthouse, leaving out my vision in the men's restroom. Violet would have had a stroke if she'd known that I'd gone in there in the first place, and if she found out I'd been so close to a potential murderer again, she'd probably try to send a note to get me excused. I had a feeling no matter my age, Violet would always see me as the little girl who needed protecting from the world.

I went home sad and confused, and even more eager to talk to Joe. I tried him again at ten o'clock with no answer. Just as I was starting to get worried, he texted.

I can't talk right now. Still working. I miss you, too.

Joe told me little about his job, but he rarely worked this late, and he always called. The only time he'd had irregular hours like this since I'd know him was when he'd lived next door and worked undercover. But Joe told me he wasn't working undercover this week and he promised that he'd never lie to me. I desperately clung to my belief in him.

Chapter Six

The air conditioning was still out in the courthouse the next morning and tempers were short. Mr. Deveraux called Detective Taylor back to the stand to finish his questioning. He didn't ask about the lapel pin the detective found in the safe. Perhaps it was out of concern that I might pass out again, but more likely he thought it unimportant. My only hope was Mr. Yates would ask about the pin in cross-examination.

Mr. Deveraux took up his usual pacing. "Detective Taylor, did you find any fingerprints at the scene?"

"We found multiple prints and ran them all. Most belonged to store employees, but we also found Mr. Decker's. We had his prints on file, seeing how Mr. Decker has a lengthy record with the Henryetta police department."

"So you proceeded to question the defendant?"

"Yes."

Mr. Deveraux paused and turned to face the jury. "And how did you know where to find Mr. Decker?"

Detective Taylor looked at the defendant. "I got his last known address from his parole officer."

"Objection, You Honor!" Mr. Yates shouted, his face reddening beyond the pink flush he already had. "The counselor is trying to sway the jury with the details of my client's past instead of focusing on the facts at hand."

"Overruled." The judge frowned. "The details of your client's past are how the police linked your client to the crime scene." He looked down at Mr. Deveraux. "Proceed."

"So you went to Mr. Decker's home and questioned him?"

"Yes."

"And what happened during the interview?"

"Mr. Decker seemed exceptionally nervous. Nervousness is to be expected considering his past record—"

"Objection!"

"Overruled."

The corners of Mr. Deveraux's mouth lifted slightly as he titled his head toward Mr. Yates. "Go on, detective. You were mentioning the defendant's overly abundant nervousness."

Detective Taylor cleared his throat. "Yes, as I was saying, a certain amount of nervousness is to be expected from a repeat offender such as Mr. Decker, but his was more so than the usual."

Judge McClary pointed his gavel at Mr. Yates, whose mouth had dropped open about to protest. He pressed his lips together in an angry grimace.

"I pushed harder with my questioning about Mr. Decker's whereabouts the night before until he contradicted himself. He first stated that he'd been home all night then said he went to the Short Stop convenience store on the corner."

Mr. Deveraux began to pace in front of the jury box, stopping in front of the stinky man to my right. "Stopping at the convenience store is hardly a suspicious activity, Detective Taylor. What made you question his story?"

"The convenience store was closed for parking lot resurfacing that night."

A satisfied look filled Mr. Deveraux's eyes, and he nodded his head toward the jurors. "So . . . Mr. Decker was lying?"

"Yes."

A woman behind me mumbled under her breath. "Um, mm, mm."

"Did Mr. Decker confess?"

"No, and even though we knew he was lying, we didn't have enough evidence to arrest him at the time."

"Yet here he is in our fine courtroom. You must have discovered evidence to tie him to the crime."

"Yes, sir. An anonymous tip was called in informing the police that Mr. Decker had the murder weapon on his premises. The informant said they saw Mr. Decker place an object under his house after the murder. We procured a search warrant and found a bloody crowbar in Mr. Decker's crawl space."

I was all too familiar with anonymous tips and planted evidence. When Sloan, a bartender I'd met at Jasper's restaurant, had been killed, Joe planted a gun in my shed and called in a tip that the murder weapon was on my property, trying to protect me from Daniel Crocker. Luckily, I'd seen him do it and was able to avoid arrest, which was good, since I'd had nothing to do with Sloan's murder.

But even though I wasn't swayed by Detective Taylor's testimony, the jurors around me were. Mrs. Baker gasped at the news, and the man to my right pursed his lips and narrowed his eyes while turning to examine Mr. Decker.

Mr. Deveraux presented the crowbar in a plastic bag, still bloodstained, as evidence. "And did you conduct DNA analysis of the blood on the crowbar, Detective Taylor?"

"Yes, the blood was determined to be a ninety-nine percent match for Frank Mitchell's. Mr. Decker's fingerprints were found on the murder weapon as well."

Mrs. Baker shook her head. The woman behind me mumbled again.

I had to admit, Mr. Deveraux made a good case. The jury seemed to believe it. If I hadn't had my vision, I might have bought his reasoning, and maybe even got past the point of wondering how Bruce Wayne could pick up a crowbar, let alone whack someone with it.

Bruce Wayne Decker sat in the same chair as yesterday. He'd been doodling on the legal pad, gripping his pen in his right hand, but when Mr. Deveraux started asking about the crowbar, Bruce Wayne put down his pen and began to fidget. It was funny how the day before, I'd thought of him as Mr. Decker, but I felt a kinship to him now. I couldn't help wondering if his dad had an obsession with Batman. Bruce Wayne wore a short-sleeved shirt and a tie and kept sticking his fingers between his collar and neck, trying to widen the gap. He looked like a man who was slowly strangling.

Then again, I guessed he was.

Mr. Yates began his cross-examination, displaying the image of the victim again. He glared in my direction, probably checking to see if I was going to pass out a second time. The heat intensified my irritation. I hadn't passed out because of the picture.

I studied the image just to prove it didn't bother me, even though my stomach churned enough to make a batch of butter. Staring at the dead man's head, I wondered how the murderer swung the crowbar hard enough to bash in the victim's right temple.

Watching Bruce Wayne, who'd resumed his doodling, I realized he was right-handed. I imagined him picking up the murder weapon and striking. It would have hit the victim on the left side, not the right. A left-handed person would have hit him on the right side.

The man in my vision was left-handed.

A clue. I squirmed in my seat with excitement, only to get frustrated when Mr. Yates didn't bring it up in his questions.

Mr. Deveraux called the coroner as the next witness to declare that the victim had died from blunt-force trauma to the head. Mr. Yates had little to ask.

Judge McClary adjourned for lunch, growling about the heat. "If they don't get this goddamned air conditioning fixed soon, I'm gonna start arresting people for contempt of court."

As soon as Marjorie Grace dismissed us from the juror room, I went outside to call Joe while I waited for Neely Kate. I still hadn't heard from him and I was starting to worry. His phone rang twice before a woman answered, breathless. "Joe's phone."

I froze, recognizing the voice.

"Hello?" she asked.

Why was Hilary answering Joe's phone? My throat closed off and I had to push out the words. "I need to speak to Joe."

She laughed, low and sexy. "He's taking a shower right now. Can I take a message?"

Fear and anger mingled into one unnamed entity. Finally, I choked out. "Tell him Rose called."

"Oh! Rose!" she exclaimed in mock surprise. "I didn't know Joe still kept you around."

I bit back several ugly things hanging on the tip of my tongue. "Just tell him I called, please."

Neely Kate found me sitting on the courthouse steps in the shade of a Corinthian column, blowing my nose into a tissue while tears streamed down my face. "Hey, what's going on? Did you pass out in court again?"

I shook my head, amazed at her casual all-knowing attitude. Then I realized that finding out about my faint yesterday wouldn't have been that difficult. Turns out, the Fenton County Courthouse would have aced the telephone game.

"No," I wiped the tears from my cheeks. "Nothing like that."

She sat next to me, touching my arm. "Hey, what happened? Was it Deveraux? Did he do something? That man—"

I wished. "No, it's Joe." Just saying his name brought a fresh batch of tears. "He didn't call me last night, and when I called him a few minutes ago, Hilary answered and said he was in the shower."

Neely Kate stiffened momentarily then relaxed, rubbing my arm. "I'm sure there's a perfectly logical explanation. Was everything okay that last time you talked to him?"

"Yeah," I sniffed. "It doesn't make sense."

"But Hilary still has a thing for him?"

"I think so."

She threw out her arms and stood. "Well, there you go! She's jealous and she's trying to break you up. I'm tellin' ya, Rose, if Joe wanted to be with her, he would have been with her before he started going out with you. Now let's go to lunch."

I stood and brushed the dirt off the back of my legs. "You're probably right."

Laughing, Neely Kate linked her arm in mine. "The sooner you realize that, the better off you'll be."

At the moment, I wasn't about to argue.

"If you like, I'll ask my Great Aunt Opal about it the next time I see her. She's psychic."

My feet stopped of their own volition and my jaw dropped. "What did you just say?"

Neely Kate scrunched her nose. "You mean about my Great Aunt Opal?" She shrugged her shoulders and gave my arm a tug.

"Everybody on the western side of Fenton County knows she's got the sight."

"What . . ." My mouth had suddenly dried out and my tongue refused to work. I swallowed and tried again. "How do you know she's psychic?"

"Because she knows stuff nobody else knows."

"Like you?"

She grinned and winked. "I'm her protégé."

I spent the rest of lunch wondering if Neely Kate's Great Aunt Opal actually had the sight or if she merely had extra-perceptive powers like Neely Kate. I suspected the latter, but I couldn't let it go.

"How is your aunt teaching you to be psychic?" I wasn't so sure being psychic was something a person could learn. I'd simply been cursed with it. I'd give anything to *un*learn it.

"She's teaching me all her ways. Tarot cards, horoscopes. But her specialty is reading tea leaves."

I tried to hide my disappointment. Her aunt was a fraud.

"I can practice reading your tea leaves if you like."

I forced a smile. "So you can predict my future?"

With a laugh, she lifted her eyebrows. "Don't you be hatin' on the ways of the mysterious and mystical, Rose."

If she only knew.

Neely Kate dropped the subject and turned out to be the perfect distraction once again, telling me about her upcoming wedding and all the drama she was dealing with her fiancé's family, who lived in the Texas Panhandle.

"They want the groomsmen to dress up as cowboys, spurs and all. Can you *even* imagine?"

No, but the most recent wedding I'd attended was Violet's and Mike's, and thinking about it made me sad. Maybe they just needed a night out together. I could volunteer to watch the kids overnight, and they could plan a romantic getaway. The thought cheered me up. *Finally*, I'd found something I could do something about.

I was desperate to talk to Joe, now more than ever. I decided to listen to Neely Kate and trust him, but I had to admit that hearing Joe deny being with Hilary would make me feel better.

Mostly, I needed his advice on how to handle what I knew about Bruce Wayne.

When we returned to the courtroom, Judge McClary was fit to be tied that the air conditioning problem hadn't been fixed. "This court is adjourned until morning!"

And I suddenly had my afternoon free. I considered heading to work but just couldn't bring myself to go there. The county was paying me for the day, no matter how long I was at the courthouse. That was good enough for me. Even if it was only eight dollars.

My cell phone rang as I walked to my car and I dug through my purse to find it. Violet's name showed on the screen. "Hey, Vi." I couldn't hide my disappointment.

"Don't sound so happy to hear from me."

"Sorry, I just thought maybe you were Joe. I haven't heard from him since yesterday."

I could almost hear her happiness in her silence.

"I'm sure it's nothing," I said, feeling the need to defend him. "He's just tied up with work is all." There was no way in God's green earth I was going to tell her about Hilary. "Hey, I was thinking, maybe you and Mike would like to go out soon and I'll bring the kids over to my house to spend the night."

"Yeah . . . maybe . . ." Her voice brightened. "But right now, I'm calling about tonight. You're home alone and last night was a bit tense, so I thought maybe you'd like to come over and we could grill out."

Grilling out in this heat sounded like asking for heatstroke, but Lord knew Mike loved his smoker like a duck loved water. And spending the evening alone with my worries didn't sound very appealing. "Yeah, that sounds good."

"Great, see you at seven. Not a minute sooner." Then she hung up.

Seven? That was odd. Usually dinner at Violet's house was around six and I never arrived at a specific time. I just showed up.

The boys next door were running around their house, digging up the azalea bushes under the kitchen window. A wave of melancholy washed over me. My daddy and I had planted those for our neighbor back when I was a little girl. Gardening was the one thing we shared that Momma couldn't take away from us.

One of the boys turned to look at me and chewed on the side of his lip. He tugged on his brother's arm. "Andy Junior."

"*What?*"

The boy tugged harder and Andy Jr. glanced over his shoulder, the shovel dropping to the ground.

The first boy squinted. "How come you look like you're about to cry?"

"I was just thinking about my daddy."

"Where is he?"

"He's in heaven."

The boy's mouth dropped open into an *O*.

The topic of death caught Andy Jr.'s attention. "What happened to him?"

"His heart gave out." Although now I wondered if he died of a broken heart. I suspect Daddy never recovered from the mysterious circumstances surrounding the death of my birth mother. "Daddy and I planted those bushes when I was about your age." I looked to the first boy. "Your name's Keith, isn't it?"

His eyes widened with fear. "Yes, ma'am."

I smiled even though I didn't feel like smiling. My own heart hurt too bad. "You know, Keith, I don't have kids of my own, but I have a niece around your age. The next time she comes over, maybe you can play with her."

Andy Jr. scoffed his distain. "I ain't playin with no *girl*."

"Well, nobody invited *you*, did they?" I asked, aware I had just sunk to the level of a six-year-old but too cranky to care. "I was talkin' to Keith."

Keith beamed, his huge grin revealing a gap in his bottom teeth.

I decided to head inside before I stooped even lower than I already had. Walking into the kitchen, I tried to shake myself from my reverie. I needed to quit dwelling on sad things.

By the time I left for Violet's, I still hadn't heard from Joe. My discomfort had turned to fear. What if something had happened to him and Hilary hadn't told me?

I pulled into Violet's driveway, surprised to see an unfamiliar car parked in front of the house. I'd barely made it to the porch when the front door flew open. Violet stood in the doorway, dressed in a skirt and sleeveless blouse, and wearing a cute pair of sandals instead of her usual barefoot style. That should have been my first clue to turn around and run.

"Rose, honey, come on in." Her voice was overly bright and cheerful, then her smile fell and her voice lowered. "Is that what you're wearing?"

I looked down at my blue capris and gauzy white blouse.

She waved her hand and stumbled as she moved out of the opening. "Never mind. You look very bohemian."

Shaking my head in confusion, I walked past her. "Violet," I whispered. "Have you been drinkin'?"

She laughed, a melodious sound I'd always been jealous of, like everything else in her life. Only now it sounded brittle. "Maybe. Just a little."

Now I was really confused. Violet rarely drank and never on a weeknight.

She pushed me out the back door and onto the covered patio, the overhead fan working overtime to stir up the air. I stopped two steps out, Violet slamming into the back of me and making me stumble.

A man wearing jeans and a polo shirt rose from the patio chair he'd been sitting in and grabbed my elbow to steady me. "You must be Rose. I've heard so much about you." He smiled at Violet, then held out his right hand. "I'm Austin Kent."

His hand hung in the air, and I was torn between shaking it and turning around and running home.

I shot a glare in Violet's direction, then turned to Austin and shook his hand. It wasn't his fault I'd been set up, and I couldn't bring myself to be rude.

Just like Violet planned.

"Hi, I'm Rose. Oh wait, I guess you knew that already." I laughed, flustered, especially since Austin was still holding my hand.

Mike, who'd kept his attention on the steaks on the grill, picked up his beer bottle and took a long swallow.

Looked like I wasn't the only one who'd been set up.

"Austin brought a bottle of wine to go with the steaks," Violet gushed. "Wasn't that sweet of him? I'll go pour you a glass."

I pulled my hand from his tight grip. "I'll go with you."

"No!" She pushed me down into the chair next to the man. "You chat with Austin and I'll be right back."

There was no way out of that one.

Austin sat next to me and I gave him a genuine smile. I couldn't very well be rude. "So how do you know Mike and Violet?"

"We all went to high school together."

"I haven't seen you around." I glanced into the yard at Ashley and Mikey playing on the playset.

Austin laughed. "I disappeared for several years. I went to the University of Arkansas in Fayetteville for my architecture degree, did an internship, worked in Little Rock and decided I missed home. I just got back to Henryetta a couple of months ago. I'm settin' up my own firm and hope to work with Mike."

Austin seemed self-assured yet not arrogant. A man who knew what he wanted in life and how he planned to get it. There was no doubt that he was handsome; his chest filled out his shirt nicely and his tan set off his hazel eyes and dark brown hair. And I had to admit, if Joe wasn't in my life, I'd have been interested in him. What surprised me was the way his eyes followed my every move. This experience was vastly different than the first blind date Violet set me up with.

Blind date. Crappy doodles. I was gonna kill Violet.

"Here you go." Violet put a glass of red wine in my hand, taking a large sip of her own. As weird as she was acting, I wondered how much she'd had to drink before I got there.

"I've never had red wine before, only white." I blurted out before I thought to stop myself. People didn't just say things like that.

But Austin smiled, making his eyes twinkle. "Then I feel privileged to have provided the selection for your first taste." He bowed his head with a wink.

He watched me as I self-consciously took a sip. It wasn't as sweet as the white wines I'd had. Austin waited for my response, so I smiled. "It's wonderful."

Austin went on to tell Violet and me why he'd chose this particular vintage (its smoky taste blended well with grilled red meat) and why that particular year (the vintage from the year before had experienced a drought). Violet rested her chin on her hand, listening to Austin as though he was sharing the secret of life. Mike continued to give rapt attention to his barbecue tongs. I longed to be over there with him.

I set my wine glass on the side table and stood. "If y'all will excuse me for a moment, I need to visit the restroom," I said as sweetly as possible.

Mike shot me an apologetic glance.

"Well, hurry up darlin'," Violet drawled. "The steaks are almost ready."

"I'm only going to the restroom, Vi. I'm not making a cross country road trip." Although at the moment, that sounded like a great idea.

Mike snickered then chugged his beer before Violet caught him.

Hurrying to the bathroom, I shut the door and pushed my back into it, the molding pressing into my neck. I took a deep breath and dug out my cell phone, hoping against hope that I'd missed a call from Joe.

Nothing.

Forlorn and having given up all pride, I called his number, preparing to hear Hilary's voice. Instead, it went to voice mail. "Joe, I really need to talk to you." My words cracked like kindling on a fire and I sucked in a breath. "I miss you. Call me. *Please*." I hung up, embarrassed over my clinginess. What would Joe think when he heard me begging him to call? I might have just sent him running into Hilary's waiting arms.

Stop it, Rose Anne Gardner. We don't wallow.

And while it was true, I felt a little entitled. If that wasn't dangerous thinking, I didn't know what was. Wallowing was never the answer, which reminded me I had another task at hand. Time to go out and face the disaster of an evening.

While I'd been in the bathroom, everyone had moved inside. Austin handed my wine glass to me and pressed his hand into the small of my back, guiding me into the rarely used dining room. Violet was going all out for the occasion.

Violet and Austin carried on most of the dinner conversation. They talked about high school and Austin's travels, and I added little, feeling out of my element. But Austin, who sat on my right, refused to accept my silence. "What interestin' places have you visited?" he asked after telling us about his last trip to Boston.

I stared at the salad on my plate. "I haven't been anywhere. Yet." I looked up. "I'd love to go to Italy."

"Which part?"

"Rome, Venice, Tuscany. There's so much history there. You can see buildings that are thousands of years old."

He grinned. "I did an internship in Venice, studying Roman architecture."

My eyes flew open in surprise.

"I have a ton of pictures I'd love to show you sometime."

As tempting as his offer was, I quelled my enthusiasm. For some odd reason, Austin Kent actually seemed interested in me and it wouldn't be fair to encourage him. "Austin, that would be really nice but I already have—"

"Rose!" Violet interrupted. "Could you help me out and bring in the cheesecake?"

We stared at each other for several moments before I stood and grabbed my plate. "Sure."

Mike picked up his plate and Violet's. "I'll give her a hand."

I followed Mike into the kitchen. His mouth pursed as I scraped leftovers into the sink, and he loaded the dishwasher.

I struggled with what to say, but he spoke first.

"I'm sorry, Rose. I told her not to do it. You're with Joe but for some damned reason, she's decided he's not good enough for you." He looked me in the eyes. "I like Joe, and even if I didn't, I wouldn't have had any part in this. It's your business, none of ours."

"Thanks, Mike." Leaning my butt into the counter, I smiled at him. "I know you wouldn't do this. Violet's not acting like herself. What's goin' on?"

"What's goin' on . . ." He picked up a kitchen towel with a snap. "Is that Violet's decided she's unhappy with her life."

My mouth dropped. "Has she said that?"

"No, not outright."

"Oh, Mike. It's probably just Momma's death. She and Momma weren't really speakin' and as horrible as she was, she was still our mother. Violet's bound to be affected by it all."

He took a deep breath and looked out the window over the sink. "I hope you're right, Rose." Mike kissed me on the cheek. "I know I'm just your brother-in-law, but for what it's worth, Joe's a good man and he's lucky to have you." Then he pulled the cheesecake out of the refrigerator and carried it into the dining room.

When I sat down, Austin asked about my job. Working at the DMV wasn't very exciting, but I had a few stories about customers to share. Austin laughed and picked up the wine bottle to fill my glass.

I put my hand over the top. "None for me. I have jury duty tomorrow."

"Jury duty." Austin leaned close. "I have to admire a woman doin' her civic duty."

"There's nothing to admire. If I hadn't shown up, I'd probably be in jail right now."

Austin laughed like I'd made a joke. I tried to keep from scowling. There was nothing funny about incarceration.

"So tell us about the case." Austin's eyebrows rose, giving him a mischievous look. "Is it exciting?"

"I can't really talk about—"

Violet leaned forward and whispered. "It's a murder trial."

His eyes lit up with interest.

"I assure you it's not as exciting as it sounds." It hit me that Joe said the same thing about his job, nearly word for word, the day before. My heart swelled, missing him more than I thought possible. For heaven's sakes, he'd only been gone two days. But I couldn't pretend to be polite and social when my heart was aching.

I stood, smiling at Violet and Mike. "Thank you for dinner, but I need to get home. The air conditioning is still out in the courthouse and it's bound to be a long, tiring day tomorrow."

Austin stood. "I'll walk you out."

Violet's mouth contorted from happy to sour and back again. How much *had* she had to drink?

I gave Austin a tight smile. "That's really not necessary."

"I insist."

I grabbed my purse and couldn't help pulling my cell phone out to see if I'd missed any calls. Austin paused to talk to Mike and I hurried outside hoping to lose him, but he stuck close to my heels.

"Rose, wait up."

I stood next to my car door and looked up at him. He really was a handsome man, but I felt no attraction to him. My heart belonged to Joe.

"It's funny that I don't remember you from back when we were all in high school."

"Well," I stalled. "You were several years ahead of me and I was pretty forgettable."

His voice lowered. "I find that hard to believe."

I sucked in my breath. "Look, Austin, you're really a nice guy . . ."

He tilted his head with a grin. "Ahh . . . not the *you're a nice guy* line. Just give me a chance. Go out with me Friday night."

My mouth twisted into a half smile. "What Violet didn't tell you is that I already have a boyfriend. For some reason she doesn't approve of him, thus her settin' this up. I'm sorry."

He sighed. "Now it all makes sense. No wonder Mike acted so weird."

"I'm sorry."

"No," he shook his head and took my phone from my hand. "You didn't do anything wrong and I'd be lying if I said I wasn't glad Violet introduced us." He punched a few buttons on my phone, watched if for several seconds, and handed it back. "If things don't work out with that boyfriend of yours, give me a call. I'm only sorry I wasn't more observant years ago or I might not have lost out on my chance."

I blushed, thankful my color was hidden by the dark. "Well, good night, Austin."

"Goodnight, Rose Gardner. I shall wait for your call."

As I drove away, I hoped Austin didn't share my gift of foresight.

Chapter Seven

I took Muffy outside, staring at Austin Kent's number on my cell phone. I wasn't interested in the man, so why didn't I delete his number? There was no doubt about it. I was hedging my bets, as Daddy used to say, but that was ridiculous. Even if Joe dumped me, I wouldn't call him. I pulled up the screen to erase his number when it rang. After I jumped and nearly dropped the phone, I saw Joe's name and fumbled to answer.

Don't sound needy. Don't sound needy.

Herding Muffy inside, I gushed, "Joe, where have you been? I've been worried sick! You haven't answered your phone for two days."

Yeah, just like that.

Joe laughed. "Slow down. First things first." His voice sounded warm and husky. "I've missed you like crazy."

I pouted, even as my body flushed at the sound of his voice. "I could tell by the way you called me."

"I couldn't help it, darlin'. I promise. I would have called if I could, but I was working into the middle of the night last night, then I misplaced my phone most of today. I only found it a short while ago."

"So you weren't taking a shower with Hilary this afternoon?" I asked, half ashamed of asking, but half dreading the answer.

"*What*? No! How can you ask me that?"

"Why don't you ask Hilary."

A full three seconds of silence passed. "I'm gonna kill her. What did she say?"

Relieved, I sank into my new fluffy sofa. "I don't want to talk about Hilary."

"Rose. Listen to me. I wasn't with her—well I was, because we work together—but not how you're thinkin'. And just so you don't find this out later and think I was lyin' to you, I *did* take a shower this afternoon at the gym after I worked out. You have to believe me."

I felt like an idiot for worrying. Neely Kate was right. "Of course I do."

"But you had doubts?"

"It's hard not to when she answers your phone in a sexy voice and tells me you're takin' a shower and I can hear the water in the background."

He groaned. "I'm sorry. I couldn't find my phone all afternoon. She must have taken it while I was in the bathroom. *At work*. We weren't alone, Rose. I promise."

"It's okay."

"No, it's not. Trust me. I'll deal with Hilary tomorrow. Are we good or do we need to talk about this more?"

"I'm good."

"I miss you."

My heart ached at the longing in his words and my voice hitched, "I miss you too."

"I'm not sure I can wait until Friday to see you."

Butterflies took flight in my stomach. "You can't come down here, Joe. You'll get in trouble."

"Come see me, Rose. Please. Take a couple of days off. Or quit. You hate that job."

I knew without a doubt I would have done it. I would have said goodbye to the DMV forever if that's what it would take to go to Little Rock. But my job wasn't what stopped me. "Oh, Joe." I didn't hide my tears. "I'd quit right now if I could, but if I came to see you tomorrow, I'd get arrested."

He paused then asked in a guarded tone, "What are you talking about?"

"I got picked for jury duty. If I don't show up, they'll arrest me."

I heard his exhale of relief.

"Wait. What were you thinkin'?"

He laughed. "Darlin', with you there's just no telling. So you made jury duty, huh? What kind of case?"

"That's why I was so desperate to talk to you. I have a problem. I had a vision about the case."

Joe didn't seem that surprised. "And?"

"Joe, it's a murder trial and the defendant's innocent."

"How do you know he's innocent?"

"I told you. I had a vision."

"Why don't you start from the beginning and tell me everything."

"Are you sure it's okay? I'm not supposed to talk about the case." I'd wanted to talk to him for two days but now worried I was breaking the law.

"It's okay. I'm a detective with the state police. I won't tell anyone, and I sure won't try to sway your decision."

It was a relief to share my problem, especially with Joe. I told him everything, starting with Officer Ernie giving me a parking ticket and ending with leaving the courthouse that afternoon. I didn't tell him about my evening at Violet's. I didn't want to make him worry, especially when I wasn't the least bit interested in Austin Kent.

When I finished, Joe sighed. "Oh, Rose. I'm so sorry. I wish I'd been around to talk. I know how hard this has to be for you."

My voice broke. "I just don't know what to do."

"I know, let's work through it, okay? What do you see as your options?"

I wiped a tear from my cheek. "My first option is to tell the assistant D.A. what I know."

"Okay, do you think that would work?"

"No." I scoffed. "He'd never believe me for one thing and for another, he'd think I was crazy. For some bizarre reason, he purposely got me on the jury. I'd almost feel like I was lettin' him down."

Joe's voice hardened. "You don't owe Mason Deveraux anything, got it? This is about you, not that stuffy-ass assistant D.A."

How did Joe know about Mason Deveraux? I didn't remember mentioning his name. "Yeah, you're right."

"What's your next option?"

"I could tell the defense attorney, but he hates me and he'd never believe me."

"Okay, next?" Joe didn't ask why the defense attorney hated me, just accepted it.

I closed my eyes, concentrating. "Maybe I could leave an anonymous tip."

"What do you think you'd say?"

I groaned in frustration. "I guess there's not much to say, is there? That the pin belongs to some mysterious man who murdered the victim, but I don't know who it is, only that he was at the courthouse on Monday morning, he likes crossword puzzles, and he has a cat."

"What's your other option?"

"I don't have any other options, Joe. Not that I can think of."

"I know one."

I sat up. "What?"

"You do nothing."

"What? I can't do—"

"Rose, trust the system. This guy is innocent until proven guilty."

"No he's not, trust me. Everyone thinks he's guilty—from the jury to the police, and as little as Mr. Yates is tryin', I suspect he thinks he's guilty too."

"Rose . . ."

"No, Joe. You're not in there. Mason Deveraux has all of this circumstantial evidence and Mr. Yates isn't fightin' any of it and the jury's eatin' it all up, which I don't understand. Even without a vision, I could tell that Bruce Wayne didn't smash that guy's head in. He's right-handed and the wound was on the right side. The murderer is left-handed."

"How in the world do you know that?"

"I saw it in my vision. He was doing a crossword puzzle and he wrote the word in with his left hand."

"Rose." Joe's voice tightened and clipped the end of my name, the sign he was frustrated with me. "That doesn't mean a *thing*."

"Of course it does. Someone right-handed would have hit the victim on the left side, how could they all miss that?"

"Rose, they were probably *fightin'*. Fights are ugly and they'd be moving around. The victim wasn't just standing there waiting to get his head bashed in."

"I'm not stupid, Joe McAllister. I know that." I growled in irritation—I'd just called him Joe McAllister out of habit.

"I'm sure they're reasoning that there was a scuffle. That's why no one is questioning the placement of the wound. You may be right, though. If the murderer is left-handed, the wound is more likely to be on the right side. But Rose, that's hardly enough to exonerate the defendant. Especially since they found the murder weapon on his property."

"Well, then what am I going to do?"

"You're going to do nothing and trust the system."

"I can't let an innocent man go to jail, Joe."

"I'm not sayin' you are, but for now, do nothing."

I sucked in a deep breath, fighting back my frustration. "Joe, that could have been me. If things had turned out different, I could be in jail right now, waiting to be tried for her murder. And I'd have been convicted, too. You *know* that."

"Rose, this isn't you. And it's not like this Bruce Wayne Decker is a fine upstanding citizen. You said he'd been arrested multiple times before."

"Yeah, for small crimes. Nothing violent. Nothing even close to this."

"But with his record—"

"Oh. My. Word," I exclaimed, hurt welling in my chest. "You're just like *them*."

"What is *that* supposed to mean?"

"You're prejudiced by his past."

"Rose, it plays a part in this."

"Joe! He's innocent."

"I know you think your vision told you—"

"You think I'm *lyin'*?"

"No! Of course not. But maybe what you saw isn't what you think."

I counted to ten, grinding my teeth into sawdust. "I think I need to go to bed now."

"Rose—"

"Good night, Joe."

I lay on the sofa late into the night too angry and frustrated to go to sleep. After watching hours of HGTV, I decided it was time to do something with Momma's room, which had been originally decorated back in the 1970s.

But why would I plan to redecorate a room when I was considering moving to Little Rock?

My fight with Joe made me wonder how much I really knew him, but that wasn't fair. Joe was a good man. Still, I couldn't help but wonder: if Violet and Mike, who'd had the perfect marriage until a few months ago, could fall apart, how could I make it work with Joe?

The next morning I woke to Muffy licking my face and daylight streaming in from the kitchen. Jerking upright, I grabbed my phone to check the time. 8:45.

Oh, crappy doodles!

Everyone in the courthouse would stink to high heaven within five minutes, so I saw no sense wasting precious time on a shower. I let Muffy out and brushed my teeth at the kitchen sink, watching her out the window. One of the boys from next door crept around the back corner of Joe's house. I stood on tiptoes trying to see what he was doing when a blur flew toward Muffy and I heard yelping.

I ran out the door faster than Mildred's cat chasing a squirrel. Muffy yelped again, lifting her foot off the ground, trying to hobble to the door. A rock lay nearby. "You get your booty out here right now!" I shouted.

The boy hid around the corner of the house, his blond hair poking out.

Leaning down, I checked Muffy's foot for signs of blood. "I see you and I saw what you did. Get out here right now and apologize to my dog."

Andy Jr. stepped around the edge, scrunching his face. "I ain't apologizin' to no dog."

"You most certainly are. Now get over here and do it right now before I march back there and drag you out myself." I surprised myself. I wasn't usually this assertive, but past experience proved

I didn't like people messing with my dog. Apparently, being a kid was no excuse.

The boy walked around the corner, leery.

"Go on now. I don't have all day. As it is, I'll be lucky if I don't get arrested."

The boy's eyes widened and he swallowed. "I'm sorry, dog."

I picked Muffy up and cradled her in my arms. "She has a name. Her name is Muffy. Say it again."

"*Oh, come on!*"

Gritting my teeth, my eyes widened and I was sure I looked like a lunatic.

The boys' face turned white. "I'm sorr . . . rry, Muffy."

"Why would you do such a thing? What did this dog ever do to you?"

He shrugged his shoulders. "I dunno."

"Would you like it if I threw a rock at you?"

He opened his mouth, then glanced at me with fear and shook his head violently.

"Nobody wants to have a rock thrown at them, dogs included. Muffy might play with you if you're nice to her."

His eyes lit up, but he sobered when he glanced my direction. "Really?"

"Well, if you can be nice, I'll let you play with Muffy sometime, but you're gonna have to earn that trust. And I guarantee if I ever see you hurt my dog again," I leaned forward and pointed at his chest, "you will regret it for the rest of your life, got it?"

He nodded, wide-eyed and properly terrified.

I stifled my smug grin. Assertive Rose, who knew?

Muffy stopped whimpering by the time I got her inside and set her down. She padded around with only a slight limp and I considered icing her leg, but didn't have time. I was going to be late enough as it was.

After a glance in the bathroom mirror, I understood why Andy Jr. looked so terrified. My hair stuck out all over my head. Mascara was smudged under my eyes, and foamy toothpaste hung from my lower lip.

I looked like a rabid Frankenstein's bride.

Throw in my threats and my talk about getting arrested, and I had just become the neighborhood crazy lady.

There was only time for a quick scrub on my face with a washcloth and a brush through my hair as I ran out the door to my car.

Oh, Lordy. I hoped to dear God I didn't get arrested. Could you rot in jail for being late to jury duty? I was about to find out.

I found a parking spot two blocks away, and half jogged to the courthouse, working up a sweat by the time I entered the courthouse. "Good mornin', Matt." I tossed my purse on the counter.

Matt checked my bag, then handed it back to me with a suspicious look.

Since the elevator was so slow, I ran upstairs, breathless when I burst into the juror room at nine-fifteen. "I'm sorry I'm late! Please don't arrest me!"

Marjorie Grace held up her hands. "Whoa there, slow down. No one's gettin' arrested. The judge is deciding whether to postpone the trial until the air conditioning is fixed." She pointed to the back of the room where everyone gathered around a table. "In the meantime, everyone has been eating a lovely breakfast casserole that Mrs. Baker brought." The way she lingered on the word *lovely* was enough to tell me to steer clear, no matter how much my stomach growled.

Bailiff Spencer walked through the door, hands on his hips. "The judge has decided to press on and try to get this trial over with."

My stomach flip-flopped. A man's life hung in the balance, an innocent man, and they were more worried about getting out of the heat and into air conditioning.

The morning dragged on. Mr. Deveraux called two witnesses who'd seen Bruce Wayne getting in and out of his crawl space. Bruce Wayne had made so much racket in the middle of the night that he'd woken several neighbors. There was also testimony from the crime scene investigator, who reasserted that blood that matched DNA from the victim was found on the crowbar, along with the defendant's fingerprints.

As the evidence piled up, my frustration mounted. When was Mr. Yates going to defend his client?

We broke for lunch and I told Neely Kate all about my evening with Violet and Austin Kent and my subsequent fight with Joe, although I glossed over the details. Not that it stopped Neely Kate from trying to get information about the trial.

"Come on, Rose. Just give me something!"

"No." I shook my head. "Don't you know I could go to jail for telling you? And if I get thrown in, what's to stop them from keeping me in there and letting me rot like poor Mr. Decker?"

Her eyes narrowed. "You know something. Spill it."

I shook my head. "No. No way. I didn't say anything."

"But you just said—"

"Neely Kate. I can't."

She puckered her mouth into a pout, but I had learned enough about her to know it was merely for effect.

As soon as I returned to the jurors' room, I could tell something was wrong. The smell, a mixture of sulfur and vomit, hit me first. I covered my face with my hand and found Marjorie Grace tending to a juror who hunched over his legs, his face pasty white.

"What's going on?"

Marjorie Grace looked up with a frown. "Five jurors have thrown up and three more are hiding in the bathroom, taking care of business on the other end, if you know what I mean."

Unfortunately, I did. "What happened? How did they all get sick at the same time?"

"Three words: Mrs. Baker's casserole." She walked over to another juror and adjusted the wet paper towels on his forehead. Turned out that wet paper towels were a staple in Marjorie Grace's ancillary medical care.

"*Food poisoning*?"

"I'm no doctor, but that's my best guess."

It was also the best guess of the doctor who showed up thirty minutes later.

Court was adjourned until further notice, and I realized I had time to get some answers. The first place I planned to look was the hardware store.

I was gonna pay a visit to the murder scene.

Chapter Eight

I was smart enough to know I needed an excuse. I couldn't just walk in and start asking questions. But as luck would have it, Archer's Hardware was the only hardware store in town and just last night I'd thought about redoing Momma's room.

Was redecorating your house a crime?

After I pulled into the parking lot, I watched the front entrance, the car's air conditioning blasting my face as I pondered this decision. If I went in, the judge might consider it a crime. But Archer's was the only hardware store in town. Surely I didn't have to put off my improvement projects until the trial was over. Joe would call this rash, but then in Joe's opinion, I should let Bruce Wayne rot in jail. I just couldn't do that. I squared my shoulders.

This was crazy, even crazier than my usual stunts. I didn't even know Bruce Wayne Decker, and I could pretty much guarantee he wouldn't do anything like this for me. But the idea of sitting by and letting them send him to the big house didn't settle well in my stomach.

I was going in.

I walked through the sliding doors, half expecting Officer Ernie or Detective Taylor to be waiting inside to arrest me. Instead, I was greeted by a girl with blue hair and a pierced lip, who hunched over the return counter.

"Welcome to Archer's Hardware." Her monotone voice and droopy eyelids suggested she was about to fall asleep.

"Hi." I headed straight for the paint department even though I wanted to wander the store and figure out where Frank Mitchell had been murdered. No need pressing my luck. Buying paint was believable. I wasn't sure I could convince anyone I was buying a plastic tube to put under my sink.

While I studied the paint cards, I realized I needed a plan. First, I had to decide what color to paint Momma's room. Next, I needed to figure out what questions to ask.

I'd painted my living room a pale yellow after Momma's death to cover up the blood splatters, and I loved the airiness. I decided to go with a pale blue and maybe even splurge on a new comforter from Walmart.

Once I picked a color I liked, I took the card to the counter and handed it to the woman next to the paint shaker machine. "Hi, I'd like two gallons in satin." Mercy, I'd come a long way since May. But how was I gonna find out information about the murder without looking too obvious?

"Sure thing. If you've got any other shoppin' to do, I'll just hold this at the counter until you're ready." She wiped her thumb on her smock, smearing a dab of green paint. Her nametag read Anne.

I needed rollers, but they were next to the counter. I picked up a package and twisted it in my hands. "Nope, this'll do it. The paint and rollers. I figured it was high time to redecorate my Momma's room. God rest her soul." I placed my hand on my chest. "After her murder and all, I just need a fresh start, ya know?"

In the process of prying the lid off the paint can, Anne stopped and blinked. "Wait. Was your momma murdered a couple of months ago?"

Pursing my lips, I nodded. "It's a shockin' thing, walking in and finding your momma's dead body." I paused. "I think that only someone who's been through something like that under-stands how truly horrifying it is, ya know?"

Anne tsked. "We had something like that happen here." She raised her eyebrows as she programmed the paint dispenser. "Our evening manager was murdered a little over a year ago. Right *here* in the store."

My eyes widened. "Oh! I remember that. What in the world is *happenin'* to Henryetta, Arkansas?"

"It's goin' to hell in a handbasket, I'll tell ya that right now."

"Did you work here when it happened?"

She shuddered. "I did, and I know what you mean about it being horrifying. I was scared to walk in the back storage room alone for months after that."

I lowered my voice. "Is that where it happened? In the storage room? My momma's was on the sofa in our living room. I found her sitting there like she was waitin' for me to come home."

She nodded and shuddered again, then jammed the paint can in the shaker machine.

"Did you get a lot of looky-loos? I had people peekin' in my living room, trying to see the bloodstains."

"Yes! It was horrible. There was this one guy who kept comin' around. He'd buy a package of screws or a broom, but nothing big or nothing you'd expect. Finally, one day Manny, he works in tools, said something to the guy about how none of us could figure out what his home improvement project was because of all the odd things he was buyin'. That's a game we do. We pay attention to the regulars and try to figure out what they're up to. But we never saw him again after that."

"That's so weird." Was that the bathroom murderer?

Narrowing her eyes, she leaned forward. "Tell me about it. But the really weird part was the murderer didn't take the money in the safe."

"What? Why not?"

"That right there is a mystery. But the night deposit hadn't been made yet and the safe was wide open. Why, there was enough money to open a bank branch right here in the hardware store but less than a hundred dollars was taken."

"Why in the world wouldn't the murderer take all the money?"

"Your guess is as good as mine. But it makes me wonder about the real reason for the murder. It sure wasn't a burglary."

My jaw dropped. This was going so much better than I hoped for. "What do you mean?"

Anne looked around and leaned close to me. "Frank was havin' some money troubles. And rumor had it he owed money to some not so nice people."

"Did the police check into that?"

She snorted. "What? And do any more work than necessary? You know their reputation."

Unfortunately, I knew only too well. Personally.

"Why'd he owe people money?"

"I have no idea. He was a nice guy and all but without a lick of sense, if you know what I mean."

"Did they find the murderer?"

"It made big news. They claimed they did. How'd you miss it?"

"My Momma didn't believe in watchin' much TV."

Anne pointed her finger in my face. "Every citizen of the United States needs to keep informed of current events. Otherwise those dadgummed militia fools, hidin' out in the woods, will be takin' over. And God help us all if that happens."

Anne made a good point.

"I got cable a few weeks ago."

She blinked, then nodded. "Are you a CNN or Fox News girl?"

"Uh," I stammered, pretty certain this was a test. "CNN?"

She puckered her mouth and nodded, walking back to the paint machine. "Good girl."

Whew. I didn't want her to stop talking. "You don't think they caught the murderer?"

Anne rolled her eyes as she took the paint can out of the shaker. "They claimed they did, although I never thought he did it."

"Why not?"

She pried the lid open and dabbed a blue dot on the sticker. "Bruce is afraid of his own shadow. There's no way he did it."

"You *know* him?"

"Yeah, he's my sister's husband's cousin's nephew."

Well, there you had it. They were practically cousins.

"Sure, he's got picked up for some petty stuff, but mostly for possession of pot and driving under the influence. A couple of shoplifting charges. Nothing big like killing someone. I don't know if Bruce could even pick up a crowbar."

I'd seen his spindly arms and had to agree.

She turned on a hair dryer and pointed it at the paint dot, killing any further conversation. I was pressing my luck being here at all. I sure as blazes wasn't going to shout any more questions at her. Anne plunked the paint on the counter. "There you go. Anything else?"

Grabbing the metal handle, I swung the paint can off the counter and smiled. "I think I have everything I need for now. Thanks, Anne."

Her eyebrows raised slightly when I said her name, then she grinned. "Good luck with your paintin'."

I paid for my paint and rollers, glad to have gotten information but suddenly paranoid that someone from the Henryetta Police Department was outside waiting to bring me in. I breathed a sigh of relief when I drove out of the parking lot.

After I got home, I opened the door to Momma's bedroom. I'd kept it closed since Joe had slept in there weeks ago, back when he'd worried someone was going to break into my house again.

The room was hot and smelled musty with a faint hint of Estée Lauder, Momma's perfume. Violet and I had disposed of all her personal items about a week after her death, but the odor must have permeated the walls. While I moved the furniture to the middle of the room, I mulled over what Anne had said about Frank Mitchell. He'd owed money to people, but why? And how much and to whom? Maybe that person killed Frank Mitchell, but how in heaven's name would I find out who it was? As far as I could tell, I was at a dead end.

I went out to the shed to get the rest of my painting supplies. Muffy followed behind me and the shrieks of the little boys next door caught her attention. While I slid the shed door open, Muffy pressed her face between the slats of the fence, studying the commotion. Heidi Joy sat in a lawn chair under the shade tree, reading a magazine and her four boys ran around the yard, jumping in and out of a splash pool. Her baby sat on a quilt, chewing on his fat fist, his eyes wide as he watched.

Muffy whined.

"What is it, girl?" I asked, squaring my shoulders. I dearly hated going into the shed, but was determined to paint. Heavens knew I needed the distraction from everything else.

After I gathered the drop cloths, tape, and paint tray, I headed back to the house. Muffy whimpered up a storm. Bending down, I rubbed her head. "What? What is it, girl?"

She barked and ran for the fence gate.

I dumped my supplies on the kitchen table. Muffy had stopped and watched me from outside.

"Okay, keep your pants on." I shook my head, realizing my mistake. "Never mind. Come on."

She ran in circles in her excitement. When I opened the gate, she burst through and made a beeline for the wading pool.

"Muffy!"

The boys shrieked when she jumped in and splashed water everywhere.

Horrified, I hurried over to Heidi Joy. "I am so sorry!"

Her eyes widened in surprise as she laid her gossip magazine on her legs. "Why?"

"My dog . . . she just jumped in your pool."

Scoffing, she waved with her free hand. Her other hand clutched a glass of ice water to her chest. "My boys love it and if your dog keeps them entertained and out of mischief, *please*, I'll sell my soul to keep her around."

I stood next to her in the shade, watching Muffy prance around. I could swear she was grinning. "They *do* seem like a handful."

"You don't know the half of it."

"How's your move goin'?"

Her lips twisted. "As good as can be expected in the middle of a heat wave with five boys underfoot."

"I can imagine." Muffy jumped up and down in the plastic pool and the boys squealed in delight. "Muffy seems to love them."

"They've been beggin' for a dog, but it's all I can do to take care of them, let alone a dog . . ." Her voice trailed off with wistful tone, her guilt evident.

"You know, Muffy loves kids. Look at her. She's having so much fun. Maybe your boys could play with her sometimes and it would be the fun of having a dog without the work."

Heidi Joy looked up, her chin trembling. "You would do that?"

Shocked at her tears, I shrugged. "Sure. Muffy would love it too."

"I'm so tired of feeling guilty all the time." Wiping a tear from her eye, Heidi Joy laughed. "There's just not enough hours in the day and Andy's at work and I'm left takin' care of these little boys.

I love 'em, I do, but sometimes I can hardly keep up. And when I tell them no every time they ask for a dog . . ."

"Well, then it works for all of us, doesn't it? Your boys get to play with a dog and Muffy gets to play with kids."

Muffy used that moment to pass gas in the pool, tiny air bubbles breaking the surface of the water.

"Ew!" the boys shouted.

My mouth dropped in horror. "Oh my word! I am so sorry!"

Heidi Joy shrugged. "It's a Jacuzzi now."

It was hot standing outside, even in the shade, and that room wasn't going to paint itself. "Muffy, we have to be goin' now. I've got a fun afternoon of painting ahead."

The boys shouted their protest and Muffy turned up her chin.

"Could Muffy stay for a little while, Miss Rose?" Keith asked, his eyes pleading.

My gaze searched out Andy Jr. and his face paled. "Andy Junior, I'm makin' you in charge of Muffy. If I find out you weren't . . ." I remembered his mother didn't know about the incident that morning, "that you weren't watching her *properly*, you and I will have to reach a new understanding."

He swallowed nodded. "Yes, ma'am."

I knelt next to the pool. "What do you say, Muffy? Want to hang out here?"

She splashed her response. Traitor. Now I had to paint alone.

"That settles it!" Heidi Joy exclaimed. "You go paint and we'll dogsit."

Reluctantly, I left Muffy in their yard after giving Andy Jr. and Keith half a dozen rules to follow. No going out front. No table scraps. No being mean to her in any way. Andy Jr. nodded, his eyes serious, while Keith petted her head. I took comfort in the knowledge that Heidi Joy was watching them too.

I spent the rest of the afternoon transforming Momma's dreary, light gray room into a soothing blue oasis, but my thoughts still tumbled. Too many things were out of sorts in my life. As hard as it was to admit, I realized that I might be pouting. Muffy would rather be with the rambunctious kids next door than me, not that I could blame her. If I were a dog, I'd rather play with kids than smell paint fumes. But I couldn't get over feeling like Muffy had betrayed me—and that she wasn't the only one.

That wasn't fair. Joe hadn't betrayed me. We just didn't see eye to eye on this trial. There was a big difference. But it was our first real disagreement since we'd officially started seeing each other, and it pricked my insecurities. Joe was in Little Rock with women like Hilary. Women who were normal, something I most definitely wasn't. It dredged up the question I continually asked myself: Why was Joe Simmons, a handsome undercover policeman, with Rose Gardner, a freak who saw visions and was the town of Henryetta's outcast?

I shook my head. I needed to trust Joe's word. He wanted to be with me, whether I understood it or not.

I reminded myself that couples fight. Even Violet and Mike fought when they were happy. But their unhappiness was like an earthquake, shaking up everything I'd believed. If Violet's world could fall apart, what could I count on?

Chapter Nine

A knock on the kitchen door jolted me out of my wallowing. I set the roller in the tray, wiping a strand of hair out my face with my forearm. Glancing at the rooster clock on the kitchen wall, I was surprised to see it was a little after six. I'd lost all track of time in my musings and the afternoon had gotten away from me. It was probably Andy Jr. and Keith bringing Muffy home.

I was halfway across the kitchen when the door flung open, catching me off guard. Releasing a shriek, I tripped backward and grabbed the broom in the corner to defend myself.

"What *is* it with you and brooms?" Joe asked, irritation making his words prickly.

I lowered my weapon, still holding onto the handle with one hand. The look on Joe's face told me I might still need it. "What are you doing here?" My own irritation overshadowed the excitement of him standing in front of me.

What *was* Joe doing here?

Joe sucked in a deep breath, still holding onto the door handle. "You scared me to death, Rose. I've been trying to call you *all day*. Why didn't you answer my calls?"

Oh, crappy doodles. Where was my phone? I panicked as I scanned the room, realizing I hadn't seen it all day. I found it on the coffee table, where I'd left it the night before. I'd completely forgotten about my phone as I raced to get to the courthouse that morning. Since I hadn't charged it overnight, I'd bet my grandma's prize-winning cornbread recipe it was dead.

While my heart leapt with joy that Joe was here, his implied accusations and assumptions lit a fire in my chest. "Why didn't *I* answer *your* calls? I could just as easily turn this around on you, Joe Simmons."

He shoved his hand through his hair, a low growl rumbling from his chest. "I told you already, Rose. I was working late Monday night and then Hilary took my phone yesterday. And trust me, Hilary has been dealt with." The hard look in his eyes left no question that he had.

My grip on the broom handle tightened. "Why are you here, Joe?"

His chest expanded and hardness on his face fell away to reveal worry. "I was scared."

"Of what? That something happened to me? You could have called Violet."

He took a hesitant step toward me. "That too, but more scared you didn't want to talk to me anymore."

I bit my lip. "Joe, how could you think that?"

"After our argument, and you hung up on me . . ."

I stared at him, unsure what to say. I was still mad at him and I'd needed space the night before, but I couldn't believe he thought I wouldn't want to talk to him anymore. Could Joe feel as insecure as I did?

My silence filled his eyes with panic. "I'm sorry, Rose. Really I am. I wasn't very understanding of your situation. I was looking at it from a police perspective, and I didn't take into account what you were thinking or how you were feeling. I wish I could take it all back and start over." He walked forward, stopping several feet in front of me.

I shook my head, tears burning my eyes. He'd driven all the way from Little Rock because he was scared I'd decided to not talk to him anymore. All my doubts about his interest in me floated away, leaving a burning lump in my throat.

He took my free hand, his eyes searching mine. "Say something, Rose."

"Joe . . ." My voice broke.

"Is that a 'Joe, I forgive you' or 'Joe, go away'? Because I'm warnin' you, I'm not leaving that easily."

I wrapped my hand around his neck, while still holding the broom.

His mouth lifted into a grin. "I'm worried you're gonna beat me with that broom."

"You deserve it."

"Maybe so, but I think I'll play it safe." He snatched the broom from my hand and tossed it on the floor. "That's better." Then his hand tangled in my hair and he pulled my mouth to his, his other hand sliding up my back.

I lost myself in him, my heart bursting with happiness.

"I don't like fighting with you," he mumbled against my lips.

"I don't like fighting with you either."

His kiss softened as his hand cupped my cheek. "God, I've missed you. Three days is too long." He crushed my chest to his, and his tongue explored my mouth, leaving me breathless.

"Ewww!" a small voice squealed.

I leaned back to see Andy Jr. standing outside the open door with Muffy at his side. "Did you take good care of Muffy?" I asked in a stern voice.

Joe squinted at me in surprise.

"Yes ma'am." Andy Jr. looked down at the ground. "I'm sorry about this morning."

"Well, thanks for entertainin' Muffy for me. Maybe you could watch her again sometime."

He grinned. "That would be awesome! Thanks!" Andy Jr. took off running to the backyard.

Joe tilted his head to the side. "Do I want to know what just happened there?"

"No." I pulled out of his embrace. "And I'm still mad at you."

With a grin, he rubbed my forehead with his finger. "It's hard to take that scowl seriously when you have blue paint smeared across your forehead."

I reached up to swipe it off, but the paint had dried. "You've been lookin' at me all this time with paint on my face?"

"It makes you look adorable and it's only on your forehead. What are you painting? I didn't know you'd planned on painting anything."

I hesitated. "Well . . . neither did I . . . until this afternoon."

His face froze as his eyes narrowed slightly. I recognized it for what it was—the Joe Simmons Arkansas State Police face.

Time to change the subject. "I'm hungry and you're gonna take me out to dinner to make it up to me. After I take a shower." I turned to walk down the hall to the bathroom.

Joe grabbed my wrist and tugging me back into his arms. "Who said I was done making up?" He slowly covered my lips with his, his tongue continuing its sweet torture.

I knew what he was doing. He'd used these questionable interrogation attempts over a month ago when he thought I was involved with Daniel Crocker. He hoped to distract me with his mouth and make me give up my secrets. "I'm taking a shower."

A slow, sexy grin spread across Joe's face as his held my hips to his. "Now that's the best idea I've heard all day."

I swatted his arm and stepped backward, breaking his hold. "Alone. I'm showering alone. That's your punishment."

"You're a cruel woman, Rose Gardner. Gettin' a guy's hopes up like that."

"You and Muffy can watch TV while you're figuring out where to take me."

"Well, hurry up," he growled, but his eyes twinkled. "I'm hungry."

I rolled my eyes. "That's why I told you to figure out where to go."

"That's not what I'm hungry for."

A blush crept up to my face. I still wasn't used to that kind of attention.

Fifteen minutes later, I emerged from the bathroom showered and in fresh clothes. Joe stood in the doorway of Momma's bedroom and turned to look at me.

"I put the paint tray and roller in a bag so they don't dry out. I like the color."

"Thanks."

"If you'd have waited until the weekend, I would've helped you."

"I know, but we got out of jury duty early today and I couldn't face an afternoon of nothing."

"You could have spent the day with Violet."

I pinched my lips. "We're not exactly speakin' right now."

His eyes widened in surprised as he led me down the hall to the kitchen. "Let's go and you can tell me on the way. The sooner we eat dinner, the sooner I can have dessert."

"You're awfully confident for a man who's in trouble."

Joe leaned down and kissed my neck. "Good thing I know your weak spots."

Dear Lord, wasn't that the truth.

We went to Little Italy, one of only two nice places to eat in Henryetta. The other was Jaspers, and I refused to go back there after the disastrous first date that Violet had arranged for me a month ago. I had no desire to ever walk through those doors again, after getting left at the restaurant by the Pillsbury Doughboy, running into Daniel Crocker, and feeling guilty about Sloan, the nice bartender who'd helped me and was murdered. After we ordered, Joe reached across the table and took my hand. "Why are you and Violet fighting?"

I had to admit it was hard to stay mad at him. He was a charming man and the dark atmosphere and candlelight in the restaurant dampened my irritation. We needed to talk about what happened the night before, but it wasn't like we could discuss Bruce's situation in public. That discussion needed to happen at home. Talking about Violet wasn't going to solve our disagreement, and I worried it would be throwing another log onto the fire. Maybe going out to eat wasn't such a good idea after all. "I don't think you want to know why we're fightin'."

He leaned back a few inches, confusion crossing over his face. "Why not?"

There was so much to tell and none of it good. Mostly, I didn't want to hurt him. "Violet's been unhappy lately."

"Why?"

"She and Mike seem to be havin' problems. It started right after Momma died." I paused, unsure whether to continue. Yet I knew honesty was the best way to go. Secrets had nearly been our undoing in the past. "If I'm honest, I'd have to say it all started after I started seein' you."

"*Me?*"

I sucked in my lip before I blew a breath away. Staring Joe in the eye, my fingers tightened over his. "Violet thinks I'm settling."

Hurt filled his eyes and I hurried to add, "It's nothing against you, Joe. She says I've never dated before and that I need more experience so I can be sure."

Joe sat in silence.

"Mike was her first and only boyfriend, and they got married soon after high school. As hard as it is to believe, I think Violet's a little jealous of me."

A scowl lowered his brow and his gaze pierced mine. "Why is that hard to believe, Rose? You're a beautiful woman and you're sweet and funny. You're wonderful."

My face grew hot. "But how can Violet be jealous of me when she has everything I ever wanted?"

Joe sat as still as a statue.

Crappy doodles. I'd freaked him out.

His voice softened. "What does she have that you want?"

I looked away. "This is embarrassing, Joe."

He put his finger under my chin and turned my face back to look at him. "No, it's not. What does she have that you want?"

After sucking in a deep breath, I released it in a gush. "A loving husband, beautiful children. A family."

His gaze held mine.

I tried to turn away in my horror, but Joe's grip on my chin tightened. Why on earth did I admit that? I'd always heard talking about that kind of stuff too early was the kiss of death for a relationship.

He smiled. "I want that stuff too."

This was a first. Other than me moving to Little Rock, the only long-term subject we'd discussed was whether five-day-old Chinese food was still good. I grinned. "You want a husband?"

Joe laughed, releasing my chin. "No. I want to be married and have a family someday."

My heart swelled with happiness, and for the first time I let myself think that far into the future.

"So why is Violet jealous of you?"

My smile fell away. This couldn't end well. "I think Violet thinks she settled and for some reason she's jealous that I have options."

"Oh." He stared out the window for several seconds before turning back, his happiness gone. "So what'd she do?"

"Huh?" My heart kick-started into overdrive.

"I know Violet well enough to know that if she doesn't want you to settle for me, then she thinks you need to be movin' on. And if you're not talkin' to her right now, she's done something. What is it?"

"Joe . . ."

"Spit it out, Rose."

The waitress showed up with our food, giving me a temporary reprieve. I was so torn. I didn't want to lie to Joe, but I sure didn't want to hurt him. I worried that telling him the truth would destroy any chance of a friendly relationship between him and Violet. But in the end, I knew what I had to do. "She set me up." I said, my voice so quiet Joe leaned forward.

"Excuse me?"

My shoulders tensed. "She set me up. With a guy."

Joe's jaw tightened and he swallowed. "You went on a *date* while I was gone?"

"No." I shook my head. "It wasn't like that. Violet invited me over for dinner last night and she'd invited someone she and Mike went to high school with. So it wasn't a date."

I was sure Violet would disagree.

"But I take it he was single?" His words were clipped and tight.

"Well, yes . . ." *Oh, my word. Could Joe be jealous?*

His eyebrows rose, the rest of his face expressionless. "And?"

"And nothing. I went over, Mike grilled steaks, and Austin and Violet caught up on what they'd all been doing since high school."

"Austin."

It wasn't a question so I wasn't sure how to respond. Violet was right about one thing: I was inexperienced and out of my element in this situation.

"Joe, I swear to you, I didn't know anything about the dinner being a set-up. I was sad and missing you and worried about," I lowered my head toward his, *"the situation with my vision,* and then Hilary had answered your phone, talkin' sexy and telling me you were in the shower, and I could hear water in the background—"

"So you did this because of Hilary?"

"No! Joe, I told you I didn't know anything about it or I wouldn't have gone."

"Really? Even after what happened with Hilary?"

"Joe, I don't want to be with anyone else but you. I wasn't interested in him at all even though he asked me out for Friday night. I told him no. This didn't have anything to do with you and Hilary. This was all Violet taking too many liberties in her big-sister role. I still would have told him no, even if Neely Kate hadn't convinced me that if you wanted to be with Hilary, you would have been already."

His shoulders relaxed. "Who's Neely Kate?"

"I met her at jury duty. She didn't get picked, but she works at the courthouse so we've been eating lunch together every day. She found me cryin' on the courthouse steps yesterday." I cringed. Why did I tell him that?

"*You were crying*?" His mouth dropped in horror. "Why?"

My mouth twisted.

"Me?" Joe groaned and covered his face with his hands. "Rose, I'm so sorry. It was nothing. I swear to you."

"I know that now."

He grabbed my hand again. "Thank goodness for Neely Kate."

"Yeah, I think she and I are friends."

His face softened. "Good. I'm glad you made a friend."

"Me too." I took a bite of my ravioli. "But we have to talk about our phone conversation later."

Joe nodded with a worried look then broke out into an ornery grin. "But first we get dessert."

After three days of my Joe famine, I wasn't about to complain.

Chapter Ten

We didn't talk much when we got home. We were too busy making up and then too exhausted to carry on a serious conversation.

In the morning, Joe and I crammed into my tiny bathroom. Since I had more time to get ready, I sat on the edge of the tub watching as he stood in front of the mirror, smearing shaving cream on his face.

"We still have to talk about my problem."

Joe spun around and leaned down until his face hovered several inches over mine. His eyes twinkled. "Problem? Darlin', as you've demonstrated over the last twelve hours, you are perfect."

Giggling, I reached up to swipe a streak of shaving cream off his face, leaving a thin line of his skin exposed. "If you kiss me with that stuff all over your face, you will regret it."

He lifted his eyebrows and laughed. "I've always had a hard time ignoring a challenge." He lowered his mouth to mine.

I squealed and leaned back to escape, nearly falling into the empty tub.

Joe grabbed my arm and righted me with a chuckle. "No need hurtin' yourself to get away from me."

"Joe, seriously."

He sighed and turned back to the mirror. "Okay."

"Joe, I'm sure he's innocent."

"Rose, you could very well be right, but I'm at a loss of what to do."

"The guy who killed poor Mr. Mitchell was hanging out at the hardware store after the murder."

Joe stilled, his razor stopping mid-stroke. He watched me in the mirror as his eyes darkened. "Please tell me you know that because you had another vision."

I pursed my lips. I had vowed to myself not to lie to him.

He closed his eyes as the muscles along his naked back tensed. "You went to the hardware store to buy paint yesterday."

Since he already knew the answer, I saw no reason to say anything.

He put the razor on the counter with a loud *whack* and spun around to face me. "Rose, you know what you did was illegal, right?"

"I had to do something, Joe."

Without a word, he grabbed a towel and stormed out of the bathroom, leaving me perched on the tub. Tears welled in my eyes. We'd been getting along so well and I'd ruined it. But my visions were part of who I was, whether I liked it or not. The good Lord knew I'd never have a vision again if I could help it, but what did Joe expect me to do? I knew Bruce Wayne was innocent, and I couldn't stand by and do nothing.

Several minutes passed, and I wondered if he was going to leave for Little Rock without saying goodbye. Surely, he wouldn't do that. Maybe I'd really blown it this time.

The phone rang, jolting me out of my brooding. I ran into the kitchen and picked up the receiver. "Hello?"

"Rose? This is Marjorie Grace from down at the courthouse."

"Oh, hi." Standing on my tiptoes, I looked out the window over the sink, checking to see if Joe's car was still there. He was leaning against the hood, talking on his cell phone, his face dark and gloomy. Obviously, he was still mad at me.

"Most of the jury is still sick with food poisoning so Judge McClary is postponing the trial until tomorrow. There's a chance we'll be out again, but for now, plan on comin' in the morning."

"Okay, thanks, Marjorie Grace."

The side door opened after I hung up and Joe pulled me into his arms and kissed the top of my head.

"I thought you were mad at me." My words were muffled as I buried my head into his chest.

Joe sighed, his arms tightening around my back. "I was, but then I put myself in your shoes."

I looked up in surprise. "You did?"

"Yeah, I understand why you went to the hardware store. Believe me I do, Rose. But do you have any idea what could happen if you get caught?"

We both knew the answer. I nodded.

"Rose, listen to me." He lifted my chin so he could look into my eyes. "Please, please don't do anything crazy, okay? Let me do some behind-the-scenes checking and see if I can come up with something."

I had no trouble relinquishing control to Joe. If anything, I was grateful I wouldn't be the only person carrying the weight of Bruce Wayne Decker's innocence. At least Joe had more resources and authority to do something. "Okay."

"Good." He kissed me lightly.

I clung to him, wishing it were Saturday.

He lifted his head with a chuckle. "Since we had another disagreement, maybe we need to make up again."

"You'll be late. I don't want you to get in trouble."

A grin lit up his face. "I fell into trouble the first time you showed up on my front porch."

Laughing, I patted his chest. "Well, I have to go to work today and I suspect Suzanne will have my hide if I'm late."

His eyebrows rose in surprise. "What about jury duty?"

"Marjorie Grace just called and said the judge has postponed the trial until tomorrow because half the jury is still out with food poisoning."

"Thank goodness you didn't eat that crazy cat lady's casserole."

"I can't believe the others *did*."

"See? You're smarter than you give yourself credit for." He picked up his bag from the table. "Walk me to my car?"

I nodded.

We went outside with Muffy, and Joe wrapped his arm around my back, pulling me close to his side. Each time he left it was harder and harder, the pain almost unbearable.

Joe stood next to his car door. We stood face to face and he picked up my hand. "You still comin' up to see me this weekend?"

"Yeah," I whispered, feeling the familiar lump in my throat. "As soon as I get out of jury duty tomorrow and pick up Muffy, I'll hit the road."

"I'll text you directions since you don't have a GPS." He cast a disgusted look at my Nova. "I'll be honest. I'm worried about you driving that thing so far. Maybe I should just come back here."

"No," I protested. "That's not fair. You always come to see me, and besides," I gave him my best wicked look, "I want to see your place."

"Then maybe you should think about getting another car."

"Maybe . . ." The Nova had been my daddy's. It was hard to consider giving it up.

"You think about it and if you decide to get a new one, I'll help you if you want, okay?"

I reached up on my tiptoes and kissed him. "I'm a lucky woman, Joe Simmons."

"I could say I'm a lucky man, so let's split the difference and say we're damned lucky to have each other."

"Works for me. You better get goin'."

"Yeah," he sighed, opening his car door. "I'll call you tonight. I promise. And I'll do some digging."

"Thanks." I gave him one long last goodbye kiss before he left. I stood in the driveway and watched his car get smaller and smaller as he drove away. My house was so empty without him. I couldn't understand how that was possible. How had he gotten so deeply embedded in my life in such a short time?

"Rose Gardner! Have you no shame?" Miss Mildred shouted from across the street.

"Good morning, Miss Mildred." Here I was, standing in my driveway in a spaghetti-strapped, slinky lavender nightie. The one I'd bought at Walmart over a month ago.

She stood on her front porch, her plastic watering container held over a pot of geraniums. She was so intent on scolding me, she'd ignored the water pouring over the edge of the pot. "There's nothing good about it when you find a—"

"—porno show in my front yard." I grumbled. "I've got it."

I was in a foul mood and poor Muffy hid under my bed to avoid my wrath, even though she had nothing to fear. I'd never take it out on her. But I couldn't help thinking she'd rather be playing with Andy Jr. and Keith instead of spending the morning with me. Not that I blamed her. I'd rather spend the morning with the boys than me too.

It was a good thing I wasn't in a good mood when I got to the DMV, because Suzanne would have snatched it right out from under me.

My boss sat at the break room table. She held a breakfast sandwich to her mouth, but when she saw me, she threw it down in front of her. It bounced and landed on the floor, rolling until it stopped at my feet.

"You!"

I took a step back toward the exit, unsure that work was such a good idea after all.

She strode over, blocking my path as she put her hand on her hip and tilted her head with a sneer. "Well, looky who bothered to show up to her *job*."

A couple of months ago, Suzanne intimidated me. Okay, she still did, but not as much. It was hard to be frightened of her when I saw her so differently. Or maybe it was that I was different. But either way, Suzanne no longer had the power to scare me, other than she was my boss.

I really did feel sorry for her. It was obvious from her teased, bleached-blonde hair and sallow skin that she'd had a difficult life. She couldn't be past her mid-thirties, but the chain cigarette smoking had carved lines around her eyes. Lines I knew she'd wasted a small fortune on creams trying to fill in.

I pushed past her. "I haven't been on *vacation*, Suzanne. I've been at jury duty."

"You got a letter or card to prove it?"

Crappy doodles. I knew I'd forgotten something. I stopped and turned around to face her. "Uh . . ."

She pinched her mouth into a smug line. "That's what I thought."

"Wait!" I opened my purse and dug until I found my letter from Fenton County Courthouse at the bottom. "Here! This is my jury summons letter."

Suzanne snatched it out of my fingers and scanned the document. "This says you were supposed to *report* for jury duty, but it don't say nothing about you stayin'."

"Suzanne! I got picked. I swear it. We just got let out today because most of the jury got food poisoning."

"Uh-huh."

I had to admit, it sounded like a lie. "I can call the courthouse if you want. They'll excuse me. Or I can get a letter when I go back tomorrow."

"*Tomorrow*? Rose Gardner, if you don't come into work tomorrow then don't bother coming back next week."

"*What*? You can't do that!"

She put a hand back on her hip in an exaggerated motion. "Just *watch* me."

I knew for a fact that she couldn't. Joe had said so. But if she tried it, maybe she'd be the one fired and the DMV would be a happier place. It's a sad day when you miss your old boss, despite the fact she tried to kill you.

Suzanne went out of her way to make my life miserable all morning. She took difficult customers from the other clerks and handed them off to me. When a customer with complicated paperwork showed up, she tossed the documents on my counter with a wicked grin. The only good thing about the day was that I was too busy to dwell on Bruce Wayne Decker's situation. In the rare moments I did, I hoped Joe had made some progress.

I'd planned on eating lunch in the break room, but Suzanne had worked herself under my skin like a raging case of scabies. I wasn't a violent person, in spite of my previous rolling-pin reputation, but I was dangerously close to snapping Suzanne's head off.

When I announced that I planned to leave the building for lunch, the other employees released sighs and relaxed in their chairs. I felt as welcome as a door-to-door vacuum cleaner salesman.

"You better make sure you're back on time! Not one minute late!" Suzanne hollered as I hurried out the back door.

The afternoon was sweltering, but thunderheads loomed on the horizon. With any luck at all, we'd get a good storm to cool things down, but if my morning was any indication of my luck, there wasn't much chance of that happening. I climbed in the car and turned the ignition over, waiting for the air blowing out of the vents to turn cold. Joe was right. While my car was reliable to get around Henryetta, I worried about driving it to Little Rock.

I briefly considered asking Violet if I could borrow her car, but knew I had a better chance of Mildred waving hello the next time Joe left.

My lunch break was a half an hour, which meant I now had less than thirty minutes before I had to face Suzanne again. If I'd done nothing else in the last month and a half, it was learning to stop squandering my life. Why didn't I just quit my job and move to Little Rock with Joe? I had to admit, the idea was tempting. I missed him. An overwhelming wave of sadness washed over me and I decided to call him. I figured I'd leave a voice mail so it surprised me when he answered on the second ring.

"How's your day goin', beautiful? I didn't expect to hear from you so soon, not that I'm complaining."

My stomach fluttered. How could he do that to me with just a phone call? "I miss you."

"I miss you too. I'm counting the hours until I see you again."

My voice lowered. "And how many hours is that, Detective Simmons?"

"About thirty more hours before I get to see your naked body again."

"*Joe!*" I protested, even as my body tingled with anticipation.

"When you asked me to help you with number fifteen on your list—do more with a man—did you think it would turn out like this?"

"Never in a million years."

"Thanks for asking." Wickedness laced his words.

My face burned, and I was unsure what to say. I cleared my throat. "Did you find out anything about Bruce's case?"

"Bruce?"

"Bruce Wayne Decker. You know, the innocent man who's bein' railroaded into a life time in jail."

"I know who you're talking about. I just didn't know you two were on a first-name basis."

I rolled my eyes. "Well, have you?"

He paused. "About that."

My breath stuck in my chest, making me regret thinking my day had gotten better. "That doesn't sound good."

"Well . . ." He paused for several seconds. "That's because it's not."

"*What*? But how can you know that already? You just got back to your office only a few hours ago."

"Right, but . . . I may have had a head start."

"What are you talkin' about?"

He cleared his throat. "I actually started making some inquiries yesterday when you wouldn't answer my calls. I wondered if you were onto something and decided to do a little diggin'."

"Why didn't you tell me?"

"Because I didn't want you to get your hopes up."

"But you don't know all the facts. I didn't tell you everything I know about the case."

"*There's more?*"

"Did you dig up the fact that Frank Mitchell owed people money?"

"Who did he owe and how much?"

I bit my lip before I answered. "Well, I don't know that part."

"What *do* you know?"

"Anne in the paint department at the hardware store said he didn't have a lick of sense, and he owed money to people."

"How did she know this? Were they friends?"

"I don't know . . ."

"It's gossip, Rose. You can't trust it."

"Well then what I am I supposed to do, Joe?"

He released a heavy sigh. "You do your civic duty and make a judgment based on the evidence presented."

My mouth dropped open. "What if all the evidence points to him being guilty even when I know he's innocent?"

"Trust the system."

The air conditioning had finally cooled the car, which was a good thing since I was blazing mad.

"Joe, I can't send an innocent man to jail!"

"Darlin', I'm doin' my best to help you, but I'm at a loss. Nothing's turnin' up. I'll make a few more calls, although I'm not sure there's much more to this case."

I sucked in several breaths.

"Are you still mad at me?"

I was mad but had to admit Joe was trying his best. None of this was his fault. "No."

"Whew." He paused for several seconds. "So what are you going to do?"

"I don't know." My anger fled, despair following in its wake. Bruce Wayne Decker was gonna go to prison. Could I really live with that?

"Just be careful, Rose. Okay? Don't do anything to get yourself in trouble."

"Okay."

I heard voices in the background. "Listen, darlin'. I have to go. I'll call you tonight, okay?"

"Okay. Bye."

I draped my arms over the steering wheel, desperately searching for an idea about what to do. Whatever I came up with, I only had twenty-four minutes to do it.

One other person had the power to put a stop to this travesty of justice, but I wasn't sure how receptive he'd be to my inside information. Nevertheless, I had to ignore my own personal discomfort and figure out a way to make him believe me. I just didn't know how I was gonna make that happen.

Sucking in a deep breath, I put the Nova into drive and pulled out of the parking lot. Time to put on my big-girl pants.

I was going to see Mason Van De Camp Deveraux III.

Chapter Eleven

The thing about wearing big girl pants is sometimes they don't fit. As I pulled into a parking spot only a block from the courthouse, I began to have second thoughts. There was no way on God's green earth Mr. Deveraux was going to believe me. I knew this as sure as I knew the sun would set around nine o'clock tonight.

So *why* was I doing this?

Because it was the only thing I knew to do.

When I went through the heavy wooden doors, cold air sent a chill down my spine. All the judge's yelling about throwing people in jail must have finally worked.

I tossed my purse onto the security table. "Good afternoon, Matt. Any word when Robbie's gonna be back?"

Ol' Matt's mouth dropped open in shock, but he quickly recovered with a scowl. "His gout is better," he grumbled. "He should be back next week."

"Well, that'll be good, huh? No more havin' to wait on Ernie."

Matt ran my purse through his scanner so quickly there was no way he could have gotten a good view of the contents. He thrust the bag at me.

"You have a nice day now." I called over my shoulder as I walked to the elevators. One of these days, I was gonna break him down and make him smile.

The directory of offices hung on the wall next to the elevator. For a moment, I worried Mr. Deveraux was so new that his name wouldn't be on the board, but there it was, plain as day in slightly crooked, white plastic letters—Mason Deveraux III, Assist. D.A. Rm 210.

I pushed the up button, my stomach spinning like the barrel ride at the Fenton County Fair. The doors opened and someone called behind me. "Rose! Wait up!"

Neely Kate hurried over and the acrobatics in my stomach slowed to a tolerable level.

"What on earth are you *doin'* here? Aren't you supposed to be home gettin' over food poisoning?"

I stepped away from the elevator, grateful I could temporarily postpone having my head handed to me on a platter. "Nah, I didn't have any of the breakfast casserole."

"Well, lucky you. I hear it's caught most of 'em *bad*." She glanced around, scrunching up her nose. "So you didn't answer my question. What are you doin' here?"

I considered telling her I was going to see Mason Deveraux, but she'd want to know why and I wasn't ready to go into that with her yet. Of course, with her knowing everything that occurred within the courthouse walls, she'd probably know the truth before dinnertime. There was nothing I could do about that. I just didn't want to be the one to tell her.

"I'm workin' at the DMV today, but I missed our daily lunch and thought I'd run over and see if you were free."

Neely Kate groaned. "I'm sorry. I wish I'd known or I would have waited. I already had lunch."

Shrugging, I grinned. "Hey, it's late and I only thought of it as I left the building."

Her eyes lit up. "I can take a break, though."

"Really? Didn't you just get back from lunch a bit ago? Won't you get in trouble?"

She waved her hand and smirked. *"Please."*

I suspected that meant yes.

"I'll only be gone a few minutes." She held up a stack of folders. "Besides I was running these to the probate department."

"If you're sure . . ."

Linking her arm through mine, Neely Kate squealed. "We can go hide in the vending machine area."

"Okay."

She stopped short and pointed to a man coming down the hall. A scowl furrowed his brow, and he stomped down the hall carrying a paper in his hand. He rubbed his hand over his head, sweeping the few strands of hair he had left to the side.

"That's my boss, Jimmy, and he's been moodier this week than a schizophrenic with PMS. We'd better steer clear of him." She led me to the basement through the stairwell, which was probably a good thing given the antiquated elevator. The thing ran so slow it probably wouldn't have reached the basement until tomorrow.

The vending machines were located in an alcove in the basement. The overhead florescent lights flickered, casting a menacing glare. My stomach growled as I faced the machines full of crackers, chips, and candy bars, suddenly remembering I hadn't eaten anything all day. A bag of chips wasn't going to cut it, but my stomach had no choice in the matter since I'd abandoned my lunch at the DMV.

Neely Kate got a Diet Coke and sat in a plastic chair. "Did you finally hear from Joe?"

"Yeah, he came down from Little Rock to see me last night."

"He drove all the way just to see you?"

"Yeah."

"That's so romantic!"

My face burned with embarrassment. "I'm gonna go see him this weekend."

Neely Kate squealed. "That's even better!"

We spent the next ten minutes hiding out from our responsibilities while I filled Neely Kate in on the latest with Joe, Violet, and my disastrous set-up with Austin.

"That's so romantic! You have two men wanting you!"

I grimaced. "What? No! Don't be silly."

She stood, laughing. "There ain't nothing wrong with being happy that two men are after you, especially when you know which one you want. You do know which one you want, don't you?"

"Of course! I'm not the slightest bit interested in Austin Kent." Although the more I thought about it, I wondered if I could say the same about Violet.

"I gotta get up to the probate office and back to my own desk or Jimmy's gonna be fit to be tied. He's got to leave early to do something at one of his rental properties. You headed back to the DMV?"

Probate was on the same floor as Mr. Deveraux's office. How was I going to explain that to Neely Kate? "Actually, I think I'll stop by the juror's room and check in with Marjorie Grace. I'll see if she knows anything about tomorrow."

"Good idea. And you can put off going back to work a little bit longer."

I checked the time on my phone. I was already three minutes late and it would take me at least five minutes to get back. Suzanne was probably stalking the back door, waiting for me to show up. "Yeah," I answered, distracted.

Thankfully, Neely Kate didn't notice and she filled me in on the latest wedding news. Her bridesmaids' dresses had arrived the day before, and instead of the soft peach color she had ordered, they were tangerine.

"That won't be so bad." I suggested. "Tangerine's a pretty color."

"Brenda, my second cousin twice removed, is a plus-sized girl and loves to go to the tanning salon and is *orange*. She's gonna look like a Skittle."

"Well, maybe there's time for her to get back to a normal color. When's your wedding?"

"In two weeks."

"Oh." I didn't see much chance of that happening.

Since neither of us was in a hurry to get back to our jobs, me now more than ever, we decided to take the elevator to the second floor. While we waited for the doors to open, it occurred to me that Neely Kate knew pretty much everything that happened in the courthouse. In fact, she knew about the Bruce Wayne Decker case before we got picked for questioning. Could I get away with asking what else she knew?

"So, this case I'm on is pretty interesting," I mumbled, staring at the numbers above the elevator doors. The *two* had been lit up for several minutes.

"Oh, yeah?" Her voice stumbled in confusion.

I couldn't blame her for sounding surprised. I'd made such a big deal about how I couldn't talk about it before, and here I was bringing it up.

She leaned her head next to mine and half-whispered. "Has Detective Taylor gotten on the stand and told his *story*?"

Trying to contain my excitement, I turned to face her. "You mean his testimony?"

Her eyes widened in mock surprise. "Oh, is that what he's callin' it now?"

"What do you mean?" My heart thumped like a jackrabbit.

She closed her eyes and shook her head. "Never mind! I didn't say anything!"

I could go about this two ways. I could beg and plead with her to tell me or I could act like I didn't want to know, which I suspected would drive her crazy. I hoped I wasn't wrong. "Pft. It doesn't take a divining rod to see he's not telling the whole story."

Her eyes lit up like she'd just woke up on Christmas morning. "So I'm right?"

Pinching my lips in an exaggerated manner, I shook my head. "I'm not supposed to talk about it."

"But you can tell he's sweeping stuff under the rug, right?"

The elevator doors opened and I nearly groaned. I wasn't done getting my information. I took small steps into the empty box and she followed on my heels.

"Rose, come on. I won't tell a soul. I swear."

After the doors closed, I grabbed her arm and leaned close. "You have to *promise* me, Neely Kate."

She raised her right hand as though she was being sworn in. "I do! I swear. I promise."

"Something's not right. It's like he's ignorin' evidence or something."

"Yes! Exactly! Like the pin they found in the safe! It didn't belong to the murder victim, but it didn't belong to Bruce Decker either. Where did it come from?"

"How do you know these things?"

She rolled her eyes. "I already told you. I have the gift. I know things. Now listen. We don't have much time."

I only wished she did have *the gift*. "Does Detective Taylor know who the real murderer is? Is he protectin' him?"

"No, nothing like that. It's pure laziness. The crowbar was under Decker's house and his fingerprints were at the crime scene. It's just too easy to slap a *Case Closed* sign on it instead of really investigating. I heard Frank Mitchell owed money to some bookies down at the pool hall."

"I heard he owed someone money too, but I didn't hear to who." Who were the bookies?

The elevator stopped on the second floor with a jerk, and the door slowly slid open.

Neely Kate glanced over her shoulder at me, then faced the front. "You didn't hear nothing from me."

"You mean that your cousin is gonna look like an orange Skittle at your wedding? And spoil the surprise for everyone?"

With a wink, she headed down the hall toward the probate office. "Thanks for coming to see me! Lunch tomorrow?"

The thought of meeting Neely Kate for lunch made me happy. "Yeah."

Mr. Deveraux's office was two doors down from the probate office, but I'd told Neely Kate I was going to visit Marjorie Grace. I might as well make an honest woman of myself and drop in to see if she was there. For all I knew, she'd gotten the day off too.

I knocked on the juror room, unsure about proper manners for such a thing. Turned out I worried for nothing. The room was empty, the lights turned off. Mrs. Baker's deadly casserole had been removed, probably handed over to Officer Ernie for evidence. Sinking into a chair, I had to admit I was relieved to be alone. I needed to prepare myself for the confrontation I was sure to have.

My cell phone rang and startled me. Snatching it from my purse, I groaned when I saw who was calling—the DMV. Suzanne was surely calling to chew me out. Maybe even fire me. Could I get that lucky?

Sucking in a deep breath, I turned off the ringer and stood. Time to get this over with.

I walked down the hall, the heaviness of my dread dragging on me while every nerve stood on end in anticipation. I stopped outside Mr. Deveraux's office door and read his name on the frosted window.

I was about to make a fool of myself.

Panic gripped me and I closed my eyes, trying not to hyperventilate. After a couple of deep breaths, I felt a bit calmer. I was the only one willing to help Bruce Wayne Decker. I couldn't let public humiliation stand in my way. My eyes still closed, I reached for the doorknob when the door swung open, and something rammed into me. I stumbled backward, releasing a squeal that rivaled the pig that had escaped at the county fair last month.

A hand grabbed my arm and jerked me forward until I collided with something hard. My eyes flew open, and my screeching stopped when I saw it was none other than Mason Deveraux III, his hand gripping my elbow so tightly I was sure I'd have bruises. My chest was firmly against his as he held me upright. His eyes were dark and angry.

"What the hell are you *doing*, Ms. Gardner?"

"I . . ."

"Are you always this annoying or is it just me you have an affinity for?"

My mouth dropped open and I vacillated from bursting into tears and giving the man a good tongue-lashing. Luckily for me, I'd cried myself out on Tuesday night.

I stiffened and twisted my arm from his grasp. "And are you always this rude or do you save it for just me?"

Mr. Deveraux stepped backward, smoothing the imaginary wrinkles from his jacket. "What are you doing here, Ms. Gardner?" His mouth pursed into his constipated look. I swore I was gonna bring him some Ex-Lax.

"Hadn't you realized, Mr. Deveraux? It's my life's purpose to annoy you. How am I doin' so far?" What had gotten into me? I'd never been so rude to anyone in my entire life.

He leaned closer, his eyes narrowing. "You're exceptionally talented, but surely even *you* have a purpose other than coming down here to pester me, on your day off from your civic duty no less. Shouldn't you be home vomiting?"

My chest heaved with my anger and frustration. This wasn't going very well and I hadn't even started yet. "I needed to *talk* to you." *Crappy doodles*! I wished I'd thought to iron out at least part of my snippy tone.

He swung his hand away from his side, his hand gripping a manila folder. A fake grin plastered his face. "Well, here I am, in the flesh. Start talking."

The blood in my veins boiled. "What in the world happened to make you so hateful?"

His arm fell back to his side and his grin turned into a scowl.

"I haven't done a thing to you other than happen to be in the wrong place at the wrong time. Trust me, Mr. Deveraux, you're the last person on the face of the earth I want to see right now."

His eyes widened in confusion. "But I thought you just said you needed to talk to me."

"*I changed my mind*!"

The sound of applause caught me by surprise. Neely Kate and two other women stood several feet away, clapping and grinning like they'd just enjoyed a show.

"You tell 'im, honey!" one of the women cheered, waving her arm into the air.

Mr. Deveraux's face reddened and he sputtered before spinning around and marching back into his office.

The two women brushed past me, one patting me on the arm and grinning.

Neely Kate rushed over and looped her arm through mine. "Oh, my stars and garters! I never would have believed that if I hadn't seen it with my own eyes!"

Embarrassment enflamed my face as the full force of what I'd done swept over me. "I . . ."

"Do you have any idea how bad every person in this court-house has been wantin' to do *that*? He's a mean, spiteful man. Don't you worry, you're not the only one to deal with his attitude, but you're the first one to call him on it."

"Am I gonna get kicked off the jury now?" I whispered as Neely Kate led me to the elevators.

"Nah, I doubt it. He'll just go pout in his office."

"But . . ."

Neely Kate pushed the elevator button. "Don't you worry your pretty little head about it. What's he gonna do? Tell Judge McClary you were mean to him? Ha! I'd like to see that."

The elevator doors opened and we walked inside. I was still in a daze.

Shaking her head, Neely Kate laughed. "I'll never forget the look on his face as long as I live!"

Neither would I.

The doors opened to the courthouse lobby and I was all too eager to escape the stares of people milling about. Had they heard what I'd done already? How was that possible?

Neely Kate patted my arm. "Don't you be worryin' about Mr. Crabbypants. You'll be fine. What's the worst they can do? Throw you in jail? Not likely."

My stomach knotted. Getting locked up frightened the bejiggers out of me.

She saw the terror on my face. "Relax! I'm teasin'."

I tried to smile, but my face was frozen. "Yeah . . ." And then I felt a vision coming. *Oh, no! Not now!* "Your flower girl's gonna get chicken pox."

Neely Kate's eyes narrowed. "What did you just say?"

"What? I didn't say anything."

She tilted her head and grabbed my arm. "Yes, you did. You said my flower girl's gonna get chicken pox."

My pulse pounded in my temples. "Did I say that?"

Her gaze pinned me down. "You did. Why did you say my flower girl's gonna get chicken pox?"

I waved my hand and released a nervous laugh. "I have no earthly idea! I don't know what's getting into me today! I have to go now." I pulled my arm out of her death grip.

"I guess . . ." She seemed unsure, but let it go. "You better get goin'. You're gonna be late."

Gonna be? I was long past late.

"See you tomorrow?" she asked.

I nearly cried with happiness. I hadn't scared her off. Yet. I had no idea how she'd react when her flower girl actually broke out in poxes. "I'll see you tomorrow." After a half-hearted wave, I walked into the afternoon heat.

Mercy, I had blown this every way possible. I was going to be late to work and maybe lose my job, and I hadn't even accomplished what I'd set out to do. Not only had I failed to tell Mr. Deveraux what I knew about Bruce, but I'd ticked him off so much there was little chance of him ever listening to me, even if I ever got enough nerve to try to tell him again.

I consoled myself with a twisted grin. In spite of everything, I'd gotten a few pieces of valuable information.

One, I'd learned that peach bridesmaids's dresses were only a good idea if you wanted a candy-themed wedding. And two, Frank Mitchell had owed money to a bookie. Maybe things hadn't turned out so bad after all.

Chapter Twelve

I'd never seen Suzanne so angry in the four years I'd known her. Not even after she'd found out the beauty school no longer offered fifty percent discounts on repeat-customer hair coloring. And that was saying something.

While her red face was a good clue something was wrong, the way she shook, starting with her chin and radiating out to the rest of her body, made a few of us think she was having a seizure. Martha called 911 but hung up when Suzanne realized what she was doing and started screaming at her.

I wouldn't have been surprised if Suzanne had sent me home, but I suspected she'd come to her senses and realized there was a proper procedure to follow. The only path to instant dismissal in the Arkansas state employment system was trying to murder one of your employees. Then again, maybe she planned to follow our old boss's footsteps.

Sitting down at my station, I stuffed my purse into my drawer, chanting, "Three more hours. Three more hours," until the words blended into a garbled mess.

Other than my encounter with Neely Kate, my day had been relatively vision-free, so I wasn't surprised when I had several right in a row. One woman was relieved but a little baffled that her purse was in her chest freezer. Another customer was none too happy to find out that his neighbor had been stealing his newspapers.

Visions were exhausting.

But my visions were a sharp reminder of how I got involved in the Daniel Crocker mess, which had led to Momma's murder and my whole involvement in the Crocker predicament. My visions had been a blessing and a curse, but they ultimately helped me save Joe and bust Crocker.

To the best of my knowledge, Bruce Wayne Decker didn't have his own visions to save him. The truth was, I probably was Bruce Decker's only hope. To my shame and dismay, I'd let my temper get the best of me and ruined any chance of getting Mr. Deveraux to believe me. He was the one person who could drop the charges and I'd blown it. But crappy doodles, that man was exasperating.

I needed another tactic, a backup plan to get myself out of the ditch I'd dug. I didn't have anything concrete to exonerate Bruce, but if I could get more information, then Mason Deveraux would be forced to listen. The problem was getting more information.

One of my customers gave me an idea when she plopped her paperwork on the counter to renew her plates.

"The address on that paperwork is wrong. Can you put my new one in the system?"

With a friendly smile, I told her I'd be happy to, but the gears in my head had already spun into motion. There was a good chance that Frank Mitchell's address was still in the system. He'd died a year ago, and it usually took longer than that to purge names. All I had to do was look up the address and just drive by poor Mr. Mitchell's house. I was bound to spot a clue—or, at least, it was worth a try.

How innocent was that? You couldn't get arrested for driving down the street, could you? But I could get in trouble for looking up his records. I'd just have to be careful.

A coworker locked the front doors of the DMV at five and I bolted for the rear exit, ignoring Suzanne's shrieks that I better show up in the morning or not come back.

Once I climbed into my car, shifting my legs on the sticky, hot vinyl, I pulled Mr. Mitchell's address out of my pocket. While the steaming air that blasted from the vents slowly cooled down, I stared at the yellow sticky note, the words scribbled in my haste. *If Suzanne had caught me* . . . But she hadn't, and there I sat with the address of a murder victim in my hand. Well, his last known address. Who knew where he resided now. God rest his soul.

I briefly considered going home. Muffy had been locked up all day and needed out. Not to mention I had a half-painted bedroom waiting for my attention, but I convinced myself this was going to be a quick drive-by. Curiosity had gotten the best of me. I'd just check out his place, then head straight home. I also considered getting Muffy and bringing her along. But if what I was doing was wrong, it seemed irresponsible to make Muffy an accessory to a crime. Again. Sometimes I was sure she still resented being forced to help me steal Miss Mildred's car when we went to save Joe from Daniel Crocker.

I grabbed the steering wheel with both hands and clenched my teeth. That settled it. A quick run past his house and then home.

Frank Mitchell's residence was in an older, rundown section of Henryetta. All the streets in his part of town had tree names: Maple. Oak. Elm. The homes in Forest Ridge were built in the 1930s and most had been neglected, Mr. Mitchell's included.

I slowed the Nova as I approached his house, gawking through the passenger window. The front porch sagged a good couple of feet on one side. One of the shutters was lopsided, looking like it would fall off if someone blew on it. A good portion of the paint had chipped away. The yard was in desperate need of cutting and the bushes in front were so overgrown that they covered half the windows. By the time I'd passed the house, I hadn't learned anything other than the house was falling apart. I needed another look.

After circling the block, I slowed down several houses before reaching Mr. Mitchell's again. The dwelling looked abandoned. Surely, it would be safe to look around.

I parked the car at the curb, one house away. As I got out, my hands shook, making the keys rattle. What in the world was I doing? What did I hope to find? I had no idea, but the urge to walk up to his house was not only undeniable but impossible to ignore.

Trying not to look suspicious, I plastered a big smile on my face and strolled down the cracked and crumbling sidewalk, taking care to keep from tripping. How would I explain breaking my leg here of all places? *I should have brought Muffy after all.* I could have said I was walking my dog, but it was too late now. I was already in the middle of doing this crazy thing.

When I reached his house, I stopped on the sidewalk. Boards with rusty nails stuck up from the porch, and I wondered how anyone went in through the front door. I moved to the driveway and started around the back of the house when I heard a voice behind me.

"What do ya think yer doin'?"

With a shriek, I turned to face the voice, stumbling backward. I really needed to stop doing that. Twice in one day was two times too many.

Staring into the face of an old man who was obviously missing most of his teeth left me almost speechless. "Huh?"

He hunched forward, his right hand cupping the top of his thick cane. The man waited for my response and he looked like a man who wasn't fond of waiting.

"I was just lookin' around . . ."

"It's been sold," he grunted, trying to straighten his back and, without success, to look taller.

"What?"

"I said it's been sold. Sold! What are you, deaf?"

"No . . . err . . ." I mentally shook myself. I needed to get it together. Obviously, I wasn't very good at this investigating stuff. "How long had it been for sale?"

"Which time?"

"How many times has this house been for sale?" I asked, dumbfounded.

"Twice. First time right after Frank died and the second just this past month. It's a cotton-pickin' shame. Frank spent the last month of his life fightin' off some guy who was using every trick in the book to get him to sell, but it was all for nothing. The damn house sold anyway." He turned around and headed back to the sidewalk, muttering under his breath.

"Wait," I called, hurrying to catch up with him. "Who was trying to buy his property? Why did they want it so bad? Was it one of the bookies he owed money to?"

The old man stopped and turned to me, leaning all his weight onto his cane as though he was too tired to stand anymore. "Yer just full of questions, ain't ya?"

I didn't respond, trying to figure out the right thing to say to get him to talk. Maybe I should have questions prepared the next time I snooped at some guy's house.

"I don't know who it was. Frank didn't say, not that it was any of my damn business anyways. And as to why they wanted it, I don't know that either. But I know they was givin' Frank the hard sell even though Frank said he'd never move. It was his momma and daddy's house, and it needed to stay in the family." He released a throaty laugh that caused a coughing fit. When he hacking slowed, he cleared his throat and spit on the sidewalk.

I jumped out of the way, swallowing my disgust.

The man got a hard look in his eye and the right side of his top lip twitched as he stared at me. If I hadn't known I could outrun him, I'd have been scared.

"You know what's funny?"

I shook my head.

"All that energy wasted tryin' to keep from selling it and his son goes off and sells it as soon as he gets the chance. What a waste." He shook his head.

"You said the person tryin' to buy his house was giving him the hard sell. What exactly was he doin'?"

He squinted up at me and his annoyance curled the corners of his mouth. "How in the Sam Hill would I know? Do I look like a mind reader to you?"

"No . . . but . . ."

He scowled, his wrinkled face twisting up like a prune. "Look, Frank was a private person. Kept to hisself. The only reason I know'd anything about it was because I found him drunk out back a couple nights before he was killed."

The pieces of the puzzle were shifting as I put things together. "Do you think the person trying to buy his house might have killed him?"

"That pot-smokin' fool didn't have enough money to buy a house."

My mouth dropped. "You mean Bruce Wayne Decker?"

He tried to stand taller again but tilted to the side. "Of course I mean that Decker kid. Who the hell else would I be talking about? That boy's on trial for Frank's murder right now."

"But how—"

"Damn, yer a nosy woman." He shook his head and grunted. This guy made me appreciate Mildred just a tiny bit more. "'Cause that Decker fool lived down the street." Lifting his cane, he pointed down the street to the house on the corner. "Right there."

The house was one of the nicest on the street. Fresh paint, a cut yard, and flowers planted along the walk.

My confusion must have been evident. The man snorted. "He didn't own that house. That's his parents' house. He lived there until a couple of months before Frank died. His folks finally wised up and kicked his sorry ass to the curb."

"Oh."

"Got any more fool questions?"

I shook my head, trying to make sense of that information. "No."

He turned his back to me and hobbled to the house next door. "My baseball game's on. If I miss something, I'm blamin' you."

Driving away, I slowed the car as I passed Bruce Wayne Decker's parents' house. I considered stopping and asking them some questions, but that wouldn't work. I couldn't very well knock on their door and say, "Hi. I'm Rose Gardner and I'm on your son's jury, but I saw a vision in the men's restroom that someone else killed Frank Mitchell so I believe your son is innocent and I'm trying to prove it."

There was no way I could pull that off. I bet dollars to donuts that they'd never believe I thought he was innocent when everyone else was ready to have a public execution. Besides, I couldn't risk it. I wasn't supposed to be investigating.

On the drive home, I tried to make sense of what Mr. Mitchell's neighbor had said. Who wanted to buy Frank Mitchell's house? It was in such bad shape, and that kind of neglect hadn't happened since Frank's death. Decay like that took years. But Mr. Mitchell was a manager at the hardware store. While he wouldn't have made enough money to get rich, he surely made enough to take care of his house. So where was his money going?

Anne in the paint department had said he'd owed money and Neely Kate said she'd heard he was in debt to bookies. I knew Joe would dismiss it as gossip, but the man had to be spending his money on something and it sure wasn't fixing his house. Had the bookies wanted his house to pay off his debts? And when he refused, did they kill him?

Muffy was glad to see me and burst out of the house, running in circles before she finally took care of her business. After I made myself a sandwich for dinner, I realized I needed to pack for my trip to Little Rock.

My stomach twisted with excitement and anticipation. I'd never been to Little Rock before, even though it was only two hours away. Violet and Mike had been plenty of times and—

Oh, crappy doodles. I hadn't told Violet I was going. No matter how frustrated I was with her, I needed to let her know or she'd worry.

I picked up the phone, wondering if she was still mad.

"Hello, Rose." My question was answered by her frosty tone.

"Hi." I tried to keep my voice friendly.

"Have you called to apologize?" she asked with a snippy air.

"For what?"

"For your rude behavior the other night."

"*My* rude behavior?"

"Yes, the way you ran out on poor Austin like that."

My blood boiled. "Are you serious? You had no right, Violet! You had no right to set me up when you *know* I'm with Joe!"

"And you know my thoughts on that."

"It's none of your business, Violet! I am not six years old. I don't need you to pick out my friends anymore."

Violet gasped. "Is that what you thought I was doing when we were little? Picking out your friends?" The hurt in her words made my stomach drop.

I forced myself to take a deep breath. "No, Vi. Of course not. You were just protecting me from the mean kids at school."

I sank onto my bed, resting my forehead on my palm. How had we started bickering again? Before Momma's death we'd hardly ever had a cross word, yet when I looked deep inside, I knew it was because I'd never found the strength to stand up to anyone. Violet included.

"So you think I'm tryin' to run your life?"

My indignation was back. "Well, aren't you?"

"Rose, it's just that you're . . ."

We both absorbed her silence.

"I don't want you to live with regrets." Her voice cracked and I knew she was crying.

"Violet, I have to live my life and make my own mistakes."

Her superior attitude was back in a flash. "So you're admitting that Joe Simmons is a mistake?"

I groaned in frustration. "No! I did not say he is a mistake. You're worried I'm makin' one, but you can't save me from mistakes. You have to let me live my life—all of it. The good things and the bad."

"I can't bear to see you hurt."

"But how do you know Joe's going to hurt me? How do you know that I won't hurt him? Or maybe neither one of us will hurt each other. Maybe we'll get married and I'll move to Little Rock, and we'll have babies and a house and live happily ever after."

"You're moving to Little Rock?" she whispered in horror.

And then I knew the reason she was so adamant I dump Joe. She was scared of losing me. The only tie Joe had to Henryetta was me and the chances of him moving here were slim. If we stayed together and got married, I'd move away and Violet would be alone.

It all made sense now. Austin had been born and raised in Henryetta. Sure, he'd moved away and sowed his wild oats, but he came back to build his life. In Violet's eyes, Austin Kent was safe and Joe Simmons was dangerous.

My voice softened. "No, I'm not moving to Little Rock."

"But Joe wants you to?"

I hated to put a deeper wedge between them, but I wasn't going to lie. "Yes."

"See! I knew it!" The tears in her voice softened her accusation.

"Violet, I told him that it's too soon. We've only just started datin'. But I can't promise that I won't move to Little Rock someday, just like you can't promise you won't."

"I most certainly can promise that! Mike's takin' over his father's construction business when he retires next year. We were born in Henryetta and we'll die here."

I sighed. "Well, it must be nice to have your life planned so nicely." The uncertainties of my own life were exasperated by Violet's carefully laid-out world.

She gasped again, which caught me by surprise. I'd been genuine—I hadn't meant to hurt her.

"I have to go, Rose." Violet sounded like she was choking.

"Wait! I have to tell you something first."

"What?" The icy tone was back.

"I'm going to spend the weekend in Little Rock with Joe. I'm leaving tomorrow after jury duty and I'll be back Sunday night."

Her silence was frightening. After several seconds, she cleared her throat. "I see. And what do you plan to do with Muffy?"

"Well, I plan to take her with me."

"*To a condo*? Doesn't Joe live in a condo in downtown Little Rock?"

I wasn't sure why I was so surprised that she'd paid that much attention to Joe's details. "Well, yeah, but we'll take Muffy for walks."

"Muffy will hate drivin' in a car for hours."

"I think she'll be fine."

"All right. Fine. I'll watch her."

My mouth dropped open in shock. "What? I didn't ask—"

"That dog gets left inside that hot box you call a house all day long while you're at work and then you plan to stuff her into a car and drive into the concrete jungle?"

"Little Rock is not a concrete jungle."

"How would you know? You've never been there."

Violet always knew exactly how to hurt me, even when she wasn't trying. "No, Vi. I haven't. But I'm goin' this weekend. And I'm staying at Joe's and guess what? I'm sleeping with him!"

"*Rose Anne Gardner*! What in *tarnation* has gotten into you?"

I had a sexual innuendo on the tip of my tongue but wisely chose to keep it to myself. "I'm old enough to make my own choices. If I want to dye my hair purple, I'll do it. If I want to spend the weekend in Little Rock, I'll do it."

"I'm not entitled to an opinion?"

"Of course you are. And sometimes I want your opinion. But there's a difference between an opinion and ramming your agenda down my throat."

Her voice softened. "You're not really gonna dye your hair purple, are you?"

I sighed, then laughed. Leave it to Violet to worry about that. "No."

"Oh, thank God, because I really don't think I could be quiet about *that*."

I caught the emphasis. "So you're gonna let me make my own decisions about Joe?"

"Yes."

"Thank you."

"But I still think I should watch Muffy. Ashley will love having her here."

I almost couldn't bear to leave Muffy for two days, but Violet had a point. "Okay."

"Why don't you bring her over before you go to work in the morning? No sense in her staying in that house all day by herself."

"I have jury duty tomorrow, but that's a good idea. I have to be at the courthouse at nine so I'll bring her by beforehand."

"Okay." She was silent for a moment. "So you really like this guy?"

I smiled. "Yeah, I really do."

"Just be careful."

I knew she didn't just mean the two-hour drive. "I've spent too much of my life being careful. I'm trying to live, Violet."

"I know. That's what worries me. I love you, Rose."

"I love you too."

We hung up, and a heaviness settled in around me. I hated when Violet was cross, especially with me, but I knew given her recent behavior that something else was going on. Maybe I'd take her out to lunch next week and try to get her to talk.

My thoughts drifted to Joe and how Violet felt threatened by him. I couldn't help worrying that sometime in the future I'd be forced to choose a side. The question was, which side would I pick?

Chapter Thirteen

Thankfully, Marjorie Grace called bright and early on Friday morning to say that we were to report for jury duty. Otherwise, I probably would have called in sick to work. The jurors were doing better, although still feeling a little peaked. The air conditioning was working, but Judge McClary said he'd recess the trial if the jurors got gastrointestinally distressed.

Nothing stood in the way of justice in Fenton County. Not even Mrs. Baker's breakfast casserole.

Dropping Muffy off at Violet's was unsettling. Violet and I tiptoed around each other, but we seemed to have reached a truce. Ashley and Mikey hopped around Muffy with glee and usually she would have joined in, but she seemed to understand that she wouldn't be leaving with me. She stood at my feet whining and I bent to rub her head. Leaning into her ear, I whispered, "You be a good girl and I'll be back on Sunday."

Her chin lifted, and she stared at me with her pitch-black eyes, breaking my heart into pieces.

I left the house in tears, which was silly. Muffy was just a dog and I'd hardly had her any time at all. But she was *my* dog, and I was gonna miss the dickens out of her.

By the time I got to the courthouse, my sober mood had lightened, especially since I found a parking spot less than a block away. I couldn't wait to leave Henryetta after court. I was beyond curious about what Joe's condo looked like and excited to see Little Rock. But mostly I just wanted to be with Joe.

When I walked into the courthouse foyer, I set my purse on the counter and an older man greeted me with a smile.

"Morning, miss."

I grinned. "You must be Robbie. How's your gout? Are you feeling better?"

His eyes widened in surprise before he began to check the contents of my purse. "Why, I sure am. Thank you, miss. How'd you know?"

"Matt was eager for you to come back."

Robbie shook his head with a laugh. "Is that right now?" He ran my purse through the scanner and handed it back. "You have a blessed day now."

I beamed. "Thank you, Robbie. You too."

As I waited for the elevator doors to open, I wondered if maybe I would. Although I was embarrassed about seeing Mason Deveraux III again, I knew he would ignore me in the courtroom. Violet and I weren't fighting. I'd discovered a clue to help clear Bruce Wayne Decker. And I was going to see Joe. How could things go wrong?

The juror's room was tense when I walked in. The people who'd gotten sick from the breakfast casserole were giving Mrs. Baker the silent treatment. She sat in the back corner dabbing her eyes with a tissue. Marjorie Grace squatted next to her, patting her arm and talking in hushed tones.

Just as I was about to go check on Mrs. Baker, Bailiff Spencer walked in and announced that it was time to go to court. I was first in line, eager to see if any new evidence would be presented to help prove Bruce innocent. I hated to think about him sitting in a jail cell all weekend.

We took our seats and waited for the judge to enter the courtroom. Mrs. Baker rested her hand on her leg, trying to hide her shaking.

I covered her hand with my own. "Don't worry. Everyone will forget all about this by Monday."

Her chin trembled and she whispered, "One of the jurors said that Judge McClary was so fit to be tied that he had to recess the trial because of . . . you know." She sniffed and glanced around. "Especially since the air conditioning finally got fixed. He said . . ."

She wiped the tears streaming down her face with a damp tissue. "He said the judge was gonna arrest me for contempt of court."

My eyes widened in surprise and I leaned closer, trying to ignore the overpowering cat food smell. "Oh, you're worryin' for nothing. He can't do that!"

She bit her lip, tears pooling in her eyes. "Are you sure?"

I nodded. "Positive." Mostly.

I had to admit Judge McClary was a cranky old coot, but surely poisoning most of the jury wasn't grounds to arrest someone.

Oh, wait.

We all stood as the judge entered the courtroom, his face twisted into a grimace. That didn't bode well for poor Mrs. Baker. I cast an anxious glance in her direction. Her face was as white as Suzanne's hair after a beauty school flunky had bleached all the pigment out.

After we were all seated, the judge banged his gavel with extra force. "This court is now in session." He glared at Mrs. Baker and I reached my hand over to hers and gripped tight.

"Since we've had a day and a half recess due to a toxic-laden casserole"—if possible, his eyes narrowed even more—"we've got a lot of time to make up. Plan on staying late, people."

His voice echoed around the room. Dismayed at his announcement, I dropped my hold on Mrs. Baker. I suspected this was going to interfere with my Little Rock trip. I tried to swallow the ill will I'd begun to feel toward her.

"Call the first witness!" Judge McClary barked.

Mr. Deveraux slid out of his seat, and assumed his usual lemon face. He'd purposely avoided looking at me, but as he stood and adjusted his suit coat, he turned his head to the side as if he was stretching his neck and his eye caught mine. If possible, his face scrunched up more. His bad mood rivaled the judge's.

"The state calls Mr. David Moore."

A man in faded jeans and a wrinkled dress shirt walked toward the front of the courtroom. His bushy, dirty-blond hair covered his ears and the top of his collar. The short steps he took, along with the fear in his eyes, suggested he was approaching a torture-filled interrogation, not a witness stand.

After he was sworn in, Mr. Moore squirmed in his seat. Even more than Bruce Wayne, and that was saying something.

"Mr. Moore," Mason Deveraux said in a deep voice. "Tell the court how you know Bruce Decker?"

"Um . . ." David shifted in his seat from one side to other while his hand drummed on the witness stand ledge. "We're friends."

"And how long have you known the defendant?"

He looked up, wide-eyed. "Who?"

Mr. Deveraux sighed and spoke slowly. "Bruce Decker."

"Oh . . ." He looked around the room and stopped when his gaze fell on Bruce. "Since we were kids."

Bruce's usual squirming had stopped, his full attention on the witness box.

"And you two are friends? Good friends?"

"Yeah."

"And what types of things do you and Mr. Decker do?"

"Uh . . ."

"Would it be accurate to say you two smoke marijuana together on a regular basis?"

Bruce's attorney burst out of his seat like someone had pinched him in the butt. "Objection, your honor! Mr. Deveraux is leading the witness."

I fought to keep my mouth from falling open. Mr. Yates was actually making an attempt to defend his client.

"Sustained." Judge McClary turned to the assistant DA and glared.

Mason Deveraux's mouth formed a thin line, but after a moment he lifted his chin and gave the witness a fake smile. "What did the two of you do together?"

"Oh, you know . . . video games . . . hang out in my parents' basement . . . smoked weed."

Mr. Deveraux turned to look at Mr. Yates with raised eyebrows as he gloated. "And how did your friend Bruce support his habit?"

"Huh?"

"Where did he get the money to buy pot?"

"Oh!" David's face lit up with understanding. "Well, he had a job at the Burger Shack for awhile. Then he worked at the Piggly Wiggly, then after that—"

"Objection, your honor," Mr. Yates shouted. "While it's true that my client has a lengthy work history, it's not necessary to go over every single place that he's worked."

"Sustained!" the judge shouted. "Let's get on with this."

Mr. Deveraux's face turned pink and he paced. "Mr. Moore, did Bruce always have enough money from his varied *careers* to pay for his weed?"

"Huh?"

"Did he make enough at his *jobs* to buy his pot?"

"Oh . . . No."

"And how did he get money to support his habit, er, how did he get the money to buy his drugs?"

"Sometimes he'd shoplift or steal small things from—"

Mr. Yates flew out of his seat again. "Objection! Hearsay!"

Deveraux walked toward the judge. "Your Honor, this has relevance, if you'll bear with me."

"Overruled. Ask your questions."

Deveraux gloated again, an unbecoming feature on a grown man. "And how did you know that Bruce shoplifted or stole things?"

"He always told me or . . . sometimes I'd help him."

"Did you ever break into houses?"

He shrugged. "A time or two."

"And did you help Mr. Decker rob the hardware store the night Frank Mitchell was killed?"

"No! I didn't have anything to do with that."

"Did Mr. Decker tell you that he saw the victim in the hardware store while he was there to rob it?"

"Yes, but—"

"And did Mr. Decker show you the murder weapon?"

"Yeah, but—"

"Did you in fact, Mr. Moore, help Bruce Decker hide the murder weapon under his house?"

David Moore frowned and looked down at his lap. "Yes."

Mason Deveraux spun around to return to his seat wearing the hint of a wicked grin. "That will be all."

Mr. Yates stood and approached the witness stand, now wearing a scowl of his own. The court was full of a bunch of cranky men.

"David, did Bruce tell you that he killed Frank Mitchell?"

The witness shook his head. "No, he said he didn't kill him."

"Did he tell you why he had the murder weapon?"

"He said when he got to the store, the back door was unlocked and he snuck in and heard two men arguing. One was Frank Mitchell, but he didn't know who the other guy was. He hid behind some shelves and watched and then the other guy grabbed a crowbar and hit Mitchell."

Deveraux leaned across his table. "Objection, Your Honor. Hearsay."

"Overruled. Continue, Mr. Moore."

David Moore looked at Mr. Yates, who nodded.

"So then what did Bruce say happened?"

"He said they scuffled around a little and then the other guy hit Mitchell in the head and he fell to the ground, bleedin' everywhere. The other guy went into the office, and then came back out and went out the back door. After the other guy left, Bruce freaked out and checked on Mr. Mitchell, but he was already dead. But Bruce figured they'd blame him for the murder and he took the crowbar with him when he left."

"Why would he do such a thing?"

"Well . . ." he looked at Bruce. Bruce nodded. "He was pretty stoned and wasn't thinkin' straight. By the time he got home, he realized he'd screwed up but wasn't sure what to do about it. So he called me and we hid the crowbar under his house."

"And why would you help hide a murder weapon? Did you know that helping Bruce hide the crowbar would make you an accessory to a crime?"

"No, I didn't really think about that. I only knew that Bruce needed my help."

Mr. Yates walked toward the witness box. "David, do you think that Bruce Decker killed Frank Mitchell?"

"Objection, Your Honor. The defense is asking the witness to hypothesize."

"Your Honor, these two men have been friends for years. Mr. Moore knows the defendant's character. His answer has relevance."

"Overruled."

It was Mr. Yates' turn to gloat. The animosity between the lawyers convinced me that I was right about Mason Deveraux picking me for the jury just to tick off Mr. Yates. But the joke was on him, since I irritated Mr. Deveraux too.

"David," Mr. Yates said. "Do you believe Bruce? Do you believe he's innocent?"

"Yeah. He can't even swat a fly without feelin' bad about it. He could never kill anybody."

Mr. Yates faced the jury and smiled.

David Moore left the stand and Bruce looked relieved until Mr. Deveraux called the next witness. "Elmer Burnett."

Bruce's face paled and I turned to get a look at the witness who'd caused him so much distress. My own face must have turned white when I caught a glimpse.

Limping down the aisle and leaning on a cane was Frank Mitchell's neighbor. The one I'd talked to the night before.

Oh, crappy doodles.

Elmer Burnett took the stand and was sworn in while sweat trickled down my neck. I sat in the front row, stuck in the middle. There was no way he could miss me. Anxiety prickled every hair follicle on my body.

Mr. Deveraux began to pace. "Mr. Burnett, how did you know the victim, Frank Mitchell?"

"I was his next-door neighbor for forty-two years."

"And you also know the defendant, Bruce Decker?"

"You already know all this so why'r ya askin' me?"

Mr. Deveraux's eyes bulged with irritation.

A few people in the audience snickered, including the juror on my right. Who still needed a shower.

Judge McClary banged his gavel several times. "Order in the court. If you can't restrain yourself from such sophomoric behavior I'll toss every last one of ya outta my courtroom. *Got it?*" The judge glared at Mr. Yates, who suddenly found the notes in front of him interesting. He looked down at Mr. Burnett in the stand. "Mr. Burnett, I know this might seem redundant to you . . . I mean it might sound like it's been said before."

"I know what redundant is. I'm not a half-wit."

The judge looked aghast that anyone dared to speak to him in such a hateful tone. "No one's saying you are. But you have to answer the questions, no matter how ridiculous they seem." He pointed his gaze at Mason Deveraux. "Or no matter how many times the lawyers object." He smirked as he looked at Mr. Yates. "You need to act like no one's ever heard this before."

"I done already told him everythin' I know. This is cotton-pickin', boll-weevil-rotting—"

"I understand your frustration," the judge said in a tight voice. "But you still have to answer the questions."

"Then let's get this over with."

"Yes, let's." Judge McClary agreed.

"Mr. Burnett." Deveraux's tone was icy. "How do you know the defendant, Bruce Decker?"

"I've known Bruce since he was a baby. He growed up a few houses down from me, the house on the corner. He lived with his parents, that's them right out there." He pointed to a middle-aged couple who were suffering from a serious lack of sleep, judging from the dark circles under their eyes. "He lived with them until a month or two before he killed Frank Mitchell."

Mr. Yates jumped out of his seat like his pants were on fire. "Objection, Your Honor. Speculation."

"Sustained." The judge faced us. "The jury will disregard the witness's last statement about the defendant murdering Mr. Mitchell." He turned back to Mr. Deveraux. "Continue."

Deveraux shook his body, just a smidge, as if trying to shake off cooties. "So Bruce Decker moved out?"

"Yes."

"Do you know why he moved out?"

"Objection, Your Honor. Hearsay."

Mr. Deveraux looked like a bulldog with a fresh bone he didn't want to let go of. "I believe the witness has information he received directly from Bruce Decker's parents."

The judge sighed. "Overruled, but rephrase the question."

"Did Bruce Decker's parents tell you why he moved out?"

"Yeah, they sure did. They kicked his sorry ass out because they was tired of all the trouble he kept getting into."

"You mean his criminal record?"

"If it weren't one thing, it was another. That boy mooched off of them his entire life and his parents were tired of it."

"Do you know where he moved to?"

"I ain't got a clue."

"Did Mr. Decker know Frank Mitchell?"

"Of course he did. They were neighbors! What kind of fool question was that?"

"Did Mr. Decker ever steal from his neighbors?"

"Bruce kept to his side of street."

Mr. Deveraux crossed his arms. "You didn't answer the question."

"Questions. Questions. That damned nuisance," Elmer Burnett pointed his finger at Bruce, "killed Frank Mitchell, yet instead of sendin' him to jail like he deserves, all you people are doing is asking questions!"

"Mr. Burnett!" Judge McClary banged his gavel.

"I'm sick of answering yer damned questions. Hell, even that girl over there came snoopin' around asking questions last night!" He pointed his finger at me and all the blood in my body rushed to my toes.

Oh, crappy doodles.

Everyone fell silent as every eye landed on me.

Then the courtroom burst with shouting.

"*Her?*" Mr. Deveraux shrieked, pointing to me.

"Objection, Your Honor!" Mr. Yates shouted.

"You and your damned objections!" Mr. Burnett growled, now pointing his cane instead of his finger. "Stuff your objections up your—"

"Order in the court!" Judge McClary banged his gavel repeatedly. "*I said order in the court.* The next person to say a word is not only thrown out but thrown into lockup."

I tried not to hyperventilate.

The judge glared at me. "Mr. Burnett, are you saying you spoke to that juror in the middle of the front row last night? The one wearing a blue dress?"

"That's her. She came snoopin' around Frank's house asking a pissload of questions."

Someone in the middle of the audience gasped.

The judge banged his gavel, his face turning red. "I warned you, not one word! Bailiff Spencer, take that man from the gallery down to county lockup."

Now I was terrified, my body vibrating like an unbalanced washing machine.

Judge McClary's eyes turned to me. "Were you at the victim's house last night?"

I couldn't lie. For one thing, Mr. Burnett would say I was and for another, I was under oath and would be perjuring myself. I had to come clean. "Yes, Your Honor."

A few people covered their mouths with their hands in an attempt to stifle their surprise.

The judge's face turned beet red.

"Your Honor, your blood pressure," the bailiff said in a low voice.

"Bailiff, throw yourself in lockup!"

"Judge McClary?" the bailiff wheezed.

"I warned you all!" His voice bellowed throughout the room. He turned his attention back to me. "Did you or did you not know what you were doing was against the law?"

"I did, Your Honor." I squeaked.

"What? Do you think you're Angela Lansbury?"

"*Who?*"

"Angela Lansbury. *Murder She Wrote.*" His face turned darker, a nice purpley-red shade, when he saw the confusion on my face. "You don't know about *Murder She Wrote?*"

I shook my head.

"What in the Sam Hill is happening to our country when young people don't know who Angela Lansbury is?" He took a deep breath, then narrowed his eyes. "What made you decide to investigate this case, Ms. Gardner? Was Mr. Deveraux not presenting enough evidence for you to find a conviction so you decided to find your own?"

"No, Your Honor."

"Then why?"

"I think he's innocent."

"*You what?*"

The room erupted in chaos, jail time be damned.

Judge McClary banged his gavel so hard it flew out of his hands and through the air, smacking Mr. Yates in the middle of his forehead.

"*Order in the court!*"

Mr. Yates crumpled to the ground with a thud.

Someone in the audience began screaming.

"*Order in the goddamned court!*" the judge shouted at the top of his lungs. "Someone find my damned gavel!"

Several people scurried around, looking under the tables and chairs.

"Well, I hope you enjoyed your fun," the judge hollered over the roar of the voices. "Because that's the last fun you're gonna have for awhile. Ms. Gardner, I hold you in contempt of court and sentence you to thirty days in county jail. Spencer, get her out of my courtroom!"

Chapter Fourteen

After a lot of chaos and confusion, the bailiff took me out of the courtroom. He didn't handcuff me, but I suspected he was too upset that he was getting incarcerated himself. Against my better judgment, I snuck a glance at Mr. Deveraux, expecting to see him gloat. Instead, he looked horrified. And guilty. Guilt over what?

I was too upset to give it much thought since my worst nightmare was coming true. The entire time I'd been suspected of Momma's murder, I'd fretted about being thrown in jail. And here I was being tossed in the slammer for tampering with a case.

What was Joe going to say?

Oh, crappy doodles. What was *Violet* going to say?

Bailiff Spencer took me down to the basement, and for once I was glad for the slow elevator. It bought me a good five minutes. He led me through the hall and stepped into the entrance of a tunnel. The gaping hole reminded me of a dungeon, and my claustrophobia kicked into high gear. My heart raced. I dug in my heels, grabbing hold of the edge of the wall, and started to cry.

"No! I can't go in there . . . I'm . . ."

The usually uptight bailiff must have been shaken up by his own pending doom. His grimace fell away and he gave me a reassuring smile. "It's okay. It's just a tunnel. We're walking through it to the county jail."

"But . . . they're . . . gonna lock . . . me up."

He sighed and gripped my elbow. "It's gonna be okay. I promise. Judge McClary can't really sentence you to thirty days. The most you'll be there is five."

I sobbed even harder. Five days? Locked in a tiny room? I fell to the floor, hyperventilating.

The bailiff's eyes bugged out and he swung his head around looking for help. Dealing with a hysterical woman who had flopped on the floor was most likely not part of a bailiff's training. He was clearly out of his element.

I sat on my bottom, snot and tears flowing when Neely Kate rounded the corner.

"*Rose?*"

"Neely . . . Kate . . ." I squeezed through my closed off throat.

She knelt beside me while poor Bailiff Spencer looked more dismayed. "What happened?"

"I'm going . . . to . . . jail."

"*Why?*"

"Contempt of court," the bailiff said. "She was investigating the case."

Neely Kate put her hand on my arm and rubbed. "Why would you do that?"

"Because . . . he's . . . innocent."

"Oh," she sighed and pulled me into a hug, my head on her shoulder, and she rubbed my back. "There, there. Judge McClary is a hothead. Everyone knows that. He'll change his mind. How long did he give you?"

"Thirty . . . days."

"Oh."

"But he can't do that," the bailiff said. "The most he can give her is five."

Neely Kate leaned back and gave me a bright smile. "See? Things are lookin' better already!"

I nodded, trying to calm down. I'd brought this on myself. While I understood that fact, it didn't make it easier.

Neely Kate handed me a tissue from her pocket, which thankfully was unused. I wiped my face, sucking in big gulps of air. Bailiff Spencer gave me an impatient look.

Neely Kate whispered in my ear, "You have to go, Rose. Are you ready?"

I nodded, my body shaking. "Okay, let's get this over with."

She helped me up while the bailiff watched, his face drawn tight with anxiety. He must've been worried I'd freak out in the tunnel.

Thinking the same thing, Neely Kate clasped my hand in hers and looked at Spencer, her jaw set in determination. "I'm comin' with her to the county jail."

His shoulders relaxed. "Thank you."

We took small steps as we eased into the tunnel. Thankfully, it wasn't very long and I could see the end within twenty feet. I kept my eyes on the other side and willed myself to put one foot in front of the other, squeezing Neely Kate's hand so tight I was sure I'd cut off her circulation.

Once we emerged, it was a short walk to the county jail, which I supposed came in handy when transferring prisoners to court. But I wasn't ready to be locked up yet. How was I going to survive days and days of confinement?

The rest of the process was a blur. Neely Kate had to leave me at the front desk. After handing over my purse and my ring, the only jewelry I wore, they took my picture against the height chart. I'm sure I looked quite the mess with my red nose and tear-streaked face, although it might have been better than some of my hideous elementary school photos. Next, they took my finger-prints and let me use the phone.

I wasn't sure who to call. I would have called the attorney Violet hired when I was suspected of murdering Momma, but I couldn't remember Deanna's phone number. I briefly considered calling Joe, but he was up in Little Rock and I didn't want him to take off work.

Fresh tears welled in my eyes and my throat closed up when I realized I wasn't going to go to Little Rock for the weekend. What would Joe think when I didn't show up?

In the end, there was only one person to call.

She answered on the second ring, hesitation in her voice. I could only imagine what she expected based on Fenton County Jail showing up on caller ID. "Hello?"

"Violet." My voice was muffled with my tears.

"*Rose?*" Panic laced her words. "What's wrong? Are you okay?"

"No, Violet." I was crying harder and I forced myself to calm down so Violet could understand me. "I'm going . . . to jail."

"Jail? *What on Earth for?*"

"For contempt . . . of court."

"What? How is that possible? Did you have a vision and blurt it out?"

"No. That's not it." I gulped back the sobs about to break free. "I was investigating the case."

"You *what?*"

"I was invest—"

"Oh, I heard what you said. I'm just not believing it."

"Violet, it's true. Can you call Deanna?"

I heard her sharp intake of breath. "This is all his fault."

"Bruce Wayne Decker's?"

"Who in the world is that? *No.* Joe McAllister. Joe Simmons. Whatever his name happens to be this week. Who can trust a man whose name's always changing?"

My mouth dropped open. She was choosing *now* to go into this? "Violet, you've got it all wrong. Joe had nothing to do with this."

"Of course, you're defendin' him. You take his side over mine even after this."

"Violet, I have no earthly idea what you're sayin'. Can we please talk about this later? I don't have much time."

"What do you mean you don't have much *time?*" Her breath came in short gasps. "Oh, my Lord! They're executing you for investigating a case?"

"No! Violet, please. I need you to call Deanna."

"Surely they won't execute you today!"

"No one's getting executed!" I shouted in exasperation. "I'm runnin' out of time on my phone call. Violet, listen to me! I need you to call Deanna."

"Oh." She seemed to have regained her wits. "I'll call her right away."

"And then I need you to call Joe. Otherwise, he won't know what happened, and he'll worry himself sick when I don't show up or answer my cell phone."

"You expect me to call that man after what he's done to you?"

"Violet! He hasn't done *anything* to me. He wasn't part of this at all. Please, Violet. I need you to do this for me."

The guard pointed to his watch. "Time's up."

"I have to go. Please take care of Muffy. I'm gonna be in here for thirty days."

"*What*? *Thirty days*? I'm calling Deanna right way. She'll get you out."

"And call Joe."

"No, that man deserves—"

The phone went dead and I looked up at the guard in horror. He shrugged. "I warned you."

As he marched me to my cell, my dismay that Joe wouldn't know what happened to me almost overwhelmed my fear of getting locked up. What would he do?

The guard stopped in front of a room with bars across the front and slid the door open. "Here's where you'll be staying."

I stood in the entrance, my feet glued to the floor. Thankfully, the jail cell wasn't as dingy as I expected. It held a cot and a toilet. But there weren't any windows and three of the walls were a light gray concrete. I wasn't sure how'd I survive five days in there, let alone thirty.

"How am I supposed to go to the bathroom?" I pointed to the toilet. "There's no doors."

The guard laughed. "You'll figure it out." He put his hand on my back and gave me a small push.

My feet dug in and I resisted. "There's been a terrible mistake."

"The only mistake I heard about was you deciding to play detective when your job was supposed to be juror."

I couldn't argue with that, and I also couldn't resist his firm push. I stumbled into the cell. The door slammed shut behind me. Spinning around, I sucked in a deep breath as panic swamped my head.

It's just a room. Just an ugly room.

A room with a locked door. You're trapped in here.

I sat on the cot, taking deep breaths to stave off my brewing anxiety attack.

About an hour later, the guard brought me a metal tray with a sandwich and a bottle of water. "Lunch time."

"Already?"

He chuckled and handed the tray though a slot on the door. "Time flies when you're having fun."

I glared. There really was nothing funny about incarceration. "I'm not hungry."

"You better eat anyway. Dinner time's not for another six hours and there ain't any snacks."

I stood and pulled the tray through the slot. "Has my attorney shown up yet?"

"Nope. The only person who's been asking about you is a blonde-headed woman who won't stop talking. She's asked to see you about ten times and we keep telling her no, but she's a persistent thing."

I couldn't resist my smile. "Neely Kate."

"Yeah, that's her."

"Just tell her I'm okay and I'll call her later. She might leave then."

"I think Scott was about to cave and let her back."

That didn't surprise me. Neely Kate was a force to be reckoned with.

"No one else?"

"Nope."

"Okay, thanks." I sat down on the cot with my tray and lifted a slice of bread. Bologna. And nothing else. I hadn't eaten a bologna sandwich since I was a kid. Wrinkling my nose, I set the tray on the mattress and leaned my head back against the wall. I decided to look on the bright side. Maybe I'd lose weight.

"I hear some inmates are repeat offenders just to come back for the bologna sandwiches."

My head jerked up in surprise. Mason Van de Camp Deveraux III stood in front of my cell, one hand gripping a metal bar. His usually neat hair looked a little ruffled. His jacket was missing and his tie hung loose, the top button of his shirt undone.

"You here to gloat?"

He pursed his mouth and leaned his forehead against the bars. "Nope. No gloating here."

"Then what are you doin' here?" Why was I always so hateful to this man?

His other hand wrapped around a metal bar. "Something's been bothering me all morning."

I swallowed an ugly retort and raised my eyebrows instead. "And?"

He sighed and looked down at the floor before leveling his gaze on me. "You came to see me yesterday, but then we had our little *run-in.*" He paused, swallowing. "I can't help but wonder why you were there. Especially in light of this morning's revelations."

Mercy sakes alive. Mr. Deveraux was not only being civil, but he was trying to be nice.

I shook my head, twisting my mouth. "That's okay. You wouldn't have believed me anyway."

His eyes burned into mine. "Try me."

I stood and moved in front of him, barely two feet away. "I probably would have chickened out, even if we hadn't had our *run-in.*"

"Why? Am I really that scary?"

I laughed in spite of my irritation. "Yes, you *are* that scary. Just about everyone in the courthouse thinks you are."

He smirked, one side of his mouth lifting into a grin. "Which explains the applause after you told me off in the hall yesterday."

"They thought you had it coming."

Tilting his head, he smiled. A genuine smile that made him appear ten years younger. When he relaxed his perpetual scowl, he was a handsome man, especially with his blond hair ruffled like it was. "I suppose I did." He paused and his smile fell, but his guard was still down. "So why did you come see me before I interrupted you with my rudeness?"

I leaned my side against the bars and sighed. "I wanted to tell you that Mr. Decker is innocent."

He turned his head to study me. "But you said you didn't know anything about the case in *voir dire.* Did you lie?"

As nice as he was at the moment, I couldn't tell him about the vision. He'd think I was crazy and they might send me to the county mental hospital instead. "No. I promise I didn't lie. But I discovered something right before the trial started. I just didn't know what it was at the time. But that's why I ran into you that first morning. It scared me enough to make me not look where I was going and I ended up running into you."

Mr. Deveraux stood up straighter, a hard look filling his eyes, and his voice lowered. "Did someone threaten you, Rose?"

"What?" I shook my head. "No. Nothing like that. But . . . it's kind of like I overheard something." Which technically was true.

"Help me understand and maybe I can get you out of here."

I narrowed my gaze. "Why would you do that?"

His forehead wrinkled and he looked forlorn. "Maybe I want to prove I'm not such a bad guy, in spite of my previous behavior."

"People might believe it if you were actually nice."

A smile brightened his face as he laughed. "You know how to cut to the heart of it, don't you?"

With a shrug, I leaned my head into the bars. "My sister would disagree. Look where I am now."

"You're in here because of me."

I shook my head. "No, that's not true."

"If I had let you tell me what you came to say, maybe I could have talked some sense into you instead of sending you off."

"And I'm tellin' you I would have probably chickened out, and things would have turned out the exact same way."

"So tell me this: why were you snooping around Frank Mitchell's house?"

"I was hoping to find out more about him and why someone would kill him."

His eyes hardened, his worldliness returning. "We know exactly who killed him."

"You've got the wrong man."

"Then tell me what you know, Rose."

What could I tell him? Joe said everything I knew was hearsay. Besides, Mason Deveraux wouldn't believe me. Not that I blamed him.

Still, an innocent man's life hung in the balance and I might be able to tip the scales in his favor. "Here's what I know: Frank Mitchell owed people money. Bookies, from what I hear. I also know someone wanted Frank Mitchell to sell his house to them. Desperately enough to upset him. I also know, from you in the trial, that hardly any money was stolen. That doesn't sound like much of a robbery to me."

"Maybe the robber panicked. He didn't plan to run into the victim and after he killed him, he was too scared and upset to think about it. So he grabbed a small out of cash and left most of it behind."

"Mr. Decker's right-handed."

He frowned in confusion. "What does that have to do with anything?"

"The murderer is left-handed."

He leaned closer to the bars. "What do you know that you're not telling me? You said right before you ran into me Monday morning that you overheard something. Where were you?"

I hesitated. There was no turning back if I told him. "I was in the restroom."

"So you think the real murderer is a woman?"

"No, it's a man."

"But . . ."

"The women's restroom was closed and I really had to go. And Matt had kept me down in security for quite some time, waiting for Officer Ernie to show up and pat me down."

"So you went to the men's restroom instead."

"Yes."

"And you were in a stall and overheard something?"

"Something like that."

"What did you hear?"

I took a deep breath. Could I tell him enough to convince him to at least investigate more without revealing my vision? "I heard a man say 'I'm going to get away with murder.'"

"That's it?"

"No, of course not. But he talked about a lapel pin. One with a dog and a tree, and he was worried it would be tied back to him."

Mr. Deveraux's face paled. "Why didn't you say something in *voir dire*?"

"What was I going to say? I had no idea what he was talking about. People say 'I'm going to get away with murder' all the time and it doesn't mean a thing. Honestly, so much was going on that I plumb forgot about it. And by the time I figured out it meant something, we were well into the trial. I didn't put it all together until Detective Taylor mentioned the pin."

His eyes sank closed. "And you fainted."

"Yeah."

"So you decided to investigate on your own? Because you thought Bruce Decker was innocent, but you didn't have any hard evidence to prove it."

I studied his shoes. They were shiny, expensive loafers, and they made it obvious that Mr. Deveraux was from money. No wonder he hated backward Henryetta so much. "Yeah."

"You know that you broke the law?"

"I think the side of the bars I'm standin' on is proof of that."

"Did you know you were breaking it while you did it?"

I raised my chin and looked into his eyes. "Yes."

"Why did you do it?"

"Why are you an assistant DA?"

"What does that have to do with the predicament you're in? I was hired to do a job. Prosecute criminals. You swore to do a job—be a juror. You broke your oath."

I sighed. Mr. No Nonsense was back. "Mr. Deveraux, just answer the question. Do you want to be a district attorney?"

"Yes."

"Then just tell me why."

He shifted his feet and pain flashed through his eyes before he could hide it.

I felt guilty. I hadn't realized my question was so personal. "You don't have to answer—"

His face lifted and his jaw was clenched, but a softness filled his eyes. "I want to uphold the laws of the state of Arkansas and put the bad guys away, as corny as that sounds. I want to protect the innocent and make the world a safer place. I want to fight for justice."

I leaned my temple against the bars, suddenly weary of it all. "And that's why I did it. I wanted justice for Bruce Wayne Decker, because no one else would get it for him. I know all too well that people are eager to find the easy target. No one was fightin' for Mr. Decker and somebody had to." Turning my gaze towards him, I realized he'd moved closer and our faces were about six inches apart.

He studied me for several moments with a serious expression, then stepped backward. "I'm going to see what I can do to get you out of this mess."

"But . . . why?"

He winked, looking young and ornery. "It's the least I can do after you pointed out what a curmudgeon I've been."

"*Curmudgeon?*" He made himself sound like he was sixty years old instead of thirty.

He shrugged with a grin, then turned to leave. "Don't get too comfortable, Rose Gardner."

I looked around at my accommodations. He didn't need to worry about that.

Chapter Fifteen

I spent most of the afternoon on my cot, examining the choices that got me into the Fenton County Jail. Should I have left it all alone and listened to the evidence presented in the trial? Despite what I knew? As I stared at the ugly gray walls, I kept reminding myself that the most time I could spend in here was thirty days. Bruce Decker would be there for years. While I admitted I should have handled things differently, I wasn't sorry I tried to help.

Thankfully, my anxiety over being enclosed had lessened since Mr. Deveraux's visit. His appearance had surprised me, proving he was definitely a conundrum. I wasn't sure whether to count on him getting me out or believe his reasons for wanting to help me. But I had little choice except to trust and hope.

There wasn't a clock in the cell so I had no idea what time it was. I only knew I'd been there for hours. What was taking Deanna so long? When I'd been taken in for questioning for Momma's murder, Deanna had shown up in the wee hours of the morning, within an hour of the phone call. Surely, it was easier to come in to the county jail on a weekday afternoon. But then again, it was Friday.

The outer door squeaked and my growling stomach reminded me I hadn't eaten for hours. If a bologna sandwich was lunch, what did they serve in the evening? Macaroni and cheese?

But instead of dinner, Joe appeared around the corner, accompanied by a grim-faced guard.

I leapt off the cot and grabbed the bars. "Joe! Violet called you?"

"No. Neely Kate called me." He frowned, his tone flat and unreadable.

I squared my shoulders. I'd gotten myself into this mess and I needed to accept the punishment. "So you came to see me?"

The guard moved in front of the door with his keys.

"I came to get you out."

"You *what?*"

While the door was swinging open, Joe brushed past the guard into my cell.

I threw myself at him, wrapping my arms around his neck and burying my face into his chest.

He pulled me close. "You'll do anything to get out of driving to Little Rock."

I laughed, choking on the lump in my throat. "I wanted to come. Truly I did."

"I know," he mumbled into my ear. After a squeeze, he dropped his arm and grabbed my hand. "Let's get you home."

"I can really go?"

"Yep, you've been released to the care of an Arkansas Police Detective." He winked.

"Really?" I asked as he pulled me out of the cell into the corridor.

The day I set foot inside a jail cell again would be too soon.

He leaned close, his voice low and sexy. "It's a hardship, Ms. Gardner, but I fully accept the responsibility of keeping you under lock and key all weekend."

The jailer's face reddened and Joe laughed. I gave the guard a sympathetic look.

Joe clung to my hand as though I might change my mind and run back into my cage. There was little chance of that happening.

"How did you really get me out?"

"I spoke with Deveraux and he said he'd been working on the judge too. Between the two of us, we convinced him to set you free."

So Mason Deveraux really had tried to get me out. Panic made my feet stick to the floor, mid-step. "I don't have to go back to jury duty on Monday, do I?"

Joe laughed. "Oh, no. Your jury duty is *done.*"

"What about poor Mrs. Baker? She didn't get jail time for poisoning the jury, did she?" Judge McClary might not have sentenced her in the morning but with all the other contempt-of-court charges flying around, I'd worried the judge changed his mind. I wasn't sure Mrs. Baker could take the stress.

Narrowing his eyes with a perplexed look, he shook his head. "Not that I'm aware." He looked like he wanted to ask about it, then muttered under his breath.

I was torn about being kicked off the jury. While I didn't want to go back into the courtroom to face Judge McClary, I wasn't looking forward to seeing Suzanne on Monday morning.

Signing the paperwork for my release, I saw Mr. Deveraux's signature on several forms. For a man who detested me so much, he'd put himself on the line. I was grateful, but wondered if he'd gloat about it. Not that I'd probably ever see him again to find out. Before my stint with jury duty, I'd never met the assistant DA. What were the chances I'd run into him again?

After I got back my purse and my ring, Joe and I walked into the early evening heat and relief overcame me. I closed my eyes and filled my lungs with sticky, humid air. I wasn't about to complain about the weather. I'd take humid Arkansas heat to the stuffy jail cell any day.

Joe wrapped his arm around my waist as we walked to his car. "Hungry?"

"Starving."

"Do you want me to make you something at home or do you want to go out?"

I narrowed my eyes in suspicion, waiting for the proverbial shoe to drop. "Why are you bein' so nice to me?"

He lifted his eyebrows in mock surprise. "I'm your boyfriend. Don't you know it's part of the job description?" He held up his hand and showed three fingers. "Be nice to you, which is rule number one and very important." One finger curled. "Number two is to make sure you eat. I need to make sure you keep up your strength for number three." Another finger dropped.

"And what ghastly duty does number three consist of?"

He pulled me against his chest and lowered his mouth to mine. "Ravage your body." Joe thoroughly kissed me on the sidewalk outside the Fenton County Jail, leaving little doubt what he intended to do later. He gave me a wicked grin. "I plan to take full advantage of number three this weekend in payment for your release."

Still lightheaded, I had trouble forming a sentence. How could he have such an effect on me? I shook my head to clear it. "Aren't you worried about getting arrested for inappropriate public displays of affection? I just got out of a jail cell. I don't plan on going back into one."

With his arm around my back, he steered me toward his car. "Ah, but you forget. I'm a state policeman, which comes with its own perks."

"You get to fondle women in public?"

He opened the passenger door and kissed me lightly. "Only women recently released from jail."

I climbed in the car, wondering why he hadn't lectured me or accused me of being irresponsible or a whole host of atrocities, instead of distracting me with kisses and innuendo.

When he pulled out of the parking lot, Joe laced his fingers with mine. "What did you decide? Eat out or cook at home?"

"I don't really feel like going out. We can eat sandwiches at my house."

He parked at a stop sign. "You still don't have any food?"

I shrugged. "It's just me. And Muffy. There's no sense cooking for just me."

He flipped his blinker on and turned left. "Well, there's me now and I refuse to eat turkey sandwiches for every meal. We're stopping at the grocery store."

While I didn't relish the idea of grocery shopping after spending all day in a jail cell, I couldn't argue with him. Besides, if we had a house full of food, we wouldn't need to go out all weekend.

Joe parked at the Piggly Wiggly, and offered to run in while I waited in the car. But I'd spent all afternoon alone and enclosed in a tight space. I didn't need any more solitary confinement. As we walked across the parking lot, he spouted off a half a dozen things he needed. My cooking was pretty good, but Joe had more gourmet tastes. Eating with him was always an adventure. I'd found that between eating alone and spending time with Joe, I didn't cook much lately. After cooking for Momma the last eight years, I was happy to let Joe take over the chore.

Joe grabbed a cart as we entered the store, and one of the baggers in the checkout lanes caught my eye. He looked familiar, with his shaggy hair and twitchy hands, yet I couldn't place him.

"Do you want to eat right away or can you wait while I cook?" Joe asked, stopping in the produce aisle.

I leaned into him as he grabbed a couple of onions. "If you're asking if I'm hungry for food, I'll just say I can think of a better use of our time than that kind of cookin'."

He stopped and turned to me, planting a kiss on my mouth before I could protest. "You're just full of surprises, aren't you?"

"Take me home and I'll show you."

His grinned widened. "How can I refuse that?"

Joe hurried through his list of ingredients, while I tried to figure out how I knew the guy bagging groceries. Something about him niggled at the back of my mind.

Joe paused at the entrance to the pet care aisle. "Do you need anything for Muffy?"

"What? No. She's good."

He put an arm around my shoulder and pulled me close. "You seem distracted. Would you rather wait in the car while I finish? You've had a long day."

"You wouldn't mind?"

"Of course, not. I'm almost done." He dug his keys out of his pocket and handed them to me. "It's still hot out there. Go ahead and start the car so you have the air conditioning. I won't be long."

"Thanks."

I walked to the exit, past a couple of women who huddled over an end cap of bakeware, whispering and watching me. I'd noticed people staring as Joe and I shopped. Gossip spread fast in Henryetta. Frustrated, I told myself that I should be used to it. I'd lived with it all my life because of my visions. But I was sure the latest topic of gossip was my recent incarceration, something many of them had hoped for a couple of months ago when they thought I'd murdered Momma. I was having quite a year. At this rate, I was bound to have my own reality TV show by Christmas.

Hurrying across the parking lot and away from all the gossiping, I saw the shaggy-haired bag boy loading groceries into the trunk of a Lincoln Town Car. He slammed the lid shut then pushed the cart toward me, looking up through his long dishwater blond hair.

I gasped, realizing he was David Moore, Bruce's friend who'd testified that morning. "Wait!" I shouted in my excitement. "I know who you are!"

His eyes widened and he hurried past me.

I followed, sure I looked like a stalker. "Stop! Please! I just want to talk to you about Bruce."

His feet froze to the ground and I almost crashed into the back of him. He turned around, and his face lit up with recognition. "Hey! You were a juror, weren't you? The one who got thrown into jail."

I smoothed my skirt, trying not to look defensive. "I wasn't the only one. Several other people were held in contempt."

"Nope." He shook his head. "You were the only one actually thrown in jail. Everyone else got released before they were even booked." He paused and narrowed his eyes. "I heard that you think Bruce is innocent."

"Yeah. I do."

"*Why?*"

I wasn't surprised he doubted me. I'm sure he and Bruce faced a lot of discrimination based on their appearance. And their habit. "Let's just say it's instinct." Since I'd been thrown in jail for trying to help Bruce, I hoped David would trust me at least a little. "Can I ask you a couple of things?"

He leaned over his cart and pushed it to the cart corral. "Just keep talkin'. I have to look busy or I'll get in trouble."

"Sure." Of course, my following him around the parking lot didn't look suspicious at all. "You said you helped Bruce hide the murder weapon. I still don't understand why he took it with him."

David glanced around then lowered his voice. "Look, Bruce is a nervous kind of guy."

I could see why the two of them got along so well.

"He saw the murder happen like *right there* in front of him and it *completely* freaked him out. Like, big time. Plus, he was pretty stoned and wasn't thinkin' straight. Daniel Crocker used to grow some pretty wicked weed."

I raised an eyebrow.

"Like I said, Bruce completely freaked and he got it in his head that he was going to get blamed for the murder even though he had nothing to do with it. So he grabbed the crowbar and brought it home. Then he called me."

"Whose idea was it to hide the crowbar under the house?"

He hung his head and refused to look at me. "It was mine. Bruce wanted to throw it into the river, but I convinced him to keep it."

"Why?"

"I thought he could use it to prove who the real killer was."

I shook my head in confusion. "How were you goin' to do that?"

"How should I know? We just planned on usin' it as insurance."

Look what good *that* did. But beating that fact into David's head wasn't going to solve anything. "Did Bruce hear anything while the killer and Frank Mitchell were arguing?"

"Yeah, Frank was shouting that he'd told the guy a million times he was never gonna sell. And the guy told Frank that he was gonna get what was owed to him."

"I thought you were going to wait in the car," Joe said behind me.

I jumped and spun around and clasped my hand to my chest. *Way to not look guilty.* "Oh, my word! You scared me!"

Joe balanced two bags of groceries in his arms. He had his cop face on, the one that told me he suspected I was up to no good. "I can see that. Care to introduce me?"

"Uh . . ." I looked from Joe to David, who gaped, wide-eyed. "Joe, this is David, and David, this is Joe Simmons. My boyfriend. A state policeman."

David's face paled and his hands shook before he took off running for the Piggly Wiggly entrance.

Joe titled his head. "What just happened there?"

"David's a nervous guy."

"So it would seem. I meant with the two of you. You seemed to be deep in conversation."

I grabbed his arm and steered him toward the car. "David? We were just catching up. Did you get what you needed? I'm starving."

Joe looked over his shoulder at the grocery store entrance. "Are you sure everything's all right with that guy?"

"Yeah, oh yeah." I waved my hand. "He was nervous because you're a cop."

"Why on earth did you tell him that?"

I unlocked the car and Joe put the groceries in the backseat.

"Because David doesn't exactly trust law enforcement officers, and if he found out that I hadn't told him, he might never speak to me again."

"And how exactly do you know him?"

"Church. I know him from church. God bless 'im." I tried to ignore the guilt that rushed in from lying to Joe. I swore I wasn't going to do it and yet the lie just fell out of my mouth.

"Huh."

Joe obviously didn't believe me, but he didn't press it either. Instead, we drove home while he told me everything he was going to cook over the weekend. Crepes for breakfast. Chicken Parmesan for dinner on Saturday.

"Where in the world did you learn to cook?"

His smile fell. "Our housekeeper."

"Your housekeeper?" I leaned closer, curious. Joe had hardly told me anything about his family or growing up, usually changing the subject whenever I asked. I wasn't going to let him get away with it this time. "You had a housekeeper when you were a kid?"

He shrugged. "It was no big deal. Everyone in the South has someone clean their house."

"We didn't."

Joe smirked. "No offense, but your mother was hardly the average Southern woman."

The Southern tradition of having a cleaning lady was usually reserved for bigger houses and working women. Definitely not the people in my neighborhood. Joe had to have been raised with money if his housekeeper cooked fancy food. "From what I hear, housekeepers don't cook."

"Well, ours did and she was good. I loved to hang out in the kitchen with her while she worked. She taught me everything I know."

The way his voice softened, it was apparent he had felt close to her. "You said your parents live in El Dorado?"

"Yeah." His back stiffened. I'd delved into territory he didn't want to discuss. But there was little doubt there were families with money and influence in El Dorado. Oil money. I decided to back off. For now.

"Well lucky for me your housekeeper taught you some delicious recipes. You know I can cook, but just home cooking stuff. Nothing fancy."

He grabbed my hand and squeezed. "I love your cooking."

I had to admit that I liked someone cooking for me for a change, but it was only fair if I did my share. "Tell you what. On Sunday, I'll make fried chicken, mashed potatoes and gravy. Homemade biscuits even."

He shot me a wicked grin "I say we move fried chicken to Saturday. And I'll have the rest of the weekend to work off all those calories."

I rolled my eyes. Did he ever think of anything else? But then again, now that he'd introduced me to it, I thought about it a lot too.

When we got home, Joe suggested I take a shower to wash away the grime of the jail cell while he made dinner. I emerged ten minutes later with towel-dried hair, wearing a pair of shorts and a spaghetti-strapped shirt.

Joe watched me for several seconds. "Perfect timing, I just finished."

A plate of sandwiches sat in the middle of the table. I put a hand on my hip. "What's this? Just fifteen minutes ago, you were beratin' me for eating turkey sandwiches."

"Those are not *just* sandwiches. These are special—pita bread with turkey and provolone, and the ingredient that makes them more than just a turkey sandwich, my secret sauce, which has won blue ribbons in three counties."

"You're kiddin' me. You entered your sauce in three county fairs?"

"Well . . . not me. Virginia. It's her recipe."

"Your housekeeper?"

He tugged on my wrist and pulled me into a hug. "No more talking."

"I'm hungry. I had a bologna sandwich for lunch." I stuck out my tongue and made an ugly face. "I sure hope your *sandwiches* are better than that."

He raised an eyebrow with a cocky look. "Are you makin' fun of my sandwiches? Just for that, you don't get one."

"And waste your special sauce? That won blue ribbons in *three* county fairs?"

"Fine. You get five minutes to eat."

"I got longer than that in jail," I grumbled as I pushed him into a chair and sat on his lap. Picking up a sandwich, I studied it to tease Joe, then took a bite. "Oh. My. Joe, this is so *good*." I mumbled through a mouthful of food.

His hand skimmed down my back to my bottom. "I told you."

"I do love a humble man."

"For that, you now have four minutes." He grabbed a sandwich from the plate and took a bite, watching me with a grin.

"What?"

He swallowed and shook his head, still smiling. "I just like lookin' at you. Then I can remember you when I'm not with you. I miss you during the week."

That was probably the sweetest thing anyone had ever said to me. "I miss you too."

I took another bite, tying to be sexy, but I laughed and the sandwiched tipped. Turkey fell out of the pita pocket and onto Joe's dress shirt, his secret sauce smearing red across the pale blue cotton. I swiped the sauce off with my finger, licking it off, but I left a stain behind. "Oops."

He lifted his eyebrow in his sexy look, the one that dared me to do it again.

I dipped my finger in my sandwich, dabbing at the sauce, and ran it down the bridge of his nose.

He set his food on the table and rubbed the sauce off his nose with his thumb, licking it off. "Mmm." His eyes widened with a wicked gleam. "You want to play that way, do you?"

I tried to squirm off his lap, but his arm tightened around my waist, holding me in place.

"No, Joe! I just took a shower!"

"Well, then it's lucky for you that you're out of county lockup and get more than one shower a day." He scooped a large dollop of sauce out of his sandwich.

"Joe!" I squealed. "It was an accident!"

"So is this." He smeared cold sauce across my cheek.

I tried to reach up to my cheek to wipe it off, but his hand at my side grabbed my wrist.

He rubbed some on the other cheek. "And so is this."

"Joe!" I choked out through my laughter.

"And this is too." His finger trailed over my lower lip but smeared on my chin with my thrashing. "You're wearing blue ribbon sauce, I'll have you know. I don't think you've given it the proper respect it deserves."

I tried to catch my breath through my giggles.

"We can't let that sauce go to waste." He lowered his head and licked my cheek.

Tingles filled my stomach. I sucked in a breath and stopped squirming.

He moved to the other side, his tongue lingering on my cheek and moving slowly to my mouth, licking the sauce from my lip and chin. His grip on my wrist loosened and I gathered my wits enough to take advantage of my freedom. I jumped out of his lap and grabbed another pita from the plate, dipping sauce out with two fingers.

Joe tried to grab my wrist, but I smeared the side of his face and down his neck, laughing so hard I could hardly see his reaction.

"Oh, Miss Gardner, you're goin' to regret that."

I winked with a naughty smile. "I don't think so." I straddled his lap, my hands grabbing the wrists at his sides.

His voice lowered. "I thought you were hungry."

I looked into his eyes and ran my tongue along my bottom lip. "I am." Leaning close, I licked the sauce, starting at his jaw and moving to the top of his cheek.

His body stiffened, his hands flexing but not breaking free from my hold.

"You're so tense, Detective Simmons. And you're covered in prize-winning sauce." My tongue slid over his jaw and to the pulse point on his neck. I sucked lightly.

His breath came in short bursts. "My girlfriend is a bit messy."

I worked my way down his neck to the top of his collar, my tongue moving in circles, followed by kisses. "Oh, dear. You have sauce on your shirt. We better take this off." I released his wrists, brought my fingers to the top button of his shirt and slid the disc through the hole.

I glanced up at his face. Unabashed desire filled his eyes, making me suck in a breath. I wasn't used to the fact that I could do that to him.

My fingers meandered to the next button and then to the rest. I spread his shirt open, my hands skimming across his t-shirt. "I think you're overdressed, Detective Simmons."

His hands circled my waist and skimmed down to my hips. "So it seems."

I pushed the shirt over his broad shoulders and down his arms, feeling his firm muscles underneath. After his dress shirt was off, I grabbed the bottom of his white t-shirt and tugged it over his head.

I stared into his face then turned my gaze to his chest, my hand following the path of my eyes. "How was I lucky enough to get you?" I whispered.

"I could ask the same thing," he said, breathless. His hands gently pushed my spaghetti straps over my shoulders, sliding them down my arms and tugging the fabric to my sides, until my shirt puddled around my waist.

We sat on my kitchen chair, me straddling Joe's lap, both naked from the waist up, staring into each other's eyes. He lifted a hand to my cheek, caressing lightly as a smile touched the corners of his lips.

Neither of us said anything, but I'd never felt closer to anyone in my whole life.

Joe pulled my mouth to his, capturing my bottom lip between his and working his usual magic, leaving me lightheaded and senseless.

I moved my hands to either side of his head. The need to be as close to him as possible overpowered every sense.

His hand tangled in my hair and he kissed me with more intensity than usual, his other hand cupping my face. He pulled back, his eyes dark with passion and something else. Fear.

"You scared the hell out me today, Rose. When Neely Kate called me and told me something bad had happened to you . . . I almost lost it right there in my office."

"I'm sorry."

"I don't think you realize how much you mean to me."

My thumb traced his cheekbone and I looked deep into his eyes. "I think I know."

"I don't want to lose you."

My gaze dropped to his mouth as I brushed my thumb across his lips. "I'm not goin' anywhere."

"I love you, Rose."

I shouldn't have been surprised, he showed me how much he loved me all the time, but this was the first time he'd said it. I looked up, amazed to see insecurity in his eyes. I smiled and placed a gentle kiss on his lips. "I love you too."

For the next hour, I forgot about dinner. I forgot about Violet and her problems. I forgot about the innocent Bruce Decker sitting in a jail cell. I forgot about everything but the man in my arms and how I was the luckiest woman alive.

Chapter Sixteen

Joe and I lay in bed, his arm lying over my stomach, our legs still tangled. He brushed a strand of hair from my face. "We have to talk about what happened today."

"When a man and a woman love each other, they—"

He placed a finger on my lips and his eyes grew serious. "You know what I'm talking about."

My tongue darted out and licked the pad of his finger.

His eyes closed and he chuckled. "That's not going to work."

"What's not goin' to work?"

"Two can play at that game." He leaned over me and kissed me until I was breathless. "Now we're goin' to talk about what happened." And to make sure he had me weak and defenseless, he kissed me again.

Damn him.

He rolled me to my side so we were chest to chest. His arm curled around my waist. His other hand stroked my neck lightly as he kissed the corner of my mouth. "Now where were we? Oh, yes." His mouth trailed down my neck. "What happened to land you in jail today?"

"This isn't fair." I gasped, my stomach tightening as his mouth sent tingles from my neck to my core.

"Nothing's fair in love and war."

His hand found my breast and I gasped. "And which one is this?"

"Both."

His mouth followed his hand and I wrapped my leg around his. "I can't think straight when you do that."

"That's the point, darlin'."

I pushed against him, my traitorous fingers wanting to explore his chest more. "Stop. I'll tell you want you want to know."

He rolled me on my back and straddled me, pinning my arms over my head. "We'll try it your way and if it doesn't work, we'll try it mine."

It was a win-win situation for me. "Okay."

"Why did you go to Frank Mitchell's house?"

"How do you know the murder victim's name?"

Joe rolled his eyes. "I spent the better part of an hour with the assistant district attorney trying to get you out of the mess you dug yourself into. Plus, I've been lookin' into it, remember? I've become very acquainted with many details of the case."

"Oh."

A wicked gleam lit up his eyes. "You didn't answer my question. Why were you at his house?"

"I didn't mean to stop and get out. I just planned to drive by. That's all. I promise."

"But you did get out?"

"Yeah."

"And did you find out anything?"

My eyes widened. "Are you seriously askin' me what I found out?"

"I thought I made that pretty clear."

"Someone had been harassin' Frank to sell his house, but he refused to sell. His neighbor didn't know who was coercing him."

"Anything else?"

"Yeah, Bruce lived on the corner across from Frank Mitchell until a couple of months before Frank was killed. His parents kicked him out. Mr. Burnett—his neighbor—claimed it was because they got tired of him moochin' off them and getting into trouble."

"And did you go see his parents?"

"I most certainly did not." I mustered up the best indignant attitude I could, not an easy task when your boyfriend had you pinned to the bed, naked.

He laughed. "You mean you hadn't had a chance to talk to them yet."

I looked away with a frown.

"Ha! I know you better than you think I do."

I lifted my hips, trying to throw him off, but he laughed and pressed harder. "Not so fast. What did you find out in the parking lot of the Piggly Wiggly tonight?"

"What are you talkin' about?"

"David Moore? Bruce's best friend? What did he tell you?"

My mouth dropped. "You know who David Moore is?"

"I already told you I knew all kinds of details about the case. Now what did he tell you?"

I narrowed my eyes. "Why do you want to know?"

"Because I want to help you, and the only way to do that is if you tell me everything you know about the case."

It took a second for his words to settle in. "*You want to help me?*"

"I told you I know you better than you think. You're not gonna let this go until you find justice for Bruce Wayne Decker. The safest way to do that is if I know what you know."

I scowled. "Well, why didn't you just tell me you wanted to help?"

He winked then leaned down, his mouth hovering over mine. "What fun is there in that?"

I lifted my head so my lips met his. He groaned and rolled onto his side, pulling me with him.

"Now tell me what he told you."

"Not much, before you showed up. He said that Bruce was stoned on Daniel Crocker's pot."

"Ah . . . my buddy, Daniel Crocker."

"When Bruce went into the hardware store, he found Frank arguin' with some guy. Then the guy hit him with a crowbar, ran into the office, and left."

"So how did Bruce Decker gain possession of the murder weapon?"

"He took it with him, and David convinced him to hide it under his house so they could use it to frame the real murderer."

"And how did they plan to do that? DNA? Fingerprints?"

"They didn't have a clue."

Joe nodded. "Sounds about right. What else?"

"He said he heard the argument. Frank was shoutin' that he was never gonna sell and the other guy said he was gonna get what was owed to him."

Joe looked surprised, then smiled. "What else?"

"That's it from those two."

"But you know something else."

He did know me. "Well, Neely Kate said Frank owed bookies and Anne in the paint department said he owed a lot of money to someone, but she wasn't sure who he owed it to."

"Anything else?"

"Yeah, some guy hung around the hardware store after the murder. I told you that already."

"And how do you know this?"

"Anne."

"The woman in the paint department? Okay. What did this man do?"

"He just hung around, lookin' suspicious, buying odds and ends that didn't make any sense."

"Anything else?"

"Other than my vision? No."

"So, Detective Rose, what do you make of this so far?"

I propped up on my elbow, looking down at his amused grin. "Well, we know that Bruce is innocent and that a man, not a woman, killed Frank Mitchell, but we don't know who he is, but I know he's left-handed and had a scar from his wrist up his forearm. And he has a pin he left behind with a dog, a tree and a bird on it. I suspect he was the guy wanting to buy Frank's house."

"And what makes you say that?"

"Because Frank told the guy he wasn't goin' to sell."

"But Decker was pretty stoned when he heard that, by his own admission, according to his buddy. And he's right. Crocker's pot was pretty potent. And often laced with other stuff."

"So it doesn't mean anything?"

"I didn't say that, but you have to take the source into consideration."

"And the guy who killed him said he was gonna get what was owed him. He must have been a bookie."

"It would seem that way, wouldn't it?"

Something in his voiced clued me in that I might be wrong. "It's the obvious fit, isn't it?"

"Yeah, that's why you have to be careful with that assumption. You're just guessing at this point, you don't have any evidence, which is why you were a suspect in your mother's murder and Bruce Decker is sittin' in the county jail. You both fit that empty hole."

"Oh." But what he said made sense. Presuming it was a bookie made me the same kind of lazy as the Henryetta police.

He lowered his voice, his tone serious. "You know you broke the law, Rose."

"I know. I can't believe you weren't mad when you came to get me."

"I was too relieved to be mad. Neely Kate scared the livin' hell out of me. I thought you were hurt or dead."

"What did she say?"

"Just that something terrible had happened and I needed to come to the Fenton County DA's office. I thought you'd been . . . I didn't want to think what might have happened to you. I tried to call Violet, but she didn't answer. I got a hold of Deveraux while I was drivin' down."

"You called Mason Deveraux?"

"Well, he is the assistant district attorney. He knew about the case, and together we convinced the judge to let you out."

"I can't believe he did that. He hates me." I thought back to our conversation in the jail. Mr. Deveraux had told me he felt guilty for being hateful. And I had to admit he wasn't very hateful during our talk.

Joe squinted. "Why do you say he hates you? I thought the defense attorney disliked you."

"They both do. But Mr. Deveraux hates me because I ran into him. Literally. Twice. He wasn't happy either time."

Furrowing his brow, Joe tucked a stray hair behind my ear. "He sure didn't act like he hated you while pleadin' your case."

I couldn't help wondering if we were talking about the same man. "Well, it was probably because he felt guilty. I went to see him yesterday after I called you. I was goin' to tell him everything, hopin' that he would believe me, but just as I was headed into his office, he was comin' out and we ran into each other. He was in a foul mood to begin with, and I was the last straw. He let loose on me. Needless to say, I gave him a piece of my mind and left."

Joe chuckled. "I would have liked to have seen that. And you're correct. He's an uptight guy. Must be from that fancy East Coast schooling."

"When he came to visit me in jail, he told me he felt bad that he'd yelled at me. He asked me if I'd visited Frank's house because of him, because he'd been so hateful, not giving me a chance to tell him what I'd come to say. Anyway, when he left the jail, he told me he was goin' to get me out."

"He did his part to get you out, and then some. I had to attest to your character, but Deveraux convinced the judge you had an over-heightened sense of justice."

My eyes widened. "Oh, Lordy! You didn't tell him about my visions, did you?"

He reached up and kissed me lightly. "No, Rose. It's not my place to tell. While I wish you'd learn to trust people more, I understand why you don't. I hope I can help you think differently."

I doubted that day would ever come, but I didn't feel like tackling the subject at the moment. "So you're really not mad at me?"

"I didn't say that. I was too scared to be mad. Neely Kate needs to give better explanations of what's goin' on."

I couldn't believe she had called Joe. How had she gotten his number? I suspected Neely Kate knew exactly what she was doing with her cryptic message. "Violet really never called you?"

His voice hardened. "No."

"What about Deanna? The attorney?"

"She showed up at the jail, but left after she realized Deveraux and I had it covered."

I stroked his cheek with my fingertips. "I'm sorry about Violet. If it makes you feel any better, I don't think it's *you*. I think it's where you live and the fact I might move to Little Rock with you."

His grin lit up his face. "You told her you might move up to Little Rock?"

"Not in so many words, but she's pretty intuitive and probably figured out that I was considerin' it."

"So you're considering it?"

"Yeah." I placed a light kiss on his lips. "I love you, Joe, and I hate it when you're gone. I'm lonely without you."

Joe spent the rest of the night demonstrating how unlonely I'd be if he were around all the time.

The next morning, Joe stood in front of the stove making crepes while I cut up strawberries at the sink, sneaking glances at him. "I miss Muffy. I want to go get her from Violet."

Joe's shoulders tensed. "I don't understand why you weren't bringin' her to Little Rock in the first place. You know I love that little dog."

I shrugged with a sigh. "Violet convinced me it would give the two of us more time if we didn't have to worry about taking care of Muffy."

Joe narrowed his eyes, making it obvious he didn't believe that explanation.

"What's done is done. I miss my dog."

He planted a kiss on my forehead. "I miss her too. Let's go get her after breakfast. And then we can finish painting the back bedroom."

With all the excitement of the last couple of days, I'd forgotten about the half-painted room. "You don't have to help me paint, Joe. I can paint next week after you're gone."

He shook his head. "I like to paint, and I want to help you. Besides, it's almost done. It won't take long."

I relented, only because he convinced me he really liked to paint. Plus, it reminded me of his offer to give me a few pointers when I painted the living room after Momma's murder. But it also reminded me that Violet had burst in and tried to ruin what I had with Joe then too, even if it had just been friendship at that point. Joe was the most wonderful thing that had ever happened to me. I wasn't going to let her stand in the way of my happiness, and I sure wasn't going to let her run Joe off.

I marched over to the phone.

Joe turned around, surprised. "What are you doin'?"

"I'm calling Violet and telling her I'm coming to get Muffy after breakfast."

He raised his eyebrows and turned back to his skillet.

The phone rang four times before Mike picked up. "Hi, Rose."

"Hey, Mike." He caught me off guard. Mike hated to talk on the phone and never answered. Violet had to be spitting mad to convince Mike to pick up.

"I heard about your ordeal."

I could only imagine what he'd heard, but there was no need getting into it. "I'm not goin' to Little Rock this weekend so I'm gonna come pick up Muffy after breakfast."

A muffling sound filled my ear. Mike must have covered the mouthpiece to relay my information to Violet.

"Um . . . Vi—I mean, Ashley was lookin' forward to spending the day with Muffy." I heard the irritation in his voice. Violet must have been coaching him on what to say.

My mouth pursed as I tried to figure out what to do. There was little doubt that it would disappoint Ashley, but I could smell a Violet power play a mile away. "Well . . ."

"Oh, to hell with it!" Mike growled. "This has gone on long enough. You and Violet need to work this out because I'm tired of being in the middle of it!"

My mouth gaped, and I must have looked as shocked as I felt, judging from Joe's worried expression.

"You come over tonight for dinner and sort this out with her."

Violet shouted protests in the background.

"That's not a good idea, Mike." I glanced at Joe. "Joe's here this weekend and with–"

"Perfect. Bring him too. He's part of this mess."

"I don't know . . ."

Joe stood in front of me. "What's goin' on?"

I whispered, "Mike wants us to come over for dinner tonight to sort this all out."

A murderous gleam filled his eyes. "I think that's a great idea."

"But . . . I don't—"

Joe grabbed the phone out of my hand.

Oh, crappy doodles.

"Mike? Joe here. What time should we come over?" He used his Detective Simmons, no-nonsense-tolerated voice. There was a long pause. "We'll be there at six. And we *will* be bringing our dog home." He slammed the receiver onto the phone on the wall, then stood in front of it for several seconds. "We're going over at six."

"So I heard."

Joe turned around to look at me, his anger fading a bit. "It's time to get this all out in the open."

I twisted the bottom of my shirt. "I suppose."

"Violet needs to accept the fact that I'm not going anywhere. The only person who can run me off is you. Do you want to run me off?" Insecurity flickered across his face before determination replaced it.

I wrapped my arms around his waist and rose on my toes to kiss him. "No, Joe. I most definitely don't want to run you off."

He held me tight, his breath whooshing out in relief. "You might have to choose. Violet may force you to choose her or me."

I buried my head into his chest. "You're a better cuddler."

He laughed and rubbed my back.

I looked up at him. "You called Muffy 'our dog.'"

He cringed in embarrassment. "Yeah, sorry about that. It's just that I've known her as long as you have and I love takin' care of her when I'm here. And I miss her."

I kissed him again and smiled. "I like us sharing something so important. It makes us more permanent."

His smile lit up his face. "I like the sound of that."

We spent the rest of the day finishing the bedroom and for the first time, I let my mind cross my self-imposed line. I let myself consider a future with Joe. But I worried about our confrontation with Violet later. Joe said he wasn't going anywhere, but he'd never been on the full receiving end of Violet's wrath. It wasn't fair that Joe had to endure her meddling. I couldn't help wondering if I was worth the aggravation.

Chapter Seventeen

"Joe, we don't have to do this."

We stood on Violet's front porch and Joe held my hand so tightly my palm began to sweat. He wore the new dress shirt and jeans we'd bought him earlier. Since he'd left Little Rock in such a hurry, he hadn't gone home to pack anything.

"Yes, we do. We're sortin' this out." He gritted his teeth, mumbling his words.

The front door opened and Mike filled the opening, an apologetic look on his face. He held two beer bottles and handed one to Joe. "You're gonna need it."

Joe took it and stepped through the door, dragging me behind him.

Mike mouthed "I'm sorry" as we passed.

I was walking into World War III. "Got another one of those?"

Mike grinned. "Comin' right up." He disappeared into the kitchen.

Violet sat on the deck and watched the kids play with Muffy in the yard. Her sunglasses hid her eyes, but she lifted a glass of wine to her mouth.

Joe stopped outside the door. "Violet, we need to talk."

Muffy saw us and ran over, jumping on my legs and begging me to pet her.

Violet lowered her glasses, eyeing Joe up and down before she pushed them back up and turned her gaze to the kids. "I don't know about manners where you're from, Joe Whatever-your-name-happens-to-be-this-week, but here in Henryetta we don't tolerate rudeness."

I gasped. I hadn't seen Violet act that catty since high school. What in the world had gotten into her?

Mike walked out with my beer and I took a big gulp, nearly choking on the fizz.

Violet turned her judgment on me. "Beer, Rose? Really?"

"There is nothing wrong with beer, Violet." Since I still held Joe's hand, I put the hand holding my beer on my hip, hoping to look indignant. Not an easy task while trying not to tip the bottle. The contents sloshed out as Muffy jumped up my leg. I'm sure it lost some of the effect, but I didn't want to let go of Joe's hand. It was important I showed her that we were a couple, whether she liked it or not.

"Joe, have a seat." Mike's tone was friendly but direct.

I sat in the wicker love seat, pulling Joe down next to me. Muffy leapt into my lap, covering me with licks.

I set the bottle down and buried my face into her neck. "I missed you too, girl."

Mike lifted the lid to his grill and turned his steaks. "This has gone on long enough and we're gonna put a stop to it tonight."

For a moment, I thought he was talking about the steaks. Mike never meddled in other people's business. Ever. But then again, he was probably tired of taking cover during Violet's tirades.

Turning around, he pointed his tongs at Violet. "Rose is a grown woman and she's entitled to date who she wants, whenever she wants. You may be her older sister, but that doesn't give you the right to run her life."

Violet gasped. "Am I supposed to sit back and say nothing while I watch her make the biggest mistake of her life?"

"You need to respect her decisions."

Her mouth pursed as she shook her head. She leaned on the chair arm, turning her attention to Joe. "We don't know anything about you. You waltz into town and put my sister in danger, then make her fall in love with you. Then you come and go as you please, makin' her miserable during the week. Now she's thinkin' about running off with you." She turned her stare on me. "I'm not a fool, Rose Anne Gardner. I know what you're thinking. But he could be a serial killer for all we know."

"Violet!" If I hadn't already told Joe that I loved him, I'd have been seething with anger that she mentioned my feelings so casually, as if they weren't mine to tell. Well, seething with more anger than I'd come over to her house with. And how did she know I loved him, anyway? I'd never told her. "You know good and well he's a state police officer. How can he be a serial killer?"

She squinted. "Stranger things have happened, Rose. What's he hiding?"

I tried to stand, but Joe pulled me back down.

"No," Joe squeezed my hand. "Let her talk. You say you don't know anything about me, Violet, but that's your fault, isn't it? Since that night you walked into Rose's house and found me helpin' her paint, you've had it out for me. Why?"

"I already told you. We don't know anything about you."

"Then ask."

For once, Violet was speechless.

"What do you want to know?"

She quickly recovered and lifted her chin. "Your family, for one thing."

"Oh Lordy, Violet!" I snapped. "That again? Can't you just let it go?" Joe wasn't comfortable talking about his family and I wasn't going to let her bully him into exposing his past.

Joe tensed, involuntarily digging his nails into my hand.

"Joe, *do not* tell her anything you don't want to share."

He took a long swig from his bottle then leveled his gaze at her. "I'm not sure what my family has to do with me and the choices I've made with my life, but so be it. You're Rose's sister. Your blessing is important to me and I know it's important to her even if she won't admit it. But let me tell you this," He leaned forward, resting his elbow on his knee. "I don't *need* your blessing. I love Rose and I'm not goin' anywhere. I'm proving it by sitting here endurin' your inhospitality and condemnation when the only thing I'm guilty of is lovin' your sister."

Her mouth opened as though she was about to say something, but she closed it without making a sound. Joe had left her speechless twice. I couldn't be more proud of him.

Mike tipped his beer with a grin and took a drink.

Joe's voice lowered into a growl. "Now what do you want to know?"

Violet inhaled, then a smug smile twisted her mouth. "Where are you from?"

"Little Rock."

"But where were you born and raised? Who are your people?"

"*Who are his people*?" I screeched.

Joe dropped my hand and put his arm around my back. "El Dorado."

"So you were born there and lived there your whole life."

"Until I went to college in Little Rock and stayed there when I joined the state police."

"And did you finish college?"

What was with her haughty attitude? She and Mike didn't go to college. Most people in Henryetta didn't. Surely she wasn't going to hold that over his head.

"Yes, Violet, I did. When I set out to do something, I do it."

That was clearly a challenge.

"So what was your major?"

"Pre-law, then law school."

I tried to hide my surprise, but Violet didn't, her mouth falling open as she peered over her sunglasses, reassessing him with this new piece of information.

"Then why are you an Arkansas State Police detective? Why aren't you practicing law?"

"Because I never wanted to be an attorney. I only went to law school to appease my father. I always intended to be a police detective."

"What does your father do?"

"He's an attorney in El Dorado."

"And your mother?"

Joe's arm stiffened.

"Joe, you don't have to answer her questions." I turned to my sister. "That is enough, Violet. This is not the Spanish Inquisition."

"What is he hidin', Rose? Your face is like an open book, and it's obvious that this is the first time you're hearin' all this yourself. How can you build a relationship on secrets?"

163

"His past is for him to share with me when he's ready. It doesn't change a thing, Violet."

"Rose, it's fine." He glared at Violet. "I hadn't told Rose because I am so completely different from my parents that I didn't want Rose to hold my family against me."

Violet's hand covered her mouth. "Oh, dear Lord. You're from white trash, aren't you?"

"Violet!"

"If your father is a lawyer, he must be an ambulance chaser."

"*Violet*!" I jumped up, but Joe pulled me back down, his arm wrapping around my waist again. He gripped my side as though he was afraid I was gonna leave him alone to face her.

"No," Joe's voice was tight. "My family is the furthest you can get from white trash. To answer your original question, my mother is not employed but keeps busy with her society work."

Violet was speechless again. Joe was going for a home run.

"My family is *the* Simmons family from El Dorado."

My head swung from Joe to Violet, unsure what that meant. But Violet knew. Her face paled. "*The* Simmons family?"

"One and the same."

"But . . . but . . ."

My heart sputtered. "Wait. I don't understand."

"His family . . ." Violet swallowed. "His family is the richest family in all of Southern Arkansas. They fill the *Inviting Arkansas* society pages." Violet would know, since she subscribed to the magazine that covered all things society in Arkansas. She pored over it every month when it showed up in her mailbox.

Fear coursed through my veins. Joe was from a rich society family and I . . . I was from Henryetta and worked at a DMV. How could I fit into that?

Joe's arm pulled me closer. "Rose, I didn't tell you because I'm not like them and I don't want to be. I've made my own life and you're part of it. They aren't."

Violet pulled off her sunglasses, studying Joe with a suspicious look. "Why not?"

"That's not the life I wanted. But since you now know that I come from an *acceptable* family, I want to drop the subject."

Violet's entire attitude changed, which nauseated me. Was my sister really that shallow?

Dinner was tense, but more on my part than Violet's doing. She was syrupy sweet to Joe, probably trying to make up for all the meanness she'd heaped on him. I kept thinking about Joe's family and Violet's discrimination.

"How's business, Mike?" Joe asked. "Your construction company still doin' well?"

"Yeah. We're bidding on a big job involving the new superstore going in over by the Forest Ridge subdivision."

My head jerked up at the mention of Frank Mitchell's neighborhood. "What does that mean exactly?"

Mike stirred his salad around on his plate. "It means they're tearing out part of the neighborhood to put in the parking lot for the store."

I set my fork down and wrung my hands in my lap. "So . . . that means someone is buying houses for the parking lot?"

"Well, yeah."

"Who's buying them?"

Joe shot me a glance with narrowed eyes but kept silent.

"The corporation that owns the store. They're in the process of finalizing the deals. Demo will start in about six months."

"What happens to the people who don't want to sell?"

"They don't have much choice in the matter. The city approved it. They have to accept a fair price."

"And is it fair?"

Mike shrugged and stabbed a baked potato from the bowl on the table, plopping it onto his plate. "I suppose it is. Most of those houses are damn near condemnable."

Violet's mouth pursed and she nodded to Ashley, who ate her food, ignoring all adult conversation. "Mike. Language."

Mike scowled.

Violet shot me an icy stare. "Why the sudden interest in real estate, Rose?"

I looked down at my steak, feeling Joe's gaze on me. "I don't know. I'm interested in old houses."

"Well, you should take Austin Kent up on his offer to show you his photos of Italy. I'm sure it still stands."

Joe's threw his fork down on his plate, the clang filling the room and stunning Violet into silence.

Oh mercy, she'd gone and done it now.

He stood up, his body stiff. "Rose, I think it's time we left."

Tears blurred my eyes as I turned to her. "How could you, Violet? Your biggest concern was that Joe's family wasn't good enough and now you know they are, so what is it?"

She placed her hands on the table, leaning forward. "Rose, honey, you know how much I love you and I can't stand by and watch you get hurt."

"What are you talkin' about?"

Lifting her chin, she shot a glance at Joe then back at me. "I don't think tonight is a good time to discuss this, Rose. How about we talk about it after Joe goes back to Little Rock?"

Joe took a step closer to me, putting his hand on my shoulder. "How about we discuss this now?"

Her face softened. "Joe, it's apparent I was wrong about you, and I'm terribly sorry about that. But in light of your new information . . . let's be honest." She pointed to him. "You're . . . a Simmons."

"So?"

"Well, Rose . . . she's . . ."

Joe grabbed my arm and pulled me out of the chair. "Come on, Rose. We're leaving."

My breath caught in my throat.

Joe pushed me around the table, but I dug my heels in. I had to know the truth.

"Let me get this straight. First you thought Joe wasn't good enough for me. Now you think I'm not good enough for him?"

Joe shook his head and tried to pull me out of the room. "Don't do this, Rose."

Mike stood next to his chair. "Violet, I'm warnin' you."

Violet bit her lip, her love for me filling her eyes. "It's not that, Rose. It's just that you . . ."

"Rose," Joe pleaded.

"No," I choked out. "I want to hear this from her."

"Honey, his family is society. They have money. How are you goin' to fit in with that? I just don't want you to get hurt." The sincerity in her eyes told me that she meant every word she said.

Joe looked angry enough to hit her. Instead, he held his breath, then said, "Rose, get Muffy."

I remained frozen in horror.

He lifted my chin and looked into my eyes. His face softened. "I love you, Rose. Don't you ever doubt that for a single minute. But I need a word with your sister, so go get Muffy and we'll head home. Okay?"

I nodded, the lump in my throat too big to speak through.

Muffy was in the backyard and I opened the back door, wondering how things had gotten to this state. Joe's angry voice carried through the glass. *I should be in there with him, not hiding on the patio.*

The door opened behind me and Ashley slipped out and wrapped her arms around my legs. "Why's everybody yellin'?"

Closing my eyes, I silently berated myself for yelling at Violet in front of Ashley and Mikey. "Grownups do that sometimes."

Muffy ran over and I knelt down to scoop her up. I grabbed Ashley's arm and tugged her closer, staring into her confused face. "People fight and they get over it. It's goin' to be okay." I kissed her forehead and stood, wishing I believed what I'd said.

Sucking in a deep breath, I walked into the house, Joe's voice echoing from the other room. "The only person hurting her is *you*, Violet."

Joe swung to face me when I entered the room, fear in his eyes before he pushed it away. "I've said my piece. Let's go."

I nodded.

"Rose!" Violet shouted as we left the room.

Joe wrapped his arm around my back, holding me tight as we walked out the front door.

She stood on the porch, watching Joe push me into the car. "Rose, honey. I love you. I only want what's best for you."

I bit my lip to keep from crying. Joe hurried around to the driver's side and drove off, Violet still on the porch shouting at me.

Neither of us said anything all the way home. I was too shocked and hurt. But as soon as we walked into the kitchen, I buried my face into Joe's chest, sobbing.

He led me into the living room and sat on the sofa, pulling me onto his lap. "It's not true. Don't listen to her, darlin'." Gripping my cheeks in his hands, his eyes bored into mine. "I love you for you and you're a hundred times better than someone from my parents' world." His hand smoothed my damp hair off my face and he kissed me. "I want you. If I wanted the type of woman my parents would choose, I'd be with Hilary."

My eyes widened in horror and I gasped.

Joe frantically shook his head. "No, it's not what you think."

But it was exactly what I thought. Joe said they'd known each other as kids. Hilary was from money too. They'd dated and lived together before Joe broke up with her. Hilary was who his parents wanted him to marry and she knew it. I was gonna be sick.

I shook my head, my tears catching my breath.

"Damn it!" he shouted, leaning his head back against the sofa. "This is all my fault." His eyes found mine. "I'm sorry. I should have told you, but I know how you think and I knew you'd feel this way. I just couldn't bear to see that look of horror in your eyes. Please, Rose. *It's me.* I'm just Joe. I hardly ever see my family. Their world isn't mine."

"I don't . . ."

He pulled me into an embrace and buried his face into my hair. "I love you and *I need you*. I don't want to live without you. Don't hold my family against me. Rose, please say something."

No matter when he told me about his family, I would have reacted the same way. Violet's words echoed in my head. "She's right."

"Who?" He leaned me back, anger filling his eyes. "Violet? The hell she is. You were right when you said you thought she was jealous. Sure, on the surface I think she's deluded herself into believing she has your best interests in mind, but she can't stand the thought of you being happy. Or even worse, better than her."

"But . . ."

"Rose. I speak to my family two or three times a year. I go home for Christmas. I don't even spend the night." His eyes burned with pain. "I am my father's greatest disappointment. I'm his only son and he wanted me to join the family business and I refused. I refused to go to my father's alma mater, Vanderbilt. I refused to practice law. I wanted to make my own life, free from my father's shadow. I've never felt as free as when I was Joe McAllister. Being with you is the happiest I've ever been in my life."

He watched me, his eyes guarded.

His family intimidated me and I suspected if Joe's father couldn't accept him having an honest job, he'd never accept me. But who was I to point fingers? My momma had been a mean, spiteful woman. My father had watched her belittle me my entire life because of the sins of his own past and never intervened. Violet had tried to run Joe off because she'd thought so little of his family and then she thought too much. If Joe could still love me, in spite of my own questionable family, how could I hold his against him?

"I want to move to Little Rock with you."

His face lit up with joy. "What? You do? Why?"

"Because I love you, Joe McAllister, and if you can put up with my insufferable family, who am I to question yours? And Violet was right about one thing. I'm miserable without you."

"You won't regret it. I swear. I love you, and I'll never let anyone hurt you if I can help it."

Sliding my hand into his hair, I pulled his mouth to mine. "I know."

Chapter Eighteen

When Joe left Monday morning, I didn't even try to pretend to be happy about it. Joe was torn between leaving me and taking me with him, even though I insisted I had to go to work and give my notice.

"I'll come back Wednesday night and I'll help you start boxing things up."

I nodded, worried I'd burst into tears.

"Are you sure you can't just call with your notice?"

"I could, but I may as well do it in person. I have to stay in town. Violet and I have an appointment with the probate office on Wednesday. The sooner we get that taken care of, the sooner I'll be free."

"Okay." He hesitated.

"You need to go or you'll be late. We can't both be unemployed."

"We could travel the world. I could take you to Italy."

"Well, the difference between your job and mine is you actually enjoy it. So you go to the job you love, and I'll figure out what I want to be when I grow up."

"You could always go back to school. I'm sure the University of Arkansas in Little Rock has an elementary education program."

He knew how much it had bothered me that I'd quit college my freshman year to take care of Momma after Daddy died. I was surprised he remembered my major. I'd only mentioned it once. But it was an option. I had my money from my birth mother. I could use it to pay for my tuition.

Joe took my hand, and I walked him to his car while Muffy ran around looking for the perfect spot to pee. "Maybe you can come up to Little Rock this weekend since this last one didn't work out."

"Sorry about that."

"Promise me you won't do anything illegal."

That was easy. I wasn't on jury duty anymore. "I promise."

"And be careful. Before you do something, ask yourself 'what would Joe think if he knew I was doing this' and if you have the smallest inkling I'd be upset, then don't do it."

That one was harder. "Okay. But you'll do some digging into who's in charge of the construction project and Forest Ridge?"

"I'll do my best, but I have a busy week scheduled. I might not get to it for a couple of days." He held up a finger when I started to protest. "I'll get to it as soon as I can. Now come here and kiss me goodbye."

He leaned against the car door and pulled me to his chest, kissing me as though he wouldn't see me for three months instead of three days.

"I love you, Joe."

"I love you too. Stay out of trouble."

I smiled. "I never used to get into trouble until you showed up."

"Somehow, I seriously doubt that. But try to stay out of it anyway."

He drove away and I looked across the street, not surprised to see Miss Mildred watching out her front door with a frown.

I finished getting ready for work, meandering through my house, amazed that I was actually going to sell it and move away. I'd lived here my entire life.

A knock at the front door shook me out of my musing. Nobody used the front door. When I opened it, I was surprised to see Officer Ernie, looking all official. My heart jumped into my throat. I'd been with Joe all weekend and hadn't done anything illegal.

"Can I help you, Officer?"

"I received a complaint I'm following up on."

"A complaint? Who complained?"

"It was an anonymous complaint, miss."

"What was the complaint?"

"You were reported for indecent acts in public." He looked over my shoulder into the living room. "May I come in?"

"No, you may not."

His eyes widened in surprise.

"We can discuss this right here."

He cleared his throat and pulled out his notebook. "You were accused of kissin' a man in public."

Crossing my arms, I shifted my weight to one side. "I missed the vote to make that an illegal act."

"Well, technically it's not illegal . . ."

I uncrossed my arms and clenched my fists at my sides. "I was in my own front yard, kissin' my boyfriend goodbye. My boyfriend, the state police detective."

He frowned, closing his notebook. "The entire police department of Henryetta is fully aware of who your boyfriend is."

"Would you like his number? You can call him and tell him about the complaint."

Officer Ernie glared. "Your boyfriend may work for the Arkansas State Police, but you are still under Henryetta jurisdiction. We're all watchin' you, missy. It would be a shame if you went back to jail."

"For *kissin'*?"

"That's how it starts, then the next thing you know, you're naked on the hood of your car, makin' love to Def Leppard's 'Pour Some Sugar On Me'."

He sounded like he was speaking from personal experience. I stared at him for several seconds, trying to purge the image from my mind. "Is there anything else?"

Disappointment turned his mouth down. He must have expected me to cower in fear. "No, but once a lawbreaker—"

"—always a lawbreaker. Got it." There was no point arguing with the man. I gave him the sweetest smile I could muster. "You have a nice day now."

Then I shut the door as he was getting ready to say something. I sure wasn't making friends with Henryetta law enforcement, but then again, they'd never liked me much to begin with. Thank goodness I was leaving this small-minded town.

Now it was time to go to work and give my notice.

Suzanne was subdued when I showed up. I expected I'd have to defend my right to stay employed even though I intended to quit, but she tried to ignore my presence, sneaking glances at me throughout the morning. She must have found out she couldn't fire me after all. And she must have heard the gossip, realizing I really had been at jury duty. I decided I'd give my two-week notice when I left for the day.

Right before lunchtime, my cell phone buzzed. I thought it might be Joe or Violet, but was surprised to see it was Neely Kate.

Lunch? ;)

I texted back. *Yes, is 1:00 too late?*

Nope, meet you at Merilees?

Yes. :)

I thought about my new friendship with Neely Kate. I may have only known her a week, but I was going to miss her.

The café had cleared out by one, and I found her sitting at a table, waving her arms. "Rose, over here!"

"How's the bridesmaids dress situation?" I asked, sitting down.

She waved my question away. "Forget about the wedding, tell me *everything* that happened."

"You mean in jail?"

Rolling her eyes, she leaned forward. "No, at the weekend softball game. Of course, at the jail. And getting out. And Mason Deveraux taking Judge McClary on to get you out."

I tilted my head sideways. "Wait. What are you talking about? And you scared the living daylights out of Joe with your message."

"Good! He deserved it after that whole Hilary incident."

"That wasn't his fault."

She pinched her lips. "Hmm." Resting her elbows on the table, her eyes glittered with excitement. "Spill."

The waitress came over, and I ordered a glass of sweet tea and a chicken salad sandwich.

"Well, look at you." Neely Kate preened. "Orderin' without a menu. You're like a pro. Now tell me what happened!"

"Not much, really."

Neely Kate raised her eyebrows. "That's not what I heard."

"I suspect what you heard is a whole lot more exciting than what happened."

"Tell me anyway."

"I got locked up and then Mr. Deveraux came to see me."

"He did? *Why?*" I couldn't believe something slipped by her.

"He said he felt guilty because I went to talk to him the day before and he yelled at me. He thought that's why I went to Frank Mitchell's house."

"Is it true? Did you go to his house because Mr. Deveraux yelled at you?"

I sighed. When she put it that way . . . "Yeah, I guess."

"But why?"

"Because I know Bruce Wayne Decker is innocent. And no one else is fighting for him."

Neely Kate nodded, accepting that I knew he was innocent without asking questions.

"I thought maybe I could get Mr. Deveraux to listen to me, but obviously that didn't work out."

To her credit, she didn't say anything about me keeping my intent from her last Thursday. "What else did he say when he came to see you in jail?"

I remember the pain in his eyes when I asked him why he wanted to be a district attorney. It felt like a private moment. Something too personal to share, like if I did I'd be violating his trust somehow, which seemed crazy. "Not much. He told me he felt guilty and he was goin' to get me out."

"And he was true to his word. Judge McClary threatened to throw him in jail too if he didn't back off, but he kept on pushing."

"Joe didn't tell me that part."

"I heard Joe went up against the judge too."

"He said he had to vouch for my character."

"He did more than that. He took full *professional* responsibility for your future actions."

"You mean his job could be on the line because of me?"

She shrugged. "Yeah, but you're safe. You're not on the jury any more so you can't get in trouble for that."

I gnawed on my bottom lip. "I guess . . ."

"So what are you goin' to do?"

"About what?"

"The case, silly. You're not gonna just let it go, are you?"

"I dunno. Before it was just me on the line. But if Joe has professionally taken responsibility for me . . ." Why didn't he *tell* me?

We spent the rest of our time talking about her wedding. She pulled out a silvery, glittery invitation and handed it to me. *Rose and Joe* was written in elaborate curlicues. "I hope you can come," she gushed.

"Oh! I haven't told you my *big* news," I said, studying the invitation.

"Bigger than gettin' arrested?"

I nodded. "I'm goin' to move to Little Rock!"

Her eyes were as wide as her hooped earrings. "He asked you to move in with him?" Then she squealed so loud that everyone in the café turned to stare.

"Neely Kate! Shh!"

"That is so *excitin'*!"

"Yeah, we'll see what Violet says."

"You haven't told her yet?"

I filled Neely Kate in on what happened Saturday night.

Neely Kate's mouth pinched in disapproval. "I'd love to get my hands on your sister."

"She didn't do it out of meanness. She really thinks she's doin' what's best for me."

Shaking her head, she frowned. "I'm not so sure about that." She glanced down at her watch. "Oh my stars and garters! I'm late." She jumped up out of her chair.

"Neely Kate. Wait a second." She turned around.

"Can you look something up for me?"

She sat back down, resting her chin on her hand. "Of course!"

"But you don't even want to know what I'm going to ask before you agree?"

She shrugged. "No. What do you want me to do?"

I leaned close and lowered my voice. "I found out that someone was trying to buy Frank Mitchell's house before he died, and he was trying to keep from selling. But his neighbor said the house got sold by his son soon after his death, then sold again not long ago. I think the second time was to a developer who's wanting to put in a super store, but I wonder who bought it the first time. Can you find out?"

She winked with a grin. "Pleaaase. I can find that out in my sleep. I'll call you with the info later."

"Thanks, Neely Kate."

"What are friends for?"

I was grinning when I went back to work, which perplexed Suzanne. The afternoon flew by, and I grinned even bigger when I handed her my letter at the end of the day.

"What's this?" she asked, squinting at the paper. "Your jury letter?"

"Nope, it's my two-week notice. It's your lucky day!"

The vinyl of my car's seat burned my legs when I climbed in, but I was so happy, I didn't care. I was actually quitting the job I'd hated for years.

Checking my cell phone, I noticed Neely Kate had left a message.

I called her on the way home, the air blasting so hard from the vents I had trouble hearing her. "Hey, Neely Kate."

"Rose! I found something out!"

Her excitement made my stomach jittery. "What?"

"Hyde Investments, a company in Louisiana, bought the house from Frank Mitchell's son."

"But shouldn't it have gone to probate?" Even though Momma had left the house to Violet, we still had to go through probate to sell it.

"No, his son's name was on the deed."

"Oh." I wished Momma had thought to do that and save us all a lot of hassle.

"Then just a few weeks ago, another corporation bought it. The company that owns the superstore."

"Hmm . . ."

"What do you make of that?" she asked.

"I don't know. Do you know anything about Hyde Investments?"

"Nope, not a thing other than it's based in Louisiana. I couldn't find out much about them from my search on the internet. If it's based out of state, could it be owned by the bookies that Frank owed money to?"

"I don't know, but it seems unlikely that an investment company in Louisiana would kill Frank Mitchell."

"Rose, there's something else." She sounded nervous.

"What?" My tongue tripped on the word.

"They're expecting to wrap up the trial on Wednesday."

The way she said it told me this was important information. "What does that mean?"

"It means you have to hurry. You can still save Bruce Wayne if you find evidence to keep him from being convicted, but if you find it *after* he's convicted, he'll have to go through an appeals process that could take years."

I sucked in my breath. "Oh no."

"What are you gonna do?"

I needed to accelerate my investigation. "Neely Kate, what are you doin' tonight?"

"Paintin' my nails and watching TV. Why?"

"I feel like playing pool."

"Um, I think it's *shootin'* pool."

Oh, crappy doodles. I had a lot to learn in a few hours.

Chapter Nineteen

Neely Kate had agreed to meet me at the pool hall at eight o'clock. I was glad for that, since it would give me a chance to take Muffy on a short walk. I'd neglected her lately with all the excitement involving my jury duty. I wondered how she'd like Little Rock. Joe didn't have a yard.

After our walk, Muffy and I shared a dinner of Joe's leftover Chicken Parmesan. Thinking about him made me miss him like crazy. I reached for my phone, debating whether to call him or not. It seemed silly to worry about calling him too much. I hadn't called him since last week, and in the meantime I'd agreed to move in with him. Surely, we were past the worrying-I'd-look-like-a clingy-girlfriend stage. Before I could dial, the phone rang and I expected it to be Joe. Instead, it was Violet. I hesitated before answering, deciding I had to talk to her sometime.

"Hello, Violet."

"Rose, I've called to apologize."

My mouth dropped open and my brain scrambled to take in her words.

"Are you there? Say something."

"Yeah, I'm here . . . I'm just . . ."

"Do you forgive me?" Her tone was snippy, not what I expected from someone truly contrite.

"Well, Violet, what exactly are you sorry about? You hurt me deeply."

Her voice lowered. "Rose, honey. I really am sorry. I know I hurt you and I don't know what got into me. Of course you're good enough for Joe. That wasn't what I meant. It all came out wrong. I watched Momma be mean to you for years, and I just can't bear the thought of someone else being mean and spiteful to you. Who's goin' to protect you?"

"I can protect myself. And if I can't, I think that Joe did a pretty good job of provin' that he could."

"Yeah, he did." She was silent for a moment. "I'm going to the Henryetta Garden Club meeting tomorrow night. The guest speaker is talkin' about roses and I know how much you love yours."

I had a rose garden in my backyard. I'd have to leave it when I moved, and the sadness that gripped me caught me by surprise.

"Anyway." Her voice was light and breezy. "I thought maybe you'd like to come with me."

"Isn't Miss Mildred president of the Garden Club? I thought they met during the day."

"Well . . . they usually do, but they're trying out some evening meetings to see if they can recruit some new blood. The median age of the Garden Club is currently around seventy-eight."

That made sense.

"So? Do you want to come? I can pick you up at six forty-five."

I had nothing else to do, and if I were busy maybe I wouldn't miss Joe so much. "Okay."

"Great! I'll see you tomorrow."

She hung up and I thought about her sudden turnaround. I was glad we weren't fighting at the moment, but I was waiting for her to pull her next stunt. I was going to have to tell her about my pending move, and I suspected it wouldn't go well.

I picked at my chicken, missing Joe again. This was ridiculous. Cold chicken made me want to cry. And it made me want to hear his voice. What in the world was wrong with me? I decided that I should talk to him now, in case he called when I was out.

He answered on the second ring. "Hey, darlin', how was your day?"

"Great. I turned in my notice."

"You really did it?" He sounded awed.

"Of course. The sooner I leave the DMV, the sooner I can move up to Little Rock."

"I can't wait."

"Me either."

"Have you told Violet yet?"

"Nooo . . . but she called and apologized."

"What exactly did she apologize *for*?"

Nothing slipped past this man. "She said what she said came out wrong. That I *was* good enough for you. She said she was worried that someone was going to hurt me and she wouldn't be able to protect me."

"Uh-huh," he answered in a monotone.

"Yeah, I don't trust her either, but I'm goin' to the Garden Club with her tomorrow night."

"I didn't know you were in the Garden Club." He sounded guarded.

"I'm not. But the guest speaker is a rose expert so Violet thought I might want to hear her since I love roses so much."

"Well, I hope you have good time." He was still reserved, not that I blamed him.

"What did you do today?"

"Oh, borin' police stuff."

"You can't tell me."

"I can't give you details. But I can tell you that we're getting ready to set up an undercover sting." Something in his voice set off alarm bells in my head.

"You're going undercover."

"Not yet."

Yet. My heart sputtered with fear. "When?"

"A few weeks."

"For how long?"

"I don't know, darlin'."

I swallowed the lump in my throat. "How long have you known?"

"A week."

"And you're just now tellin' me?"

Joe sighed. "I'm trying to get out of it. I put in for another transfer."

"Why? You love your job."

"I love you more."

I was torn. I didn't want him to go undercover, but I didn't want to be the reason he gave up something he loved. "Then why am I movin' to Little Rock when you're not even gonna be there?"

"It's not like Henryetta, Rose. I don't have to live there. I'll see you at night."

"But you'll still be in danger?"

"A policeman is always in danger, Rose."

And there was the crux of it. Other than his time in Henryetta, I tended to picture Joe behind a desk since he usually called me from his office during work hours. But the reality was that his job was much more dangerous and I could lose him at any time.

"Say something."

Honesty seemed the best way to go here. "I don't know what to say."

"Tell me that you still love me."

"Oh, Joe." I closed my eyes and leaned my forehead into my hand. Joe had never lied to me about his job. I knew full well what I was signing up for when I started seeing him. What gave me the right to hold it against him now? "Of course I love you. I'm just tryin' to calm my fears."

"I know. I'm sorry. I've never really had to think about someone worryin' about me."

I smiled even if he couldn't see it. "Well, you do what you need to do. I love you and nothing's goin' to change that."

"You're amazing," he sighed.

I wasn't so sure that he'd be saying that if he knew where I was planning to go later tonight. But his undercover plans took away the guilt of my own secret mission.

I told him about eating lunch with Neely Kate and what she'd found out about the investment company buying the murder victim's house.

"It's definitely worth checking into."

"Neely Kate also said they were goin' to wrap the trial up on Wednesday. If I don't prove Bruce Decker's innocent by then, he'll have to go through appeals and that could take years. Is that true?"

"Yeah, that's most likely what would happen."

My cold chicken wasn't sitting well in my stomach.

"Rose, this is not your responsibility. I appreciate that you feel that you have to help him, but think about what he was doin' when he saw the murder. He was robbin' the hardware store. He was going to go to prison for that anyway."

"For how long?"

"Five to ten years, most likely. Out in three to six years for good behavior."

"And second-degree murder?"

"At least twenty."

I sighed. "I gotta go."

"Don't be mad at me."

"I'm not, I promise. But I told Neely Kate I'd meet her later. Girls' night out." There, I'd told him. No guilt.

"You have fun and be careful."

"I will."

"I love you, Rose."

"I love you too, Joe."

I glanced at the clock, 7:15, which didn't leave me much time to get ready.

Standing in front of my bathroom mirror, I put on my makeup. While I'd never been to a pool hall, I suspected that if I was going to get information, I had to dress up more than I usually did. And by dress up, I meant wearing the right costume.

The situation reminded me of the night I went to meet Daniel Crocker at the Trading Post, a local bar. Crocker had threatened to hurt Violet if I didn't show up with a flash drive that was supposed to be full of information.

But that was different. Tonight I was going to the pool hall on my own free will. And I was meeting Neely Kate. Completely innocent.

As long as I kept telling myself that, maybe I'd believe it.

I left the house at ten to eight. I'd considered wearing jeans, but it was too doggone hot. Instead, I wore a white skirt and a silky light blue blouse. I'd bought it a couple of weeks earlier to go out with Joe but hadn't worn it yet. I hated to waste it on the pool hall, but the black blouse I'd worn to the Trading Post had gotten ripped open by Daniel Crocker. The only other sexy thing I owned was my red dress, and that was too fancy. I just had to make do. There wasn't time to shop for slutty clothes. My hair was curled and I had on twice as much makeup as I usually wore. With Neely Kate's help, I might be able to pull this off.

As I drove, I tried to figure out a plan. I didn't know anything about the bookie, other than he or she worked at the pool hall. I'd just have to wing it. Besides, Neely Kate was smart and worldly. She'd figure something out.

The parking lot wasn't very full when I parked, but then, it was a Monday night. Business probably wouldn't be booming. Staring at the building, I realized I didn't know what kind of car Neely Kate drove. She might already be inside. My hands wrung the steering wheel while I tried to figure out what to do.

A man walked past my Nova, casting a quizzical glance my direction. If I didn't go in, I was going to look suspicious.

Sucking in a breath to steady my nerves, I got out of the car. *Here goes nothing.*

A flashing neon sign advertised beer in the window and the smell of it hit me when I opened the door. I expected the place to be dimly lit, but the lamps over the tables created puddles of light, brightening up the room.

Scanning the hall for Neely Kate, I quickly realized she wasn't there. My heartbeat picked up. I was on my own.

I could do this. I survived my encounter with Daniel Crocker at the Trading Post, and he'd planned to kill me if I didn't provide the flash drive. Then I reminded myself I hadn't gotten myself out of that mess at all. Joe had. And Joe was two hours away.

Oh, crappy doodles.

What on earth was I doing here?

If I turned around and left now, I might not get any information at all. I should at least get a drink and think this through.

I ordered a bottle of beer and sat on a stool. It was next to a small table against the wall and gave me a good view of the premises. After taking a good look around, I decided most of the men didn't look scary. Most looked like guys wanting to spend a night away from their families, hanging out with their friends. But a group of three in the back reminded me of Crocker and his men. They swaggered around a pool table, leaning on their sticks like the world was theirs for the taking. I watched them for a second before turning my attention elsewhere. But not before I noticed the gaze of one of the men fall on me.

I'd bet a lifetime supply of Suzanne's tanning lotion that those were the men I needed to talk to.

Where was Neely Kate?

The guy who'd turned his attention to me sauntered my direction. I took a big chug of my beer, hoping it would give me the courage I lacked at the moment.

The man sat in the chair across from me. He was a good-looking man with dark hair and a neatly trimmed beard, but he had an edge to him that made me uncomfortable. Muscles stretched his t-shirt and tattoos peeked out under his sleeves. Resting an elbow on the table, he held his beer bottle over the table edge and leaned forward. "Well, hello there, gorgeous. What's a girl like you doin' in a place like this?"

Even with my lack of experience, I knew that had to be a tacky pickup line. The question was how to handle it. I decided to go with my instinct. After taking another long drink, I set the bottle down. "Is that the best you've got?"

Where had this Sassy Rose come from? It had to be the beer. I loved beer.

He tilted his head back and laughed, a deep throaty sound. When he recovered, he winked. "I think that earns you a drink." He went over to the bar and brought back two bottles, handing one to me. Holding up his beer, he grinned. "Here's to what's looking like an interesting evening."

I clicked my bottle into his, then took a drink.

"Are you here all alone?" He put his arm along the back of the chair across from me.

"I'm waiting for a friend. She should be here any minute."

His mouth lifted into a slow lazy grin.

I suspected I'd just said the wrong thing. To hide my shaking hand, I took another drink. Crappy doodles. I'd been here less than ten minutes and drank one and a half bottles of beer. I needed to slow down.

"You wanna shoot some pool while you wait for your friend?"

"Let me check if she's tried to call." Searching the contents of my purse revealed my mistake. I'd charged my cell phone before I left. And never unplugged it.

I had two choices: leave or stay. The whole purpose of me being here was to get information and I suspected my opportunity had just presented itself. I smiled. "Sure."

I took a long sip of my beer and set it down before I slid from the stool. He stood in front of me, extending his hand. "Skeeter."

"Uh . . ." I couldn't tell him my real name. "Jane."

Instead of shaking my hand, he held onto it, slipping his other arm around my back. "Well, Jane. How good are you at pool?" He led me to the back corner, where his two friends watched, not bothering to hide their grins of approval.

Where in the dickens was Neely Kate?

"I've never played."

His eyebrows raised and he studied me. "Then what's a nice girl like you doin' at a pool hall all alone when you've never played before?"

His friend handed him a bottle and Skeeter pressed it into my left hand, still holding onto my right. "My friend . . . Sasha . . . she's getting married next week so we decided to get a little loose and crazy and do something we've never done before. Like play pool . . . I mean shoot pool." Why did I always babble when I was anxious?

Skeeter hovered over me, making me nervous. The condensation from the cold bottle dripped down my fingers, tempting me to take another drink to bolster my courage.

"I like loose and crazy," he said.

I pulled my hand from his and took a step back, holding my bottle in front of me. "Then it's your lucky night." Before I realized what I was doing, I'd taken another long sip, then set the bottle down with a clang.

Skeeter's butt rested against the side of a pool table, his hands behind him, drumming on the edge. He smirked. "I guess it is."

He was too sure of himself to suit me, and the beer had begun coursing through my veins. "You gonna show me how to do this or what?"

His eyes widened in surprise. "Eager, huh? I like that. I'll get you a cue."

While he was gone, his friends checked me out. I gave them the best haughty look I could muster. A difficult task when I couldn't feel my face.

An arm slipped over my shoulders and I looked up in to Skeeter's face, his beer breath blasting me. He handed me a pole. "This here's the cue stick. You line it up with that white ball and hit it so that the white ball hits another ball and sinks it into a pocket."

His condescending tone rankled my nerves. "I've heard of pool. I just haven't played it."

Skeeter chuckled. "Just trying to make sure you know the *rules*."

I looked into his face, wondering if I had missed something in my beer-hazed state.

His arm dropped from my shoulder and he moved over to the table. Grabbing a rack from the wall, he scooped up the balls and rearranged them, then rolled the rack back and forth until he had them where he wanted them. He lifted the wooden rack and left the balls in a perfect triangle. Bracing his hands on the table edge, he leaned forward, staring at me. "Do you know what to do now, Jane?"

It took me a second to realize that he was talking to me. "Yeah, you have to get the stripes or the solids into the pockets."

"And who gets to decide who's stripes or solids?"

"I dunno."

"The person who sinks the first ball." He picked up his cue and leaned over the table then struck the white ball. It slammed into the triangle, sending balls everywhere. Several dropped into the holes.

Showoff.

Still hanging over his pool cue, he leered at me.

Where the *hell* was Neely Kate?

Skeeter took a long drag of his beer and set it down on the table. "Come 'ere and let me help you hit the ball."

"I can do it by myself." Grabbing my stick, I walked over, try-ing not to wobble in my heels. I stopped at the side of the table, directly in front of the white ball. "So what do you pick? Solids or stripes?"

He slid closer, resting his hand on my shoulder. "How about I go easy on you. There's more stripes left on the table. I'll let you have solids."

Hunching over the table, I rested the cue on the ledge, lining it up with the white ball and a red ball behind it, aiming for the pocket. I stared down the length of the stick and slid it between my fingers like I'd watched Skeeter do. Then I pulled and hit it, the white ball smacking the red ball and shooting it into the pocket. I stood up with a grin.

"I believe you've been holding out on me, Jane."

I lifted my eyebrows.

"What do you say we make this more interestin'?"

"What do you mean?"

"I'm a wagerin' man. Let's wager on the game."

Skeeter was a wagering man. Ten to one he knew the bookie that Frank Mitchell owed money to. Still, it was a fool's bet. And I didn't even know what was at risk. "Not a chance."

He turned his back to the table and crossed his arms across his chest. "Scared?"

I put a hand on my hip and jutted it out. "My momma didn't raise no fool." Where did *that* come from? Damn beer.

He chuckled sliding closer. "You don't even know what the wager is yet."

I rolled my eyes. "I don't need to. We both know I made a lucky shot. I've got no chance of winnin' against you."

"What if I played you with one hand behind my back?"

"Why would I do that? What am I gonna win?" More important, what was I going to lose?

His eyebrow waggled. "What do you want?"

I swallowed my instinctive gag. *Not you.* But I knew what I wanted. I just didn't know how to go about asking for it without giving myself away. "You know, when Susan—I mean Sasha— and I were coming here tonight, we wanted to try new things. You know. Playin' pool and . . ." I lowered my gaze and glanced up through my eyelashes. "Placing a bet," I whispered. "I heard you could do that here."

A wicked grin spread across his face. He licked his top lip. "I can help you with that."

"And if you win?"

Reaching up his hand, nice and slow as though I was a wild animal that might run away, he brushed the hair off my shoulder and looked into my eyes. "A kiss."

I shook my head with a frown. "No way. I don't even know you."

"You'll know me better after you kiss me."

Crappy doodles. Why had I played my hand already? Now that he knew I wanted to place a bet, the only way he was gonna help me was if I accepted his wager. And as sure as Miss Mildred would complain about Muffy peeing in the front yard, Skeeter, the wagering man, didn't make bets he knew he'd lose. I was between a rock and a hard place.

Stupid beer.

I scanned the room looking one last time for Neely Kate and spotted a clock by the bar. 8:35. I had to accept the fact that she wasn't coming. I was in this alone.

I was so close . . .

Lifting my chin, I gave him my sternest glare. "I want a practice game first. Then I'll decide if I want to accept your wager."

With a wink, he stepped away from me. "It only seems fair. It's still your turn. I'll even make it easy for you. You don't have to call which pocket the ball goes in before you shoot. That's one of the rules."

"So why are you breakin' it?"

"Trying to increase my odds of gettin' you to accept my wager."

Not a chance. "Well, aren't you the gentleman?"

He laughed loud and long. "Most definitely not."

I turned my attention to the pool table, focusing on the balls spread across the green felt. It was shooting balls into holes. How hard could it be? I found a blue one close to a hole but other balls were between it and the white.

His voice lowered. "I'll help you if you want."

"I don't need your help."

He laughed again.

My hand began to tremble and I grabbed my beer bottle, drinking a gulp as I circled the pool table. *Go home, Rose. Don't do this.* But I wasn't in any real danger. There were other decent people playing pool. Skeeter couldn't do anything harmful to me in public. I just wouldn't agree to his wager and I'd be safe. Plus, I found a clear shot with the white ball and a green one.

Skeeter leaned his hip against the other side of the table. "So what do you want to bet on?"

Lining up my cue with the ball, I concentrated on the table. Maybe I wouldn't need his wager after all. "I dunno. What *can* I bet on?"

"You don't even know what you want to bet on? Then why do you want to place a bet at all?"

Unsure how to answer, I stalled and took my shot. The white ball hit the green one, but the green one missed the hole. I looked up at him. "It's kind of one of those bucket list things. But I was supposed to do it with my friend, Susan. I guess she stood me up."

"I thought her name was Sasha."

My breath stuck. "Oh, yeah . . . it is. Silly me. Susan's her sister . . . Her twin sister." I was proud of myself. That sounded convincing.

Skeeter moved around the table toward the white ball and I scooted the opposite direction.

"So what *can* I bet on?"

He didn't try to hide his amusement. "Pretty much anything. Sports. Horses. The Oscars."

"Um, sports."

Lining up his cue stick, he lifted his face to look at me. "Baseball?"

"Sure."

He hit the ball and several balls split off, two sinking into pockets.

Thank goodness I didn't make that wager. "So how would I do it?"

Moving around the side of the table, he shrugged. "You can do it online. Lots of people do these days."

"What if I want to bet in person?"

He bent over the table and winked. "Then I guess you need me, don't ya?"

"How does it work?"

"Well, first you have to figure out what team you want to bet on. Do you even know any baseball teams?"

I grabbed my beer bottle to stall, surprised that I'd already finished it. How many was that?

Skeeter waved with a finger toward the bar.

"Um, I know the Little Rock Travelers."

He laughed and shot again, another ball going into the pocket. "They're minor league, although you can bet on them too. But most people don't. Most people bet on major league teams."

A waitress brought over two beer bottles, handing one to me.

"Oh, no." I waved my hands in front of me.

Skeeter motioned for her to put the bottle down.

"How do you know so much about this?" I perched in a chair, not an easy task given the fact I was a bit unsteady.

"Because, Jane . . ." He moved closer to me, making me sorry I'd sat down. He had me cornered. "If you want to place a bet, I'm who you need to talk to."

"Oh."

He picked up my beer and handed it to me. "Tell you what, I'm feeling generous tonight. How about I help you place a bet, without this pool wager?"

"Why?"

"Why not?"

"Okay."

His grin shifted from amused to calculating. "It's your shot. I missed."

Did he? I thought he'd got another one in.

He grabbed my elbow and accompanied me to the table, handing me the pool stick I'd forgotten. "There's a perfect shot for you right there." He pointed with his finger, his hand still holding his beer. "See it?"

I was having trouble focusing, let alone seeing the perfect shot. "No."

He set his beer aside. Pushing gently on my back so I leaned over the table, he lifted the cue stick and placed it on the edge next to me. Skeeter squatted beside me, his face inches from mine. "Pool is physics. Were you any good at physics in school?"

"Not particularly."

"It's all about trajectory and rotation."

"Sounds complicated."

"It kind of is."

"Is being a bookie complicated?"

He smirked. "Do you always say what pops into your head?"

"Only when I drink a lot of beer."

"Then you definitely need more beer."

I most definitely didn't. "Well, is it?"

"Is what it?"

"Is being a bookie complicated?"

"It has its moments. Right now you need to focus on this shot." He rested his chest on my back, his arms extending next to mine. "Look down the cue stick and aim it for the right side of the ball, not the middle. See?"

I squinted one eye shut. "I think so."

"If you aim for the edge, the ball will shoot off in the opposite direction and hit that green ball on the side and send it into that corner pocket. Do you see it now?"

"I think so."

His hand curled over mine, holding the cue. "Now, nice and smooth." He slid my arm back then forward, and the tip of the stick hit the edge of the white ball. It spun away to the left and struck the green one, which rolled into the corner pocket.

My peripheral vision faded. I was getting a vision. *No*! I saw my hand throw a bottle across the room and a string of obscenities filled my ears. "That was a sure bet." Skeeter said in my vision. "I don't take losing thousands of dollars lightly. Somebody's gonna pay for this mistake."

"You're gonna lose a lot of money," I said, then scrunched my eyes closed in terror.

He stood, pulling me up with him and turning me around to face him. His eyes narrowed. "What makes you say that?"

Warnings were going off in my head and I tried to back away, but his body and arms had me pinned against the table.

"Why're you so interested in betting, Jane?"

Jane? Oh, right. I was Jane. I obviously wasn't very good at this undercover stuff. "I told you. It was on my list of things to do."

"People who place bets just place 'em. They're not interested in the business of it. Even if this is an act, you seem too naïve to be a cop. Who are you?"

"I told you—"

"Sweetheart, I didn't get where I am today by letting things get past me. What are you doin' here?" He leaned over me, still sounding amused, but his eyes had a hard edge.

"I think I want to go now."

"Not until I get some answers."

"I believe the lady said she wanted to go," a deep voice challenged. Turning my attention to the voice, my eyes bulged when I saw Mason Deveraux III holding a pool cue in one hand, a no-nonsense look on his face.

What had I gotten into now?

Chapter Twenty

"Who the hell are you?" Skeeter tensed, his body still pressed against mine.

"I am someone you *don't* want to mess with. I suggest you step away from the lady unless you want to see enough legal injunctions brought upon your establishment to shut you down before sunrise."

Lifting his hands in surrender, Skeeter backed away from me. "I didn't hurt her. I just wanted to know why she was being so nosy."

"Being nosy seems to be what she does best. I'll be takin' her home now." Mr. Deveraux tossed the cue to the empty table next to him and reached for my arm. "Come on, Rose."

"*Rose?*" Skeeter bellowed. "I knew Jane wasn't your real name!"

Mr. Deveraux cringed at his mistake as he pulled me toward the door.

"My purse!" Teetering on my heels, I made it to my table and retrieved my bag, with Mr. Deveraux still gripping my arm.

"Good Lord, how much did you have to drink?" he muttered.

"I don't rightly know."

Why did I admit that? I hated beer.

"We'll see each other again, *Rose*," Skeeter shouted from the back corner.

"Not if I see you first," I said, then giggled.

Mr. Deveraux pulled me out the front door and onto the sidewalk. "You have an uncanny knack for making enemies."

I tilted my head, staring up into his face. "Things were going pretty well until you got here."

He snorted, a rumbling sound in the back of his throat. Leave it to Mason Deveraux to make a snort sound pretentious. "I saw how well you were doing when he had you trapped against the pool table."

"Yeah, well . . . it was going well up until that part." I opened my purse and started digging.

"What are you doing?"

I glanced up, curling my lip at his stupid question. "I'm lookin' for my keys."

"You're *not* driving anywhere. You're drunk."

Crappy doodles. He was right. I ran a hand through my hair and scanned the parking lot as I searched for another option. Putting my hand on my hip, I glared. "Well, then how am I gonna get home?"

"I'm taking you." He grabbed my arm again and dragged me to a dark sedan in the second row, separated from the other cars.

"Why? What are you doin' here anyway?"

"Neely Kate called me."

What was the deal with Neely Kate calling men to come rescue me?

"She told me that she was supposed to meet you here, but her grandmother had chest pains and she had to rush her to the hospital. She tried your cell phone, and when you didn't answer she called me."

I plopped my bottom against the trunk of his car, crossing my arms over my chest. "No offense, but why would she call you?"

He shrugged with a scowl. "Good question."

I suspected that he knew and wasn't telling me. "Again, no offense, but why did you *come*? You don't even like me."

His grimace softened. "I know I come across as an ass, but I am actually capable of being nice."

I giggled. He'd called himself an ass.

"God, you're as drunk as a skunk. Get in the car."

I put my hands on my hips. "You can't tell me what to do."

"Get in the car or I'll call Detective Taylor and have him arrest you for disorderly conduct."

Mumbling curses under my breath, I started to open the passenger door but stopped short when Mr. Deveraux got there first. "You might be an ass, but you *can* be a gentleman when you want to."

"Be sure to tell my mother, to make up for my earlier offenses." The door shut before I could respond.

After he got in the car and drove toward downtown Henryetta, I realized he was headed toward my house. But then again, most of the population of Henryetta lived this way. "Don't you need my address?"

"Nope."

"Why not? *Are you takin' me to jail?*" Oh Lordy. Had I done something illegal?

"No, Rose. Calm down. You're not going to jail. I got your address from your juror form. If you weren't at the pool hall, I was gonna go by your house to check on you."

"*Why?*"

"I told you. I *am* capable of being a gentleman."

"No. *Really.* Why?"

His mouth twisted as he pondered how to answer me. "Neely Kate was worried about you. And with just cause." He shot me a stern look before facing the road. "Why are you still investigating this case?"

"Who said I—" Oh. Neely Kate.

"So, why are you doing this?" His hands gripped the wheel and his shoulders tensed. "Did you know Bruce Decker and not reveal it in *voir dire*?"

I scrunched up my face in disgust. "Why do you keep assuming I lied during *voir dire*? I didn't."

"Then help me understand. You've turned this whole case upside down since you plowed into me that first day."

"That was an accident and you know it." I watched the mailboxes on the side of the road fly by. My head started spinning and I leaned back in the seat, closing my eyes. "I told you that I knew he was innocent from what I overheard in the men's restroom." Opening my eyes, I turned to face him. "But also because I know how hard it is when everyone, including the police, thinks you're guilty just because all the puzzle pieces fit. Who was going to help Bruce Wayne Decker if I didn't?"

He gave me a quick glance. "Who helped you?"

I shook my head in confusion. "What are you talking about?"

"The police were planning to arrest you for your mother's murder. They were waiting for corroborating evidence to back it up. Even your boyfriend thought you were guilty when he first met you."

"How do you know that?"

"I read your file. Just like I read your juror file to get your address."

"*I have a file?*"

"You were a suspect. Of course you have a file. But answer my question: who helped you clear your name?"

Who helped me? Not Joe. Not until the end, and by then I'd figured out most of the pieces myself—even if most of my figurin' was an accident. Not Violet. She was too wrapped up in her own family. "Me."

"That's right. You. *You* figured out that Daniel Crocker was behind all of it. *You* shot him and apprehended him. *You* stood up for yourself. Why can't you let Bruce Decker stand up for himself? Why do you feel responsible for his justice?"

His questions were making my head hurt. "I don't know."

He pulled into my driveway and shut off the engine. He peered into my face, his gaze intense. "Rose, I don't think you realize the danger you put yourself into tonight. You are not a police detective. Playing Nancy Drew could get you hurt or worse."

I squared my shoulders, indignant at his lecture. "Well maybe if the Henryetta Police Department did their job, I wouldn't have to. Did I do anything illegal?"

He leaned his arm on the steering wheel and exhaled. Goodness, even that sounded stuffy coming from him.

"No, since you're no longer on the jury, what you did wasn't illegal."

"So why did you come get me?"

"I told you, Neely Kate called me and told me that she couldn't—"

"Yeah, I know about that part. Why did *you* come get me?"

"Because I know about Skeeter Malcolm. You don't want to mess with him, Rose."

"Do you think he could have killed Frank Mitchell? Was he Frank's bookie?"

Leaning his head back against the headrest, he groaned. "Will you just forget about Frank Mitchell and Bruce Decker for *one minute* and *listen to me*? Skeeter Malcolm is very protective of his business, and you were there snooping around and askin' questions. Malcolm has no idea why but now, thanks to me, he knows your first name. It won't take much digging on his part to put two and two together and find out who you are. I don't think you should stay home alone tonight. Why don't you go inside and grab some things and I'll drop you off somewhere."

Where in the world was I gonna go? Not Violet's, things were still too tense, and there was no one else to stay with. I was too tipsy to drive to Little Rock. I lifted my chin and tried to look dignified. "Thank you for your kind offer, Mr. Deveraux, but I think I'll be fine here."

"I think we're past formalities at this point, Rose. Call me Mason."

"Well, thank you, *Mason*." His name felt weird rolling off my tongue. "But I just want to go inside my house and go to bed."

"I'm not sure that's safe."

"Why? Because Skeeter Malcolm killed Frank Mitchell and now he's coming to shut me up?"

"*Will you let that go*? Bruce Decker killed Frank Mitchell."

I grabbed the car door handle, so angry I could spit. "You asked me why I was fighting for Bruce Decker when he wasn't fightin' for himself. Well, I'm doin' it because it's the right thing to do. You say you became an assistant district attorney because you want justice. If you were really wanting justice, you'd be figurin' out who the real murderer is." I pushed the door open then turned to face him again. "Thank you for coming to my assistance. And I'm sorry for my rudeness, both tonight and in the past."

He sighed. "I'm sure I deserved every bit of it."

"Nevertheless, I'm sorry."

"Will you *please* consider going somewhere else tonight?"

I paused, my back to him, my feet out the door and on the driveway. "I have nowhere else to go." Why did I admit that?

Damn beer.

He sighed again and pulled his cell phone out of his pocket. "Then I'll see about getting the police to do some drive-bys. Just to be on the safe side."

"The Henryetta Police are gonna be thrilled about that."

"They'll deal with it. Here." He handed me a business card with a phone number written in ink. "My cell phone is on there. Call me if something happens. *Anything.*"

"Why?"

He groaned in frustration. "That again? Because I told that jerk your name. If he comes looking for you, it's partly my fault."

I climbed out of his car. "Thank you and good night Mr— er, Mason."

"Good night, Rose. And *please* be careful."

He stayed in the driveway until I was in the house and the lights were on. I let Muffy out, but encouraged her to hurry up and do her business. I checked my cell phone while I waited for her outside. I had several missed calls, mostly from Neely Kate, one from Violet and three from the number written on Mr. Deveraux's— *Mason's*—business card. Thankfully, no calls from Joe. I wasn't ready to tell him what happened. I knew I'd have to tell him, just not tonight.

I lay in bed, half-terrified someone would break in to get me. I hadn't lived with that fear since I was in the mess with Momma's murder, and I really hadn't missed it. Muffy snuggled against my body. I swore she glared at me, before a stench filled the air.

"Look, I know I haven't been the best pet owner lately . . ."

The stench grew worse. I grabbed a pillow and covered my face. "Muffy! Stop that right now!"

She spun around again, then laid her head on my leg and looked up at me with innocent eyes.

"Oh, no you don't! I know that was you, and I promise to be better, but I need you to be a guard dog tonight."

Nestling into her covers, she turned her backside to me. The smell that reached my face told me what she thought of that.

"Arg! Muffy, if I wake up dead tomorrow morning, I'm not gonna be happy!" Even in my drunken state, I knew what a ridiculous statement that was, but I was too tired to reason it out. Instead, I succumbed to my beer-induced sleepiness.

The next morning I woke up to light streaming in my bedroom window. Despite Mason Deveraux's dire predictions, no one had snuck inside in the middle of the night. However, I had a more pressing issue. When I sat up, a piercing pain shot through my head and my stomach rolled.

One more reason I hated beer.

I ran into the bathroom, barely making it to the toilet. There was no way I could go to work, and I found myself secretly happy to have an excuse to stay home. It was a sad day when you were thankful for a hangover, proving it was a good thing that I only had eight more days left at the DMV.

It was no surprise Suzanne gave me an earful when I called her. "Don't you bother coming back, Rose Gardner!"

My pounding head couldn't take the shrieking in my ear. "Thanks, Suzanne. I won't." I hung up, feeling wicked. Not only had I just quit, but I'd hung up on my boss too.

Momma had been right. Beer really was the fount of wickedness.

By mid-morning, I was feeling a bit back to normal and I needed to figure out what to do with myself for the rest of the day. Looking into Bruce Decker's case wasn't an option. Skeeter Malcolm wasn't someone to mess around with. And in the light of day, sober except for my headache, I realized how naïve I'd been the night before.

I couldn't just waltz in and grill shady characters. Shady characters tended to be suspicious by nature, and simply asking questions put me in danger. And the fact was, if I couldn't ask questions, I had no other means to get answers. I was at a dead end. But the most disturbing realization of all was that Mason Deveraux had saved me from a compromising situation. Joe would have a fit if he knew. No, *when* he knew. I had to tell him, as difficult as it was going to be.

Sitting on my sofa, flipping through over a hundred channels and finding nothing to watch, I surprised myself by realizing Mason Deveraux was right. I had no business being in the middle of this mess. I needed to leave the investigating to trained professionals. I'd saved my own hide when I was suspected of murder. Bruce Wayne Decker needed to take care of his own exonerating. All I'd done was stir up trouble and maybe even put myself in danger.

I cast a glance toward my kitchen door. I told myself there was no shame in being scared. Only fools weren't scared when in harm's way, but it still seemed odd. This was Henryetta, Arkansas for heavens' sake. How dangerous could it be?

Daniel Crocker's image popped into my head.

I jumped off the sofa and hurried to my room to get dressed. Suddenly, packing boxes for my move to Little Rock sounded like a great plan. But I didn't have any boxes. And I also didn't have a car since I'd left the Nova at the pool hall. Groaning, I realized I'd either have to get a cab to take me to get my car or ask Violet. Since I didn't feel like getting grilled and lectured, I called a cab.

Taxis weren't a common occurrence in our neighborhood so when one pulled in front of my house an hour later, several faces peered out windows. The faces belonged to members of the Neighborhood Watch, also known as the Busybody Club. Since Miss Mildred was the most diligent of them all, she was president by default. I waved to her when I climbed in the cab's backseat, trying not to gag from the thick smell of cigarette smoke.

The cab driver didn't seem surprised when I told him where to go, even though I was secretly cringing. I hoped to high heaven I didn't run into Skeeter again. I really needed to think about carrying a weapon, but I was too afraid of guns and my purse was too small for my rolling pin.

But I'd worried for nothing. The parking lot was nearly empty, and no one hung around outside when I paid the taxi driver and got into my car. The memory of last night seemed like a bad dream until I noticed a piece of paper stuck under my windshield wiper.

My pulse pounded in my head as I climbed out and grabbed the slip, then jumped back into my car and locked the door. I carefully opened the paper as though the contents were going to jump out and bite me. I found a short message scrawled in block letters.

I don't like people messing in my business.

Moving to Little Rock seemed like the best idea since the Earl of Sandwich came up with his ingenious discovery. But moving meant packing.

I needed boxes.

I decided the hardware store was the best place to stop. Wandering the aisles proved fruitless—they must have been reorganized since the last time I'd bought packing supplies. Since I was close to the paint department, I decided to ask at the counter. Anne stood next to the paint machine, staring off into the distance. A smile brightened her face when she saw me and walked over.

"Hey, I remember you. How'd your paintin' project go? You back for more?"

"Oh! It went great. My boyfriend ended up helping and I was done in no time." I waved my hand. "This time I'm lookin' for boxes. Moving boxes. They aren't where I found them last time."

"Take a look-see over by the lawn and garden aisle. I think the new manager moved 'em over there."

"Thanks, Anne."

She grinned when I said her name.

I started walking away when she hollered after me, "That guy was back this weekend."

My breath caught in my chest, and I slowly spun around to face her. "The looky-loo guy?"

Pinching her lips together in a grimace, she nodded. "Yep."

I took several steps closer. What was I doing? I was no longer interested in the Bruce Wayne Decker case. I reminded myself that Mason Deveraux was right. Bruce needed to stand up for himself. *Turn around and walk away.* Instead, I moved next to the counter, leaning close to Anne. "What was he doin'?"

"He was snoopin' around the back."

"Why?"

"Good question. The plumbing manger caught him back there and asked him what he was doin', but the guy ran off before he answered."

"Was he in his thirties? Big muscles and with tattoos on his arms?"

She shook her head, confused. "No, he's a short bald guy."

"What?" That didn't match the description of any of the men I saw last night.

"Yeah, dress pants and shirt. Tie. Professional guy. Kind of mousy."

I sagged into the counter. That wasn't Skeeter or his pals at all.

"And it's the same guy who kept showing up after the murder?"

"Yep, one and the same."

That didn't make sense. If it wasn't Skeeter, who was he? It had to be the guy who wanted to buy Frank Mitchell's house. And if Skeeter wasn't the murderer, then I wasn't in the danger that Mason Deveraux thought I was.

Stop thinking about it, Rose. You've let this go. You're not working on this anymore.

But I couldn't let it go. It was information that could possibly prove Bruce Wayne Decker's innocence. The only problem was I didn't know what to do with it. Mason Deveraux wouldn't listen. Loading boxes and packing tape into my cart, I realized there was one other person I could talk to. I just wasn't sure how receptive he'd be. But I'd already made a fool of myself all over town. What was one more place?

It was time to talk to the accused himself. I needed to talk to Bruce Wayne Decker.

Chapter Twenty-One

Getting in to see Bruce Wayne Decker turned out to be harder than I thought. I found the number for William Yates's office and told the secretary I had information that might help Bruce Decker's case. When I told her my name, a long pause resulted before she told me she'd pass my message along.

I took that as legalese for "he'll call when the next ice age covers Henryetta with a glacier."

I was gonna have to take matters into my own hands.

Judge McClary usually broke for lunch right around noon and it was already eleven-forty-five when I found a parking space two blocks from the courthouse. I camped on a bench outside the courtroom and waited for Mr. Yates. Five minutes later, the doors opened and the occupants of the courtroom spilled out. As the crowd thinned, Mason Deveraux emerged, talking to his assistant. He had nearly turned the corner when he caught a glimpse of me.

He stopped and leaned over to the man next to him, who nodded and continued down the hall. Mr. Deveraux approached, a grim look on his face.

William Yates still hadn't come out, and I didn't want to miss him.

"Rose, is everything all right?"

I stood, clasping my hands in my nervousness. "Yeah, everything is fine."

"You look upset. What are you doing here?"

"I'm waiting for someone." I bit my lip.

"I see." He shifted his weight and glanced down the hall then back at me. "The police drove by your house multiple times last night. They didn't report anything suspicious. Did you have any trouble?"

"No, everything was fine." He blocked my view of the courtroom doors and I shifted to the side. "Oh, yeah. I forgot something." I dug into my purse and pulled out the note. "I found this on my car when I picked it up this morning."

When he read it, his body stiffened and he looked into my face. "This is a threat, Rose."

I didn't have time to be distracted by Mason right now. "What? No. It just says he doesn't like people messin' in his business."

He crossed his arms across his chest. "You can't be serious. You honestly didn't think this meant anything?"

William Yates pushed through the double court doors, a frown puckering his cheeks.

"Well, of course it did. It meant he doesn't like people messin' in his business, and I don't intend to. Especially since I know he didn't kill Mr. Mitchell."

"Finally. That's the first sensible thing I've heard you say since I met you."

"A bald guy killed Mr. Mitchell and Skeeter Malcolm definitely isn't bald." I pushed past him. "Now if you'll excuse me, I have to talk to Mr. Yates."

"Rose!" Mr. Deveraux shouted as I hurried after the defense attorney. "Rose!" He grabbed my arm and pulled me to a halt.

"He's gettin' away!"

I squirmed, and he gripped both of my arms. "If you will stop and listen to me, I'll make sure you get a personal meeting with him. That's what you want, right?"

I huffed in frustration. "Well, yeah . . . and Bruce Wayne Decker too."

He rolled his eyes and shook his head. "You have to take this threat seriously. I want to know what you're planning to do about it."

I was hot and my headache made me cranky. I jerked my arms free from his grasp. "I don't know, Mr. Deveraux. There's nothing *to* do."

"Why won't you go stay with your sister?"

I put my hand on my hip, my temper flaring. "How do you know I have a sister?"

"Your file."

He stood there so arrogant, discussing my life as though it was merely the contents of a file. But then again, for him it was.

"How dare you!"

His eyes widened and he stiffened. "Excuse me?"

"*How dare you*? You read about my life, the private things *in my life*, like the fact I have a sister, or throwin' in my face that Joe didn't trust me when he met me. What gives you the right to snoop into my business and toss it around like it means *nothing*?"

His face reddened. "That is not what I intended, Rose. I was merely trying to find out—"

"Why didn't you just ask me?"

"*What*?"

"If you have a question about my personal life, ask me. Stop reading about me in a file. It's violating!"

Taking a deep breath, he turned to the side and rubbed his chin. After staring at the wall for several moments, he exhaled and dropped his hand to his side. "You're right. I've been very crass about the facts of your personal life. I apologize. But I swear I didn't mean to violate your privacy. The first time I read your file was when I was convincing Judge McClary to let you out of lockup. I promise you that I did it with the best of intentions."

I started to protest, but he held up his hand.

"Yes, I know. You think I should have come back to the county jail and asked you, but time was running out. Judge McClary only gave us until five o'clock to convince him to let you go. If we didn't get the paperwork signed by five then you would have spent the weekend in jail."

I groaned, now feeling like the most ungrateful person alive.

"And then last night, I was working late in my office when Neely Kate called. So I looked up your file, which was still on my desk. Neely Kate had given me your phone number, but I wanted your address to run by your house."

I sat down on the bench, suddenly weary. When would I stop jumping to conclusions?

Mason perched beside me, leaning forward with his elbows on his legs. He clasped his hands in front of him. "I had no intention—"

I fought back the tears burning my eyes. "Stop. I shouldn't have assumed the worst of you. You've helped me twice now and what have *I* done? I've been rude and ungrateful. I'm sorry."

He leaned back, pressing into the wall. "We sure do seem to bring out the worst in each other."

I wasn't sure what to say to that, but it seemed to be the truth. We sat in silence for several seconds before he cleared his throat. "I don't have enough evidence to charge Skeeter Malcolm with anything at this point, so my hands are tied. But you have to take this threat seriously, Rose. You have to take some type of precautions."

I wiped a tear from my cheek. "Okay. I will."

"What are you going to do?"

"Um . . . Joe's comin' down from Little Rock tomorrow night. Maybe I can go back with him on Thursday morning."

He nodded. "Good. That's good. What about tonight?"

"I'm supposed to go to a Henryetta Garden Club meeting tonight, so I'll be out."

"You shouldn't stay at your house overnight."

"What do you think Skeeter's gonna do?"

"I don't know. Maybe nothing. Maybe . . . something."

"Do you think he's capable of murderin' someone?"

He turned his head so that his gaze held mine. "Yes. I do."

"Oh."

"Now you see my concern?"

"Yeah." I looked down at my lap. "Do you think he's killed people who owe him money?" I didn't think Skeeter had done it, but it didn't hurt to ask since he seemed to be leveling with me.

He released an exasperated sigh. "Rose," he growled. "Let it go."

"It's a yes or no question. If you answer, I'll spend the night at my sister's."

He stood, and I was sure he wasn't going to respond. He tugged at his tie. "You promise me that you won't spend the night at your house?"

I made an X over my chest. "Cross my heart and hope to die."

His face paled. "Wrong choice of idioms at the moment." He shifted his weight and his eyes hardened. "I'm scared to give you my honest opinion. I'm worried what you'll do with the information."

"I promise not to tell anyone."

"That's not what I meant." He paused. "You seem so head-strong about proving Bruce Wayne Decker innocent. I hate to throw fuel onto your burning fire for justice."

"So the answer is yes?"

"Yes." He looked sorry the moment the word left his mouth. "*Stay away from Malcolm*. Got it?"

"Yes."

"I want your word, Rose."

"I promise. And thank you."

"Now if you'll excuse me, I'm about to eat humble pie."

"What does that mean?"

One side of his mouth lifted into a wry grin. "I made you a promise, Ms. Gardner. I told you that I'd get you a meeting with William Yates, although I can't guarantee his client will be present. I'm Mr. Yates's least favorite person in the world so this is going to take some doing. But I'm a man of my word."

It was funny how my opinion of him had changed in only a few days. "I believe that you are, Mr. Deveraux. Thank you."

"Stick around the courthouse. I'm sure this meeting will occur during the lunch break. I'll call you when I know something."

He disappeared around the corner and I collapsed on the bench. Never in a million years would I have believed Mason Deveraux would help me. Even if it was obviously against his better judgment.

I had to admit I was surprised that Mason was so concerned that Skeeter would try to hurt me. Sure, I'd asked some questions, but the more I thought about it, I wasn't any type of threat. Skeeter was just trying to scare me with the note. Especially if Skeeter hadn't murdered Frank Mitchell. I didn't even know if Skeeter was Mr. Mitchell's bookie, although I suspected he was. But my instinct told me the bald guy hanging around the hardware store was the real murderer, and it was obvious he wasn't Skeeter. Why had the bald guy come back?

Ten minutes later my phone rang and caller ID showed Mason Deveraux's number. "He'll meet you at twelve-forty-five in room 216. Don't be late."

"Thank you."

"This wasn't easy to arrange so I hope you get what you need out of it."

"Thanks."

At 12:44, I stood outside of room 216. I half-expected Mason Deveraux to show up and escort me in, but was thankful for his absence. What I wasn't prepared for was the sheriff's deputy stationed outside the door. What did Mr. Yates think I was capable of doing?

I reached up to knock, but the deputy pushed the door open.

Sitting at the table was William Yates. And next to him sat Bruce Wayne Decker.

Once I crossed the threshold, the door closed behind me.

Mr. Yates's left hand tapped the table with an ink pen. "I hope this isn't a waste of our time, Ms. Gardner."

"I'll try my best to make sure it's not."

"Have a seat." He motioned to the chair across from him, then scribbled a note on the legal pad.

Pulling out my seat, I couldn't help staring at Bruce. He seemed smaller close up. More fragile, which struck me as ridiculous. Joe was right. Bruce was a criminal. Yet there was a difference between Bruce and Daniel Crocker, and Skeeter Malcolm. Crocker and Malcolm were hardened men who thought nothing of disposing of people in their own way. I could see it in their eyes. But Bruce was soft and made me think of a dried-up autumn leaf, tossed around in the wind and easily crushed.

"Do you plan to stare at my client all day, Ms. Gardner, or do you actually have something to share with us?"

"Oh, sorry." I slid onto the chair and placed my hands on the table. I had no idea where to start. Maybe I should have spent more time going over my speech and less time obsessing over my personal life. I looked into Bruce's face. "First of all, I know you are innocent."

Relief filled his eyes, but Mr. Yates snapped me back to reality. "And exactly *how* do you know this?"

"Um . . . I overheard the real killer in the bathroom."

Mr. Yates tensed then rolled his eyes. "And what did he say? What did he look like? How did you hear this in the bathroom? Did you see Jesus in your toast this morning too?"

I pursed my lips in disapproval. "There's no need to be snippy, Mr. Yates. In case you hadn't noticed, I went to jail tryin' to get evidence to prove Mr. Decker is innocent."

"That doesn't mean a thing. In today's media hungry, five-minutes-worth-of-fame craze, people do stupid things to get attention. Who's to say you didn't get used to the attention with your own mother's murder? Maybe you miss the spotlight, so now you're trying to recapture it with this cockamamie story."

I squinted in disbelief. "Is that really what you think I'm doin'? Tryin' to get my five minutes of fame?"

Mr. Yates pushed back his chair, the legs screeching across the floor. "I've heard enough. I've done my end of the bargain. We're done here."

Bruce looked down at his hands, which were folded neatly on the table. "No."

Mr. Yates's eyebrows rose. "What?"

Bruce looked up and held my gaze. "No. I want to hear what she has to say."

Shaking his head, Mr. Yates patted Bruce's arm. "I understand your desperation—"

I cleared my throat. "Why didn't you point out that Bruce is right-handed?"

"What in tarnation does that have to do with anything?"

"Mr. Mitchell's head wound was on the right side."

"*So what?*"

"The murderer is left-handed."

He paused, staring at me with a hard look. The overhead lights reflected off the top of his nearly bald head. "And how do you know this?"

I couldn't tell him about my vision "I just do."

"You just do." Disgust drenched his words and he resumed tapping the table with his pen in a steady beat. "My client is curious, so indulge us with what else you *just know*."

"I know the pin belonged to the murderer and he's worried it will be tied back to him. But he thinks he's goin' to get away with it."

Bruce's mouth hung open as he took in my words. Mr. Yates looked bored.

"Before Frank Mitchell's death, someone had been trying to buy his house, but Mr. Mitchell refused to sell. Whoever wanted it was pushing Frank hard. Hard enough to make him so upset that he got drunk and stumbled around in his backyard a few days before he was murdered. Then a couple of months after he died, his son sold the house to an investment company in Louisiana. But it recently sold again to a corporation that is putting in a superstore. They bought his house to make a parking lot. I also know that Frank owed a bookie a lot of money. But I don't think the bookie killed him."

Mr. Yates's eyes bulged. "Why not?"

"After the murder, a man kept showing up at the hardware store, getting all nosy about the murder scene. Finally, one of the employees asked him why he kept showing up and buying weird things and he stopped coming in. But this weekend, he came back and he was trying to get to the storage room, where the murder took place."

Mr. Yates's face paled. I guessed I knew more than he thought I did.

I turned to Bruce. "The employees say he's bald and mousy and usually wears nice clothes, like he's a businessman. Do you know anyone like that?"

Bruce chewed on his thumbnail and shook his head. "No."

"Can you tell me what happened the night you were in the hardware store?"

Mr. Yates leaned forward, glaring at me. "Do not answer her. My client is not taking the witness stand."

"He's tellin' me, not the witness stand. I'm tryin' to help him."

Bruce looked down at the table, studying a groove in the wood.

Hunching down, I tried to make eye contact. "Bruce, I saw David last week. At the grocery store, after I got out of jail, which I got thrown into for tryin' to help you. David told me that you heard Frank Mitchell arguing with his murderer. Is that true?"

He nodded, then moved on to a hangnail on his index finger.

"David said you heard Frank say he was never gonna sell and the other guy said he was gonna get what was owed to him."

He gave three sharp nods of his head. Yes.

"Did you hear anything else? See anything? Anything at all?"

"No."

Mr. Yates banged his hand on the table and leaned forward, the light reflecting off the top of his bare head. "Bruce, I am warnin' you. Do not talk to this woman. She can walk out of here and use anything you say against you."

Bruce cringed, curling up his shoulders and trying to hide is face.

I softened my voice. "Bruce, I promise you that I only want to help you. I know you took the murder weapon because you thought they might pin the murder on you. You wanted to get rid of the crowbar, but David wanted to keep it as insurance."

"David Moore needs to keep his thoughts to himself." Mr. Yates growled through clenched teeth.

"Bruce, will you please tell me what happened?"

He took a deep breath and stretched his hand out across the table. "I decided to rob the hardware store. I'd just lost my job and my parents had kicked me out." With a grimace, he rubbed his eyes. "I didn't want to do it, but my rent was due . . ." I was surprised how soft and timid his voice was. How could anyone think him capable of murder?

"So what happened when you got there?"

"I expected that I was gonna have to break in, but the back door was standin' open, so I slipped through. As I walked along the back wall to the office, I heard yellin'. So I got closer and hid behind some shelves. Two guys were fightin' and shoutin' at one another. Frank, he kept yelling 'I'm never gonna sell, you rat bastard.' And 'crawl back into the hole you crawled out of.' Things like that." Bruce's eyes lit up. "Oh! And he called the guy *cue ball*."

"Then what happened?"

"The other guy, he kept shoutin' 'I'm gonna get what's owed to me' and 'I'm gonna get what I deserve' which seemed really weird. Finally, he picked up a crowbar and whacked Frank on top of the head."

"And then he went into the office?"

"Yeah, he was in there for several minutes before he came out and ran out the back door."

"Did you get a look at the guy? Can you tell me about him?"

"No, he was wearing black clothes and a black stocking cap."

"Even though it was April?"

Bruce shrugged.

"Was he tall? Short? Fat? Skinny?"

Rubbing his forehead, Bruce closed his eyes. "I think he was as tall as Frank. Not skinny, but not fat either."

"Just average weight?"

He shrugged. "Yeah."

I tuned my attention to Mr. Yates. "How tall was Frank Mitchell?"

"How should I know?"

"Won't it be in his file or something?"

"He wasn't very tall." Bruce cut in.

I'd forgotten that Bruce grew up across the street from the victim. "How tall do you think he was?"

He shrugged again. "I dunno. Maybe five-six. Five-seven."

"And you didn't see the killer's face or hair?"

"No, he had on that hat and it was too dark to see his face."

"So after the man left, you grabbed the crowbar and left too?"

Bruce looked down, chewing on his pinkie fingernail. "There's something else I never told anyone."

Mr. Yates sat up straighter. "Why not?"

"Because it freaked me out and I tried to ignore it."

"What happened?" I whispered.

His eyes looked wild and crazy. "After the other guy left, I walked over to Frank and his eyes were closed."

That didn't make sense. "But the pictures of him at the scene showed his eyes were open." I'd never forget that blank stare.

"Yeah, they were in the picture."

"But . . . how . . . ?"

"After I walked over, his eyes popped open. Frank was still alive when I got to him."

"And you're just now telling me?" Mr. Yates bellowed.

Bruce shook his head, squeezing his eyes shut. "I was scared. And ashamed."

"Why didn't you call 911?" I asked, horrified.

"Because I wasn't thinkin' straight." He looked up, his eyes filled with unshed tears. "He stopped breathing a little bit after I got to him. There was so much blood." He rubbed his hands, as though trying to scrub it off.

"Did he say anything?"

He swallowed and nodded his head multiple times. "Yeah, he kept sayin' *Duane* over and over."

"Duane?"

"Yeah."

"Do you know anyone named Duane?"

Biting his lip, he shook his head. "No."

I glanced at Mr. Yates. "Can we tell the police this?"

He looked down his scrunched-up nose at me. "What exactly will we tell them and what do you expect them to do about it? They have their suspect and they're damn near close to their conviction. There's nothing to tell."

Bruce's head jerked up in alarm.

"But . . ."

"Thank you for your persistence, but let it go."

"But . . ." He was really going to ignore this?

Mr. Yates stood, his face hardening with his obvious dislike of me. "We are due back in court so that will be all, Ms. Gardner. Tell Mr. Deveraux I look forward to the use of his fifty-yard-line tickets to the Arkansas-LSU football game this October."

"What?"

"That's what he offered to set this up. I hope it was worth it. Most people would gladly give up their firstborn for those tickets."

Mr. Yates pulled Bruce out his chair and toward the door in the back of the room. Bruce glanced over his shoulder, fear in his eyes.

I stumbled from the room and into the hall, trying to absorb everything I'd learned.

One, Mr. Yates didn't want my help.

Two, Mr. Decker wanted my help but was afraid of Mr. Yates.

Three, I didn't know much about football, but according to William Yates, Mason Deveraux just gave him coveted tickets as a favor to me.

Why on earth would he do that?

Chapter Twenty-Two

I knocked on Mason's office door, wondering if he'd even be there. Bruce Decker and Mr. Yates were headed back to court, and I was sure that Mason would be too.

But he opened the door, a grim smile on his face, walking past me and calling over his shoulder, "How'd your meetin' go?"

I hurried to catch up, falling in step beside him. "I'm not sure. I'm still tryin' to figure that out."

"That bad, huh?" He stopped and pushed the elevator button.

I ignored his question. "Why'd you give him your football tickets?"

His face paled and he shifted his weight. "How'd you find that out?"

"Mr. Yates."

Mason clenched his jaw. "That damn son of a bitch." Then he glanced down at me, his eyes widening in embarrassment. He sighed and rubbed his forehead. "Excuse my bad manners. *Again.* That was unconscionable."

"I dislike him too."

His hand dropped and he smirked. "Well, he doesn't like either one of us, so it's one big love fest."

"You still didn't answer my question."

The elevator door opened and I followed him in.

He pushed the number three. "That's hard to explain."

"Lucky for you this is the slowest elevator in the world."

He turned to me and grinned, the grin that lost his stuffy-pants attitude. He looked approachable like this. "I guess the best answer is there's lots of reasons. I've been inconceivably rude to you. And I gave Skeeter Malcolm your name, putting you in danger. While you shouldn't have been there in the first place," he narrowed his eyes, "at least you were smart enough to use an alias and I blew it. And finally," he paused, watching me for a minute. "You have made this boring, backward town more tolerable with your antics. It only seemed fair and reasonable to give you something in return."

I put both hands on my hips. *My antics?* Who did Mason Van de Camp Deveraux III think he was? Indignation and anger prickled inside me. "Let me get this straight. You're sayin' that you helped me because I'm entertaining? Like a show?"

His eyes sank closed for a second, then opened. "That's not what I meant."

"And is that why you came last night instead of sendin' someone else? *Because I'm entertaining?*"

The elevator doors opened and his face tightened in indecision. "I swear to you, that's not what I meant and that's not why I came instead of sending someone else."

I took several deep breaths, trying to calm my temper.

"Look Rose, I have to go to court, but I don't want you thinking that I see you as a circus sideshow."

"*You see me as a circus sideshow?*"

People in the hall stared into the elevator car. The doors started to close and Mason pushed the door open button. "No. I'm trying to tell you that I don't, although I'm doin' a very poor job of it. Let me explain it later, okay?"

Tears burned my eyes. "Just go to court, Mr. Deveraux. Tell me how much the football tickets were and I'll reimburse you."

He walked out of the elevator, anger and confusion in his eyes. "No. I don't expect you to reimburse me." Taking two steps backward, he gave me a pleading look. "I have to go."

"I'm not stoppin' you."

"I don't want to leave you upset and thinking the worst of me."

Hurt and anger had curled inside me like a snake and attacked. "Don't worry, Mr. Deveraux. I thought badly of you long before I discovered this."

Pain filled his eyes before his usual disdain replaced it. "Then I guess there's nothing left to say."

He walked into the courtroom as the elevator doors closed. I struggled to keep from crying. What was wrong with me? Why was I so hateful to that man? I was torn between being grateful for his help and horrified that *my antics* entertained him. The hurt on his face at my parting words stabbed my conscience. I needed to talk to someone.

Neely Kate.

Her office was on the first floor and she knew everything about everything when it came to people. She'd know what to do, although I suspected there wasn't anything *to* do. I just needed to get over my pain and humiliation.

When I entered the personal property tax office, I found her at a desk behind the counter. She looked up and saw my face, her smile falling. "Rose?" She jumped out of her seat and came around the counter, pulling me into a hug. "What on earth happened?"

"I don't know exactly. I'm so confused."

Neely Kate lifted her chin to peer around the corner. "I'm takin' a break, Jimmy."

"Of course you are." A sarcastic male voice echoed from the back.

Putting her arm around my shoulder, she pushed me out the door. "Have you had lunch yet?"

"No."

She steered me toward the courthouse exit. "First things first. You need food. Let's go to Merilee's."

"But haven't you already been to lunch?"

She waved her hand in dismissal. "Don't worry about it. Jimmy'll grumble, but he won't do anything. He's been distracted over all the pension mess and I've been getting away with murder."

I winced at her choice of words, but she didn't notice.

Once we were seated in the café, Neely Kate started her inquisition. "Is this about Joe?"

Shaking my head, I blew my nose. "No."

Her eyes flew open. "Oh my stars and garters! Is this about last night? I'm so sorry I didn't show up, but my grandma got chest pains and made me rush her to the hospital."

I'd completely forgotten about her grandmother. Some friend I was. "Is she okay?"

She looked confused. "What?" she waved her hand. "Oh, yeah. It was nothing. Heartburn. It doesn't matter how many times we tell her not to eat the ten-piece buffalo hot wings special at Big Bill's Barbeque, she still does it. Every time." She leaned over the table. "Did Mr. Deveraux show up?"

"Yes, but I cannot believe you called *him*, of all people. And until just a few minutes ago, I couldn't believe he actually came."

"What happened a few minutes ago?"

I sniffed. "He called me entertaining."

She squinted in confusion. "What's wrong with that?"

"That's not what he said exactly. But that was his point. To be more exact, I think he said that my *antics* had made his stay in this boring town more tolerable."

Her face was expressionless as she waited for me to continue.

"He insulted our town."

"Who doesn't?"

"He insulted *me*."

She looked confused again. "Which part insulted you? I missed it. Rose, I think that was his stuffy way of saying he likes you."

"*What*? No."

She stared at the wall, deep in thought. "Who knew that Mr. Crabbypants had some humanity deep down?"

"Why did you call *him* to come check on me last night?"

Turning back to me, she shrugged. "Because he had enough guilt in him from your jail experience that I knew he'd help you. Besides, would you rather I call him or Officer Ernie?"

"Neither," I grumbled.

The waitress brought our food and I attacked my hamburger, realizing I hadn't eaten since the night before.

"Stop being such a baby."

I shot her a glare since I couldn't protest with a mouth full of food.

"Think about it. Mason Deveraux is new to town. A town he doesn't want to be in. He's a mean ol' cuss, even if he isn't old.

He's stuffy. He's arrogant. And he's got everyone in town scared of him."

There was no arguing with that.

"Then you run right into him and tell him off. And you keep doin' things to throw him off his carefully polished pedestal. For once, someone's not kowtowing to him and is meetin' him toe-to-toe instead."

I wasn't sure I liked where this was headed "What are you sayin'?"

"I'm sayin' that Mason Deveraux is lonely, clearly by his own doin', but lonely nevertheless. He doesn't have any friends in this town. Maybe he wants to be your friend."

"Me?"

"Sure. Why *not* you?"

I shook my head. "I don't know . . ."

She shrugged and poked at her salad. "Maybe I'm wrong, but that rarely happens." She lifted her gaze with a wink.

I couldn't help laughing. I suspected she was right about that part.

"Besides, he seemed concerned about you when I called him last night. What happened when he showed up?"

I filled her in on all the details of the evening.

A faraway look filled her eyes. "Mason Van De Camp Deveraux III stood up to Skeeter Malcolm. I would have liked to have seen that."

"You know about Skeeter Malcolm?"

She snorted. "Who doesn't?"

Me. Obviously. "And you didn't think it was a bad idea to go there last night?"

"Well, no. There's nothing wrong with shooting pool. But when I couldn't go, I had a feelin' you'd go and do something crazy and make Skeeter suspicious."

Why did everyone always expect me to do something crazy? "I don't think Skeeter killed Frank Mitchell."

"Why not?"

I told her what I'd learned from Anne in the paint department.

"That does sound suspicious."

"She says he's a short, bald man. But Skeeter and the guys he hung out with aren't short or bald. Did you find out anything else about that investment company?"

"No . . ."

"Maybe Frank's murder didn't have anything to do with him owin' money. Maybe it was the person who wanted his house. What if they're two separate things? Did you know there's a super-store going in at the edge of Forest Ridge neighborhood?"

"Now that you mention it, Jimmy said something about it. Some of his rental properties in that neighborhood got bought up." She watched me for a minute, her brow furrowing. "Rose, how did you know one of my flower girls was gonna get chicken pox?"

I nearly choked on my food. "Uh . . . I heard it was going around."

"Well, Misty broke out all over in spots this morning." Neely Kate bit her lip and slowly shook her head. "How do you know Bruce Decker is innocent?"

My heart thumped wildly. "I told you already. I just know." My chest tightened and I had a hard time getting out the words.

Her gaze pinned me down. "You have the sight."

Panic filled every cell of my body. "What are you talkin' about?"

"You know things like I know things." She tilted her head, examining me. "I can see your aura. It's a bright blue. You have the sight."

Auras were new. I wondered when she'd learned to read those. I laughed. "That's the silliest thing I ever heard."

She gave me the closest thing to a glare Neely Kate was probably capable of. Her eyebrows rose. "Is it?"

I looked down at my food while my brain scrambled to find the best way to handle this. I would give anything to share the knowledge of my curse with her, but what if she wouldn't accept me? I'd had a friend once back in middle school who I'd thought I could trust. We both agreed to share our biggest secret, but when I told her mine, and she realized it was true, horror and fear filled her eyes. She never spoke to me again. Neely Kate claimed to be open to the mysterious and the mystical, but what if she reacted the same way? What if I lost my only friend? "So . . . what if I did have the sight?" I lifted my chin enough to catch her gaze. "What would you think?"

She remained perfectly still for several seconds. "So you *do* have it?"

I blinked. I didn't see any way out of this. "Yes."

"I *knew* it!" Neely Kate shrieked and she clapped her hands. "I can't believe it! You have the gift!"

My eyes widened in horror. "Neely Kate! You can't tell anyone!"

She settled down and narrowed her eyes in confusion. "Why not?"

"Because people think I'm a big enough freak without knowing this."

Scoffing, she waved her hand. "They're just jealous."

I was pretty sure that wasn't it. "*Please*, Neely Kate."

Her hand covered mine and she smiled. "Calm yourself. If you don't want me to tell anyone, I won't, but I don't see why not. How strong is your gift?"

The food in my stomach became a ten-pound weight. "I don't actually consider it a gift. More like a curse."

Her eyes widened. "Why on *earth* would you think that?"

"Because I have no control over them—"

"Most clairvoyants don't."

"And whatever I see just pops right out of my mouth."

"Huh." She titled her head. "Okay, that's different."

"People think I'm nosy and gossipy because I know things I shouldn't."

She chuckled. "I know lots of things I shouldn't, and look at me."

True, but Neely Kate was made of sturdier stuff than I was.

Could I tell her everything? I'd come this far. "My momma thought I was demon-possessed."

Neely Kate paused and tilted her head. "You're kidding me, right?"

I shook my head.

"Rose, I'm so sorry."

I shrugged. It was in the past, even if the pain jumped out from time to time, nipping at my slowly building confidence.

"You most certainly are not demon-possessed. You're one of the sweetest people I know. I'm so glad we're friends."

I glanced up at her in disbelief.

"I need to ask you something serious." A stern look crossed her face.

My stomach twisted with dread. "Okay."

"So is my wedding going to be destroyed by my fiancé's family?"

I squinted in confusion. "How would I know?"

"With your gift."

"I just told you I couldn't control them."

"You can't make yourself see things unless it just pops into your head?"

"Well . . ." Joe had once convinced me to force a vision, and when I tried I saw his murder. There was no way I was gonna do that again.

She saw my hesitation. "You *can* make it happen."

"Only once and it was awful. I saw Joe die."

"But Joe's still alive. That couldn't have been a vision."

"Not everything I see happens. Sometimes things are different. I saw myself dead on Momma's sofa, but it ended up her, instead. I saw Joe dead, but I stopped it from happenin'."

She leaned over the table, her eyes wild with excitement. "All the more reason for you to tell me about my wedding. If something bad's gonna happen, I want to be able to put a stop to it."

"Neely Kate, I don't know. I've only tried it one time. It might not even work."

Her mouth lifted into a smug smile. "Well, you'll never know if you don't try, right? Consider it practice. You just never know when it might come in handy."

Joe had pretty much suggested the same thing, but I didn't see how that was possible. Neely Kate sat across from me, giving me puppy-dog eyes and pouting. How could I say no to that? I sighed, closing my eyes. "All right . . ."

She grabbed both my hands in hers and pulled them toward her. "Thank you, thank you! You have no idea how much this means to me!"

I hoped she felt that way after I had a vision. *If* I had a vision. I looked around the café to see if anyone was watching. The customers all seemed intent on their own conversations. "Okay, let me hold your hand and I'll concentrate on you and the wedding and see if something happens. That's what I did with Joe, only I thought of him and Daniel Crocker."

Nodding, she placed our linked hands on the table. "Okay."

My eyes sank closed and I pictured Neely Kate and thought about her wedding and her bridesmaid dresses. Tension knotted my shoulders and just when I thought it wasn't going to work, I felt the familiar tingle.

I walked down the aisle, a puffy white dress swirling around my legs. A handsome man stood at the altar, wearing a black tuxedo. His mouth lifted into a wide smile. A multitude of groomsmen and bridesmaids crowded on the sides, too many to count, but I spotted Neely Kate's orange cousin right off.

Candelabras covered the back of the altar and lined the side aisles, casting a beautiful candlelit glow. Then the older man next to me placed my hand into the groom's and I stepped up onto the altar next to him, my heart bursting with happiness.

"You're goin' to have a beautiful wedding." I forced the words past a lump in my throat, tears stinging my eyes.

Neely Kate's grip tightened, her eyes wild with worry. "Then why are you about to cry?"

"Oh, Neely Kate. It was just so beautiful." A tear slid down my cheek. "Your fiancé is such a handsome man. And I saw The Skittle, but everything else was so beautiful that I hardly noticed her. And you were so *happy*." I choked on the last word, still overwhelmed with feeling. I'd never experienced emotions before in a vision. Did I feel her happiness because it was so strong or because I'd forced the vision?

"Really?" Neely Kate bit the side of her lower lip.

"I promise."

She pulled me into a hug. "Thank you, Rose! Thank you so much!"

I smiled. That hadn't turned out so bad. I'd made a vision happen and it hadn't been something awful. And Neely Kate was clearly relieved. I had done that for her, and pride and happiness washed over me. I felt needed. "How many people are in your wedding, anyway?"

Neely Kate looked up at the ceiling and ticked off her fingers. "There's a maid of honor, five bridesmaids, two junior bridesmaids, three flower girls, one best man, seven groomsmen, two ring bearers and four ushers."

"I don't even think I'll have that many guests at my wedding."

She snorted with a laugh. "Nah. I bet Joe would invite a lot of people."

Knowing who Joe's family was, Neely Kate was probably right.

"Joe and Violet had a big knock-down, drag-out fight this weekend and Joe told Violet about his family. They're the Simmons family from El Dorado."

Neely Kate's mouth formed an O and she quickly covered it with her hand. "*The* Simmons family?"

"Why does everyone but me know who they are?"

"Girl! Have you been living under a rock? They're practically royalty."

I frowned, stabbing a French fry into my ketchup. "Lucky me."

"Why didn't Joe tell you about them?"

"Because he knew exactly how I'd respond—not in a good way." I pulled out my wallet. "In any case, we're miserable without each other so I gave my notice at the DMV yesterday. I planned to move up in a week or so, but Mason thinks I should leave town with Joe on Thursday morning. Because of Skeeter."

"Wow. That's fast. You're still gonna come to my wedding, aren't you?"

"You really want me there?"

"It wouldn't be the same without you!"

My heart burst with happiness again, only this time it was my own happiness and not Neely Kate's leftover emotions from my vision. "I wouldn't dream of missin' it! It's not every day you get to see a Skittle walk down the aisle." I laughed. "Twice."

"Ain't that the truth." Frowning, she stood. "I gotta get back to work, but if you come back to the office with me, I'll show you a picture of the dresses."

I almost mentioned that I'd just seen them, but I wasn't eager to go home to my lonely house. "How can I refuse?"

Following Neely Kate back to the courthouse, I realized how much I was going to miss her. Sadness squeezed my heart. I'd finally made a friend, a friend who knew about my visions and didn't think I was a freak. When I moved, I was going to lose her.

I stood at the counter while Neely Kate dug in her drawer. "I know it's here somewhere."

"Well, look who finally showed back to work." Neely Kate's boss rounded the corner, his words dripping with sarcasm.

Neely Kate kept rifling through her drawers. "Don't be getting all worked up, Jimmy. Ah! Here it is!" She pulled a folded magazine page and handed it to me. "Now these right here are lavender, but mine are tangerine, even though they were supposed to be peach."

I quickly scanned the page and handed it back, watching Jimmy out of the corner of my eye. He didn't look very happy and I didn't want to get Neely Kate in trouble. "Your wedding is goin' to be wonderful."

A dreamy look covered her face. "I've been imaginin' this day my whole life."

"I'll let you get back to work. If you find out anything about Hyde Investments, let me know right away."

"Sure."

Jimmy glared at me then barked, "*Neely Kate*! You have work to do."

She jumped in surprise, whispering, "He's not usually this snippy."

He walked over to the counter, scanning me with interest. "I don't think I've ever seen you before. Are you one of Neely Kate's many cousins?"

I smiled, trying to smooth things over for her. "Oh, no. We met on jury duty last week." My peripheral vision faded. *Oh no. Not now.*

I saw a hand pressing something into my hand.

"I believe this is yours," a man's voice said and the vision faded.

"You're gonna get something back that's yours." I blurted.

Jimmy studied me. "Am I now? What are you, a fortune teller?"

I cringed. "Something like that."

Neely Kate jumped out of her seat. "Jimmy, don't be silly. I told her that you were missing your lucky penny. It's her way of tellin' you she hopes you find it."

He scowled. "I've been looking for it everywhere. I'm about to offer a reward." Jimmy kept his eyes on me. "Neely Kate, aren't you going to introduce me to your friend?"

Neely Kate rolled her eyes. "She has a boyfriend, Jimmy."

"I'm not askin' her out on a date," he grumbled.

"Fine." She huffed. "Rose Gardner, this is Jimmy DeWade. Jimmy, Rose."

"Nice to meet you, Rose." His mouth lifted into a smile that looked painful. "So you're the juror that caused all the ruckus."

There was no denying it. "Yeah."

His eyes hardened. "They don't take well to ruckuses around here."

"Tell me about it." Suddenly, Mason Deveraux popped into my head and melancholy washed over me. If Neely Kate was right, I needed to apologize. Again. I was forever apologizing to that man. "I've got to go."

"Stay out of trouble." She winked.

"I'm going to the Henryetta Garden Club meeting tonight with Violet. How much trouble can I get into there? See you later, Neely Kate."

She moved closer to her desk. "Lunch tomorrow? Noon?"

I grinned. "Sure."

Jimmy stood at the counter, watching as I walked out the door.

Chapter Twenty-Three

I felt bad leaving Muffy again. Rose Gardner, the homebody who never set foot off her property unless she was going to work or church, was suddenly a social butterfly, flitting all over town. But poor Muffy paid the price, getting left behind. I considered calling Violet to cancel. I didn't really feel like spending the evening perched on a folding chair being polite to a bunch of old women. But I still hadn't told her I was moving to Little Rock on Thursday morning and I planned to do it while we were out.

I cringed. Joe didn't even know I was going to Little Rock with him Thursday morning. While he'd be thrilled with the end result, there was no way he was going to be happy about the cause. I'd call him after the Garden Club meeting.

One confrontation at a time.

The neighbor boys were playing in their backyard when I got home, and Heidi Joy chased after them, looking frustrated. I smiled. I had a couple of hours before Violet was going to pick me up—plenty of time to make a pie to take next door. The police had taken the wooden rolling pin used to kill Momma, but I still had the marble one. I'd make two pies and prove to Joe that I could bake when he showed up the tomorrow night. Plus, it got me out of packing boxes.

I made the piecrust dough and stuck it in the freezer to cool it off before rolling it out. Since I didn't have any fresh fruit, I decided to make French Silk pies instead. An hour later, I walked next door, pie in hand, while Muffy followed behind, jumping around in excitement.

Heidi Joy had moved to her chair, reading a magazine under the shade tree while the boys ran in and out of their plastic pool. Enough grass floated on top of the water to stuff a straw mattress.

I held the pie toward her and smiled. "Welcome to the neighborhood!"

"Oh, my! What do you have there?" Heidi Joy stood and waddled toward me. Her t-shirt stretched across her rounded tummy.

I stifled my gasp of surprise. Heidi Joy was pregnant. She was still early and she'd worn loose shirts before, so I hadn't noticed. How in the blazes would they fit another child in that tiny house?

"Oh. It's a French Silk pie. Sorry it's late."

She grabbed the pie out of my hands. "Honey, the words *French Silk pie* and *sorry* shouldn't be anywhere near each other."

I laughed. "True. You might want to put that in the fridge. It still hasn't set up long enough, but I'm goin' out tonight and wanted to make sure you got it."

"Thank you so much!" She cast a glance around the yard, uncertainty wavering across her face.

"I'll watch the boys if you want to run that in."

"You don't mind?"

"No! Of course not. Muffy's havin' fun with them."

Heidi Joy ran inside and I sat on the quilt next to the baby. He looked up at me with wide eyes while he alternated chewing and sucking on his fist.

"Does that hand taste good?"

"He ain't gonna answer you." Andy Jr. sat in the middle of the pool, dead grass clinging to his chest. "He don't talk yet."

I laughed. "Is that so?"

"We ain't got to play with your dog all weekend."

"My dog has a name. Muffy."

"Yeah, I know."

I shook my head.

"I heard you tell my mom that you was goin' out tonight."

"I am."

"Can Keith and I babysit your dog?"

I raised an eyebrow.

"Can I babysit *Muffy*?"

"Well . . ." That would appease my guilt over leaving her, but I still wasn't sure I trusted Andy Jr.

"I promise to take extra good care of her. She likes me. See?"

Muffy stood on her back legs in the pool and licked Andy Jr.'s face.

"Let's talk to your mom first."

Heidi Joy was thrilled to let Muffy stay. "She'll entertain my boys. Anything that keeps them busy is a welcome relief!"

The boys set about teaching Muffy how to sit. *Good luck with that.* That dog had a mind of her own. But she looked happy, so I relented. And although I knew she'd be happier with the kids, it was hard to leave her.

My kitchen sink was full of dirty dishes, but I only had forty-five minutes before Violet was going to pick me up and I needed a shower. The dishes could wait. Joe said he had a dishwasher in his condo. Maybe I'd never have to wash dishes again.

Violet pulled into the driveway right at six forty-five. I went out the side door, watching Muffy in the neighbor's backyard. It was obvious she was having fun. I was worrying for nothing.

"You look very pretty tonight." Violet said when I climbed into the passenger seat.

I'd worn a floral pink skirt and a white blouse with a pair of sandals. I didn't trust her motives and decided to be on guard. "Thanks."

"How's Joe?"

I clasp my hands in my lap. "He's good. He's coming down tomorrow night."

"That's good." She smiled, her voice cheerful.

She was definitely up to something.

The meeting started promptly at seven in the Henryetta Southern Baptist Church fellowship hall. Miss Mildred caught a glimpse of me after she sat down and frowned. I was probably contaminating the Garden Club with my demon-possessed presence.

Two more days and then I wouldn't have to put up with her meanness.

The thought made me happy. After seeing my huge smile, her eyebrows lowered in suspicion.

The speaker, Mrs. Annabelle Perkins, was a self-proclaimed prize-winning rose expert, but after looking at the fine print in the program, it became apparent that her award was third place in the Fenton County Fair. Five years ago.

Loneliness for Joe washed over me. I hadn't talked to him in twenty-four hours and I needed to hear his voice. I leaned over and whispered in Violet's ear. "Let's leave early."

She pinched her lips together in disapproval and shook her head. "Rose Gardner," she hissed in my ear. "If you want to fit into this town, you need to make more of an effort."

Scowling, I reached into my purse for my phone. I didn't want to fit into Henryetta. I wanted to run away and never look back.

She must have known what I was thinking. Wearing a smug smile, she whispered, "You think the Henryetta Garden Club is stuffy? They're *nothing* compared to Joe's family and the company they keep. Consider this practice."

I had no idea if her plan was to truly help me fit into high society or make me aware of the hole I was digging myself into with Joe, but either way, I wasn't happy. Especially when I saw I'd missed a call from him. I rose from my chair, planning to leave the room to call him back, but Violet grabbed my wrist. "Don't you dare. You sit in that seat until this is over."

A blue-haired woman in front of us looked over her shoulder and glared.

Yep, I was fitting in just fine.

I sent Joe a text message. *Stuck in this boring meeting with Violet and I can't hear your message yet. I miss you.*

A half-minute later, he texted back. *The voice mail has a surprise. :)*

Now I really wanted to hear his message.

Violet frowned at my phone.

I had two choices. I could make an excuse to go to the bathroom and irritate Violet more or I could wait. I wanted her as happy as possible when I told her I was moving.

I sent Joe a text. *I have a surprise too.*

Does it involve sexy lingerie?

No. I blushed and stuffed my phone into my purse.

An hour later, the speaker finally stopped chattering.

Violet stood and pulled me to my feet. "We need to introduce you to the Garden Club board."

I had no interest in meeting the board. I wanted to hear my message from Joe. "Violet, I really have to pee."

Puckering her mouth, she shook her head. "No, you don't. You have the bladder of a whale. You're just tryin' to get out of meeting people. Come on." She looped her arm around mine and dragged me to the front of the room.

"We already know Miss Mildred. Why are we doing this?"

"Stop your whining. You want to be a grownup, then it's time to act like one."

I had no idea what meeting the old regime of the Garden Club had to do with being a grownup. I was sure millions of United States citizens were considered grownups without the pleasure of glad-handing the Henryetta Garden Club. But escaping from Violet's death grip would cause a scene, which definitely was not a good way to stay on Violet's good side.

"Fine." I huffed.

She spoke through gritted teeth as we stood in the reception line. "Can you at least *try* to look like you want to be here?"

I plastered on a fake smile. "Better?"

Violet beamed. "Yes."

Miss Mildred looked like she sucked on a lemon when Violet and I approached her.

"What a wonderful presentation, Miss Mildred." Violet shook her hand. "Having the meeting in the evening was a wonderful idea. Look at all the new faces!"

She wrinkled her nose. "Not all of them are desirable."

I rolled my eyes.

We moved to the next woman, who looked like she was a hundred years old. She couldn't have stood more than five feet. Her hair was pure white and I'd seen fewer wrinkles on a raisin.

"Miss Eloise?" Violet shouted, grabbing the woman's gnarled hand. "I want you to meet my sister."

"You have a blister?"

Violet shook her head. "No. My *sister*. My sister Rose."

"Roses? Yes, the program was about roses."

Violet smiled and moved to another woman.

I gave Miss Eloise a warm smile as I moved past, but a gold glint on her lapel caught my eye. A pin with a tree, a dog and a bird.

My stomach cartwheeled and I turned back to her. "Miss Eloise, what a lovely pin you have!"

She looked confused. "Eh?"

Violet moved closer to me. "Rose, she's hard of hearing."

I swung my head to face Violet. "I think I've deduced that already, Violet, thank you very much. I need to find out about her pin."

"What on earth for?"

"I just do, you move on if you like." I had no desire to be part of the Garden Club board gauntlet, and most of the other members seemed to be steering clear of Miss Eloise.

Violet muttered under her breath and greeted another member.

I stood directly in front of Miss Eloise, pointing to her lapel. "Your pin," I shouted. "What does it mean?"

Her eyebrows rose. "My *pin*?"

I nodded vigorously. "Yes!"

"It was my grandmother's."

If the pin was her grandmother's, it was well over a hundred years old. "What does it mean?"

"Eh?"

"What does your pin *mean*?"

"I'm mean? Well, I never . . ." She started hobbling away.

Grabbing her arm, I shook my head. "No!" I dug in my purse, looking for something to write with. A program lay on a chair by us and I snatched it up, scribbling in large block letters. I held it in front of her.

WHAT DOES YOUR PIN MEAN?

She leaned closer, then pulled a pair of reading glasses from her pocket, perching them on her nose.

Anxious for her answer, I fought to keep from fidgeting.

She read the note and her face lit up. "Oh!"

I breathed a sigh of relief.

"I don't know."

"What?" I screeched.

If looks could kill, Violet would have me stuffed and mounted to the wall.

Miss Eloise patted my arm. "But I can tell you that only four people had them. My grandmother and her three best friends."

"Who were her best friends?"

"Eh?"

Frustrated, I took the paper back and wrote my question.

"Oh! Rosemary and Mary Beth Dickens, and Viola Stanford."

I wrote out *WHAT WERE THEY FOR*? and held it up to her.

"They were friendship pins, dear. A way to show they were a group."

DO YOU KNOW WHERE THE OTHER PINS ARE?

She shook her head, a forlorn look in her eyes. "No, I know that Roberta Malcolm had one. Her grandmother was Viola. Roberta threw herself into the gutter when she married into the Malcolms. A bunch of malcontents and wastrels."

That sounded like Skeeter Malcolm.

I lowered my face to hers. "And the other two?" I said slowly enunciating the words.

"I think Rosemary married a man named White. I don't know about the other."

"Thank you, Miss Eloise! Thank you so much!"

Miss Eloise pinched my cheek. "That's a good girl, interested in Henryetta history. You were born and raised here, weren't ya?"

I nodded. "Yes, ma'am."

"Don't you listen to the young people today. Who you are is tied to where you're from. Henryetta is in your blood."

I couldn't have disagreed more, but she wouldn't have understood and I didn't want to be rude after the information she gave me.

I hurried over to Violet, who was deep in conversation with the speaker, Mrs. Perkins. "Violet, I have to go. Now."

"What on earth is so important that you have to go now?"

She was right. What did I have to rush to? Who was I gonna share my information with? I could tell Joe, but at this point, I knew he was placating me, trying to keep me out of trouble. Could I tell Mason Deveraux? I doubted he'd care. And besides, I'd been inexcusably rude. I doubted he wanted to hear from me anytime in the near future. Surprisingly, the realization filled me with sadness.

Mrs. Perkins stared at the program in my hand with pure evil in her eyes.

I glanced down to see if anything I'd written could be construed as rude. The front of the leaflet featured Mrs. Perkins's face, which now sported a drawn in curlicue mustache and devil horns.

My eyes widened in horror. "Oh, no! I didn't . . . this wasn't . . ." I stopped. There was no way out of this. I pointed to a row of chairs. "I'm just gonna wait over there."

Violet didn't say a word to me and continued her conversation with Mrs. Perkins as though my interruption had never occurred.

Traitor.

While I waited for Violet, the Henryetta social debutante, to stop making her rounds, I sat in the now deserted front row, trying to figure out who might have the other two pins. Part of me wondered if I should bother—the Malcolm family had been known to have one, and Skeeter was already on my suspect list. But Joe's words echoed in my head. Just because a puzzle piece appeared to fit in a spot, it didn't mean it belonged there.

I briefly considered calling Mason despite our last argument. I'd tried to find him after I left Neely Kate earlier, but he'd been in court all afternoon. Even if I apologized, he probably still didn't want to hear from me, not that I blamed him. But he'd said he couldn't charge Skeeter because he didn't have enough evidence. Was this important enough to make a difference? I doubted it and a friendship pin sure wasn't important enough to be calling Mr. Deveraux on his off hours, even though he still might be working. It could wait until morning.

After what seemed like an eternity, Violet wandered over, looking less surly. I'm sure the empty plate smeared with cake frosting had something to do with that.

"Are you ready to go?" she asked, her snippy tone barely in check.

"Does a bear—"

She shot me the look she saved for Ashley and Mikey when they misbehaved. The expressionless face with one eyebrow slightly raised. "A simple yes or no will do, Rose."

"Yes."

She threw her plate away as we exited the church hall. Her bad mood had lessened, but she was still a bit cranky, and I hadn't even told her my news yet. As she pulled out of the church parking lot, I knew it was now or never.

Chapter Twenty-Four

Wringing my hands in my lap, I squared my shoulders. "Violet, I need to tell you something."

Her head swung side to side and her smile was forced. "No, I need to tell you something first."

I groaned. "If this is about Joe, I don't want to hear it. I'm sick to death of you belittling him."

"It's about me." Her voice was barely a whisper.

She sounded so serious and so scared, my chest squeezed tight. "What is it?"

"Mike's leaving me."

Violet drove down Main Street as though it were an ordinary evening, like the world hadn't just split open and threatened to swallow us all whole.

"I don't understand."

She inhaled through her nose, her chest expanding. A tiny smile tugged at her lips. "He's tired of me."

"Oh, Violet. No. It's just a rough patch is all."

She pulled up to the four-way stop at the main intersection in town and turned her head to look at me. "No. It's more than that."

"But you both were so happy. Before."

Before Momma died. Before I had a midlife crisis at twenty-four. Before I stopped being Violet's full-time project. Before Violet realized our childhood had been based on a lie.

A tear ran down her cheek. "Were we? I don't even know anymore."

"But . . ." I didn't know what to say. I couldn't fix this.

"We married so *young*," Violet sighed, hunching over the steering wheel. "We were babies. We hardly knew who we were let alone what we wanted in life."

"What *do* you want in life?" I whispered.

She released a tiny sob with a laugh. "I don't even know. I don't know who I am anymore. I'm Mike's wife and Ashley and Mikey's mom, but who am *I*?"

I'd done so much soul-searching of my own the last couple of months, I couldn't even imagine going through it with a family to worry about.

"Do you still love him? Does he love you?"

"I think I love him, but not like I used to. And he says he loves me, but I'm not who he married. Funny, he's not who I married, but I'm still here."

I was the first to admit she'd put Mike through hell. Her disapproval of Joe. Her flirting with Austin Kent. But still . . .

"He says it's a break." Her laugh was bitter. "But we both know what that means."

"Do you think . . . ?" I wasn't sure how to ask without hurting her more. "Do you think there's someone else?"

She pulled into my driveway and let the car idle. "*What*? No. Don't be silly. It's Mike we're talkin' about."

Mike was a good-looking man and had been unhappy for at least a couple of months. An affair didn't seem as preposterous as Violet made it out to be, but now didn't seem like a good time to bring it up. "So what are you gonna do? Like . . . for a job?"

She rested her forehead on the steering wheel and groaned. "I don't know. I didn't go to college like you did."

"I only went a semester and a half before Momma made me come home."

Twisting her face, she peeked over the arm that gripped the steering wheel. "It's more than I've got."

"You'll come up with something. What do you think you want to do?"

She sat up, her classic Violet determination etched into her face. The shadows from the fading sunlight made her look older. "I love flowers. You and I both do."

"We can thank Daddy for that."

Her hand lifted to her mouth and she bit her finger. "I've considered taking my half of Momma's house money and using it to open my own flower business."

"Oh." Violet didn't know the first thing about running a business and there was already a florist in town, even if they were snippy. "Well that might work . . ."

"I thought maybe you'd want to go into business with me."

My mouth dropped open. "*Oh.*"

Her face lit up and her eyes radiated excitement. "I've been researching this for a bit. If we both put in money as collateral, we can get a small business loan. Did you know they give loans to women to start their own small businesses?"

"Violet, I don't know . . ."

"I was thinking maybe we could open a nursery and we could figure out something to sell in the winter, like Christmas trees. Maybe have a gift shop with it."

"Violet . . ."

The happiness left her eyes and she looked sadder than I'd ever seen her in my life. "Just think about it, okay? I can't do this alone."

"How long have you been considering all this?"

"A year."

I froze in surprise. This had been going on longer than Momma's murder. "Why didn't you tell me?"

She shrugged, looking away. "Mike thought it was a silly idea and wouldn't hear of it. I tried to tell him that the construction business could be partners with the nursery. But he told me it was flighty and frivolous, and my job was to take care of our children and the house."

It made sense now, her desire—her *need*—to create the perfect house and the perfect children. "Violet, I'm so sorry. You are capable of doin' whatever you put your mind to."

Clasping my hands, she pulled me closer. "You don't have to decide tonight but think about it, okay? You hate your job at the DMV. This could be good for both of us."

How was I going to tell her I was moving to Little Rock? "I turned in my two-week notice yesterday."

"You did? Why?"

"I'd had enough of Suzanne. You're right. I hated that job."

"So what do you plan to do?"

"I haven't figured it out yet." Technically, that was true.

"See?" she squealed, excited again. "It's fate!" She pulled me into a hug. "You think about it tonight and we'll talk more about it tomorrow after the probate meeting."

I'd almost forgotten about the probate meeting with all the other craziness in my life. Which reminded me that I hadn't asked Violet if I could stay at her house for the night.

Violet loosened her grip. "I have to go. When I get home, Mike and I are sortin' out the details of his leaving."

There was no way I could ask her now. "Do you need me to watch the kids?"

"Oh no. Mike's mom is watching them."

"Does she know what's going on?"

Her face hardened. "Not yet. I'm gonna let Mike tell his parents."

I was sure that wouldn't go over well. "Okay. You take care of yourself and call me if you need anything."

"Okay."

"I love you, Violet."

"I love you too, Rose."

I got out of the car and watched her drive away. My whole world quaked beneath me, making me question everything.

Joe and I weren't like Violet and Mike. But how could I be sure our relationship would work? The truth was that life didn't come with guarantees. Every decision was a risk. I just needed to make sure the odds were on my side.

Odds. I'd promised Mason Deveraux that I'd spend the night somewhere else. I'd convinced myself that it was overly cautious, but knowing Skeeter's family had possession of the same kind of pin found at the murder scene made me reconsider. Where was I going to go? I could stay in a motel but most wouldn't allow dogs. Maybe Muffy could stay with Heidi Joy and her boys.

With a lump in my stomach, I knocked on their front door.

Heidi Joy answered the door, the baby on her hip. "Hi, Rose! Your pie was delicious. Thank you so much!"

"Thanks for watchin' Muffy. Was she any trouble?"

"Oh, no! None at all. She's curled up on the bed with the boys right now while Andy reads them a bedtime story."

I smiled hesitantly. "Heidi Joy, I have a huge favor to ask. Do you think Muffy could spend the night with you tonight? I have to go somewhere and I can't take her with me."

She winked. "Got a rendezvous with that hot boyfriend of yours?"

My face caught fire. "Well . . ."

"Of course she can stay. The boys will love it."

"Thank you. I'll pick her up around lunchtime if that's okay."

"Have fun. But not too much fun."

I blushed again. I only wished I was going to be having fun with Joe. Tomorrow night couldn't get here fast enough.

I headed home, figuring out what I needed to do. Pack a bag and check into a motel. Violet had all the probate paperwork— I just needed to show up at the courthouse at ten in the morning.

How was I going to tell my sister that I was leaving Henryetta? Could I really leave her alone? Before, I thought she'd have Mike, but now she needed me more than ever. And she wanted me to go into business with her. The idea of owning a nursery had filled me with more excitement than I cared to admit.

What about Joe?

I forced the tears burning my eyes to go away. I didn't have to make a decision tonight. Joe was coming tomorrow and I'd tell him everything. He'd help me figure out the right thing to do.

Instead, I thought about the new evidence and how it wasn't enough to change Bruce Wayne's case. Neely Kate had said the trial would probably be over on Wednesday. While I might have more information, I'd failed Bruce Wayne Decker. I consoled myself with Joe's suggestion that Bruce would have gone to prison for breaking and entering anyway. Anything else I found out could be used in an appeal. It wasn't ideal, but it was the best I could do.

I unlocked the side door and turned on the kitchen light, but was greeted by darkness. I flipped the switch several times. Nothing. Déjà vu swept through me. I told myself I was being silly. I couldn't remember the last time I'd changed the light bulb. The light was burnt out was all. Nevertheless, I hurried toward the living room, eager to get my things and get out.

I bumped into the side table in the living room, and the lamp crashed to the floor. With a groan, I turned to head back to the kitchen when I saw a dark figure in the hall.

Someone was in my house.

I screamed, running for the still-open side door. The intruder was faster. He shoved me into the kitchen table and pushed the door closed.

My heart hammered against my ribs. I had to get out. Stepping backward, I threw two kitchen chairs into the center of the room. I turned and ran for the front door, the sound of screeching wood behind me. I had a good head start, but my fingers fumbled with the stiff deadbolt.

A body slammed me into the door, pushing the air from my lungs.

"I wish you'd stayed out of it." The man growled into my ear.

My chest heaved as I fought to catch my breath. "I'm sorry! I promise I'll stay out of it."

"It's too late for that." His fingers dug into my arm and he yanked me away from the exit.

He was dressed in black and wore a hood over his head. He wasn't much taller than me.

This was the person who killed Frank Mitchell.

Panic erupted and I instinctively tried to jerk out of his grasp.

His hold tightened and I cried out in pain. He was stronger than me, which meant I needed more than strength to get away.

"Look, I'm really sorry," I gushed. "I don't know anything. I don't even know who you are. If you just leave, I won't tell anyone."

"It's too late for that now." He dragged me toward the hall and I grabbed the upholstery on the sofa, screaming. The couch scooted across the floor as he continued pulling.

His free hand hit my arms, trying to break my hold. "Let go!"

It took him several whacks before he loosened my hands. I reached around and scratched his face under the hood.

His arms dropped, freeing me. I ran for the kitchen and tripped on the chairs in the middle of the room.

"Stop!"

I threw a chair at him and lost my balance, falling into the counter. He grabbed a handful of my hair and jerked me backward.

"Help!" I screamed. "Somebody help me!" My hands skittered across the counter, seeking out any kind of weapon, and settled on a long cylindrical object.

My rolling pin.

Wrapping his arms around my chest, he pinned my arms to my sides and dragged me backward toward the hall.

I kicked his legs and screamed, my throat burning. The rolling pin was clutched in my fist, but I couldn't raise my arms.

He lifted his right hand to cover my mouth. "Shut up!"

I bit hard on his finger and he cursed, shoving me down.

I rolled to my side and scrambled to get up. "*Help!*"

He reached for my arm and I swung wildly with the rolling pin, connecting with his side.

He grunted and let go, then hit me across the face.

Fuzziness filled my head, but I tried to hit him again when he whacked my arm. My weapon rolled across the hardwood floor.

"Leave me alone!" I screamed, kicking his legs.

"Rose!" A male voice shouted, followed by pounding on the front door.

The intruder fell on top of me, crushing me and covering my face with his hands, cutting off my breath. I bucked trying to throw him off while opening my mouth and biting him again.

His hand slipped and I gulped air.

"*Help me!*"

My attacker's fist hit my cheek and my vision faded. I fought against it, knowing I needed my wits about me to get out of this.

The banging on the door grew louder. "Rose!"

The man stared at the door, then wrapped his hands around my neck and squeezed.

Glass shattered behind me, but everything was fading. Suddenly, the pressure was gone and I gasped for air.

I rolled to my side and struggled to get to my feet, too dizzy to stand. A figure approached from the front window.

Panic flooding my head, I crawled into the kitchen, my limbs slow to react.

"Rose!"

Arms wrapped around me, pulling me off the ground.

I fought against him, my screams sounding hoarse.

"Rose, it's me. You're safe."

I looked up into Mason Deveraux's shadowy face, then fainted.

Chapter
Twenty-Five

I came to on my front porch. Red flashing lights slipped through my cracked eyelids. I heard Mason's terse voice. "Are they searching out back?"

"Yeah."

My eyes fluttered open. I was lying on the porch and something soft was under my head.

"Send someone to pick up Skeeter Malcolm *now*." Mason paced in the yard in front of my porch, running his hand through his hair.

"We both know it's a waste of time." I recognized the voice, and my hazy vision confirmed it was Detective Taylor. He stood to the side, watching Mason with a guarded expression.

Mason stopped pacing and faced the detective, and although his back was to me, I knew he had an arsenal of snotty looks at his disposal. I suspected he was using one. "Just do your goddamned job for once," Mason spat through gritted teeth.

The policeman looked like he was about to strangle the assistant district attorney.

I tried to sit up. Pain pierced my head at the movement, and I groaned.

Mason spun around and was next to me in two steps. "Don't try to get up." His hand pushed gently on my shoulder. He looked up, his eyes wild. "*Where's the ambulance?*"

"I'm fine. Let me up."

"You lost consciousness and you have an obvious head wound. You need to lie down." Mr. Stuffypants was back.

I brushed his hand away. "No I'm fine. I pass out when I get really scared. Well, and probably from being strangled. But, really. I'm okay."

His eyes widened and he held me down. "Someone give me a flashlight!"

"I'm not dying and I'm not bleeding." I felt blood trickle down my cheek. "Okay, I'm not bleeding to death. I'm sure it's just a scratch. Let me up."

He looked doubtful but helped me sit.

I winced at the throbbing in my face.

"Rose, please—"

I swung my legs over the side of the porch and smiled, even though it pulled the sore muscles in my cheek. "See? I'm fine."

A crowd had already begun to gather in the street. The good folk of Henryetta could count on Rose Gardner to put on a neighborhood show. Before tonight, my events had been restricted to the weekend. Apparently, I was branching out into weekday shows now. I needed to start selling tickets.

"You are far from fine. What the hell were you doing here? You promised you wouldn't stay here. You gave me your word, Rose."

"Calm down. I wasn't stayin'. I was just grabbin' some stuff to take to a motel."

"A motel? You were going to stay *alone*?"

While I appreciated his concern, his attitude was irritating. "You never said anything about not being able to be alone."

"You told me you were going to your sister's."

"And I was goin' to until she told me earlier this evening that her husband was leaving her."

Officer Ernie walked over with a long flashlight and narrowed his eyes at me.

Mason took the flashlight and flipped it on. "I want to look you over, but the light's going to be bright so you might want to close your eyes."

"Mr. Deveraux—" A blinding light made my eyes squeeze shut. "Is this really necessary?" I asked, irritated.

"Yes." He grunted. After several seconds the light left my face and I felt him lift my hand. I opened my eyes to find him examining my arm.

"I'm fine."

He put my arm down with a gentleness that surprised me. Over his shoulder, he shouted, "Where is the ambulance?"

"It was on another call," someone shouted back.

"Where's the other ambulance?"

"It's in the shop. It hit a deer this morning."

Mason grumbled, then turned back to me. "Are you dizzy? Do you feel like you're about to pass out?"

"No. I keep telling you I'm fine."

He paced again, more agitated than I'd ever seen him. "If they don't keep you at the hospital, we have to find somewhere for you to stay tonight. I'll have Taylor put you under twenty-four-seven guard."

"Mr. Deveraux, stop overreactin'."

He stopped and turned to face me, his eyes burning with anger. "Overreacting? *Overreacting?*" He pointed to the front door. "Your bathtub was full of water, Rose. *He was going to drown you!*"

"What?" I felt lightheaded and began to sway.

He hurried over and sat next to me, wrapping an arm around my back. "I'm sorry. God, I'm so sorry. I shouldn't have blurted it out like that."

"Mason." I looked up into his face. "I'm okay. See?" I wasn't sure why I was so surprised about the tub full of water. The man tried to strangle me on my living room floor.

"I almost didn't stop to check on you. I almost didn't go to the door." His voice hitched.

"Why *were* you here?"

"I came to check on you. I called you a couple of times to make sure you went to your sister's, but you didn't answer. So when I left my office, I drove by and saw your car in the driveway. I kept thinking you were mad and you'd be even more furious if I showed up. I figured that you probably wouldn't answer the door. I almost left when I heard you shout that you wanted to be left alone."

Fatigue surged through me with a ferociousness I wasn't prepared for and I rested my head against his shoulder. "It's okay. I'm not mad." Neely Kate's earlier statement came back to memory. He wanted to be friends. As foreign as the concept had seemed at first, it sounded nice. Mason Deveraux III was an egotistical man, but he had moments when he let his guard down. I liked the man I saw when that happened.

"I . . . sometimes what I say . . . it just doesn't . . ."

"Shh. It's okay. Thank you. You saved my life. That makes up for anything you didn't mean to say."

His arm tightened around my back, as though the intruder was waiting for Mason to let his guard down so he could snatch me away. He rested his cheek on top of my head. "You scared the hell out of me. If I'd been here two minutes later . . ."

"But you were here. See? *All's well that ends with the bucket in the well* as my grandma used to say."

"Uh, I don't think that's right."

"Wisdom according to my grandma. She was the oracle of LaFayette County. What she says goes."

He turned to look into my face, confusion in his eyes, when Joe's angry voice made me jump. "What the hell is going on here?"

Oh dear. This had to look bad. Mason was sitting next to me on the porch in the dark, his arm around my back, leaning into my face and probably looking like he was about to kiss me.

Mason sat up, dropping his arm and looking guilty. "It's not what you think."

"Try me." Joe stood six feet away in my yard, hands clenched at his sides, chaos swirling around him.

My anger let loose. "You walk up and find half the Henryetta Police Department in front of my house and the first thing you notice is that it looks like the assistant district attorney is sitting too close to me?"

He didn't say a word, but the anger I'd seen in his eyes faded.

Mason stood. "Rose had an intruder in her house. The police are here investigating." After my reaction to his blurting out the intruder's intent to drown me, Mason must have decided to ease his way into it with Joe.

"And you didn't think to call me?"

"Joe, calm down." I stood up and my legs gave out. Mason grabbed me before I hit the ground, but Joe walked over and shoved him out of the way.

"Get the hell away from her, Deveraux."

Mason backed up. "I assure you, Detective Simmons, it's not how it appears."

"When you told me you'd keep an eye on her, I didn't know what you *really* meant."

"Joe!" I'd seen Joe jealous before, but nothing like this. "If it wasn't for Mason Deveraux, I'd most likely be dead in my bathtub right now, so you treat him with respect. He saved my life."

His body stiffened. "What are you talking about?"

"If you would stop jumping to conclusions I could tell you. Someone was in my house when I came home from the Garden Club meeting and attacked me. He meant to kill me. Mason showed up and scared the guy off."

"Are you okay?"

"I'm fine."

"And what were *you* doing here?" Joe asked.

Mason had recovered, his condescending attitude returning. "I was here making sure she'd gone to her sister's like she promised me earlier in the day. But I'm sure you know how stubborn she is."

"I'm very acquainted with her stubbornness." Joe angled his body, making his statement a challenge. "Why did you make her promise to stay with Violet?"

"I felt responsible for giving her name to Skeeter Malcolm. And when he put that threatening note on her windshield this morning—"

Joe took a step forward, shouting, "Why the hell would you give her name to Skeeter Malcolm?"

I put my hand on Joe's arm. "Joe, this is my fault, not his. He showed up at the pool hall and saw that Skeeter had me cornered and he helped me get away but accidentally called me Rose."

"*What the hell were you doing with Skeeter Malcolm in the pool hall?*"

I'd never seen Joe so angry and took a step backward. "You know who Skeeter Malcolm is?"

"Of course I know who Skeeter Malcolm is. Who the hell doesn't?"

Apparently, I was the only one.

"Detective Simmons," Mason said, his hands clenched at his sides. "She's been through hell tonight and she doesn't need the stress at the moment."

"Excuse me?" Joe challenged.

"Joe, please." I tried to sit down, but my head spun and I started to fall.

"Rose?" Joe's voice softened, his arms around me.

"Where the hell is the ambulance?" Mason shouted. "This is goddamned Henryetta, not some metropolis."

"Ambulance?" Joe asked, the word sounding strangled.

"She was attacked, Simmons," Mason seethed. "Which part of that do you not understand?"

"She said she was fine."

"And I suspect she'd say that if she had a gaping abdominal wound. She needs medical attention. If you would stop having a fit and *look at her*, you'd see she's not fine."

Joe led me to one of the chairs on the porch and helped me sit down.

A light flipped on inside the house, spilling through the open front door. Joe gasped, staring at me.

"I'm fine, Joe. Really."

A police officer stepped out the front door. "Mr. Deveraux, we have the lights set up. Do you want to walk through the crime scene with us?"

Joe flinched.

"Coming." Mason glared at Joe, his face hardening. "I suspect you want to go in?"

Joe glanced over his shoulder at the front door, then back at me. "I don't want to leave you alone."

I groaned. "Will you just go already? I'm sick to death of tellin' everyone that I'm fine. *I'm fine*!"

Mason asked Officer Ernie to keep guard. "If she needs anything, call me."

Officer Ernie nodded, sterner than usual. After Joe went inside, the policeman moved closer, his gaze on the yard. "I checked on the ambulance. They got a flat tire but should be here soon."

"I don't need an ambulance. Everyone's overreactin'." I sighed, leaning my head into my hand. The pounding had gotten worse.

"Do you want me to get you something? A glass of water?"

"No, I'm *fine*."

Five minutes later Joe burst out the front door. "Rose, where's Muffy?"

"She's next door with the neighbors. I left her there since I was going to go to a motel." I looked out into the crowd. Sure enough, Heidi Joy and her husband Andy stood at the edge of the crowd. I bet they were rethinking their decision to move in next door.

"Thank God. After . . . I was . . ."

"What did you find in there?"

"Rose, for once let the police take care of it."

My back stiffened. "That's my house, Joe. This happened to *me*. I have a right to know."

Mason walked out the front door. He cleared his throat. "The police said the suspect escaped out the back window, which is how they think he got in."

My stomach rolled. "That window's seen a lot of action, huh?" I joked.

Joe didn't look at me.

"They haven't found the attacker yet, but they're bringing Skeeter Malcolm down to police headquarters to question him."

Skeeter's name reminded me of Miss Eloise's information. "Wait. I didn't get a chance to tell you. I found out that Malcolm's family had a pin like the one found at Frank Mitchell's murder scene."

Joe took two steps back. "Will you let it go, Rose? You are not qualified nor trained to do this. You've put yourself in danger, *unnecessary danger*, as evidenced here tonight."

While I couldn't argue with him, the anger in his voice strangled my heart. "I didn't . . ." My voice broke as I tried to ignore the pain from Joe's outburst. "I didn't do anything dangerous to find that out." I looked into Mason's sympathetic eyes. "When I was at the Garden Club meeting, Miss Eloise was wearing an identical one and I asked her where she got it. It was her grandmother's. She and three friends had them to symbolize their friendship. Miss Eloise didn't know what they meant, but she knew that one had been in the Malcolm family, another in the White family and the fourth she wasn't sure about."

"That's good, Rose. Thank you. I'll pass it along, but the police will want to question you about it too."

"I'm going to talk to Taylor." Joe bounded off the porch.

I watched him walk away, trying to stuff down my hurt. "They want to question me? I didn't do anything wrong."

"No one thinks you did anything wrong. They need a statement about what happened."

"I want a lawyer. I want to call Deanna."

Mason squatted next to me, his face level with mine. "Rose, I assure you that you don't need an attorney. If you like, I'll sit with you during questioning, and if there's anything I don't think you should answer, I'll let you know."

"But won't you be the one *prosecutin' me?*" I was getting hysterical, but I couldn't stop myself. Joe was leaving me.

Mason turned to watch Joe. "He's coming back. He just needs to feel like he's doin' something."

I didn't want to be alone. I was more scared than I thought, but what scared me most was the thought that Joe had had enough of my shenanigans and wouldn't come back.

Mason sat in the chair beside me and put his hand on my knee. "Do you remember when you were picked for the jury? You went through *voir dire*, right?"

I tried to settle down. Crying wouldn't solve anything and it sure wouldn't bring Joe back. "Judge McClary wasn't very happy."

Mason laughed. "That's an understatement. I can't prosecute you because I couldn't be impartial. Someone else would have to do it. But I promise you, you are not a suspect."

"Okay."

"Don't worry. We'll find who did this." His voice faded and his mouth stretched as if he was in pain.

There was more to his look than just worry about me. "You told me that you're an assistant DA because you want to protect people. Did something bad happen to someone you care about? Is that why it's important to you?"

He nodded, looking straight ahead.

"Who was it?"

A grim smile lifted one corner of his mouth. "My sister."

"Was she okay?"

His face hardened. "No."

"Did you find who did it?"

He turned to look at me, his eyes dark and brooding. "Yes."

Mason sat with me until Joe returned several minutes later, then he got up and walked away. I expected Joe to get angry that Mason had sat next to me again, but instead Joe sighed and pulled me into his arms.

"I love you, Rose."

Nodding, I held back my tears.

The ambulance never showed up so Joe took me to the hospital himself. I spent an hour in the ER before going to the police station to give my statement. True to his word, Mason sat next to me during questioning, despite the fact it was well past midnight. Joe sat on the other side, not saying a word, but cringing when I gave the details of the attack.

The three of us stayed in the room when Detective Taylor left.

Mason put his hand on the table and looked at Joe. "Malcolm had an alibi."

"Well, of course he did. He wasn't going to do this himself."

"Joe, Malcolm didn't have anything to do with this and you know it."

"How do you know that?" I asked, my fear rising at their seriousness.

Mason turned to me. "Because the intruder filled your tub with water and most likely intended for it to look like an accident."

"I still don't understand."

"Malcolm would never send someone so sloppy. You have multiple contusions on your face and bruises on your arms and legs. Even if he had succeeded and staged your murder, the Henryetta Police wouldn't have believed it was an accident."

I wasn't so sure about that. "So who was it?"

Mason swallowed then flexed his hand. "You might be onto something with your theory of Bruce Decker's innocence."

Joe slammed the table. "Don't encourage her, Deveraux."

"I respect her enough not to lie to her. Can you say the same thing?"

My heart skipped a beat. What did he mean by that?

Mason continued. "We don't know who it is, but if the assault wasn't tied to Malcolm, then we have to presume that you've upset someone else with your investigation. I'm going to ask the judge for a recess tomorrow morning so we can question you on what you know."

More questioning? But Mason insinuated they would listen to my evidence for Bruce Decker's innocence. Wasn't that what I wanted?

"And then she's done." Joe said. "She's out of this mess for good."

Mason nodded. "Take her somewhere for tonight and bring her to the judge's chambers at nine."

Joe stood and took my hand. "Come on. You need some sleep."

I doubted I'd ever sleep again. We got into Joe's car and drove to a motel. If the clerk thought it odd that we were checking in at two in the morning, he never let on.

When Joe shut the door he locked both locks and looked around the room before setting his gun on the bedside table.

"Do you think you'll need that?" I asked, pointing to the weapon.

"I will if I find the bastard who did this."

Stepping toward him, I put my arms around his neck and pressed my body into his chest.

He buried his face on my shoulder. "If Mason Deveraux hadn't shown up . . ."

"I know. But he did. How did you get to my house so fast?"

"Didn't you listen to your message?"

"No, after I found out about the pins from Miss Eloise, accidently insulted the guest speaker, and then found out that Mike is leavin' Violet, I got distracted."

"So basically it was a normal night for you?"

I shrugged. "I guess."

"My message was that I was comin' tonight. I have something to work on in Magnolia tomorrow. Since it's closer to Henryetta than Little Rock, I decided to come spend the night with you."

I kissed him. "Lucky me."

"Let's get you undressed and tuck you into bed."

"I don't have any pajamas."

"I'll keep you warm."

I almost protested that I wasn't in the mood, but I was pretty sure that wasn't his intent.

He helped me undress and climb under the covers, then he removed his shoes and jeans and slid in next to me, pulling me into his arms.

"Never a dull moment with you, Rose."

I didn't think it was a compliment.

We lay in the dark for a couple of minutes, Joe's steady heartbeat in my ear.

"So Mike left Violet?"

"Yeah." Crappy doodles. I never called her to tell her what was going on. I hoped she didn't find out from somebody else what had happened tonight.

"I know they've been having problems, but I never saw that one coming."

"Me neither. She's thinking about starting her own business, a nursery selling flowers and Christmas trees."

He was silent for a moment. "Are you okay, Rose? Really?"

"Now I am. I'm always okay when I'm with you."

"I don't want to lose you."

"I'm too stubborn to be gotten rid of that easily."

He snorted, his breath blowing the hair on the side of my face. "I love you." His breath evened and he soon fell asleep.

I lay awake for hours, trying to purge the images of the evening from my mind. As I finally drifted off to sleep, I saw Mason Deveraux's face as he looked at Joe, saying, "I respect her too much not to lie to her. Can you say the same?"

Had Joe lied to me? What would he have to lie about?

When I woke up the next morning, Joe sat in a chair next to the bed, working on his computer.

"What time is it?"

He looked up at me then back down at his computer. "Nine."

"Don't I have to go meet the judge?"

"That's been postponed to later today."

"Oh." I sat up, and groaned. My entire body ached. "Don't you have to go to Magnolia?"

"Someone else is doin' it."

I closed my eyes, guilt washing over me. It was a wonder he hadn't lost his job because of me. He was acting so strange, maybe he was mad about that. "I still have to go to the courthouse. I have that probate meeting at ten."

"I have an appointment with the Henryetta Police so I'll drop you off, and maybe you can go home with Violet."

I nodded. "Okay."

He spun around in his seat, leaning over his legs. "Why didn't you call me and tell me what was goin' on?"

"Which part?"

He stood up. "Rose, you shouldn't have to ask *which part.* Why didn't you call me with any of it?"

"I don't know . . ."

He sat next to me. "Yes, you do. You knew I wouldn't like it. You've been reckless and irresponsible."

I wasn't sure what to say. He was right.

"Thank God you're movin' to Little Rock so I don't worry about you every minute of the day."

The thought of moving away from Henryetta suddenly filled me with panic. How could I leave Violet? "Joe . . ."

His eyes widened. "You're still movin' to Little Rock, aren't you?"

I looked down at my hands, twisting the sheet around my fingers. "It's just that with Violet being all alone now . . ."

His voice hardened. "And whose fault is that, Rose?"

I closed my eyes. "I know."

"I told you that one day you'd have to choose."

My heart was breaking. How did I choose between the two people I loved most in the world? "I know you see the bad in her, but I promise you that there's so much good. I wouldn't have survived all those years with Momma without her. She protected me from Momma and from everyone else."

His hand stroked my hair, his voice softening. "I know you both thought she was protecting you, but she was stiflin' you. Hiding you away instead of havin' you face your fears and the gossip around you. Keeping you sequestered only enforced that there was something wrong with you and there's not, Rose."

He was one of the first people to believe that. I released a sob. "She loves me."

He leaned close, tenderness in his eyes. "I love you too."

"I don't know what to do. I'm miserable without you, but I'll be miserable knowin' what she's goin' through all alone."

"You have to make this decision. I can't make it for you and neither can Violet."

Gently pushing me down, he kissed me with such tenderness, I cried harder.

"That wasn't supposed to make you upset."

I was losing him. I felt him slipping through my fingers. "I just love you so much."

Leaning on his side, he traced the bruises on my cheek and my neck with his fingers. Tears filled his eyes. "I don't think I can keep doing this. Worrying about you here. Worrying what trouble you're going to get into. Worrying that someone is going to call and tell me you're dead."

"I'm sorry," I choked out.

"I love you. Do you know how much I love you?"

The fear in his eyes last night had showed me how much he loved me.

"I didn't . . . I tried . . ."

He smiled, but it was sad and forlorn. "I know. You can't help it. This is you. This bundle of chaos is who I fell in love with. How can I ask you to change what makes me love you?"

"I'm sorry."

He leaned down and kissed me, his hand caressing my cheek, careful to avoid my bruises. I kissed him back in desperation and fear. We made love with a tenderness we'd never shared before and I cried the entire time because I knew what this was.

Joe was telling me goodbye.

Chapter
Twenty-Six

I was late to the probate meeting, not that I cared. Violet was the executor of Momma's will and the only thing bequeathed to me was the box my birth mother had left me. I didn't care about any of it. I'd been reluctant to move from Momma's house, but I recognized it for what it was now—a fear of change. I'd spent most of my life living in fear. Why should I act differently with this?

I slipped into the room and took a seat next to Violet. She shot me an irritated look when she saw I was in the same clothes as the evening before, but she didn't seem surprised by my bruises. Which meant she'd heard about the attack from someone else.

I was in for an earful later.

The judge however, took in my contusions and stopped the proceedings. "This is probate court, miss. The criminal court is on the third floor."

"I'm in the right place. Agnes Gardner was my mother."

His eyebrows rose, but he continued while I tuned him out.

My mind drifted to the pin Miss Eloise wore the night before. I decided to run by the library and look up Miss Eloise's grandmother and her friends. The Henryetta Historical Society took great pride in recording the history of its citizens. If I could find out who the other women had married and who their children were, then I might be able to find the White family. Maybe they would know who might have the missing pin.

I knew I should stay out of it. Now that Mason believed me, I should let the police take care of it. I stifled a snort, getting another look from Violet. Letting the police take care of it was a terrible idea. Still, Mason might make them investigate the leads I'd found. Especially since he seemed so convinced that Skeeter Malcolm wasn't involved in my attack.

Besides, was going to the public library a crime?

And I had to make a decision about my move to Little Rock, but Joe was right. I was a bundle of chaos and I suspected it didn't matter where I lived, whether it was Henryetta, Little Rock, or Antarctica, I'd find trouble. The trouble I found was what drove a wedge between us.

Did I want to change?

I'd spent my entire life trying to make Momma happy. Did I want to spend the rest of it trying to make Joe happy?

I stifled a sob, knowing the answer. I didn't want to accept it. Joe was the best thing that ever happened to me. Was I really going to throw that away?

The more immediate question was if I should go to Little Rock with Joe this afternoon. Did he even want me to come?

When the proceedings ended, Violet and I met the estate attorney in the hall. I realized that my life was packed full of attorneys and judges. Shoot, Joe was an attorney, even if he wasn't practicing.

"I'll keep in touch, Mrs. Beauregard," the attorney told Violet, cringing at the sight of my bruises.

After he went around the corner, Violet turned on me. "You have a lot of explaining to do, Rose Anne Gardner."

"Okay, but not here in the hall."

"Fine. We can go to the coffee shop across the street."

"Okay."

We crossed the lobby toward the exit as Mason entered through the front doors.

"Rose!"

Violet's eyes darted from him to me as Mason walked toward us. "Do you know him?"

"Yeah, that's Mason. Mason Deveraux. He's the assistant DA."

"You're on a first-name basis with the assistant DA?"

Mason's eyes widened in horror as he approached. "I didn't think it was possible, but you look worse today than you did last night."

I scowled. "In light of your previous heroic behavior, I'm going to ignore the rudeness of that statement, Mr. Deveraux."

Violet gasped. "Rose!"

"It's quite all right." Mason laughed. "It has been well-established that the majority of my social interactions are rude and hostile." He winked at Violet.

Mason Deveraux winked?

"Mason, this is my sister, Violet Beauregard. Violet, this is Mason Deveraux, my rescuer."

Mason's face reddened. Who would have thought?

Shaking Violet's hand, Mason grinned. "Rose exaggerates."

"Savin' my life twice is far from an exaggeration."

"I don't think we can count the first time unless you actually planned to drink and drive. I prefer to think that you were calling my bluff."

Violet studied Mason with a hungry look, as though he were a New York steak. "Nice to meet you, Mr. Deveraux."

"And you as well, Mrs. Beauregard." He grinned at me. "See, Miss Gardner? I'm capable of polite conversation. Be sure to tell your courthouse groupies."

I laughed. This new Mr. Deveraux was a welcome change.

His expression turned more serious. "How are you today? Really?"

I'd never been more miserable in my life, either physically or emotionally. "I'm fine."

"Are you still going to Little Rock tomorrow?"

Violet froze, waiting for my answer.

I stared at the floor, trying to figure out what to tell him. Finally, I looked up, tears in my eyes. "I don't know."

Mason studied me for several moments. "I see."

"Can we talk about this later?" I was about to breakdown in the courthouse lobby. I'd had enough embarrassment the last few days to last me the rest of the year.

"Of course. We can discuss it this afternoon when we meet the judge. But if you don't go to Little Rock, we need to make other arrangements."

I nodded. "Okay."

"I'll call you when I know what time the judge will see us. In the meantime, if you need anything, call me. If it's an emergency and you can't get me on my cell, call my office. They know to contact me if you call."

"Okay."

"I mean it, Rose. And stay out of trouble."

"I was thinkin' about spending the afternoon in the library."

He narrowed his eyes as though he didn't believe me.

"What trouble can I get into in the library?"

His mouth pinched into a grimace. "Honestly, with you, who knows? Just be careful." He turned to Violet and smiled. "It was nice to meet you, Mrs. Beauregard, but I'm late for a meeting. Rose, I'll see you this afternoon."

Violet watched him walk away and nudged me with her shoulder. "You are in so much trouble."

"Why? What did I do now?"

"I can't believe you didn't tell me about him or about him savin' you. You've got a lot of explaining to do."

"There was nothing to tell."

She raised her eyebrows in disbelief as we exited the building.

"He's the assistant DA. He and Joe got me out of jail when I was found in contempt of court. And he showed up Monday night at the pool hall and helped me out of an uncomfortable situation."

"And why on earth were you at the pool hall?"

"I don't think you want to know."

Violet let it drop until we'd gotten our coffee and sat down. I told her about going to the pool hall, Mason accidently telling Skeeter Malcolm my name, and Mason's concern that Skeeter might try to harm me.

"What were you thinking, quizzin' Skeeter Malcolm? Have you lost your mind?"

"*You* know who Skeeter Malcolm is?"

She rolled her eyes. "Who doesn't?"

I groaned. At this point, I bet even seven-year-old Andy Jr. knew about Skeeter.

"And why didn't you tell me you needed a place to stay?"

"You were going through your own problems. You sure didn't need mine dumped on your doorstep."

"But last night . . ."

"Violet, you had just told me that Mike was leaving and you were going home to sort out the mess. If the roles were reversed, would you have asked to stay with me?"

"I guess not." She glanced out the window, then back at me. "Now tell me what happened last night."

I told her sketchy details, not wanting her to get too upset. The few details I shared were enough to make her pale.

Violet bit her trembling lip. "You were almost killed."

"I'm fine. Thanks to Mason."

"So that's why you were going to Little Rock?"

"One of the reasons."

Violet waited.

"Joe asked me to move to Little Rock with him."

I expected her to yell or argue. Instead, she inhaled and looked down at her hand on the table. "When were you going to tell me?"

"I was going to tell you tell you last night, but then you told me about Mike and . . ."

"So why aren't you going tomorrow?"

"It's complicated."

She looked up with sad eyes, but her mouth lifted into a wry grin. "My brain isn't *complete* mush after bottles, diapers and sleepless nights. Try me."

I twisted the coffee cup in my hand. "I can't leave you, Violet."

"Rose . . ."

"It was hard enough considering leaving you before you told me about Mike, but now . . . You need me."

Violet reached across the table and grabbed my hand. "Rose, you can't stay because of me. If you do, it will be just like Momma guiltin' you into taking care of her. You hated it and felt trapped. I don't want you to hate me."

"Last week you told me you were scared that I'd leave and move away."

"I was and I still am, but I want you to be happy."

"But what about the nursery?"

Sadness filled her eyes. "That's my dream, not yours."

The more I thought about it, I wasn't so sure.

"What else is holding you back, Rose? I can see it on your face."

"I don't know if I'm the person Joe wants me to be."

"What on earth are you talking about? That man loves you more than the air he breathes."

"Part of the reason he wants me to move in with him is so he can keep an eye on me and so I'll stay out of trouble. But you know I can't guarantee that nothing will happen in Little Rock. What if I move up there and find out he's tired of me? What will I do then?"

"He's not goin' to get tired of you."

I hoped she was right.

"There's something else holding you here. What is it?"

Unease nagged the back of my brain, but something Joe had said earlier that morning had nudged it forward. "I think by moving, maybe I'm trying to run away from my problems."

Violet sipped her coffee and waited.

"I thought I could be someone else if I moved away and I could run from all the pain from our past, but now I'm not so sure. Maybe I need to learn to accept and learn to love Rose Gardner of Henryetta before I can be Rose of somewhere else."

"Then maybe you have your answer."

I bit my lip, tears falling down my cheeks. "I'm going to lose Joe."

She grabbed my hand again. "If he loves you enough, he'll understand."

Would he?

"And if he's fool enough to let you go, he doesn't deserve you. Don't you worry, Rose, there's plenty of other men to choose from."

I laughed through my tears. "You mean like that blind date you set me up with? Steve, the Pillsbury Doughboy?"

She cringed. "No, and I'll regret that for the rest of my life. Austin Kent, for one."

"I'm not interested in Austin Kent."

"Of course you're not. You only have eyes for Joe. But if you find yourself in the position of being single, I assure you that other men would be interested."

I leaned over and hugged her. "Thank you."

"What are big sisters for? Maybe shaking up my own life has helped me look at things differently. I love you, Rose. I want you to be happy."

"Thanks, Vi. I love you too."

"I have to go pick up the kids. Were you supposed to go home with me?"

"How did you know that?"

She smiled. "Joe sent me a text."

"Yeah. But I'm supposed to eat lunch with Neely Kate and I want to go to the library."

"Are you sure it's safe?"

"You heard me tell Mason about the library, and he didn't try to stop me."

She stood. "Okay. Do you want me to drop you off anywhere?"

"No, I'm not done with my coffee and Neely Kate can probably take an early lunch. Then I'll just walk to the library. It's only two blocks away and there are lots of people around. I'll be fine."

"Call me if you need me to come get you."

"Thanks."

I watched through the window as Violet walked to her car. Her change in attitude surprised me. Joe most likely wouldn't be happy that I didn't go home with Violet. I sighed, my heart heavy. Just one more offense to add to my ever-growing list. But if I decided to go to Little Rock tomorrow, I wanted to have one last lunch with Neely Kate.

I texted Neely Kate, and told her I was at the coffee shop and ready whenever she was. She answered back a few minutes later, saying Jimmy was going out for awhile and she'd let me know when she could go.

Since I had some time to fill, I figured I ought to use it to think about my future. I decided to make a list of reasons to go to Little Rock and a list of reasons to stay in Henryetta. I grabbed the coffee receipt and started the Little Rock list first, coming up with twenty-nine reasons.

Waking up with Joe every morning. Having someone to kill bugs. He cooks really well. He's sweet to Muffy. He's a good cuddler. He's a wonderful man. He helps me wash dishes. He believes in me more than I do sometimes. He puts gas in my car. He mows the lawn for me. He helps me paint and says he likes it. He likes to try new things with me. He's content to just be with me. He likes to play with Ashley and Mikey. He holds my hand when we go for walks.

He doesn't snore. He rubs my feet. He gives me backrubs. He's thoughtful. He's a very handsome man. He thinks I'm beautiful. He helps me figure out problems. He thinks I'm intelligent. He's not embarrassed by my visions. He loves me. He misses me when we're not together. He wants to have a family one day. He makes me happy.

I'm miserable without him.

I turned the receipt over and started the reasons to stay, staring at the paper a good five minutes before only coming up with one. But once I wrote it down, my eyes welled up with tears and I knew without a doubt I'd made my decision.

I stared at the three words through blurry vision, sure I was making the biggest mistake of my life.

I'm not ready.

Choking back my tears, I picked up my phone to call Joe. Now that I had my decision, I felt the need to tell him as soon as possible. His phone rang as a man walked in the door of the coffee shop. Jimmy DeWade, Neely Kate's boss, stood just inside the entrance holding a folded newspaper under his arm. He glanced around the room, catching my gaze. His mouth lifted into a half-smile, but his eyes were cold. My breath stuck in my chest when I saw the scratches on the side of his face and my head grew fuzzy.

Joe's voicemail message kicked in, but I was frozen in horror.

Jimmy DeWade. *Duane.*

"He's here," I wheezed before Jimmy walked over and took my phone out of my hand. Stunned, I was slow to react. He hung up the call and tucked it in his front dress shirt pocket, sitting across from me.

"Fancy meeting you here."

I was still trying to catch my breath.

Jimmy grinned, the scratch marks across his cheek stretching. "I think it's time we had a chat."

Chapter
Twenty-Seven

Jimmy's mouth lifted into a lopsided grimace. His hand twitched on the table, giving away his nervousness.

I noticed the scar on his arm, matching the one in my vision. Why hadn't I looked him over more closely the day before?

"You've got nothing to say in broad daylight?" He removed the paper from under his arm and laid it on the table, lifting an edge to expose a gun. "Don't think about doing something stupid. We don't want someone to accidentally get hurt."

"You'll never get away with this, Jimmy."

"Sweetheart, that is so cliché. Seriously. I expected better from you, but in case you hadn't noticed: I already have got away with it. I just have to keep you from talkin' any more than you already have."

My cell phone rang in his pocket and his eyes filled with irritation and worry.

I needed to get myself together. I fought this man off last night in the dark. Alone. So why was I freaking out now? I took a deep breath. I could use the phone call to help me. "That's probably my boyfriend. The state police detective. He's at the Henryetta Police Department, which is only a couple of blocks away. If I don't answer, he'll rush right over and check on me."

Jimmy looked down at his gun.

"You know, if you leave now, you could have a good head start. I'll even let you take my cell phone. I've got plenty of minutes left this month." That was a lie. I'd used most of my minutes with Joe.

He reached into his pocket and read the caller ID. "Mason Deveraux."

My pulse pounded in my temple. "That's the assistant DA."

Growling, he pushed a button to make the ringing stop and put the phone on the table. "I know who Mason Deveraux is. The question is, why is he calling you?"

"He's expectin' me to come over to the courthouse. If I don't show up, he's going to send the police out looking for me."

He cocked his head, suspicious. "I don't believe you."

I flashed my sweetest smile. "You can call him and ask him if you want."

"Why in the world would I do that?"

"You said you don't believe me. That way you'd know that I wasn't lyin'."

The phone rang again.

"Good Lord. Do you run a call service?" he asked, disgusted. He picked up the phone and checked caller ID. "Joe."

I smiled again. "My boyfriend. The state police detective."

"You already said that."

"Just tryin' to help you keep everyone straight."

He rubbed his eyes, and I was about to hop up and run for the back door when he dropped his arm and reached for the newspaper. "Don't even think about it."

"I have to pee."

"No, you don't."

"I do. I swear it. I have the bladder of a thimble, not to mention coffee goes *right through me*, if you know what I mean."

"You can wait."

"I can't be held responsible for accidents." I grumbled, but the longer we sat here the longer I'd stay alive. There was no telling what he had in mind when he said *have a chat*, although his attempt to kill me the night before gave me a pretty good idea.

Waiting was good, although Violet was the only one who knew I was here. No, Neely Kate knew and was meeting me for lunch. I nearly groaned when I realized Neely Kate wouldn't come until Jimmy went back to the office and Jimmy was detained, plotting my murder. I needed to stall him until I figured out what else to do. "Why did you come to my house last night?"

He snorted, his eyes bulging. "You're kidding, right?"

I tried to look innocent. "Why would I ask if I knew?"

"I thought my motive was pretty clear when I tried to strangle you."

My nausea brewed. "How'd you pass off your scratch marks?"

"Cats are vicious things."

They didn't look like cat scratches to me, but this was the normally mild-mannered Jimmy. No one would suspect anything ungentlemanly from him. "You still didn't answer."

"I already—"

"No. *Why?*" I tried to keep my voice light and breezy, not an easy task when talking about your attempted murder with the man who tried to do it. "I get that you wanted me dead." I laughed. "Hello, anyone could figure that out. Even the Henryetta Police Department."

Jimmy's eyes narrowed in irritation.

"Come on, even you—especially you—have to admit that the HPD's investigating skills are like two dogs in heat lookin' for an acorn."

He smiled with a shrug. "Well . . ."

"You're gonna be like a local legend, you know it?" I asked, excited. "You're gonna be known as the guy who outwitted the HDP."

He shook his head in confusion. "Wait. How do you figure that . . . ?"

I lifted my coffee cup. "To the guy who outwitted the HDP." I started to take a sip then put it down on the table. "Oh wait. You don't have a drink. I'll go get you one, my treat." I grabbed my purse and stood. "What can I get you?"

"Sit back down."

"It's really rude to drink in front of you, especially when we're drinking *to you*."

"Sit. Down."

I sat. "You don't have to be so grumpy about it."

He sighed in exasperation. "Here's what we're gonna do. We're gonna get in your car and drive out Highway 82, out past Watson's Garage. You're pretty acquainted with that area, aren't you?"

I was only too familiar with it and he knew it. That's where Daniel Crocker's operation had been based. Muffy and I had traipsed through the woods and brush around there to rescue Joe. If Jimmy DeWade planned to take me out there, they wouldn't find me for a long time. If ever.

Trying not to hyperventilate, I half-smiled, half-grimaced. "There's a teeny-tiny problem with that plan. I don't have a car."

"What?"

I shrugged. "This seems to be a *thing.*"

"What the hell does that mean?"

"Well . . . when I had to meet Daniel Crocker at the Trading Post, I had no car. And when I saved Joe from the warehouse, no car again. I'm noticing a trend here."

He muttered then glared at me. "Fine. We'll take mine."

"To the woods?"

"No, through the drive-thru of Chuck and Cluck. Of course, to the woods."

Oh, crappy doodles. *Think of something!* "What about my diary?"

"What diary?"

"The diary I have hidden in my house listing all the evidence I have against you."

He studied me for a moment before breaking into a grin. "You don't have a diary. If you did, you would have given it to the police already."

I snorted. "The Henryetta Police don't believe a word I say. They probably think I faked my attack last night. I wouldn't give them my evidence. They'd just waste it. I'm savin' it."

"Saving it for what?"

Oh, dear. For what, indeed? "For my meeting with Mason Deveraux this afternoon. And the judge." I nodded. "Yeah, I'm bringin' it to them this afternoon."

He looked perplexed by this unexpected dilemma.

"Not to worry," I said. "We can just swing by my house and pick it up."

"Why in the world are you helping me?"

"My momma, God rest her soul, taught me to be kind to those less fortunate than myself."

He snorted. "You consider me less fortunate?"

For all of his recent boorish behavior, Jimmy DeWade had been the epitome of a Southern gentleman. I hoped there was still part of that in him. I gave him a stern look. "Is your momma a God-fearin' Christian woman, Mr. DeWade?"

He tugged at his collar.

"Is your momma still *alive*?"

He looked down at the newspaper. "Yeah."

"I can only imagine what she's gonna say when she finds out what you're up to."

Chuckling, he glanced up with an evil look. "I thought you said I was gonna get away with it. The Henryetta police are a band of imbeciles."

My eyebrows rose. "Ah, but a momma always knows, doesn't she?"

His smile fell and his face paled. "Enough talking. Time to go."

I couldn't believe that line worked. "I still have to pee."

"You can pee when you get home."

Was he going to try to drown me again? My heart tried to throw itself from my chest. *Calm down.* I'd done pretty well so far, in fact, I couldn't believe how well I'd done. But we were still in a public place. If he got me alone . . . I felt like I was going to throw up.

My phone rang.

Jimmy shook his head with a sneer. "You're quite the popular girl, aren't you?" He picked it up. "Joe."

"That's my boyfriend, the state—"

"—police detective. Got it."

I grimaced and gave him a sympathetic look. "Yeah, here's the thing about Joe. You don't want to tick him off. He's got this *really* bad temper."

The phone continued to ring in his hand. His grip tightened. "How bad?"

"Did you hear what happened to Daniel Crocker's brother when Joe busted their ring a couple of months ago?"

"Daniel Crocker didn't have a brother."

I cringed. "Yeah, that's what they *want* you to think. If word had gotten out what Joe did to him . . ." I shook my head. "Let's just say, after Clinton was governor, the state police learned how to sweep messes so far under the rug that entire towns have been known to disappear." Lordy. Where had that come from? I tried to ignore the fact that I had become a bald-faced liar. Apparently, facing my impending murder brought out a scrappiness I didn't know I had.

He stared at the phone, then stuffed it in his pocket. "Yeah, right."

I shrugged. "Don't say I didn't warn you."

Picking up the newspaper, Jimmy stood. "Time to go."

I glanced out the window. Officer Ernie was meandering across the street toward the coffee shop, his mouth set in his no-nonsense purse. If only I could stall Jimmy a bit longer.

But Jimmy followed my gaze and noticed the officer. He pushed me toward the hall. "I think we'll take the back door."

Before I lost sight of the window, I saw Joe running down the street, a good fifty feet away. He'd probably found out where I was from Violet. If we left the coffee shop, how would he know where to find me? Joe was going to be furious that I hadn't gone with my sister.

Panic tightened my chest and I stopped moving.

Jimmy pressed the tip of the gun in my back. "I know you're thinking 'Oh, he won't shoot me in public,' but you're wrong. I killed Frank Mitchell and I tried to strangle you last night. I'll shoot you. But you're more valuable to me alive right now, so the choice is yours. Stay here and get shot, or go with me."

One last glance confirmed Joe wouldn't reach me in time. I had no idea how much damage Jimmy's gun would do, but I wasn't willing to take the chance.

"I'll go with you." My breath caught and the words came out in a squeak. My irritation rose, momentarily overshadowing my fear. I didn't want to give this man the satisfaction of hearing that I was afraid.

"Smart girl." He poked the gun into my back and I marched toward the back door, praying I'd made the right decision.

We exited into an alley, the heat hitting me as soon as we walked out the door.

"Goddamned heat wave," Jimmy grumbled. "The AC's out in my car." He shoved me to the right and had me walk in front of him. "Where's yours?"

I frowned, the heat and the situation making me cranky. "I already told you that it's not here."

"I know *that*. I asked you where it's at."

"I suppose it's in my driveway."

"Does the A/C work?"

I looked over my shoulder at him in disbelief. He wanted to drive to my murder scene in air-conditioned comfort. "Not very well."

"Wait a minute." He shoved me against the brick wall of the coffee shop. A dumpster hid us from view of the street at the end of the alley.

I tried to swallow, a lump of fear getting in the way. He was going to shoot me outside next to this smelly dumpster. "I've changed my mind. I want to go back inside."

He shook his head in disgust. "You can't change your mind *now*."

"Well, I did anyway. If you're gonna shoot me, I'd rather die in the air conditioning instead of dying next to the trash."

"I'm not gonna shoot you. I'm trying to figure out what to do about the car."

"Oh."

He rubbed his chin, looking toward the street.

"What are you trying to figure out?"

"If I drive my car to your house, it's going to be seen by your neighbors."

"We could take a taxi."

"*What*?"

"I bet it'll have air conditioning."

"We can't take a taxi."

"Why not?"

His eyes widened as though I'd said the pope was Jewish. "You know, the whole *hostage* thing."

"Oh . . . right . . ." So much for staying around people.

"We'll just have to take my car."

I shrugged. "You'll be fine. My neighbors are a bunch of blind and deaf old women. They never notice anything."

He grabbed my arm and pulled me around the dumpster and toward the street, stopping at the edge to peer around the corner. "There's cops crawling everywhere."

"It's the end of the month and I bet they're handin' out jay-walking tickets. You know, to boost the revenue."

"Or they're looking for *you*."

"Yeah, they don't like me very much. You know, you can just leave me here and I won't tell anyone about you."

"The only way you're walking out of this alley is if you leave with me."

So much for options. "Where's your car?"

One side of his mouth lifted into a smirk. "That's what I thought."

The back door to the coffee shop opened. I hoped to God it was Joe.

Jimmy dragged me onto the street and around the corner, cutting diagonally across the street to a parking lot before I could see who it was coming out of the coffee shop. We stopped next to a light blue VW Bug, the old kind from the sixties. The car was a rust bucket, and Jimmy had to tinker with the lock to get the door to open.

Putting his hand on top of my head, he pushed me into the front seat.

I was starting to panic again. "I think it's only fair I warn you that I get carsick."

"Great." He rolled his eyes. "Now stay put in that seat or I'll shoot you, got it?"

I judged my odds of getting away as he made his way to the driver's door and decided they weren't very good. For one thing, it was a small car and thus a short trip around the back. And for another, the door would probably get stuck as I was opening it.

My nerves were getting the better of me and I started talking. "Lucky for you, your car's seen better days so if I get sick, it won't make much difference. You know, you'd think with all that income from your rental properties you'd be able to afford a new car."

"Shut up," he growled and shoved my head to my lap when a policeman walked around the corner.

My forehead hit the dashboard on the way down. "Oww!"

"Shh!" The gun lay across his lap, daring me to try something. I needed to come up with a plan.

"So where's this diary of yours?"

"What? Oh, it's . . ." Oh crap. I needed a location that would slow him down. "It's in my shed." It would take forever to go through the contents of my shed. Especially since everything had been thrown in there haphazardly after the Henryetta police emptied it looking for a gun.

"Why the hesitation? You lying to me, Rose?"

"Well, it's not like I want to just hand all my evidence over to you, now is it?" I grumbled.

"I guess not."

"But then I saw your gun and realized I better tell you the truth."

"Smart girl."

I wasn't so sure. I was barely hanging onto control, my wits starting to slip. I needed to stall him and I wanted to hear why he killed Frank Mitchell. "Can I get up now? I'm getting a crick in my neck."

"Yeah . . ." He lifted his hand off my head and I sat up, stretching.

"So you wanted to buy Frank Mitchell's property because the superstore was goin' to buy up land around there?"

"Still Miss Nosy, huh?"

"I figure I'm entitled to know what I'm dyin' for."

"Fair enough, although you seem awfully calm for someone about to meet their maker."

I was far from calm, about to start screaming any minute, but I suspected that was the surest way to get shot with the police milling around. Instead, I held my hands up. "And I'm prepared. After Momma's accident, God rest her soul, I figured you just never know when evil's gonna strike. Best to always be ready."

Jimmy shifted in his seat, glancing in the rearview mirror.

I turned around to get one last glimpse of Officer Ernie walking the opposite direction. I was on my own.

Oh, crappy doodles. I really was in trouble now.

Chapter Twenty-Eight

I needed to keep him talking until I figured something out. "The thing about evil, Mr. DeWade, is it often starts with the best of intentions and not even knowin' it's evil, don't you think?"

"Why're you asking me?"

"Well, you know . . . the whole *murdering* thing and all. I figured go straight to the source."

His face paled and he ran his hand through his hair. "I'm not evil. I was just getting what was comin' to me."

"And I bet Frank got what was comin' to him too. You were just carrying out justice. Like a vigilante." My eyes widened with excitement. "Like Batman!" My shoulders dropped and I tilted my head. "No, wait. Wouldn't Bruce Wayne Decker be Batman with his name and all? No, that can't be right. I don't think Batman ever went to jail . . ."

He shook his head, growling. "Bruce Wayne went to jail."

"Are you sure? But what about Batman? I mean, he's Batman! Who could arrest Batman? And wouldn't they take off his hood when they took his picture? Or did they take the picture with his hood on? Because I had to take off my *ring* so I can only imagine they'd take off his hood."

"*What the hell are you talkin' about?*"

"Bruce Wayne Decker. The innocent guy waitin' to be convicted."

"No, you got it wrong. It wasn't anything like that."

"Well, then what was it?"

He exhaled in a huff. "I just wanted what was mine."

"You said that already. What did Frank Mitchell take from you?"

His brow furrowed and his eyes turned dark. "Frank Mitchell didn't take anything."

I rolled my eyes. "That makes no sense. If he didn't take anything from you, why did you kill him?"

"You talk too much."

"And you told me you'd tell me why I was dyin'. So far, I've got nothing."

"I've spent over twenty years working for Fenton County. I hate it. It's a soul-sucking job. But I figured I'd put in my time and then retire on my pension. But a year and a half ago, Fenton County stole our pensions and ruined everything."

"I heard about that, but Frank Mitchell didn't have anything to do with it, did he?"

"If you'd just be quiet, I'd tell you."

Jimmy was halfway to my house and I still hadn't come up with a plan other than digging through my shed, which wasn't any kind of plan at all.

"Like I said, I was gonna retire early on my pension, but that got screwed to hell."

"I work at the DMV, or I did until yesterday, and that has to be a worse job than working with Neely Kate. You don't see me whackin' people with crowbars."

He gripped the steering wheel with both hands, his body shaking as he grit his teeth. "It wasn't like that!"

"Then what was it like?"

My phone rang in his pocket. "Damnit!" He pulled it out. "Your buddy, the DA." He shoved the phone at me. "Answer it."

"*What?*" I fumbled to snatch the phone from him, dropping it in my lap.

Jimmy picked up the gun and pointed it at me. "Tell him something to make him stop calling."

My breath came in short bursts and my face started tingling. *Get a grip, Rose.* Hyperventilating wasn't going to help anything. "Hello?"

"Rose! Where the hell are you?" Mason's angry voice shouted through the earpiece.

Jimmy flinched. He must have heard the yelling.

"Uh . . ."

"Tell him you went to lunch with a friend."

I put my hand partway over the phone and whispered, "He's never gonna believe that. He knows Neely Kate is covering the personal property department until you get back."

I tried to laugh into the phone, which came out sounding like the squeaky breaks on Miss Mildred's Cadillac. "You said I'm in trouble? Because I didn't show up for court? I'll try to make it in later."

"Rose, are you in trouble?" Mason whispered. "And it has something to do with Neely Kate? Someone she works with?"

I released a snort. "What are you gonna do? Put me in jail?"

"Where are you, Rose?" Mason sounded frantic. "Does someone have you?"

"Well, I don't care what Joe says." I tied to sound indignant, but it wasn't working so well. "Tell him . . . tell him . . ." I choked on a sob. "Tell him I love him anyway."

Jimmy snatched the phone out of my hand and ended the call, a grim expression on his face. "That didn't go the way I wanted it to, Rose."

Anger seethed in my gut. "Well, this whole morning hasn't gone the way I wanted it to, so consider us even."

"You're forgettin' who has the gun here."

"Then shoot me already!"

"Not until you get that diary."

That meant I had a little time. He wanted the nonexistent diary and was willing to delay my execution until he got it. However, he seemed agitated enough that I wasn't sure that he'd take the time to drive to the woods before finishing me off.

Thinking about Joe opened the door to my fear and it swamped my head, stealing all my senses. I shoved it back before I started bawling. I suspected Jimmy would rather deal with a babbling woman than a sobbing one.

"I still don't know why you killed Frank. I know you're a murderer and all, but you're still a Southern gentleman and I would hope you'd keep your word."

"Well, you keep interrupting."

"I'm not interruptin' now!"

"After the pensions were stolen, I was eating lunch at Merilee's. I happened to be sittin' behind two zoning employees and they were discussing the rezoning for the superstore. I already had two rental properties in Forest Ridge, but realized if I bought houses in strategic locations, I might get more money. Most of the owners were willin' to sell. They didn't know anything about the superstore and with the economy being so bad, I practically stole those houses out from under 'em."

"Except for Frank."

"His house was dead center. But that stubborn son of a bitch flat-out refused. He was in debt up to his eyeballs and I kept raising the offer but nothing. They had to get sixty percent of the owners to agree or the deal fell through. If he refused to sell, they might have moved the parking lot further north and I'd be stuck with all fifteen houses."

"But I don't understand. Killing him didn't help anything. He couldn't sell it if he was dead and his son sold it to an investment company in Louisiana."

He grinned. "Owned by my third cousin. We split the profit from the sale to the superstore."

"So it couldn't be tracked back to you. It would look suspicious if you bought it a couple of months after he died."

"Exactly, although the Henryetta Police had already arrested Bruce Decker. Besides, I didn't mean to kill Frank. I just wanted to scare him. But we got to arguing, and the next thing I knew, I picked up a crowbar off a shelf and whacked him."

"And you stole the money to make it look like a robbery."

"Yeah, I would have taken more, but I realized I'd lost my grandmother's pin and I was searching for it. I heard a noise in the warehouse and took off before I remembered the cash."

"Not that it mattered. The police didn't care."

"Gotta love the Henryetta Police Department."

I didn't see the point in disagreeing.

Jimmy was only a block from my house. I needed to come up with something fast. "But an innocent man is takin' the blame. You don't feel guilty about that?"

"I did at first. Until I realized he had a long arrest record."

"But nothing violent."

Jimmy shrugged.

"What about me?" I didn't mean for it too sound strangled. I took a breath and forced myself to sound brave. "I don't have an arrest record. I'm an innocent citizen."

He laughed. "You are far from innocent. I'll admit, I felt bad when I first decided you had to go, but it's you or me. And let's face it, you've annoyed a lot of people."

Jimmy pulled into my driveway and I pondered the truth of his statement. Maybe I'd annoyed half the town, Jimmy included, but that wasn't a crime worthy of execution.

I wasn't going out without a fight. Jimmy DeWade had messed with the wrong woman.

Miss Mildred walked out her front door, watering can in her hand and I knew exactly what she was up to. Only a fool would water her flowers in the heat of the day, and while Miss Mildred was a lot of things, a fool wasn't one of them.

For once, I might be able to use Miss Mildred to my advantage.

Jimmy looked through the windshield. "Is that your shed?"

"Yeah, but I need the key. It's inside."

"Okay, we'll get the key then wander back there. Do anything stupid and I won't hesitate to shoot you, got it?"

I didn't see the point of all of this. Jimmy had noticed Miss Mildred out on her porch, but maybe he was fooled by her age, especially after I'd told him she was blind and deaf. Well, he was in for a rude awakening. Not only could Miss Mildred give a perfect description of any suspect from fifty feet away, I wouldn't be surprised if she couldn't draw the photographic likeness herself.

"I still have to pee." My bathroom had a window. If he let me go take care of business, I could climb out and run for help.

"You keep saying that but so far, you seem to be doing fine."

I lifted my eyebrows in indignation. "Would you rather I pee on your seat and leave DNA evidence?"

"Fine . . ."

It took me three pushes to get the passenger door open. Jimmy walked around the back of the car and stood next to the door. As I climbed out, I glimpsed Miss Mildred crossing the street with a broom in her hand.

Oh crappy doodles.

"I've had enough of this nonsense!" she shouted.

Jimmy's mouth dropped open.

She waved the broom over her head and stopped three feet in front of us. "What kind of a neighborhood do you think this is, Rose Gardner? How many different men have you had here this week? Three?"

I struggled to get my wits about me. "Yes, ma'am."

"You're running a brothel outta that house and I've plumb had enough!" Miss Mildred whacked Jimmy on the head with the broom.

"Oww!" he shouted, covering his head with his arms. His gun fell to the driveway.

"Rose!" I turned toward the sound of the voice and saw Heidi Joy standing in her front door, her mouth gaping at Miss Mildred. Muffy appeared at her feet and took off running, barking as she went.

Miss Mildred's beating continued, her momentum picking up. "Get out of here, you filthy vermin! This is a God-fearin' neighborhood and we don't allow filth in!"

Jimmy had accidentally kicked the gun under the car. I dropped to my knees, but Jimmy still had enough sense to realize what I was doing and lunged for me.

We fell to the ground, me on my stomach and Jimmy lying on my back. I tried to get to my knees to throw him off, but he pushed me back down.

Miss Mildred moved over and hit him on the head with renewed force. "Devil! Satan! *Fornicating*! In broad daylight!"

I stretched my hand under the car, the gun only inches out of reach. Jimmy crawled up my back, but I lifted my shoulders and we rolled around grunting. He got both feet planted into the driveway and slammed down onto my back, throwing me to the ground.

"Never," Miss Mildred shouted, getting in several swings, "have I seen such *filth*!"

Muffy stood next to us, growling while Jimmy and I continued our tussle. She lunged, but Jimmy and I rolled into the front yard, away from my brave dog's teeth.

"*Heathens*!" Miss Mildred shouted before turning the hose on us.

Jimmy jumped to his feet, yelling, his eyes dark and dangerous as he faced his five-foot-two nemesis.

I took advantage of his distraction and crawled to the car, reaching for the gun.

Sirens filled the air, still a distance away.

Releasing an ominous growl, Jimmy charged Miss Mildred, who continued to spray him with the hose. Muffy jumped and bit Jimmy on the leg. Howling, Jimmy bent down to swat her off, but Muffy latched onto his arm. Jimmy squealed in pain and dropped to his knees.

Miss Mildred continued to douse him, holding the hose with both hands. "*Damn Yankee carpetbagger scum*!"

Gasping to catch my breath, I moved toward them, pointing the gun at Jimmy.

Joe's car skidded to a halt in front of my house. He threw open his door and tore across the yard, sliding to a halt when he saw us. He stared in disbelief.

Oh crappy doodles.

Two police cars pulled up behind Joe's and police swarmed the yard, all circling around, pointing their guns and not doing anything.

"Joe . . . I can explain."

Joe's face was expressionless. "You can explain *this*?" He pointed to the sight in front of him.

Jimmy screamed while Muffy nipped his arms. Miss Mildred had turned the nozzle on the hose to high. And I stood next to the mess holding a gun.

Maybe I couldn't explain.

I waved the gun in the air. "This isn't mine."

Joe and the police ducked, shouting.

"Rose, toss the gun to the ground!" Joe said, easing himself toward me.

Was he mad enough to arrest me?

I dropped the gun and it landed on the grass with a thud. "Joe, I swear! *I didn't do anything*! I was just sitting there mindin' my own business."

He pulled me into a hug. "I know. It's okay."

I breathed a sigh of relief.

"Trouble seems to find you wherever you go, Rose Gardner. I give up."

I titled back my head, my stomach flip-flopping in dread.

His mouth lifted into an ornery grin. "I wouldn't have you any other way."

Then he kissed me to prove it while mass chaos swirled around us.

But by now, Joe was used to it.

Chapter
Twenty-Nine

Joe and I walked out of the courthouse, his arm around my waist. Storm clouds brewed on the horizon, and a cool wind swept through the streets of Henryetta.

"Looks like our heat spell may have broken." I said, breathing in the sweet smell of rain and hope.

Joe nuzzled my ear. "It depends on which heat spell you're referring to."

I giggled and nudged him in the ribs as Mason Deveraux descended the courthouse steps toward us.

"Congratulations, Rose." Mason grinned. "You were right. Bruce Decker was innocent just like you said all along. He's been released and James DeWade has been charged with the second-degree murder of Frank Mitchell. The police in Louisiana are picking up his cousin for questioning."

I squinted in confusion. "But I thought Bruce would still be prosecuted for robbing the hardware store. How can he be released?"

"He didn't break in—the back door was open. And the only thing he stole was the crowbar."

"Oh."

His eyes softened. "So what's next for you? I heard you officially quit your job."

I looked up at Joe, my heart fluttering with nervousness. "I'm not sure yet."

Mason held out his hand and I took it, his fingers holding my hand with tenderness. "I wish you happiness with whatever you do."

I smiled up at him. "Thank you, Mason."

Mason turned his gaze to Joe, his eyes turning cold. "Simmons."

"Deveraux," Joe said in his detective voice.

I looked up at Joe, narrowing my eyes. "What was that about?"

"It's between the two of us. Don't you worry about it." He led me to a bench on the sidewalk. "We need to talk."

My stomach tossed around my insides.

We sat down, and Joe draped his arm around the seat back behind me.

He was silent for several seconds, his face serious. "This morning I decided to break up with you."

I looked down at my lap, a lump filling my throat. "I know."

"It's just . . . you just . . . you drive me crazy."

A tear fell down my cheek, dripping onto my lap.

"You're like this storm of confusion and unpredictability, and I don't know how to handle it."

Why was he doing this here? In downtown Henryetta? "I know."

He rubbed his face with both hands. "I have no idea what you're goin' to do next, and you scare the hell out of me."

I looked up into his face, biting my lip. "I'm sorry."

His hand reached up to my cheek, careful of my bruises. "But the thought of life without you scares me even more."

I held my breath, not sure what he meant.

"I'd made up my mind. I was going to break up with you as soon as I knew you were safe. But the thought of never seeing you again, or holdin' you. Or kissin' you." His lips lowered to mine, kissing me with a surprising tenderness. "The thought sent me into a panic. You're full of excitement and spontaneity. You're like a roller coaster ride, and I suspect life with you will be a series of ups and downs, but I don't want it any other way. I love you, Rose."

"I love you." I reached for his face, crying with relief. I kissed him, hoping my next words didn't send him away. "But I can't move to Little Rock with you."

He leaned back, staring into my eyes. "I know." Sadness filled his voice.

"It's not just Violet—"

"I know." His mouth lifted into a small smile. "I found your list at the coffee shop."

"Oh." I closed my eyes for a moment. I still had Joe. Why was my heart breaking so? "What are we gonna do?"

"I guess we'll just keep doin' what we're doin'."

"I guess." I was miserable doing what we were doing.

"What are you goin' to do about a job? You're not going back to the DMV, are you?"

"Shoot, no. I don't know, maybe . . . Violet wants us to go into business together."

"The nursery?"

I looked down at my lap, suddenly unsure. "Yeah."

Joe lifted my chin. "Is this something *you* want to do? Not Violet. *You*?"

I nodded. "Yeah. I do."

"Then I think it's a great idea."

"Really?"

"Look out, Henryetta. The Gardner sisters are about to take over."

I grinned. "Yeah."

He leaned over and kissed me so thoroughly I was sure Miss Mildred would turn the hose on us if she could see.

"I don't have to go back to Little Rock until tomorrow morning."

"Then I say we go home and finish this conversation there."

Joe stood, pulling me up against him and kissing me again. "I think that's the best idea I've heard all day. By the way, I particularly liked number sixteen on your list."

"Which one is that?"

"He is a *very* handsome man."

I laughed. "Obviously, I left off 'Joe is a very *humble* man.'"

We walked to his car arm in arm, Mason's words niggling the back of my head. If we were getting everything out in the open, I needed to know this too. "Joe?"

"Yeah, darlin'."

"What did Mason mean last night when he said that he didn't to lie to me, and could you say the same?"

Joe stopped, uncertainty washing over his face.

"Joe?"

He squared his shoulders, hesitating. "I had help getting you out of jail last week. Deveraux and I had tried everything and the judge was fit to be tied, so I called in a favor. I made Deveraux promise not to tell you."

I steeled my back. "What did you do?"

Swallowing, a hardness filled his eyes. "I called my father."

"I don't understand."

"My father has a lot of influence in the state. A lot. He used his persuasion."

"Your father used his influence to get *me* out of jail? Why would he do that? He doesn't even know me."

"Because I asked him to. What you don't understand, Rose, is that asking my father for something always comes with a price."

"And you asked for it anyway?"

"I couldn't leave you in jail."

"I'm sorry." Why was I always telling him sorry?

Joe shrugged. "Water under the bridge."

"What was the price?"

"What?" He tried to act confused but failed, instead looking like he was hiding something.

I lowered my voice. "What was the price, Joe?"

He shrugged. "I don't know yet. Dad called it a future favor."

My stomach tightened with fear. "I hope I was worth it."

He tilted my head back and looked into my eyes. "I would do anything for you. Do you realize that?"

I nodded. He'd proved it multiple times.

He winked. "Now take me home and show me how much you love me."

I tilted my head with a grin. "I don't think one night is long enough to show you that."

He kissed me with the promise of happiness and love. "Then we'll just have to spend the rest of eternity workin' on it."

That sounded good to me.

Acknowledgments

Thank you to my critique partner, Trisha Leigh, who tolerates my insanity with very few eye rolls. (That I know of.) And thank you to Derek Dodson for agreeing to read my first draft, even if he didn't realize what he was signing up for. Trisha and Derek were flooded with pages in a very short period of time after my writing marathon in a week and a half. Thank you for fitting me into your busy schedules and giving feedback in a very short period of time!

Thank you to my beta readers: Rhonda, Anne, Lori, Wendy, Brandy and Kay Bratt. I sent them *Twenty-Nine and a Half Reasons* and asked for feedback in two weeks. They all sent back their notes within two days. I love when readers can't put my books down!

Thank you to Marcy, Marjorie, Anne, and Heidi, who won a contest a year ago and each named a character in the book. (Marcy: Neely Kate; Majorie: Marjorie Grace; Anne: Anne; Heidi: Heidi Joy) I was a little worried about making it work, but it turned out to be so much fun. In fact, I'm planning to do it again for *Thirty and a Half Excuses*.

Thank you to Mandie Metier with her invaluable help with courthouse questions as well as zoning issues. She saved me a ton of legwork. I love Facebook and I love my friends who are so will and eager to help.

Thank you to my developmental editor, Alison Dasho, who sent back her edit notes on my first draft—full of Rose love! She had minor change suggestions, but they made a huge difference, making the story even richer. I love that she can read my characters and come up with psychological insight to them that *I've* missed.

Thank you to my copy editor, Jim Thomsen, who takes my words and makes them even shinier. After six books together, I love that he gets me.

Thank you to my proofreader, Annette Guerriero. She's meticulous and she loves my books. Total win for both of us.

And finally, thank you to my readers. I write for me first, because if I didn't love what I was doing, you all would notice. But I write for you second. I love that I entertain you and make you laugh and cry. I love that you think of Rose and Joe and Violet as real people. There are a million books out there and you chose to read mine. The significance of this is not lost on me.